The Fragrance Shed by a Violet

Murder in the Medical Center

SECOND EDITION

The Fragrance Shed by a Violet

Murder in the Medical Center

Lin Wilder

The Fragrance Shed by a Violet

Lin Wilder

S E C O N D   E D I T I O N

ISBN: 978-1-942545-17-0
Library of Congress Control Number: 2015949006

Cover Image Credits: Spring Wild Flowers ©Konstanttin,
Morgue ©Katarzyna Bialasiewicz

Wilder Books
An Imprint of Wyatt-MacKenzie

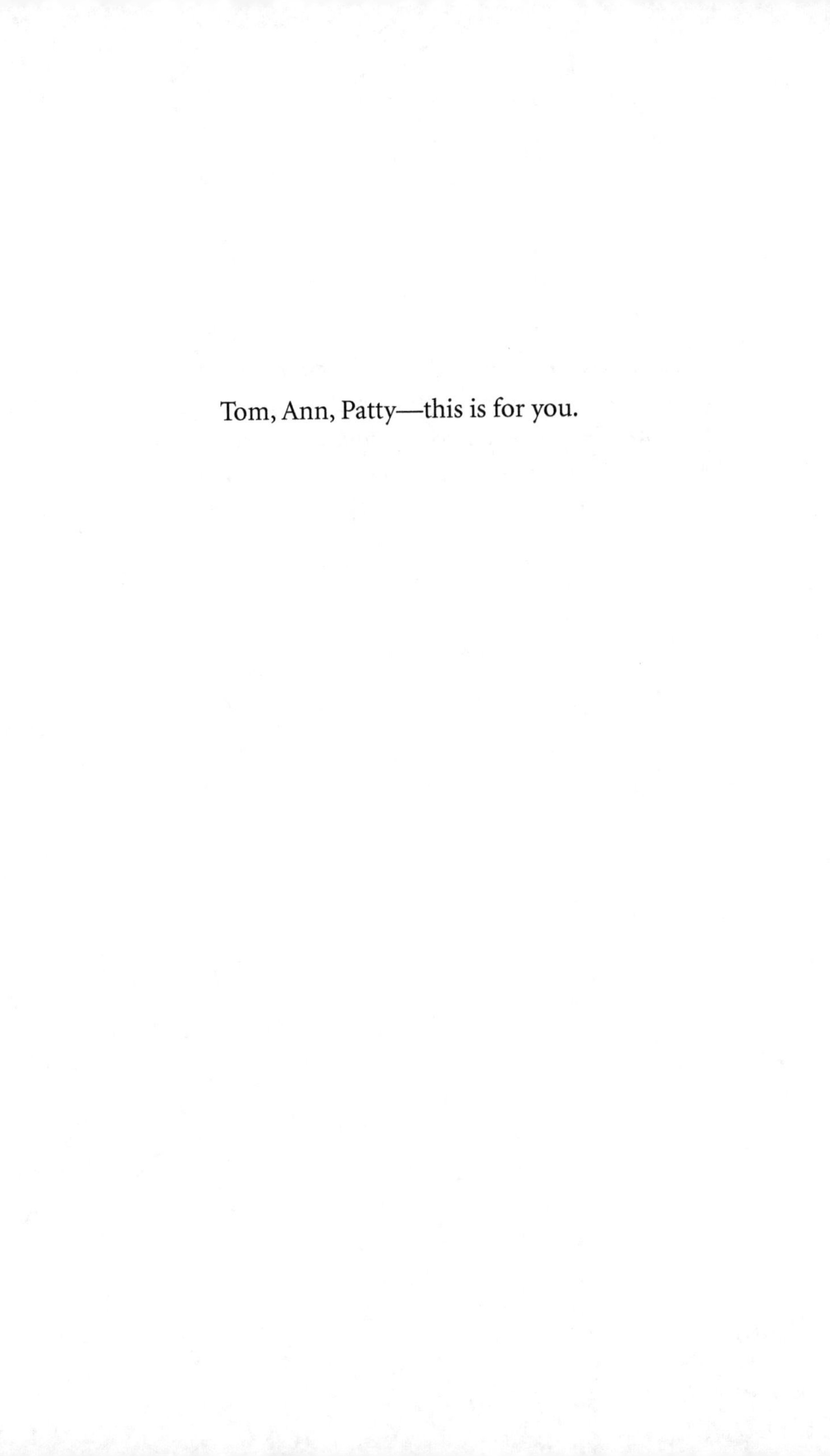

Tom, Ann, Patty—this is for you.

*He who learns must suffer. And even in our sleep pain
that cannot forget falls drop by drop upon the heart,
and in our own despair, against our will, comes
wisdom through the awful grace of God.*
—Aeschylus

She lay listening to the unfamiliar night sounds: the pacing of other sleepless prisoners, the occasional echo of a heavy-footed guard making his rounds. Mostly though, she waited for the terror of the dream to subside, for the iron bands around her heart to loosen, and for the awful pressure on her chest to lighten so that she could breathe. And she waited for her heart to climb back down into her chest and out of her throat.

The dream was a familiar one. It had begun four years before following the sudden death of a fifty-two-year-old man whose heart she had catheterized. Dr. Lindsey McCall had surgical hands—a reference to the skill and dexterity that she brought to the Cardiac Catheterization Laboratory at Houston General Hospital. A colleague had made the comment during rounds one day during her cardiology fellowship at Houston General, and it had stuck.

There had been no reason for his death. Nate Morrison was a healthy senior executive with Southwest Oil, one of the largest oil conglomerates in the world. During his annual physical, Morrison had been referred to Houston General for a work up based on nonspecific changes in his cardiac diagnostic tests. Upon reviewing his tests, Lindsey had suspected that the man's coronaries might be clean—free of coronary artery disease. She was well aware of the numbers. Of the sixty thousand cardiac catheterizations performed each year in the United States, over 30 percent revealed clean coronaries: absence of plaque in the vessels supplying the heart with oxygenated blood. And the procedure was not benign. Complications of cardiac catheterization were not uncommon and ranged from mild hematoma to death. In twelve years, Lindsey had done over five hundred cardiac catheterizations and more than three hundred angioplasties. She had never lost a patient.

But close to 75 percent of the revenue of her department came from referrals from doctors practicing in Texas and the Houston metropolitan area; the physicians at Southwest Oil referred hundreds of patients to Houston General per year, usually for an angioplasty or cardiac cath. Furthermore, McCall was well acquainted with the financial realities of her profession—turning down lucrative procedures such as cardiac catheterizations was not smart.

For some reason she could no longer recall, she, rather than one of the cath lab nurses, had gone to see this man the night before the procedure. While she had been reviewing the potential complications with her patient and obtaining his informed consent, Morrison had asked with a wink, "Just how many patients have you lost in your twelve-year career, Dr. McCall?"

His quick-grinned response to her answer had been, "Well then, let's you and I make sure that I'm not the first, deal?"

Lindsey could picture that conversation as if it had happened a moment ago. Fourteen hours later, he was dead.

As she had done hundreds of times before upon awakening from the dream, Lindsey lay there second-guessing herself—asking all the questions that had been asked by his family, by the morbidity and mortality committee at the hospital, and by her chairman of medicine. The final diagnosis had been sudden death caused by a massive left ventricular infarct most likely from coronary spasm. Neither his family nor the hospital held her responsible. There had never been even the suggestion of negligence on her part.

Her technique had been flawless. She had been calm and confident throughout the two-hour procedure, explaining what she was doing to her patient and laughing at his quick-witted responses. Lindsey had completed the injection of dye into the man's left anterior coronary artery, and after satisfying herself that it, too, was free of plaque, had almost completely extracted the catheter from his coronary in preparation to end the procedure when she heard the startled cry of her technician.

"Lindsey, he's fibrillating, he's fibrillating!"

For just a second, her gaze met that of her lead tech, Ben, who responded to her unspoken question. "He's been in sinus rhythm for the whole exam—there was never any arrhythmia, not even a PVC!"

Ben was referring to premature ventricular contractions that are frequently harbingers of serious cardiac arrhythmias. Lindsey trusted this guy implicitly; they had worked together for over ten years. If Ben said there had been no warning of this potentially fatal arrhythmia, she believed him. So she and her staff went to work, certain that in just a few minutes, they would get control and be back to the routine work of winding down the procedure.

But they couldn't.

They had worked for over three hours, along with six members of the hospital's on-call code team who had responded to the emergency in the Cath lab. They were never able to restore a normal cardiac rhythm, despite massive amounts of antiarrhythmic and other emergency drugs and numerous attempts at electrical defibrillation.

It was the head of the code team who called the code, suspecting that Lindsey was unable to do so. She had dropped her hands and stood staring at the futile electric signals displayed on the cardiac monitor, at the virtually unrecognizable semi-nude and mottled body of Nate Morrison and remembered joking with this man the night before. She remembered his smiles, good humor, and, most of all, his vitality. Then she walked out of the lab to tell his wife that her husband was dead. To tell her that he had had no coronary arterial disease but that he had died. And that she had no idea why.

That was the last time she had accepted a patient for catheterization.

The chairman of Medicine at Houston General had spent hours with Lindsey during that first year following the death of this patient. He had known her since she had been accepted into the cardiology fellowship almost fifteen years earlier and had followed the young woman's career at first with interest and later with excitement. For that entire year, Lindsey had been exceedingly grateful to Bayer for his concern and, yes, the love she knew he felt for her. She had tried, God knows, she had tried to return to the cath labs at the hospital, but she could not do it. Just opening the door to the labs and beginning to scrub for the procedure evoked a panic reaction so severe that she could not tolerate it. And the idea of seeking a psychiatrist for treatment was unacceptable to her. Naturally, many of her colleagues in Houston and around the country had suggested that some of the newer antianxiety drugs could mitigate her reaction, but the only one who could force her to seek psychiatric and pharmacologic help was Dr. Bayer, and he refused to do so.

During their last conversation on this matter, a luncheon he had scheduled to discuss her future at the medical school,

Lindsey managed to convince Dr. Bayer that she would now have the time and the energy to focus on her drug research. And once more, that wonderful man had supported her. He had even shared her excitement when she explained again the vision she had for a modification of the digitalis molecule.

Dr. Simon Bayer was known to many as the cardiologists' cardiologist. He, too, had been excellent in diagnostics, research, and in education. Author of several textbooks and principal investigator of countless experimental drug protocols, Dr. Bayer was internationally admired and respected. But in close to forty years as chairman of Internal Medicine at Houston Medical, Dr. Bayer had never before seen the talent exhibited by this young physician.

Early in her fellowship, Lindsey had talked with Dr. Bayer about her preliminary doctoral work exploring alteration of the molecule for digitalis. At that time, he had listened politely. Lindsey remembered sensing that her chairman believed she was chasing windmills—the drug had been around forever, after all.

For centuries, physicians have treated heart failure with digitalis. Its effect on strengthening a failing left ventricle—the main pump of the four-chambered heart—remains unparalleled. But the drug has serious systemic side effects ranging from mild to potentially fatal depending on dosage and frequency. Lindsey had become interested in the drug in high school when her mother had been diagnosed with idiopathic cardiomyopathy—heart failure of unknown origin—at the age of forty-three.

Cardiomyopathies are a strange and almost-universally-fatal type of heart failure. Thought to be caused by a virus, the actual mechanism of disease is poorly understood. But the course of the disease is all too well known: increasing heart failure and incapacitation over time and death if not treated with heart transplantation. Despite living fifty miles from the premiere transplant center of the world, the Texas Medical Center in Houston, Lindsey's mother would not consider transplantation. That she lived for close to thirty years without surgical intervention was regarded as a minor miracle by her physicians. Then, as now, digitalis was the drug of choice for heart failure, and so the balancing act of dosing had begun—sufficient medication to keep the heart out of failure but not so much as to cause severe nausea and vomiting and toxicity to the heart.

Before her illness, Lindsey's mom had been physically active with many outside interests and lots of friends. Although she had never worked outside her home, she had been active in volunteer and church work. The disease completely changed her personality; Ann became incapable of focusing on much other than her symptoms and the acute anxiety brought about by the facts of her illness and incapacitation. Formerly a dominant force in the McCall family, Mrs. McCall rapidly took on the role of a cardiac cripple. Unable to accept that her lifestyle need not change so long as she rested frequently and did not unduly exert herself, the terrors of her diagnosis imprisoned her and her family. The results were all too predictable. Lindsey's dad, a bit of a workaholic by nature, accepted the more risky assignments at NASA, and Paula, now twenty-three and a graduate nurse, took on the care of her mother by default. For Paula, a gravely ill mother provided the perfect excuse to avoid the realities of an already unhappy life.

Only thirteen at the time, Lindsey handled the virtual loss of her mother through intense study: of the heart, of her mother's disease, and of the drugs that manage heart failure, specifically digitalis. This intellectual response to loss, crisis, and fear worked exceedingly well for the young girl and would become her primary response to trauma throughout her life.

At the age of seven, Lindsey had decided that she would be a cardiologist and a research scientist; the acute onset of Ann McCall's illness served to augment and crystallize Lindsey's ambition. Throughout her junior and senior high school years, the young girl persuaded her chemistry and biology teachers to support her determination to alter the digitalis molecule in ways that would optimize its inotropic, or strengthening, effects on the heart, while mitigating its toxic effects.

Lindsey's chemistry teachers were impressed with the exceptional motivation she demonstrated at her age. Recognizing and respecting his daughter's ambition, Tom McCall, Lindsey's father, a NASA test pilot, made certain that Lindsey received the best of what the Clear Lake Texas schools offered in their advanced science courses. Therefore, Lindsey received quality tutors throughout the six years of junior and senior high school. Lindsey McCall's cardiac models were entered at each science fair and, without fail, received first prize.

By the time of Lindsey's talk with Dr. Bayer, Lindsey had been studying digitalis off and on for close to thirty years. But actual research in the laboratory had been limited to her doctoral studies. After explaining the preliminary work she had done, and the abstract of her dissertation findings that had appeared in *Science* the year after she received the doctorate, she quietly asked, "So do you still think that I'm chasing windmills, Dr. Bayer?"

He had placed his hand on hers and smiled affectionately as he said, "Lindsey, you lost me three models ago; it has been too long since I've done basic science research. But here is what I can do for us." Noting her widened eyes at his use of the pronoun *us,* Dr. Bayer continued speaking in that measured, thoughtful, and precise tone of his, "Yes, of course, Lindsey, the medical school will benefit in immeasurable ways when you develop this drug. And you *will*, I have no doubt at all that you can do this. The clinical benefit of your work is immeasurable, and the monetary gain to both the medical school and the company with the patent is in the billions."

Waving off her attempts to thank him for his trust and confidence in her, Dr. Bayer explained that a close friend of his had just taken over as CEO of Andrews, Sacks, and Levine (ASL), one of the largest drug companies in the world, a company that badly needed new drugs since the patents for the company's top three drugs were due to expire within the next twenty-four months. According to Dr. Bayer, Hank Reardon, ASL's new CEO, owed him some favors; Bayer would set up the meeting between Lindsey and Reardon within the next couple of weeks.

∾

Now fully awake, lying on her cell bed, Lindsey considered the irony of her current circumstances. She almost laughed out loud in the dark at herself—at least the terror of this dream was familiar and lay buried in her past; her real nightmare was no dream, no mere memory. And she could feel the fear uncoil, stretch, and begin to take her over once again. Closing her eyes, she began to pray:

∾

Let nothing dismay thee.
All things pass.
God never changes.
Patience acquires all that is strived for.
She who has God finds that she lacks nothing.
God alone suffices.

I feel that the dormant goodwill in people needs to be stirred. People need to hear that it makes sense to behave decently or to help others, to place common interests above their own, to respect the elementary rules of human coexistence. They want to be told about this publicly … Goodwill longs to be recognized and cultivated. For it to develop and have an impact it must hear that the world does not ridicule it … people want to hear that decency and courage make sense, that something must be risked in the struggle against dirty tricks. They want to know that they are not alone, forgotten, written off.

—Vaclav Havel

1

Kate Townsend wondered for the one hundredth time that evening why she felt so numb. This should have been the happiest night of her life. Her face was actually sore from the constant smile that had been fixed there for the last ninety minutes as colleagues from all over the country had approached to congratulate her at the open bar preceding the award ceremony that had now started.

The newspaper had spared no expense in planning the gala; Eleanor and Marguerite Philbin had arranged that the exclusive River Oaks Country Club adjust the Banquet Room's seating capacity to comfortably accommodate the fifteen-hundred-plus journalists representing over one thousand newspapers, and Kate truly appreciated the grace and dignity of the elegant building and its staff. Located at the end of San Felipe in the heart of the affluent River Oaks neighborhood in Houston Texas, the River Oaks Country Club was synonymous with celebratory events by and for prestigious and powerful Houstonians. The building was opulent yet understated with its clean antebellum sweeping design and simple lighting.

Although this evening was the culmination of years of sacrifice and dogged determination on her part, Kate felt hollowed out, empty. Applause had interrupted her boss, Jeff Simmons, more times than she could count as he proudly spoke about her series of articles that had resulted in the award of the Pulitzer Prize for his newspaper, the *Houston Tribune.* It had been over fifty years since the paper had been granted a Pulitzer, and its financial survival had been in question until Kate's series had electrified the Houston and the national media. Looking around the dinner table at the faces of the leading characters of what she had come to believe was a modern tragedy, she saw reflected on their faces emotions ranging from jubilation to studied neutrality. Immediately on her left sat Paula Livingston, the older sister of Dr. Lindsey McCall. Although she was over fifty and a mother of three children, Paula was an extremely attractive woman.

Paula confused Kate. She had met with her countless times in the last six months or so, yet she remained a mystery. Her ironclad self-control was unnerving. During their first couple of interviews, Kate had found Paula's conversation to be consistent with a loving but concerned older sister to Dr. Lindsey McCall. With her background as a cardiac ICU head nurse and her enormous blue eyes that seemed to reflect a deep and genuine sincerity, Paula had been an extremely effective witness at her sister's trial. It was likely her testimony that had been the most critical factor in the decision of the jury to convict Dr. Lindsey McCall of murdering her dying mother. Yet there were some inconsistencies that Kate had sensed in the story that Paula had told. Those inconsistencies plagued Kate. And so did the fact that Kate had been aware of them almost from the beginning; yet she had been unable to break through

Paula's facade.

Paula sat staring at her glass of wine, wishing she could get to her flask without going to the bathroom again. She had promised herself that she would not drink tonight—of all nights—but while getting dressed, she realized that she could not face this evening and these people without fortification. So she went to the liquor cabinet to retrieve one of the five liters of Absolut vodka she maintained at all times.

Just one drink, she remembered thinking, *just one, that's all I'll need.* But by the time she was ready to leave the house, she had made the trip to the cabinet three times. By now Paula had realized that this long evening would be tolerable only if the dinner wine were fortified by lots of vodka. She had watched Kate Townsend studying her and was aware of the confusion with which Kate regarded her. Paula had become extremely adept at hiding her motives and emotions over the years. And she was observant to the point of vigilance—she had to be. Being finely tuned to the covert behaviors and non-verbal signals of others was an essential attribute of any successful closet drinker. That's what Paula called herself, a closet drinker: certainly not an alcoholic. Yet Paula's compulsion to drink was growing—as was her tolerance—and when she allowed herself to dwell on it, she got really frightened.

Catching Dr. Christine Stewart's gaze, she smiled and rolled her eyes as if to convey her boredom at the endless speech by the newspaper's editor, Jeff Simmons. She murmured to Kate to excuse herself and silently left the table. Imagining that many pairs of eyes were following her exit from the room, Paula forced herself to move slowly. As she walked through the banquet hall, she thought of Lindsey—the absent star of this show—and laughed to herself thinking, *My "little sister," how unnecessary all this really was.*

Thoughts of their last conversation—if you can call it

that—brought back the rage that Paula had felt then: fury at Lindsey's arrogance, her certainty, the coldness with which Lindsey had declared her "diagnosis" of Paula.

Now in the restroom, Paula breathed a sigh of relief as she took the flask from her purse and emptied it in three long swallows. Eyes stinging, she looked in the mirror to check her eyes. *Good,* she thought, *no redness, just a little teary, easily attributable to the tragedy that had befallen my brilliant little sister ... perfect.*

Returning the now-empty flask to her purse, Paula checked her watch and was stunned to see how little time had elapsed since her last bathroom break. This interminable evening had at least two hours to go before it was over, and she was out of vodka. Checking the panic that began to arise, she leaned into the mirror once more, whispering, "Girl, we can do this—we'll take only a couple to help us through the next few hours." And she reached into her purse again.

This time she pulled out a prescription bottle of Zoloft and stared at the label: "One to two capsules every six hours for severe anxiety, Christine Stewart, MD." Shaking out two of the capsules, Paula thought again of Lindsey and the arguments that had started all this. It was eight months ago almost to the day. The two sisters were standing in the hall of their mother's Clear Lake home, arguing. Paula had been begging Lindsey that entire month it seemed: first, to use her research drug to see if it could help their mother as her failing heart grew weaker and weaker and for one more prescription.

"Just one more, Lindsey, then I promise you, I'll never ask again." She had been sobbing.

"I've been up all night with Mom."

She had even dropped to her knees as she begged her sister for the drug.

God, Paula thought now, *did I really do that? Kneel before her as if she were some kind of deity?*

Disgusted and humiliated at the memory of her own desperation and Lindsey's cruelty, Paula mumbled a familiar curse to her absent little sister and thought, *I am so glad you finally get to be the lonely one, Lindsey, the frightened one—now it's your turn.*

Lindsey had stared down at Paula, who was sobbing as if her heart would break; stared as if her sister were someone she'd never seen before. And then Lindsey had said in that clinical, detached voice that Paula and their mother detested, "No, I am never writing another one Paula, ever. You are addicted to these things. You have a problem—a big one—and I am no longer going to be a part of it."

And she had not let it go there. No, while Paula had been awkwardly trying to regain her balance and get up off her knees on the slippery floor, "Dr." McCall had continued to berate her.

"And, Paula, I want you to see a friend of mine about your drinking. You're out of control, and I'm afraid you'll hurt yourself, one of your grandchildren, or one of your patients. He is a good guy and has worked with a lot of addicts. Dan will even go with you to the first few AA meetings."

All this was said in Lindsey's calm and measured voice. Paula had once accused her of practicing on tape recorders to achieve that modulation and that pitch.

Lindsey had paused and was stepping back to a table in the hall for a pen and paper to write down the name of the shrink that she wanted Paula to see.

Paula's hatred of her sister had been so intense that she had stopped the hysterics and began to think clearly. She thought back to a scene many years before when she'd first realized the depth of her animosity toward her younger sister, Lindsey. It was the night of Paula's junior prom, and she was happier than she had ever been in her young life. She was the head cheerleader that year, and Tony, a guy already out of the navy, had asked Paula to her junior prom. She'd talked her mom into spending over $750 dollars for her dress and knew that she looked beautiful. Her mother and father had asked Paula to pose for some pictures and planned to take more when Tony arrived. As her dad was happily snapping the photos, he'd been singing strains from the song "The Yellow Rose of Texas."

But then her seven-year-old sister walked out and stood in the hallway, saying nothing at all, just staring at them all. Her little friend Julie was with Lindsey, as usual. Julie was the only friend the weird little kid had.

Paula could hear Lindsey's seven-year-old voice all too clearly: there was an eerie adult and decisive tone to it. And Paula did not miss the look that passed between her dad and mother. How that kid had learned that her dress cost $750 was completely beyond Paula, but the magical moment was gone. Both she and her mom had persuaded and cajoled for all they were worth, but Tom McCall was adamant. Now he'd learned that they had deceived him. How many times had Paula and her father had serious talks about her penchant to lie her way out of the scrapes that her impetuosity got her into? Too many for Paula to remember.

∾

Shaking herself free of the awful memories of that night, Paula screwed the cap back on the bottle of pills, checked her appearance one last time, and returned to the dinner, a smile plastered firmly on her face. As she returned to their table, she saw that Kate seemed to be concentrating on something; Kate did not look up when Paula took her seat.

Next to Paula sat Hank Reardon, the chief executive officer of Andrews, Sacks, and Levine, one of the leading pharmaceutical companies in the world. Of the nine people at her table, Kate had found Hank Reardon to be one of the most delightful surprises of her life. In the course of her research for the series on new drug investigation, Reardon's generosity of spirit had provided her with an unparalleled view of the world of academic medicine and clinical research. She remembered her nervousness when she was introduced to this powerful businessman. And her stunned response to Reardon's invitation to the Lausanne Corporate Offices for Andrews, Sacks, and Levine during their WebCor meeting in Dr. Christine Stewart's office.

Without Hank Reardon, Kate mused, there would have been no series, or at least no Pulitzer Prize-winning series. The man had quite literally opened his heart and his life to Kate. That week in Switzerland had been magical, miraculous really, and Kate Townsend was well aware of the privileges she had been granted. Feeling the weight of her gaze, Reardon shifted his attention from the podium to Kate and grinned at her with his electric-blue gaze. Smiling back at him, Kate was struck by the depth of her affection for one of the ten wealthiest men in the world.

Reardon's sorrow had been genuine when he spoke of Lindsey during Kate's interviews with him. He spoke openly of their disagreements, but it was clear to Kate that he had admired McCall's insistence on controlling the methodology of her research and the early conclusions of her stage one clinical trial. It was, Kate recalled, just those arguments that drove the final nail into the relationship between Lindsey and her boss, Christine Stewart.

The three people seated next to Reardon were openly thrilled; smiles and toasts abounded at that corner of the large table. In this age of increasing public skepticism about the effectiveness of drugs, and suspicion about the actual science behind the development and introduction of new drugs, this new drug had provided a windfall both for Reardon's company and for Houston Medical School. Kate had read recently that shares in ASL had tripled in price in each quarter of this past fiscal year simply on the forecasted FDA approval of the modified digitalis drug now marketed as Digipro. Yet Reardon looked the same tonight as he had each time that Kate had met with him: intensely focused on the people and events unfolding about him. Inscrutable, she thought; no wonder he was so effective. Only the bruised, bluish shadows under his eyes betrayed the deep grief he was feeling at the recent death of his wife, Peg.

And next to Reardon sat the group from Houston General Medical School: Lindsey's former boss, chair of internal medicine, Dr. Christine Stewart; Dr. Anthony Miller, the president of the medical school; and Dr. V. Samuel Lister, the CEO of the Health Science Center. Although Dr. Stewart had been the only Houston General physician called to testify at Lindsey's trial, Kate had extensively interviewed both Miller and Lister to understand the complexities of academic medical centers in general and of clinical research in particular. They had been pleasant and accommodating, and had filled in extensive details for Kate upon her return from Switzerland.

Kate had enjoyed this part of her investigation more than almost any other of her series. In fact, she and Jeff had disagreed about the prominence that Kate had decided to give clinical research in her articles. Kate had argued successfully that clinical research, the drug industry, and academic medicine were black boxes and would be of significant interest to the public. Of her four articles in the series, it was this information in the first and second articles that had captured the attention of the national and international media.

Dr. Stewart interrupted Kate's reflections with a quizzical look. Realizing that she had been staring at Christine, Kate smiled warmly at the woman and hoped that her smile looked genuine.

Stewart was smart, ambitious, and was apparently excellent in her field. Academic medical departmental division heads were still predominantly male, even in the new millennium. Christine Stewart was a notable exception. Not only was she a cardiologist at Houston General Medical Center, but she was also chair of internal medicine at the medical school. Even today, when women account for more than half the medical school graduates in the United States, only 14 percent of cardiology fellows are women. And Stewart was one of only three female chairs of internal medicine in the country.

In the 1980s when both Christine and Lindsey were cardiology fellows, the numbers were even lower. Kate mused again on the improbable odds of two such unusual women arriving in the same place at the same time. That was one of the many ironies that had caught her attention when she had first begun her investigation of this case. Here were two female cardiologists: the subordinate Lindsey McCall and her superior Christine Stewart, who were so intensely competitive that only one had survived. It had seemed like a caricature to Kate in the beginning—like an old women's liberation joke gone bad. She knew that Christine and Lindsey had never worked together until Christine had been recruited from California to replace Dr. Simon Bayer, Lindsey's longtime mentor and friend, and wondered how differently this thing would have played out had Dr. Bayer not retired.

Sighing, Kate thought once again about Lindsey and wondered how that she held such admiration for someone she had never met—respect, profound sadness, and a deepening sense of responsibility for her plight.

Dr. Christine Stewart was a twenty-first-century academician. With her medical academic credentials from Stanford and Columbia, she obtained an MBA from Wharton in the late eighties and began to write about the financial tsunamis headed toward the specialties and academic medicine.

Teaching and research are very expensive endeavors and require very deep pockets. As the funding climate had changed, and federal grant dollars were reduced in the difficult economic turndown, all medical schools were forced to look beyond competitive government subsidies. It was only natural that medical schools turn to pharmaceutical companies. In a sense, these new revenue streams were obvious business partners for the struggling medical schools. The pharmaceuticals required the intellectual firepower of the academic medical centers and the AMCs badly needed money to replace funds lost from the turbulent changes in the federal subsidy, insurers, and costs of litigation. Ironically, it was Dr. Lindsey McCall who had brokered the largest research grant ever received by the Houston Medical School. Her ten-million-dollar grant, along with several others, placed Houston General Medical School among the top ten medical schools in the country for research dollars.

By the time Christine Stewart accepted Houston Medical's offer to replace Simon Bayer as chair of internal medicine, she had become extremely well-known nationally. To some, she was perceived as a necessary adaptation to the many shocks occurring in academic medicine; to others, she was a species to be observed and treated as potentially lethal.

A soft comment from her right brought Kate back to the here and now. It was Eleanor, speaking so that only Kate could hear her. "Kate dear, it looks as if Jeff is winding up, and you'll be introduced in just a few minutes. May I take this moment with you alone, my dear, to tell you how very proud you have made Marguerite and me?"

Kate turned to face the eighty-plus-year-old woman and, for the first time, grinned with a real face-splitting grin, not the perfunctory smiles of these last few hours. How she had come to love these two women! Of all the regret that the last year had brought, certainly her relationship with the two sisters was not one of them. Marguerite and Eleanor Philbin owned the *Houston Tribune.* They had privately told Kate that they were in the last stages of a merger with one of the syndicates when Kate's series broke. The three had met several times to plan Kate's series on clinical research, which had been so unexpectedly and so overwhelmingly successful. Although the sisters fit perfectly under the rubric of old Houston oil money, Marguerite and Eleanor Philbin were each a unique combination of wisdom, elegance, and wit. The face that was turned to Kate now was beautiful, aristocratic, and full of love. Eleanor gazed directly into Kate's eyes and whispered, "Stop worrying about Lindsey and enjoy your accolades; you deserve this evening, Kate." And she reached for Kate's hand to squeeze it.

Kate was so surprised at the woman's insight that she could feel her eyes start to tear up and her throat close; she had said nothing to anyone about any of her deepening concerns about McCall. Certainly not to Jeff, nor to Eleanor nor Marguerite, for the paper was still recovering from the financial toll of the years of diminishing circulation. In fact, the contract for the book sat unsigned on her desk at her home office. And one of the many demons now assaulting Kate was the knowledge that she could not sign that contract. The book was to be based on her series, and its appearance on the market would very likely assure the newspaper's continued soaring circulation. Yet, she knew she couldn't offer this prospect to the owners.

Kate sat rigidly, willing the wave of emotion to subside. But she held on to Eleanor's hand, gripping it tightly. Finally,

Kate recovered enough to draw a deep breath and another until she could look back at Eleanor and smile once more.

"Thank you," she whispered, "thank you ever so much."

The older woman nodded and drew Kate's head down to whisper once more, "Kate dear, I know what is bothering you, but I believe this will all work out for her. Come see us, and we'll talk about our plan for Lindsey; it's a good one."

Truly stunned, Kate turned to look at this woman, who now felt both like savior and oracle and murmured, "Eleanor, how could you know? I've not spoken with you about any of this."

That dear face broke into a thousand wrinkles as Eleanor smiled back to repeat, "Come and see us this weekend, and we'll all talk. Now, dear girl, Jeff is about to introduce you as the star of this show, so go on up there and accept the kudos. You have worked hard—very hard—but there is more to do. And we'll all get it done. Jeff knows it, too."

As Kate turned to look and listen to Jeff's glowing introduction, she realized that the crushing weight of the burden she had been carrying was gone. With Eleanor's astonishing revelation, Kate no longer felt like Dr. Lindsey McCall's only hope. Suddenly Kate was excited, really excited. She stood to walk toward the stage, smiling and thinking, *This thing is not over. It's just beginning.*

Standing at the podium, she turned to look at Jeff to thank him for his lengthy and somewhat laudatory introduction. Grinning, she started to speak, then stopped as she realized that no one could hear her since the entire room was on its feet, clapping wildly, and that the tall, lanky shadow standing by the door could be Steve. Still smiling, Kate stared across the huge banquet room, and the shadow moved into the light. Yes, Dr. Steve Cooper was back.

There are two kinds of truth, small truth and great truth. You can recognize a small truth because its opposite is a falsehood. The opposite of a great truth is another great truth.

—Niels Bohr

2

About Seven Months Earlier

Kate and Jeff had come to the *Houston Tribune* as a team. He had been her editor at the *San Francisco Gazette*, and they had forged an extremely close professional and personal friendship. So when he got the offer from the struggling *Houston Tribune*, one of Jeff's conditions for accepting the job was that Kate would be hired as one of the senior crime reporters. Jeff was hired to turn the financials around, but the paper still struggled after a year of just about all the magic Jeff Simmons could apply.

Then Kate found the seventy-five word inconspicuous story about a Texas Medical Center cardiologist indicted and convicted of homicide. Buried in the Texas Medical Professional Review site, Kate literally stumbled on it when she entered a typo in the Google search bar as she was doing some research on an entirely unrelated subject. Kate had never heard of a physician being indicted for murder. It just did not happen, she had thought at the time. And she had worked the crime desk for four news services in five states.

How had a story of this magnitude escaped the press and the local Houston news? For a moment, Kate had stared at the article and reread the piece for the third time. For that matter, how had *she* missed it? How had she missed the notice in the police blotter? For crying out loud, she was head of the crime desk at the *Trib*, how on earth could she have missed a two-week murder trial? The small article in the Professional Review Organization site made no mention of the dates or any other details other than that Dr. Lindsey McCall, a former cardiologist at Houston Medical Center, had been found guilty of intentional homicide. Quickly googling "Lindsey McCall," Kate scanned the first few pages of several hundred hits. Paging through the series, she found no entries about this case. Unbelievably, this story was unknown.

Kate was acutely aware that there were other hungry reporters searching for the perfect tip: that once-in-a-lifetime confluence of human interest, intrigue, and scandal. This was it.

She knew she had to calm down, for she was incredibly excited, and when she got like this, she could not think straight. She closed her eyes and practiced the meditative techniques a therapist had taught her years ago: "Breathe in, breathe out, focus on your breath and only your breath."

As always, the technique worked, and she now knew her next steps. Glancing at her watch, she steeled herself for the call, for she hated using Jim in this way, but she had no other options and little time. If she had stumbled on this, so could a thousand other reporters.

Convicting an internationally known and respected cardiologist for homicide based on misuse of an experimental drug seemed fantastic, absurd. Then a few phone calls corroborated the basic facts; Dr. Lindsey McCall was currently in a Huntsville jail, serving out her two-year sentence for intentional homicide.

As she waited for her call to Jim in the Houston DA's office to go through, she thought about the few facts she had learned about this case. And the more she considered it, the more remarkable it seemed. In her ten-year review of all fifty states, there were no cases where a physician had been indicted for homicide. And yet Dr. Lindsey McCall had not only been charged but convicted. What was it about this place? Kate wondered for probably the one hundredth time.

Her musings were interrupted when Jim picked up. After they had exchanged initial pleasantries, he confirmed the facts that she had read online. The victim had been the doctor's mother and that the homicide indictment was based on McCall's use of her own unapproved research drug on a human—a human who happened to be dying and who happened to be her mother. Kate recalled thinking that if she'd seen a movie with this story as the plot line, she'd have walked out; it was so absurd. Yet there it was, five hundred words of pure gold. Kate ended the call with an apology and a rushed, "Thanks, Jim, I've got to try to reach Jeff before he leaves the office. I'll get back to you, I promise."

Although it was getting late on a Friday afternoon, Kate figured Jeff was still in the office. When he picked up his private line, he growled, "This better be good, Kate. I promised Ellen that I'd be home early and that we would be on time— for once—for our reservations at Café Annie's."

Kate knew that Jeff and his wife were extremely protective of their Friday date-nights. That was most likely one of the primary reasons the couple was still very happily married, despite the passage of seventeen years and the appearance of five children.

Once Kate had outlined what she had discovered and the way she would like to put together her proposal for presentation to the newspaper's board of trustees, Jeff's response was a whispered, "Holy shit, Kate, we can't present this to the board. If someone slipped and mentioned it, one of the major news services could pick up on it, and we'd lose out. Hold on for a few minutes while I do some checking."

She smiled as she heard the click of the hold line. Kate was delighted that he saw the urgency and was as excited as she was about the potential here. She loved working for the guy. He was smart and didn't play games. More than that, he was never afraid to make a decision.

While waiting, she switched her home office phone to speaker and continued listing the work that had to be done for this proposal so it would be in some shape to present on Monday. Sighing, she realized that she would have to cancel her date tomorrow night.

Maybe, Townsend, she thought to herself, *the fact that you work every blasted minute of your waking hours is the reason you have no social life—nada.*

"Okay, Kate, we have a meeting in my office with Marguerite and Eleanor at seven sharp. You get to work, now I gotta get—" Apparently realizing that she had not said a word, Jeff barked, "Kate, are you there? Say something."

"I'm getting my nose to the grindstone, which is where it will stay all weekend."

She laughed as she heard the dial tone.

Kate spent half that Sunday night putting together the proposal to sell Jeff on approving an investigative series on this case. She knew he would go for it but suspected that the main problem would be funding the necessary research trips to do the clinical investigation articles she knew were essential to the series.

Monday morning, Kate barged into Jeff's office with barely a knock and took no note of the two women who sat at his glass conference table. Tossing his copy of her proposal into his lap, Kate continued the conversation they had ended six hours earlier—at 1:00 a.m.

"Jeff, I added a page explaining why I think the investigational drug research, including a site visit to the primary research site at Andrews, Sacks, and Levine, is so necessary. If you turn to page 12, you'll see the bullet points covering my rationale and—"

Cutting her off with a grin, Jeff casually asked Kate if she'd like a cup of coffee and would she like to say hello to Eleanor and Marguerite Philbin. Mortified, for she remembered now that Jeff had said he would see if the owners of the paper could join them for this meeting, Kate could feel the heat rise in her cheeks. Both Kate and Jeff understood that there was no time to waste here. That a case of this magnitude had not been uncovered by another reporter was nothing short of miraculous for the *Tribune* but if Kate learned about it, then so could their competitors, both locally and nationally. Decisions had to be made quickly and discreetly. Thankfully, the Philbin sisters were masters at discretion, and both enjoyed intrigue.

Recovering somewhat, Kate smiled awkwardly and extended her hand first to Eleanor and then to Marguerite, exclaiming as she did so, "I am so sorry for my rudeness, please forgive me."

Marguerite was the first to answer in a soft Houston drawl, "Kate, dear, Jeff has already briefed us on the urgency of this matter, and we have both reviewed your preliminary proposal this morning before we came to Jeff's office. We have just a few questions if we may."

Three hours later, Kate had her green light and an additional $75,000 added to the budget she had drafted the night before. The Philbins were consummate businesswomen, Kate learned in that two-hour meeting. Their questions and suggestions were incisive, and their connections were of critical importance to Kate. But the best part of the meeting was that the two women grasped the potential galvanizing effects of this investigative series upon *Houston* immediately. When they lobbied Jeff harder than she did for the inclusion of the two-article in-depth look at academic, clinical research, and big pharma (the moniker given the pharmaceutical industry by their detractors), Jeff had thrown up his hands in mock despair and laughingly agreed to the entire format as Kate had written it.

Marguerite and Eleanor Philbin were not only very wealthy native Houstonians, but were also devout Catholics, a fact that had been revealed to Jeff and Kate at the meeting. The relevance of those three attributes was evident in not-for-profit boards of trustees like hospitals. Therefore, both women had served on the boards of a majority of the Texas Medical Center (TMC) hospitals.

The TMC boasted over two hundred thousand workers in forty-two institutions covering over one thousand acres, about the size of the financial district in downtown Manhattan. Located on South Main Street in central Houston, it is currently the largest medical complex in the world.

But the pride of Houstonians also held an irresistible allure when it came to human drama and intrigue. Kate knew this intuitively, but Eleanor and Marguerite had related some personal anecdotes of their own about a few former TMC physician and administrative misalliances that were both appalling and hysterically funny. The stories were told with promises of confidence, of course, but the one point that Jeff and she had disagreed on—what the meat of this story was—was resolved.

Kate believed that people—all people—took a perverse pleasure in learning of the misfortunes of someone thought to be smarter, richer, or nobler. She argued for the introductory piece, giving a brief overview of the case against Lindsey and then introducing her *Houston* readers to the realities of medical research in the twenty-first century.

The daughter of a retired California cardiac surgeon, Kate had grown up listening to her dad and his partners trying to cope with the rapid changes affecting their medical billings and of the intense competition for the research dollar. To a majority of Americans, the nut and bolt of what drove academic medicine and clinical research was a black box. Kate was sure that readers of all ages and occupations would be eager to open up that box and peek inside.

Jeff disagreed, because he was wary of making powerful enemies within the TMC. His strong feelings were the residual reaction to a slander lawsuit filed against him while working in Boston; the suit was filed by a surgeon whose patient's death was the focus of his story. While Jeff was explaining what had happened all those years before, it was apparent that he was reliving the entire dreadful nightmare. Kate had known some of what had happened but never the whole story. She was speechless, for she had never seen Jeff this upset.

Very gently, Marguerite leaned over to touch Jeff's arm. "Jeff," she said softly, "such a thing will not happen here in *Houston*. I will not allow it."

Although her voice was not raised, its tone was emphatic. Marguerite's light-blue eyes were fixed on Jeff, and when, after a few seconds, he'd continued staring down at the glass table they all sat around, Kate watched the long, spidery fingers clamp down and squeeze his arm. Hard. Saying nothing, he looked up at her, and their gazes locked. Marguerite simply nodded her lips tight.

Amazingly Kate watched Jeff relax and nod as well as he took the elder woman's hand and shook it, saying, "You know, Marguerite, I believe you. I really do, I guess I'm not accustomed to having a boss I can trust."

Following a long silence, Marguerite asked, "Kate, dear,

how do you plan to start?"

Kate thought how she normally detested being called "dear," but out of Marguerite's mouth, it sounded endearing and loving. She answered, "Get started how? I'm sorry, Marguerite, I don't know what you mean."

"Well," replied the older woman, "I think the proprietary nature of the research labs at the medical school and at Andrews, Sacks, and Levine may pose an obstacle to a *Houston Trib* reporter attempting entry to do an investigative series on a new drug, don't you?"

With a startled laugh, Kate acknowledged the truth of the statement and exhaled very slowly.

"Actually, Kate," replied Eleanor, speaking for the first time since the pleasantries of the meeting had concluded an hour earlier, "I have a couple of thoughts since I currently serve on the board at Houston Medical Center Hospital. I have met Mr. Reardon at several medical center functions, and I found him to be a most unusual businessman." Eleanor's bright-blue eyes twinkled as she scanned the bullet points of Kate's proposal. "I think Mr. Reardon will find this project every bit as intriguing as Marguerite and I."

The older woman paused to sip some coffee and then continued, "I'll make a couple of phone calls: first, to Mr. Reardon and then to Dr. Stewart when I get home later this morning. I'm certain Christine will be more than happy to set up a meeting between you and Hank Reardon." She grabbed a small sterling silver-enclosed notepad from her purse and jotted down a few notes, then glanced up and addressed Kate as she refocused the attention of the group on Dr. Christine Stewart.

"This is very timely," Eleanor remarked, "for it was just two months ago that Dr. Stewart received a commendation from the trustees for her ten-million dollar grant from Andrew,

Sacks, and Levine. Her predecessor, Dr. Bayer, had begun the process with the ASL new chief executive officer, Hank Reardon."

Eleanor paused to sip some coffee, and as she did, Jeff commented, "That grant is based on the research done by Dr. Lindsey McCall, on that modification of an old heart drug, right? In fact, it was the one that she used to kill her mother, right?"

Kate was watching the interchange as she attempted to determine whether she should join the comments; she happened to notice an almost imperceptible expression flash across Eleanor's face as Jeff finished speaking. Eleanor looked almost angry, but the expression disappeared so quickly that Kate wondered if she had imagined it. A large part of Kate's skill as a reporter lay in noting such flashes of emotion, and she wondered why Eleanor would show anger at Jeff for asking about Dr. McCall's use of the drug. Reflecting back on what she'd seen, she realized that Eleanor had reacted to Jeff's phrase "kill her mother." As she sat turning that over in her mind, Kate looked up to find three pairs of eyes staring at her.

"Uh, it looks as if I've missed something here?"

Patting her hand a bit indulgently, Eleanor laughed and replied, "Kate, dear, I am sure you are exhausted after the weekend of work you've put in. I doubt that you got more than a few hours of sleep. I was asking if you would like me to call Dr. Stewart to let her know that you'll be setting up a meeting with her this week."

Delighted, Kate bobbed her head and squeezed Eleanor's hand as she said, "Yes, please. Would you do that as soon as you can get to it?"

The whole problem with the world is that fools and fanatics are always so certain of themselves, and wiser people so full of doubts.
—Bertrand Russell

3

By eight fifty-five Wednesday morning, a mere two days after Eleanor had made her introductory call to Dr. Stewart's office, Kate sat waiting for her nine o'clock meeting with the new chair of internal medicine.

Although Houston's traffic problems were legendary, traffic within the downtown and medical center areas was normally pretty light. So Kate had turned onto Ross Sterling Drive in front of Memorial Hermann Hospital by about quarter past eight. She'd done some research on the TMC before moving to Houston the year before and knew that the TMC was like Texas: huge. She recalled that there were over sixty independent medical institutions and with eighty thousand or ninety thousand physicians, researchers, and employees in the sprawling twelve miles of incorporated TMC prime real estate. Even with all those facts, however, she had not imagined the immensity and complexity of the place.

Precisely at nine, the door to Dr. Stewart's office opened, and there stood the chair of internal medicine. To Kate, Dr. Christine Stewart looked exactly as she had during the extensive media blitz thrown by the local Houston television stations upon her arrival to the city. About five foot eight and relatively slim, Stewart stood clothed in a light wool herringbone designer suit that looked like a Dior, accessorized with black low-heeled pumps. Her pumps were definitely Ferragamo,

Kate thought as she examined the new chair of medicine. Dr. Stewart's outfit had to have cost her somewhere close to twenty-five hundred. These observations and many more ticked through Kate's mind as she stood and extended her hand to the woman standing in the doorway of her office. Dr. Stewart looked more like a Fortune 500 CEO than a physician, Kate reflected as she smiled a hello to the attractive blonde.

"I can't thank you enough, Dr. Stewart, for meeting with me on such short notice."

Waving Kate in and directing her to sit at a tastefully decorated coffee table and three decorator chairs, Christine Stewart smiled warmly as she laughingly responded, "Kate, one would have to be a fool to refuse the chair of the board of trustees the favor of a sixty-minute meeting."

Christine's keen gray eyes noted Kate's expression at her comment, so asked her, "You did not know that Eleanor Philbin is chair of the board at the Houston General Medical School?"

For only a moment, Kate considered smiling back into the gray eyes and lying, but she knew her surprise had been registered by Stewart.

"Eleanor told me that she was on the board but failed to mention that she was chair." Surprised at her own thoughts, Kate mentally shook herself to regain her objectivity as she wondered what it was about this woman that had evoked such pettiness. Recovering, Kate continued with a smile, "Regardless, Dr. Stewart, I am certain that your schedule is extremely full, so I do appreciate your assistance."

This time, Dr. Stewart nodded and agreed, "Well, Kate, you're correct. I am booked very tightly today and therefore can spare only about forty-five minutes with you. But my chief of cardiology, Dr. Steve Cooper, has a bit more time today and is willing to take you to see Dr. McCall's research laboratories if that would be useful to you."

Without waiting for Kate's response, Dr. Stewart declared that Eleanor had explained to her the purpose of Kate's visit and that she had placed a call to Hank Reardon in Zurich earlier that morning. She expected a call back at any time now.

"If your goal is to understand the basic issues of academic clinical research with emphasis on Dr. McCall's breakthroughs with Digipro, then you'll want to go to Zurich so that you can see the corporate headquarters for ASL."

Just as she completed her last comment, there was a discreet knock on the door, and upon opening the door, Dr. Stewart's secretary quietly announced that Mr. Hank Reardon was on line two. Standing, Christine motioned to Kate to follow as she approached a large conference table on the opposite side of her office. There sat a computer and several phones. Touching a couple of buttons on the computer, Christine clicked on Web-Com, and there appeared the face of the internationally known corporate magician known as Hank Reardon, smiling his signature grin.

"Top of the morning to you, Christine. I take it this is Kate Townsend sitting next to you?" Without waiting either for Kate's nod of the head or her verbal *yes* that accompanied it, Reardon continued, "Have you been to Zurich, Kate?"

Again, responding only to Kate's nonverbal signals, Reardon nodded and smiled at her negative.

"Good, if you can get here by the weekend, I can pick you up at the airport and take you to our labs. Oh, right, Christine." Reardon acknowledged a frown from Dr. Stewart. "Kate, my daughter, Liisa, is the head scientist of the Digipro research project for ASL and will be in Zurich until Monday afternoon. You can meet with Liisa before she has to leave on a business trip. Okay, Dr. Stewart? Have we covered all that you had mentioned?"

There was that engaging smile again, but as Kate stared at the computer screen, there seemed to be something other than amusement in Reardon's startlingly blue eyes as he waited for Christine Stewart's response. When Kate heard Stewart's voice, she was surprised when she heard her name. Ignoring Reardon's last comment, Stewart's cool gaze was on Kate as she said, "Well Kate, if you have your schedule, maybe you can give Hank an idea of how soon you can leave for Zurich?"

Pulling out her Blackberry with her left hand, Kate looked first at the unsmiling face of Christine Stewart and then at the electric-blue eyes of Hank Reardon on the screen as she replied, "I'll be there as soon as I can book a flight."

And then he was gone.

Stewart turned to Kate as she checked her watch, a gold Rolex, and asked, "How can I be of help to you in the remaining time we have together today?"

Trying mightily to appear as if she booked international flights with corporate moguls on an hourly basis, Kate collected herself and answered, "Perhaps you can give me your view of the prospects for this new drug and its impact on the public at large."

As Kate opened her briefcase to retrieve her tape recorder and legal pad, she was momentarily overwhelmed with how quickly this thing had taken shape. Only three days ago, she'd been surrounded by discarded drafts of her proposal. And here she was beginning the research for her first two articles. *Amazing*, she thought, *unbelievable really.*

Clicking her recorder on, Kate also started taking notes as Dr. Christine Stewart began to talk about the implications of a centuries-old drug suddenly rid of toxic side effects for the treatment of heart failure. Stewart's response was polished and informed by her twenty-first-century approach to academic research. Kate had read many of Stewart's early and recent articles in *Circulation, New England Journal of Medicine,* and *Lancet.*

She was well published but not in clinical research. Rather, Christine Stewart had risked and received censure from her academic colleagues with her defense of collaboration between corporate pharmacology companies and academic medical schools. To Stewart, such cooperation was essential for the continuation of academic research in the new age of diminishing federal research monies. There were no alternatives; therefore, what had been termed *collusion* by many of her predecessors was simply reality to Christine Stewart.

The meeting passed quickly. Suddenly, Christine was standing and introducing her to her chief of cardiology, Dr. Steve Cooper. Following Dr. Cooper out of Dr. Stewart's office, Kate had turned to thank Christine once more, but the door had been quietly closed. Steve Cooper caught Kate's gesture and shrugged as he asked, "Shall we go to Lindsey's lab now?"

As she nodded her assent to Cooper, she took note of his casual use of Dr. McCall's first name. Kate realized that she'd spent an hour with Christine Stewart and that Dr. Lindsey McCall's name had been mentioned by Stewart only one time and in a manner that suggested that the two barely knew each other.

How weird is that? thought Kate as she hurried to catch up with Dr. Cooper.

For in much wisdom there is much sorrow,
And he who stores up knowledge stores up grief.
—ECCLESIASTES 1:16–18

4

Dr. Steve Cooper stood at the side of the door to let Kate enter the small three-room suite of offices identified only by number. Each room was painted that ubiquitous and nondescript institutional yellow and faintly smelled of chemicals that Kate could not identify. Kate stood looking around and caught Cooper staring at her. As her eyes met his, Cooper smiled and said, "Pretty unimpressive, isn't it? Lindsey and I were cardiology fellows together, and Dr. Bayer gave her this research space before she completed her fellowship. Dr. Bayer was the chair of medicine before Dr. Stewart." Cooper wandered around the small room as he spoke, acting as if he had never seen the space before. Then he turned back to Kate and smiled. "Dr. Bayer thought Lindsey was the best and the brightest of us all." The smile faded and then he frowned. "She worked here many nights and most of the weekends that she was not on call." Pointing to the shelving lining the upper halves of the walls on two sides of the small room, Steve asked, "See all those notebooks stacked on the top shelves? If you page through them, you'll see her notes on all the experiments starting from 1987 to 2004, the year that she did it."

"The year that she did it." Kate echoed Cooper. "You mean when she came up with the new molecule for Digipro?"

A dark eyebrow lifted in surprise. "Right, sorry, she had been working on this even before medical school, so over twenty years."

Kate sensed there was more that the man wanted to say, so she said nothing, absorbing the silence of the place—the surprising austere, almost bleak sense of the atmosphere here. Several minutes passed in silence while she paged through the early ledger books. Each page was filled with precise penciled notes detailing the names and dates of dated sequential experiments. Most of the notes were composed of acronyms and abbreviations. When she picked up the last one, which was dated 2004, and turned to the last page, July 15, she saw the same carefully penciled notes. Then nothing.

Glancing over her shoulder to read that last entry, Cooper whistled softly, "I would have written *eureka* in the last entry, or at least a *yahoo*; but not Lindsey. You'd never know that this one was the last experiment or that she had any pride at all in finally conquering the side effects of digitalis." Then so softly that Kate had to strain to hear him. "'Course by then, she'd stopped caring."

Kate was no novice reporter. Excellent interviewing skills were the number-one tool of a journalist, and Kate had long ago learned that silence elicited far more information than did interrogation. Rather than focusing on the next question, the skilled interviewer used silence to map out the verbal and facial territory of the person being interviewed. It was often the nonverbal cues and facial expressions of a person that provided the real meaning behind their words.

While Christine Stewart seemed to be one of those rare people capable of suppressing the verbal and facial "tells" for any good interviewer's interpretation, Steve Cooper looked like an open book. His dark eyes were lively, and his facial expressions suggested ironic amusement at the world around him.

Kate had accompanied her father on countless Saturday morning rounds, and she remembered the easy camaraderie between her dad and the cardiologists with whom he worked. They acted like members of a brotherhood and spoke with one another in the verbal shorthand unique to doctors. The respect they had for one another's opinions was always evident, even when opinions differed and massive egos were defending themselves. Steve Cooper could have fit easily among those men, but she could not imagine Christine Stewart as one of the group, and she wondered about that. Not because Stewart was a woman, at least from the perspective of the men, Kate thought; it was more a sense of distance dictated by Stewart herself. Of course, surgeons are a different breed, and the distinct tension Kate felt between Cooper and his chair could possibly be attributed to gender. But Kate sensed that Cooper was not the type of guy to resent a female boss. There was definitely something else at work here, and she wondered about it.

By now, the silence had stretched to the point that Cooper decided to fill it with possible points of interest like the tiny cages for the rats (now empty) that had been used in McCall's early experiments and the small hoods under which the animals were anesthetized. As Cooper talked, Kate heard affection, respect, and sadness for the plight of Dr. Lindsey McCall. All of these had been absent from Christine Stewart.

When Dr. Cooper had arrived to pick up Kate, his boss had simply nodded to him. Christine's gesture had seemed stiff and unusually formal—seemingly accentuating Cooper's status as the underling.

She decided to take a risk with this guy.

"You and Dr. McCall were good friends, Dr. Cooper?"

Intense brown eyes looked down at her. Kate was not short; at five foot ten, she was accustomed to meeting the gaze of most men at eye level. Not Steve Cooper, though, who had to be five or six inches taller than Kate, who was wearing heels.

"It's Steve, and right, Lindsey and I are—not were—good friends. Christine Stewart and I are not. Dr. Stewart also told me to take you on a tour of the new animal research labs. Are you ready to do that or is there more here you'd like to see?"

The two comments were said nonchalantly, as if the second naturally followed the other. The doctor's drawl was curiously devoid of emotion. Kate wondered if Dr. Cooper—Steve— were expecting some kind of response from her. Was this an invitation or a challenge? But Kate decided to play this carefully for now. She guessed that Steve Cooper may be a man who just said what he thought, but her innate caution took precedence when a story as big as this one was brewing.

And this one was huge.

Sidestepping his comment about Christine Stewart, Kate replied, "Thank you, Steve, and it's Kate. I think I've seen enough of Dr. McCall's labs for now. Yes, I would love to see the new research labs."

"To dare is to lose one's footing momentarily. To
not dare is to lose oneself."
—Soren Kierkegaard

5

Sighing deeply as she sank into the plush leather seat on the Swiss Air nonstop flight to Zurich, Kate thought gratefully of Eleanor's suggestion—command really—that she fly first class to Zurich. Kate considered herself unpretentious and normally abhorred self-indulgence.

But this was nice. Very nice.

"Yes," she heard herself reply to the smiling blond flight attendant, "I would love a scotch on the rocks. Do you have Macallan by any chance?" *Right, Townsend, you're not an elitist. No, not you, but the first chance you get, you glom down a single malt scotch,* she scoffed silently to herself.

Reflecting on the past five days that felt more like a year, Kate was astonished at the amount of work she'd been able to get done on this series. The first installment had copious notes already drafted into a loose format, and she would complete it by Friday night in Zurich and fax it to Houston for Sunday publication on the front page of the *Houston Tribune* once she'd met with Hank Reardon and Liisa to fill in major gaps in her story.

She was pleased with it, and she was without a doubt her own worst critic. But this had seemed to write itself, almost from the beginning.

Aware that the progress was certainly not by her efforts alone, Kate was deeply grateful for the efforts of Jeff, of Marguerite and Eleanor Philbin, and most recently, of Steve Cooper. She and Steve had spent most of Wednesday afternoon together as Cooper successfully waved aside her reluctance to consume an entire day of his assuredly busy schedule.

Of course, she thought now, it didn't hurt that she liked this guy, as in *really* liked him.

Dangerous, she knew. Steve Cooper reminded her of her dad. And Kate's father was her favorite person on this earth.

When Cooper had walked her to her car after showing her the new animal research building around five in the afternoon that Wednesday, he had asked if she were free for dinner the following night. Floored, Kate had stammered out a *yes*, and the next evening they had spent four hours drinking red wine and savoring filets at one of Steve's favorite restaurants in River Oaks.

Driving away from Kate's apartment Thursday late afternoon, Steve had promised that Marfreless, the bar where they would stop before dinner, was a special bar that served only the very best vodka, one that had no neurological effects like drunkenness.

They drove down West Gray Boulevard and took a right onto Peden, right around the corner from the River Oaks Theater. Steve drove and parked in a lot at back of the theater, but instead of turning left to walk down the street of the posh shops and restaurants, he turned right and walked back into the parking lot. Kate, suddenly noticing that he was not beside her, had turned to see him standing in the parking lot, waiting patiently.

When she caught up with him, she started to ask where they were going, but he placed a finger over his lips and walked back through the parking lot to a white metal staircase, under which was an unmarked blue door. He opened the door and stood there waiting for her to catch up.

"Be careful," Steve said, "it's very dark, so wait until your eyes adjust to the light."

Kate could see very little as they entered a narrow entryway, which dropped down just a bit as she walked along. Soon she could make out a soft light and could negotiate her way without falling.

Thankfully, she reached the level floor without incident and followed Steve into the dimly lit bar. She glanced around at the charming place and saw several small, square tables to her right; two long couches in front; and an about-thirty-foot-long bar, which extended almost the length of the place. Above the bar hung an eight-panel Japanese silk screen softly illuminated by the lights of the hundreds of bottles of vodkas and scotches openly displayed. Completing the understated elegance and intimacy of the place was a classical piece playing softly in the background.

Joining Steve at one of the small tables, she took a seat across from him as he finished ordering their drinks from a very tall, slim young woman dressed in tight jeans and sweater with at least four-inch stiletto heels. As Kate watched the girl saunter over to the bartender to order their drinks, she noted wryly that the young woman moved gracefully and confidently on the heels, as if she were a model at one of the fashion shows.

Glancing back at Steve, she saw that he'd been watching her watch the waitress, and she smiled as she said, "I'm admiring her grace on high heels; it sure exceeds mine."

Nodding, he asked, "So what do you think of Marfreless? I have been coming here for over twenty years. And, Kate, I hope you're ready for the best vodka martini in Houston. You do drink vodka martinis, I hope?"

"As a matter of fact, I do, and yes, I'm ready for a great one. Thanks, Steve."

As she smiled into his dark eyes, she noted once more the vitality apparent in his eyes and his expression—and a touch of the ironic air that seemed to emanate from him.

Picking up her drink, she leaned closer to him and touched his glass as she toasted, "To the home of the best martinis in Houston." Sipping her drink, Kate exclaimed, "Wow, you're right, Dr. Cooper, this is a superb martini. I like your Marfreless a lot, but I'm not sure that I could ever find it again unless I can remember where the blue door is. The return customers must really want to find this place. Clever."

Popping one of the huge olives into his mouth, Steve chewed contentedly.

"So why have you decided to help me, Steve?"

Swallowing his olive quickly, the doctor snapped back, "Okay, Kate, why does an investigative reporter for the *Houston Tribune* doing a series on murder in the Texas Medical Center decide to start with an exciting subject like academic clinical research? And why does same reporter seem completely disinterested in said murder? Evidenced by her total lack of questions about same? Did I say that I was interested in helping you? How do you know that I'm not just a bored cardiologist looking for female company tonight?"

Returning Cooper's gaze steadily, Kate answered only the last of the questions he had thrown at her, "Because I don't think boredom is something you ever experience, Steve … maybe exhaustion, overwork, overexertion, insomnia."

Interrupting her with a rueful laugh, Steve held up one hand and cried out, "Enough! Ms. Townsend, you have exposed me!" Laughter fading, Cooper frowned as he regarded Kate. "Honestly, Kate, I don't know that I know the answer to your question as yet. Not completely, anyway. Christine asked that I give you the tour the other day. And that was no problem as I had a really light schedule. I hadn't been in Lindsey's labs since this whole thing broke loose, and I did not expect the reaction I had upon going back there."

There was silence as he thought about what he was saying and what he meant to convey to Kate. And she sat there, comfortably waiting for him to continue his thoughts.

Unusual, Cooper reflected silently. Most people would be attempting to suggest to him the emotions that he was feeling either because they were uncomfortable with silence or because they wanted to control the conversation.

He had known a few reporters and most had trouble keeping their mouths shut.

Not this lady.

"You asked if Lindsey and I were good friends the other day, and I remember correcting your use of the past tense to that of the present. Since then, I've been thinking about why I did that. Lindsey has been in jail for over six months, and she refuses to see me. From what I hear, she won't talk to anyone, even her lawyer.

"So it's been a good year or so since we have talked. It was before the trial that we last had any kind of a conversation, and she wasn't in very good shape to speak to me about anything of substance back then. But I've loved Lindsey McCall ever since I met her in our fellowship program. So, yes, Kate, Lindsey's probably the best friend I've ever had."

Steve stared over at the Vermeer for a few minutes as he stirred his martini absently. Returning his gaze to Kate, he said, "I used the word *love,* Kate, because *like* isn't strong enough, but there is no romance between Lindsey and me. There never was.

"Watching her perform in the cath lab was a thing to behold. She was the best in the department. Dr. Bayer said she was the best he had ever seen in over fifty years of practice. She was certainly better than I would ever be. I knew that already when we were still fellows. But the thing with Lindsey was that she was never out to prove anything to anyone. So her proficiency in the lab, in research, and in the clinic was something she took for granted. She had gifts and knew it. And I miss her. You have no idea how deeply I miss her."

There was that look of irony again as he shook his head and added, "Until I walked into those research labs of hers, *I* didn't know how much I miss her. Guess I managed to suppress all of that once it all hit the fan."

Steve seemed to mentally collect himself as he shrugged and grinned. "Sorry for the extensive rumination here. Are you sure you're not a shrink dressed up as a reporter? I've only known two people who listen as intently as you do, and both of them went into psychiatry."

The question was rhetorical, Kate knew, but she responded, "I learned very early in my career that the real story wasn't what people said first or even second. Most of us move so fast through our busy lives that we never stop to reflect about how we feel or what we know. Until something happens that forces us to do it."

Kate was enjoying getting to know this man. Her gut had been right: this was a man who called it the way he saw it— rare in these days of political correctness. Once more, she thought of the comparison she had made to her dad; only this time, she didn't fight it. She smiled as she thought of the similarities between the two men.

Of course, the smile did not go unnoticed. In answer to the quizzical look he gave her, Kate explained, "I think that you and my dad have some things in common, and I realize that I've not previously met anyone who has reminded me of Dad."

Acknowledging her comment with a nod, Steve said, "I'll take that as a compliment, Kate. I like to think of myself as genuine—that I don't play mind games with people or with myself. But I've not been a good friend to Lindsey these last six months; I've not been a friend at all." Hesitating, considering what to say next, he continued, "So twenty minutes after you asked the question of why I was helping you Kate, I've figured out why. So now it's your turn. Why are you going after the most salacious story in the TMC in the last seventy-five years as if it were an academic dissertation?"

Slipping her miniature tape recorder out of her purse, Kate took another sip of her drink and outlined the general sense of her planned series, briefly reviewing her plan to begin the first article with what she called the "black box" of academic clinical research: the process and the funding sources. Then she would move to the relationship between academic medicine and the pharmacologic industry as a logical extension of diminished support from the federal government.

Steve's expression was one of focused concentration as Kate spoke, but she noticed a frown between his dark eyebrows.

"Steve, what are you thinking? I can see the question formed on your forehead."

"Well, yeah, Kate, you're doing a series on a murder in the TMC, and you're starting with a dry subject like clinical research? Isn't that like doing a story on the mom who murdered her kids and explaining the birth process? You're a crime reporter, not a medical reporter, right?"

Kate's hands came together in a clap as she delightedly exclaimed, "That's exactly what we discussed at our Monday meeting. I may discover that you and my editor, Jeff, are right when we run the first article on Sunday, and no one from the major news services picks it up, Steve, but here is why I am going to start this way.

"I'm sure that you are aware of the trouble that American

newspapers are in, Steve. And since you have leveled with me, I'll tell you that the *Houston Tribune* is in serious financial trouble. We need readers—all kinds of readers from all age groups, professions, and ethnicities. This story needs to appeal to all of them to sell. Most people get their news from the television or the Internet; no longer is it the daily newspaper. But in the eighteen months that I have lived in Houston, I have learned there are two loves in this city: the Texas Medical Center and NASA.

"Of course, my first article will highlight the murder conviction of one of the TMC's best and brightest. In fact, I'm toying with this as a title, 'Murder in the Texas Medical Center.'" She lifted an eyebrow and looked quizzically at Steve to gauge his reaction.

Placing his hand on his forehead, Steve groaned and said, "Kate, you're not serious, are you? Good God, tell me you're not serious."

Even in the dimly lit bar, Kate could see Steve's face turn ashen. She realized that the consequences of this story had not dawned on him until now. Somehow the politics and betrayals and who knew what else had been safely hidden. The lightness and bantering of their cocktail hour was over. So she decided to explain further.

"Steve, there are a host of reasons that the series needs to be written. I'll mention only a few, and you know them better than most of us because you live in the medical world. But first, we live in a medical age that dominates a majority of the lives of Americans: Arguably the best-educated generation of Americans, we have a love-hate relationship with doctors and with drugs.

"Of the baby boomers, over half are on antidepressants. You cannot watch a television show without being inundated by advertisements for a chemical answer to every malady known to man and woman. And of course, the diseases increase with each decade. Restless leg syndrome and female incontinence are only two examples. My dad laughs each time those ads appear on TV. I remember one of my dad's friends explaining to me that he knew antibiotics were of no help to patients with a virus, but if he didn't prescribe one, the patient would either complain to the manager of the HMO or go down the street to the competition."

Noting Steve's quizzical look, Kate explained that her dad had been a cardiac surgeon at Stanford and that she had been included in his weekend rounds while growing up.

Taking advantage of the interruption, Steve picked up his martini glass and waited until Kate picked up hers. Then he leaned over the table to gently touch her glass with his and sipped his drink without taking his eyes off hers. His gaze was intense, deep, and sexy. And Kate could feel the heat all the way down to her toes. She was grateful for the dimly lit bar, for she could feel the flush in her cheeks as well. Without changing his expression, Steve smiled crookedly and commanded, "Drink, Kate."

"And then there are the drug companies. Intent on supplying this medically fixated baby boomer generation a cure for everything from hair loss to old age, we've witnessed quite a menu of drugs being withdrawn from the market because of *side effects*, ranging from minor to fatal." Kate frowned in concentration as she recited a partial list, "Redux, Seldane, Prolulsion, Rezulin, Lotromax—to name just a few of them, Steve. And the majority of Americans know next to nothing about the drug industry; most of us go to the doctor with a problem, expect a pill to fix whatever the problem is without ever questioning whether the drug is necessary or will even help us." Kate was on a roll. She could feel the familiar sensations of being on the hunt: the thrill of discovery coupled with the exhilaration of something brand-new and always that undercurrent of anticipation that this could be the story that might warrant the Pulitzer. Aware that she was most likely overwhelming Steve, Kate reigned in her enthusiasm by taking a long sip of her martini and slowly chewing one of the huge olives in the clear-crystal-stemmed glass.

Looking up from her drink, she met Cooper's intense gaze with silence and lifted eyebrows.

"Okay, Kate," Steve said slowly and thoughtfully, "I suspect you are right about the need for public education on all things medical, including drug companies and their growing influence on our health, for better or for worse, but where does Lindsey's indictment and conviction for murder fit into your scenario?" Steve was finding himself interested in this bright and provocative reporter. Kate was more than attractive, but the angular planes of her face and cheekbones were too sharp to be considered conventionally beautiful. And Cooper found that he was eager to hear her assessment of the bizarre circumstances surrounding Lindsey's arrest and conviction.

"I don't know."

Of all the responses, he had expected to hear, that one was not among them. Echoing Kate's words, Cooper stared at her. Steve had heard so many theories from friends, colleagues, and the nursing staff about this case that he'd been positive Kate's would have been similar to one of the stories he had already heard. He realized that no one he knew had admitted that they didn't know; in fact, he seldom heard that phrase from anyone these days; everyone seemed certain of everything. Steve started to smile and laugh with delight. "Let me get this straight, you're planning a series of articles under the title 'Murder in the Texas Medical Center,' but you don't have a working theory to explain why an internationally known cardiologist and researcher would have murdered her mother by using her unapproved research drug."

Kate's gaze did not veer from Cooper's as she asserted, "Quite right, Dr. Cooper."

After several seconds had passed in silence, Cooper realized that Kate had no need to elaborate, make excuses, or explain herself in any way. *What an intriguing woman this is,* he thought as he extended his hand to her and suggested that they go grab some dinner. Steve settled their argument about the bar bill by assuring Kate that the tab would be hers the next time they had martinis at Marfreless. As he stood at the long bar waiting for the bill, Steve realized that he had been engaging in magical thinking about Kate. Knowing that he was not being rational, Steve had hoped that Kate would provide an answer that made sense to the peculiar events that had taken place at the medical center and had been momentarily disappointed when Kate had pled ignorance. A good part of the intrigue that Kate Townsend held for him was just that, Cooper mused as the bartender handed him the credit card receipt to sign. Scribbling his signature in the well-known indecipherability of doctors, Cooper smiled to himself as he thought, *But if anyone can unravel the Gordian knot of Lindsey's conviction, I'll place my bets with Kate Townsend.*

The Uses of Sorrow

Someone I loved once gave me
a box full of darkness.
It took me years to understand that this, too, was a gift.
—Mary Oliver

6

Dr. Lindsey McCall grinned ruefully to herself in mid sentence as she realized that she had been praying Julie's prayer out loud over and over; she'd lost count of the number of times she had spoken the words of a fifteenth-century saint. And she wondered at the solace she felt from saying the prayer. Lindsey was frightened, and she had good reason; the events of the last several weeks had potentially calamitous consequences for her, for Huntsville Prison, and maybe even the entire prison system. Yet she knew she had done the right thing. Deep down, in places she'd never before tried to access, she sensed that the risks she had taken were known, understood, and strangely appreciated. And she wondered again at the prayer and the serenity that seemed to overwhelm her with each recitation.

Julie Grayson had been Lindsey's best friend from first grade through their graduation from Rice University. Most of their friends and families were puzzled by the closeness of the two girls and were surprised that the friendship had lasted through high school and then college. To outsiders, the two girls could not be more different: while Julie was a devout Roman Catholic and had considered a religious life as a young girl, Lindsey had attended the family's Episcopal Church only because her mother had insisted that she go. She had walked out of her Saturday morning confirmation class at thirteen and had never returned to church. Although both girls were excellent athletes, Julie excelled in the team sports of soccer and varsity basketball and volleyball, while Lindsey was drawn to the solitary sports of track and swimming. Julie's ambition was marriage and family, while Lindsey's pursuit of a career track of cardiovascular research and medicine never wavered.

Lindsey's mind drifted back to how she had "met" Julie's Spanish saint: it was a Saturday afternoon in May, and the two young women were cramming for their senior exams in the room they shared at Rice University in Houston. Julie was a double major in mathematics and theology. Julie was fascinated by St. Teresa of Avila and had read each of the nun's four books. She had just finished St. Teresa's autobiography and was undeterred by Lindsey's protests of disinterest.

Lindsey could feel Julie's intense scrutiny as she insisted that Lindsey listen to some of St. Teresa's writings that Julie favored. One of the many things that Lindsey loved and admired about her friend was her independence from the influence of her peers. In the early eighties at Rice University, few college students were devoutly religious; fewer still were interested in fifteenth-century Catholic saints. So Lindsey had put aside her biochemistry texts and surrendered to her passionate young friend. An hour or so later, Lindsey had learned more than she had ever cared to about the unusual relationship between St. Teresa of Avila and St. John of the Cross.

But the book was interesting enough that Lindsey had borrowed it and had read it later that weekend, committing several selections to memory, one of which was the Let Nothing Disturb Thee prayer that had been found on a bookmark after the death of the saint. Julie had always been the only one who could penetrate the intellectual veneer that Lindsey used to protect herself from a family broken apart by illness, jealousy, and loss. Both of the girls' fathers had worked at NASA and had been close friends until the crash of the plane that had killed Lindsey's dad. With his death, Lindsey had shut down emotionally. But that Saturday in May, Julie's enthusiasm had been infectious. Lindsey recalled the delight that she had felt at some of the folksy wisdom and humor of this woman, St. Teresa, who had achieved union with her God.

They had opened up a bottle of Kendall-Jackson cabernet and toasted St. Teresa at least five times. And at last when the wine began to erode Lindsey' rigid self-control, the conversation turned to the personal.

"Linds," Julie had asked gently, "how are things with your mom and with Paula?"

Julie knew better than anyone how jealous Lindsey's older sister was of Lindsey. She had seen it ever since the two friends had been small girls. Julie and Lindsey had practically grown up at each other's houses and were as comfortable at each other's dinner table as they were at home.

Lindsey and her dad had been the best of friends; anyone could see that and did—including Lindsey's mother and sister. Ann McCall was subtle about it, but the nonverbal signals between Paula and her mom when Lindsey and her dad engaged in one of their animated conversations were hard to miss, so Julie had picked up on them. Although Mrs. McCall's cues were never as visible as Paula's outbursts, they were evident to Julie and became more frequent as the girls grew older.

Julie knew, too, of the manipulative skills Paula used with

Lindsey's mother. Julie remembered the scene between the then seven-year-old Lindsey and seventeen-year-old Paula that seemed to be the start of the split within the McCall family. She and Lindsey had been in Lindsey's room when they heard Lindsey's mom yell, "Tom, get the camera. We need a picture of Paula on her prom night!"

As Julie and Lindsey came out of the bedroom, Paula was posing on the landing of the circular staircase in the front room, and Lindsey's dad was dutifully taking pictures from several different angles. Julie remembered the dress and how much older it made Paula look. At seven, she was no judge of fashion, but Paula had looked like a movie star that night. The dress was low cut and white and clung very tightly to Paula's petite but voluptuous body. Of course, Paula was basking in this rare and undivided attention from her father.

The moment shattered into a million irretrievable pieces when Mrs. McCall unthinkingly turned to her younger daughter and cooed, "Lindsey, darling, just wait until you are old enough to be elected prom queen and go to your senior prom!"

And to the astonishment of everyone there, Lindsey's grave response, though said very quietly, seemed to echo through the huge entry way of the McCall's entryway.

"Mother, no way will I spend $750 on a silly dress. I'll need every dime for med school."

For just a moment, no one said a word. Julie could still remember how the hair on the back of her neck had stood up, as it did right before the thunder rolled and the lightning began to crack.

All energy in the room seemed to evaporate as Lindsey's dad calmly put down the camera and looked at his wife and older daughter as he said quietly, too quietly, "I thought that we had agreed that $750 was too much for a prom dress. Did we not discuss this in exhausting detail last week?"

The question was rhetorical; neither Paula nor her mother bothered to answer him. Both the older and the younger women were staring at Lindsey in shock. Her father's voice was quiet. Julie had never heard Tom McCall yell, but his blue eyes—the exact same shade as Paula's—were glacial. As he walked out of the room, Paula's eyes filled with rage as she glared at Lindsey. But Lindsey had turned back to Julie and asked her to come back to her bedroom to finish their game. As they left the room, Julie knew that Lindsey never saw the stunned expression on her mother's face nor did she notice Paula.

The death of Lindsey's father during their freshman year had worried Julie for more than the obvious reasons. Lindsey and her dad seemed to be able to communicate without words. In contrast, the "mom" side of the McCall family—Paula and her mother—chatted about all kinds of things. Lindsey and her Dad always seemed to be in the family but not of it. Both of them were intense and naturally laconic. At least that was how it seemed to the young Julie. It was as if Ann McCall and her older daughter, Paula, were figuratively jumping up and down and constantly talking to get the attention of Tom McCall. While Lindsey was—well, she was just Lindsey—never seemed to be aware of all the drama that permeated the family. Because she never tried to get her dad's attention, he seemed to be drawn closer and closer to Lindsey. Tom McCall delighted in his younger daughter: her intensity, intelligence, and way of looking at the world around her were easy for him to understand. As a test pilot for NASA, Lindsey's father had seemed larger than life to everyone but his younger daughter.

They looked nothing alike. In fact, Lindsey strongly resembled her mother, Ann. Both were blonde with intense, green eyes. It was Paula who looked so much like her father that her grade-school pictures were compared to Tom's by Ann. Tom and Paula were both dark and small with eyes that were not just blue but cerulean, a startling contrast to their dark-brown, almost black hair. Tom would frequently joke that there was no way NASA would hire him now, for he was too short for the hiring standards of the eighties.

Julie decided in the early years of her friendship with Lindsey that the connection between the two family members of each "set" of McCalls was a deep and complicated interplay of personality traits. Ann McCall had been a stay-at-home mom in a neighborhood where most of the women were working professionals as well as wives and mothers. So when her seven-year-old daughter announced that she planned to save all her money for medical school, Ann McCall had no frame of reference for ambition like that. Paula, although a difficult teenager, was someone whom Ann could relate to. Paula wanted to marry and have children. And, of course, the onset of Ann's illness coincided perfectly with Paula's need to get away from a husband she married impulsively and a child who had come much too soon in the turbulent marriage.

Lindsey and her dad seemed like two peas in a pod. From that momentous evening when Lindsey had announced the direction of her life, her father never doubted the girl. It was a given: Lindsey would be a cardiologist as well as a cardiovascular research scientist. Other parents might dismiss such a statement as a passing phase, but Tom never did. Julie wondered if Lindsey's focus would have been so unwavering if her dad had been less supportive. And it didn't really seem like support when you were around the two of them. It was more that Tom McCall recognized his younger daughter—understood her in a way that no one else could.

They had been freshmen at Rice when his test plane crashed. Julie had driven a dazed Lindsey home to Clear Lake to suffer through the fiasco of what Julie privately referred to as "funeral by Paula."

Julie's concern for her friend was not unfounded. The death of Lindsey's dad meant that the delicate balance of power in the family would tip in Paula's favor. And from the beginning of that dreadful weekend, Paula made it clear that the gloves were off. Paula would call the shots and was confident that their mother would support everything Paula wanted: two against one.

And in fairness to Ann McCall, how could she not? At least that was how Julie had interpreted the strange dynamics of the three remaining McCalls. Paula had taken charge of her care from the beginning. With the confidence bred by recent nursing school training, Paula had seen an opening in the stricken family and grabbed it.

At only one point during the interminable weekend Lindsey had offered a counter to Paula's endless recitation of duties to be assigned to this friend, to that neighbor; Julie's folks were named for half of the list, but she wisely kept that observation to herself. Paula was now planning the funeral: it would be Monday at nine in the morning at the Trinity Episcopal Church in Clear Lake, and there would be these hymns sung by the choir.

"Dad never went to that church, Paula. Dad never went to church—period. Mom, how can you lie there and let Paula plan a funeral that Dad would despise?"

Lindsey's voice was flat, and her tone was not combative, but Paula erupted. "You are *not* controlling the way *my* father leaves this earth. You manipulated every part of his life and worked it so that he never had time for Mom or me. Yeah, Lindsey, you and Dad excluded Mom and me every chance you got. I got so sick and tired of hearing Dad rave about his perfectly brilliant Lindsey. Don't you dare pretend you're a member of this family now, of all times. Mom and I are planning this funeral, and there is nothing you can do about it. If you don't like what we're doing, don't come. You just go back and do what you do best: ignore your mother and pretend that all your stupid studying will help her. Oh and of course, leave all her care to me. Don't ever offer to help out."

By now, Paula was screaming, her eyes bulging, and her face scarlet with rage. Her last few words were slurred, and Julie wondered if she had been drinking, although it was only ten thirty in the morning.

Lindsey turned to look at her mother, saw the tears streaming down her face, and said very quietly to Julie, "Let's go."

They walked out of the house, and Lindsey never said a word as Julie drove them back to Rice. Lindsey did not attend the funeral, and Julie did not know if she'd seen her sister or mother since that ghastly weekend.

Now, three years later, Lindsey echoed Julie's question, "How are things with Paula and Mom?" She was sobbing out the words, crying so hard that she was coughing and choking. Stunned at her friend's outburst, Julie had sprung from her bed to that of her friend and held her as tightly as she could while the sobs racked Lindsey's body. Julie said nothing at all while she waited out the emotional tsunami overwhelming her friend.

Once Lindsey gained control of herself, she shocked Julie again as she hesitantly asked, "Jules, I'd like to go to mass with you in the morning. Would you mind?"

Julie suppressed the shout of joy that she wanted to bellow and answered, "Sure, Linds, I'd love to have you join me—I'll even let you pick the time. We can go to the seven, the nine, or the eleven—any of those will work fine for me." This was a sacrifice, for Julie was always at the 7:00 mass at St. Vincent de Paul Catholic Church on Sunday mornings. When the girls had started at Rice, one of the very first things that Julie did on their first weekend was to find a Catholic church that she liked and that had the selection of daily and weekly mass times that could work with the schedule of a busy Rice University student.

All these years later, Lindsey could recapture the events and feelings of that Sunday morning. Even as a college student, Lindsey had trouble sleeping, so upon waking at four thirty in the morning, she had slipped quietly out of their room at five that Sunday morning to get in her daily run; normally, she liked to do ten miles but this morning she knew she'd only have time for a quick six. She knew that Julie's preference was the early mass and had no interest in disturbing Julie's routine.

Lindsey loved running at this time of the morning when only she and the birds were stirring. It had been spring, and the campus was redolent with the fragrance of the profusion of azaleas blooming all over the campus. Running along the inner asphalt track, Lindsey had marveled at her desire to go to church, with Julie puzzling about how that had come to be. She remembered chuckling as the St. Teresa prayer began in her head. Finishing up her run with her last three on the dirt track that ran alongside the perimeter of the university, she had arrived back in their room in an hour and was already showering by the time Julie awoke.

The two had been uncharacteristically silent as Julie drove her red Mazda down Rice Boulevard to Buffalo Speedway and pulled into the church parking lot at about six thirty. Parking her car, Julie had turned and smiled at Lindsey as she declared, "I ought to have you with me more often, Linds. I'm usually dashing in right at seven."

Julie had said nothing more as they walked through the glass doors of the cavernous church. She walked up the long linoleum corridor, stopped at the third pew on the right to genuflect, and slid down the bench where she sat to pull down the kneeler and knelt to pray. Lindsey knew that for Julie, Lindsey, and the world for that matter, was gone. She had seen Julie in meditation for years and knew the depth of her friend's concentration and focus. Lindsey mimicked Julie's actions and looked about her as she knelt next to her. There were about ten to twenty people already there, she had noticed as the two had walked up the long aisle approaching the altar. A few were young adults, it seemed, but the majority looked to be in their forties and fifties. All of them appeared to be deep in prayer.

As Lindsey knelt in the silence, she thought back to the last time she had been in a church; she had just turned thirteen and agreed to attend confirmation class to appease her mother. The Episcopal priest at St. John's Episcopal Church in Clear Lake, Philip Rivers, was no match for ten teenaged sons and daughters of Clear Lake's top citizens; most of the class was composed of kids like Lindsey with one or both parents a scientist, astronaut, or physician employed by NASA. Few members of the class were content to accept the bland and uninspired answers given by the priest to questions about mysteries of the Christian faith. Halfway through the first two-hour session, Lindsey had zoned out, figuring this would be a ten-week endurance test. But the third class had gotten her attention because the subject that morning was one of the central tenants of Christianity: Transubstantiation or Consubstantiation, whether the bread and wine imbibed during the rite called the Eucharist or communion was substantially changed to the body and blood of Jesus Christ, or was it merely a commemoration of Christ's death on the cross? Lindsey had wondered about this herself and was, therefore, listening to the verbal exchange between Mr. Rivers and Jennifer Garland, the daughter of an astronaut at NASA. Jennifer had not accepted the explanation that Mr. Rivers had given her; as Lindsey listened to the increasingly heated exchange, she sympathized with the young girl because Rivers was evading the basis of Jennifer's argument. When Rivers curtly dismissed Jennifer's last comment and began to change the subject, Lindsey had opened her mouth for the first time in the class.

She could recall the horror on Rivers' face when Lindsey had calmly asked, "Well then, Mr. Rivers, are we cannibals when we eat the consecrated wafer and drink the consecrated blood?" The unfortunate Mr. Rivers had turned a most unhealthy shade of red and had announced that the class was over for the day. Lindsey had not returned to church after that Saturday until now.

Lindsey could not deny the sense of peace she had felt upon walking into St. Vincent de Paul Catholic Church at six thirty that next morning. Kneeling next to Julie, who was deep in communion with her God, she felt the silence as a tangible thing. Lindsey finally had risked a look up at the huge crucifix dominating the altar of the church, realizing that she had looked everywhere but up at that cross. As she had stared at that quintessence of agony and sacrifice, she thought of a paper Julie had written the year before for her theology class. Julie had started her paper with the sentence "The problem with the Catholic church is the crucifix."

Both girls were excellent writers, but Julie had asked Lindsey to read the article to check her argument for logical inconsistencies. Although Lindsey did not agree with Julie's main premise, that there was meaning in suffering, she had thought her friend had done an excellent job of presenting her arguments about a subject that held no interest for Lindsey. But now, gazing up at that crucifix, she realized just what Julie had really been saying behind the logical and philosophical arguments she had presented in her paper; it was right there in the enormous, tortured, and disfigured Christ hanging before her. Unbelievably gruesome, Lindsey mused as she had continued to stare upward, unwilling to take her eyes away from the nails buried deep into the flesh of the hands and the feet, at the thorns digging deeply into his head; startled, she realized that the wrap around his emaciated waist and loins was a convention. Of course, he would have been completely nude, wouldn't he?

Lindsey thought of the lovely filigreed gold cross her mother always wore; the cross without the dying Christ was the sanitized version, much more comfortable to contemplate than this God-man displayed in an attitude of such shocking powerlessness and hideousness. And she had found herself asking what on earth could require such pain and suffering and wondering what kind of God would require such an agonizing death from his own son.

Later on the way back to the dorm, Julie had asked Lindsey how she had felt being back in church and had smiled when Lindsey had responded with one word: "Curious." After a short pause, Lindsey continued, "Julie, do you still have a copy of that paper you wrote on suffering for your theology class last year?"

Turning her head quickly to her right to look at Lindsey in surprise, Julie had queried, "What on earth made you think of that paper, Lindsey?"

"That paper … do you think you still have it?" had repeated Lindsey, now somewhat impatiently.

While turned back to the growing Sunday-morning traffic on Buffalo Speedway, Julie had nodded as she replied, "Yes, Linds, I know where I filed it. I'll get it for you when we get back to the dorm, okay?"

Hearing no response from Lindsey, Julie had once more quickly gazed at her and saw that she had not heard a word that Julie had just said. Lindsey had her thousand-yard stare on and was somewhere deeply lost in thought. Julie laughed at the irony; she had worked harder on that paper than almost any other she had written while at Rice and had known it was excellent. She had asked Lindsey to check it for logical inconsistencies as a ruse, for she had known there were none. Julie had been devastated by Lindsey's typically detached response to the paper; it was evident that none of her words had provided any solace to her isolated friend. "So here we are, Lord, almost two years later, and now she wants to read it, amazing. You are so amazing, thank you."

"Julie, were you asking me something just now?"

"Linds, I was just telling you that I'll get that paper for you when we get back to school."

Midway upon the journey of our life I found myself in a dark wood where the right way was lost.
—Dante, *The Divine Comedy*

7

"Julie," Lindsey whispered into the semidarkness, "how I wish that I could see you now."

Immediately upon uttering that self-pitying thought, Lindsey mentally rebuked herself as she recalled the many times Julie had called her in the last several years. And always, she would hear Julie's message at home or office voice mail and would plan to call Julie later, when she had the time. But she never did. And recently, Lindsey lost count of the number of times that Julie had driven all the way out here from Friendswood. "Why did I refuse to see her?" she asked herself. "My best friend—maybe the only one I have ever had—and I won't see her?"

That day had been three months to the day since she had arrived in Huntsville, and it felt like three years. Not that she was treated badly by the guards or other inmates—quite the contrary in fact. If there were a universal response to her from both guards and other prisoners, it was curiosity.

Lindsey looked about the eighty square feet she now called home. Palatial by Huntsville Prison standards, her cell had a desk with an attached stool. Piled on the desk were three neat stacks of books. Above the desk were two small storage units where she kept a hairbrush, dryer, and a few cosmetics. As she surveyed her meager possessions from her prone position on her bed, Lindsey considered the life she had been living a mere six months ago as if it had been lived in another universe.

During those first few hours following the long bus ride from Houston to Huntsville, the reality of her new identity was made evident in countless trivial and major ways: the fingerprinting, the many photographs, and the distribution of the prisoner handbook. Lindsey recalled some of the smirks on the faces of the inmates in line with her as she had read the 112-page State of Texas prisoner handbook, relieved to have something to hold on to and to occupy her mind. She must have been in a daze, which had started on the day she had been arrested. Although she tried to remember her trial, there were days during the two weeks of testimony that she could recall almost nothing. She sometimes wondered if she had even been there; in many ways, she thought now, she had not. The shock and exhaustion of all the events that had culminated in her arrest, she knew, had protected her from feeling much of the horror of listening to the hours of testimony from ostensible friends, colleagues, and her sister, Paula. Lindsey wondered if she would ever feel something other than sorrow for Paula. Lindsey thought back to the many one-sided conversations with Todd Kensington, the defense attorney who had shown up the day of her indictment, now sighing as she realized yet again how frustrated the man had been by her silence.

One of the biggest surprises in store for her was how protective of her were the other inmates even before the incident that cinched her status as notorious among all inmates and guards at the prison. Although all the other prisoners were men, she was never afraid of assault. Lindsey had never been all that interested in movies, but the few that she had seen painted prisoners and guards with the classical personalities attributed to petty bureaucrats and their victims, and Lindsey had accepted the typecasting as reasonable. She'd been wrong.

Certainly there were a couple of guards who fit her stereotype: fat, stupid, and lazy. But the majority of them were kind, even apologetic. And most called her Dr. McCall even though she frequently explained she could no longer practice medicine in the state. She had stopped asking the guards to call her Lindsey rather than Dr. McCall when Luke Preston had reminded her that she had still graduated from medical school and had passed the examinations, so wasn't she still a doctor? She had smiled at that comment and at him that day. It had been a long time since she had smiled like that.

The relative "freedoms" enjoyed here were also surprising. The prison library was fairly well supplied with reading material, and there were miles of running paths available for those who had been deemed to be at low risk for escape. Like her.

All Texas state prisoners are initially assigned to the Byrd Diagnostic Unit in Huntsville; some remain there for the entire duration of their sentence, while others are reassigned once their classification status is determined. Following a series of paper-and-pencil tests evaluating basic intelligence, psychological and educational profile, and oral interviews with trained prison personnel, a judgment is reached about each prisoner's security or custody level.

Although Lindsey was evaluated at a level 1 status based on her test results, she received an administrative segregation classification because of her high-profile status. There had been extensive national television coverage of her case following the *Houston Tribune*'s series of articles entitled "Murder at the Texas Medical Center." When she was assigned a permanent cell at the all-male Huntsville prison, it was because the wardens believed her to be at less risk from male prisoners than from female.

It was the sense of time here that was so strange. Everything seemed to be slowed down; moments seemed to last for years, especially at night. Lindsey understood that she'd never really thought about time—had never thought about anything but her next goal. Her life had been directed by time, of course. But she had always felt on top of it as if the interminable deadlines were the road signs mapping her life. And the final destination? She had never thought about it.

Life had seemed exquisitely simple for Lindsey McCall; there were clear, tangible goals, and life was a series of attaining one then moving onto the next. Even as a child, she had never questioned the design or discipline she had imposed upon her life; she had loved its order and the associated milestones along the way. Seldom did she stop to question any of her goals. Lindsey's life and the course it would take had been crystal clear to her from grade school.

During grade school and junior high, there had been many conversations between Lindsey and her mother about the narrow range of Lindsey's interests. Ann McCall worried about her younger daughter's isolation and disinterests in the kinds of activities her sister, Paula, and most other young girls engaged in. Although Lindsey had attempted to be polite during these sessions, she found these talks exceedingly boring, a fact that became obvious to Ann McCall as the years went by; eventually these talks would invariably end with hurt feelings that could not be assuaged by anything Lindsey said. They could not have been more different, she and her mother. While her mom was undeniably an intelligent woman, her goal in life had been to be a wife and mother from the time that she had been a small girl. The ambition and determination of her younger daughter had been something that her mother had enjoyed displaying to her friends in Lindsey's grade-school years. But by junior and high school, Lindsey's mom was totally bewildered by her brilliant young daughter. The acute onset of her mother's cardiomyopathy further confounded their relationship, serving only to widen the gap between mother and younger daughter as Lindsey's passion took root and grew.

The walls of Dr. Lindsey McCall's former office were covered with framed evidence of her academic achievements, certifications, awards, and honors. In a field where the presence or absence of such accoutrements dictated promotion and tenure, the practice made sense. A majority of academics throughout the world had such displays; it was part of the prevailing culture of the scholar.

The list had impressed so many: medical and doctoral educations completed in six years, a fellow in the College of Cardiology by thirty-two, and a potential Nobel Prize winner at thirty-seven. Milestones, hundreds of them; yet meaningless to her now, she realized, as she reflected on her life up to now.

Here, in this place, she was forced to acknowledge doubts, conflicts, and sorrows, which she had been extraordinarily adept at ignoring. Most terrifying to Lindsey was the admission to herself that the loss of her career, her research, even her ability to practice medicine—her entire life—was not what bothered her. It was the fact that it didn't—that she missed nothing about her former life—nothing at all, that was what bothered her the most.

These shifting memories began to seem like a movie as if an unseen director were taking her back through various phases of her life. Suddenly she recalled the Saturday night when she had finally cracked the molecular quagmire that had paved the way to Digipro. She'd known she had found the answer; she had been certain of it.

It was midnight, and she had fallen asleep from sheer exhaustion at home. For more years than she could count, Lindsey had pursued the equations and thousands of exquisitely subtle magnetic variations of the molecular structure for digitalis, which would preserve its unique effects on the myocardial sarcomere, yet obviate the pernicious effects on the conduction and the gastrointestinal systems.

She had been dreaming her very favorite dream when suddenly she had awakened with the answer. In the dream, Lindsey and her dad were roaring through the atmosphere in one of Tom McCall's test fighter planes; the stars were so close that Lindsey knew if she could just reach out of the windows of the plane, she could grab and hold on to them.

When her eyes snapped open, the memory of that flight evoked a broad grin.

It had happened only once because NASA could have fired Tom McCall for his irresponsible decision to take his ten-year-old daughter on a test flight at four in the morning. She and her dad had snuck stealthily out of their Clear Lake home at three- thirty that morning to make the thirty-minute drive by four; Lindsey had never been as happy or as excited before or since as she was that morning. When the test pilot and his daughter got to the enormous NASA complex, Tom McCall cautioned his little girl to stay low and to run when he did; he wasn't worried about the early hour because the tower personnel were quite accustomed to the unusual flight times of their best test pilot, but it was the presence of Lindsey. McCall appreciated the risk he was taking, but he also understood the profound influence this experience would have on his brilliant little girl, and he would not deny it to her. Tom McCall knew that Lindsey would come as close to heaven as is possible for any living person, and he hoped that the experience would further solidify the young girl's ambition.

That dream had been the catalyst for the solution to so many problems in her life that she always wondered if her dad were still able to help her in some mysterious way. Lindsey's yellow jeep was right in front of her house where she'd left it a few hours before, having been too tired to drive it into the garage. Now as wide awake as if she'd had eight hours of sleep instead of two, Lindsey raced through the quiet streets of West University to get to her lab. Only a very short distance from the Texas Medical Center, West U was populated mostly by medical center nurses and doctors who could afford the steep prices that a West University house commanded. Usually Rice Avenue and Holcombe Boulevard were patrolled by West U cops looking to stop a careless driver for exceeding the thirty-five-mile-an-hour speed limit. But at this hour, all was quiet.

Lindsey had stood impatiently tapping the identifying badge that was her entry into the locked-down Houston Medical Center complex as she waited for the yellow elevator to take her to her fifth-floor research lab. The sprawling building was identified by colors. Each of the medical school departments occupied suites of offices in one of the blue, orange, yellow, green, or red sections of the building. Although somewhat garish, the color system served to be of much more directional use than the office numbering system, rumored to be based on the Dewey decimal system in explanation of its indecipherability. At Houston Medical, all research animals were housed in the Center for Laboratory Animal Medicine and Care. But the animal welfare committee at the medical school granted permission for certain researchers to work in a satellite lab near their office. Animal welfare committees had proliferated quickly during the early years of animal research in medical schools. By the late eighties, all institutions that used animals in research were required to establish these committees to assure that use of animals was actually necessary to answer an individual researcher's question and to assure that the animals were protected from unnecessary pain and suffering.

Lindsey unlocked the door of her small, two-room research suite and took down her log. It was the notoginsenoside, or R1, that she had been adjusting for years now in her formula; she believed that merely adding an additional hydrogen ion to the protein would take care of the minor problems remaining in her new drug. Use of the atomic force microscope from a physicist colleague allowed her to make the adjustment. After noting the reconfiguration of R1 in the formula in her log, Lindsey prepared one last injection of her altered medication for her last experimental rat.

The fundamental problem with the use of digitalis for acute and chronic heart failure lay in the toxic effects caused when large doses were required, as was the case for patients with severe heart failure like Ann McCall. The drug had been the mainstay of treatment for hundreds of years because no other drugs could match the inotropic effects of digitalis. The healthy heart adjusts its output on a moment-by-moment basis according to the needs of the individual or animal. During exercise, the cardiac output of an individual may be close to six thousand milliliters per minute while at rest barely half that amount.

By the time Lindsey was close to deciphering the alterations to the new molecule that became Digipro, she was aware—at some level—that her mother would most likely not benefit from the drug. Once chronically present, heart failure damages every major organ system in the body. To function effectively, the heart, like any pump, must empty completely before filling again for the next contraction. If either the force of the contraction is diminished by disease to the heart or the ability of the heart to empty completely is diminished as in tying off the pulmonary artery in an experimental rat, the end result is multisystem organ failure.

In treating the acute heart failure she had caused in her

experimental rat, Lindsey's goal was threefold. First, she needed to counteract the damage to the contractile force of the animal's heart with a large dose of her altered digitalis. Then she had to make sure that the toxic effects in the conduction and gastrointestinal systems had been eliminated, and last she had to act very quickly before the rat experienced the effects of chronic heart failure.

Lindsey was reasonably confident that the new configuration of the drug was working according to her specifications, but she needed to make sure the effects were lasting. At ten that same morning, Lindsey had extubated the rat and continued to monitor his cardiac pressures. Although he seemed fine, she decided to administer another half dose of the drug and waited another two hours while she monitored his venous and arterial pressures and electrocardiogram. After three more hours, he had been stable as a rock, so she had taken all the lines out and closed up the incisions she had made.

She also remembered how she had felt at that moment. And it was nothing; she'd felt nothing at all. Her whole life had been consumed by this marathon. Everything had been oriented toward this goal, and she had done it, finally, after all those years. Reflecting back on that day, about two years before, Lindsey could remember feeling puzzled at her own indifference at achieving what had been her goal for over thirty years. All she remembered was a somewhat robotic drive home, falling into bed, and sleeping for almost twenty hours.

During the endless days at Huntsville, the brainless busyness of her two jobs, the one in the library during the evening hours, and the activity of her day job in the infirmary, provided a sixteen-hour respite from this obsessive questioning of her life and the choices that had brought her here. Of course, she was aware that with what had just happened between her and the physician assigned to Huntsville Prison, the infirmary job may be done. She wondered if you could get fired from jobs for which you received no pay and the thought made her chuckle grimly. Texas is one of the few states in the country where all prisoners work, and none receive any pay for the work.

∼

We must be willing to let go of the life we have planned, so as to have the life that is waiting for us.

—E. M. FORRESTER

8

The Present

Rich Jansen was no ordinary warden. With a twenty-year background as a homicide detective within the Harris County Sheriff's Office, Jansen had accepted the governor's offer to be chief warden of the seven Huntsville prisons with a combination of relief and trepidation. A severe injury had forced his early retirement from the sheriff's office, but his exemplary record while working in the homicide department had won him a host of admirers, among whom was the current Texas governor Gregory Bell. Bell had become governor just as the federal government returned control of its judicial system to his state. In the late eighties, a Federal Judge named Justice had upheld a class action suit filed by hundreds of prison inmates against the entire Texas prison system claiming inhumane treatment. The suit resulted in three decades of Federal oversight. The Texas governor then gained national attention with the successful multibillion-dollar bond implementation resulting in an astounding100 percent increase in prison capacity. Known to be tough on crime, Bell had also gained national notoriety with his refusal to pardon over fifteen prisoners on death row at the Ellis Unit in Huntsville. There were consequences from the publicity in the shape of intense scrutiny of the death-row prisoners by the media, ACLU, and a host of other agencies.

He hated to admit it, but he was excited by this assignment. He liked Bell and believed him to be good for the state. He was aware of the man's presidential ambitions and thought he could vote for the guy if it came to that. He and Bell were about the same age and shared some of the same beliefs.

These past few months after his forced retirement had been difficult for the retired cop. While Rich knew that the grieving that had finally erupted had been healing, Rich was not accustomed to long bouts of self-pity, and after two months of feeling sadness the depths of which seemed bottomless and never-ending, he had gone to talk with a longtime friend at the Co-Cathedral of the Sacred Heart in downtown Houston.

Father John Tobin had officiated at Rich and Laura's wedding long before there was a cathedral in Houston; he had baptized their son, Rob; and had presided at Laura's funeral mass. After the mass, Father John had walked up to Rich and lightly placed his hand on Rick's shoulder. Waiting until Rick returned his gaze, the priest's piercing eyes seemed to bore into his soul.

"It will get bad, Rich, and when it does, I want you to call me."

Rich had nodded and agreed, dry-eyed, and had not shed a single tear until this past summer when it had seemed as if the grief would kill him. The day after Laura's funeral, Rich had been back at the office commandeering his ten-man department of homicide detectives. He had managed to keep his emotions in a box for over four years, until he got shot and was forced to stop.

Throughout that long, hot summer, the pain of her loss would so overwhelm him that he could only lie in his bed, sobbing, the vigilant Max at his side, ever ready to hand him a paw or a lick. When he realized that he had lost fifteen pounds he did not need to lose, he went to see Father John and had continued to visit him every week thereafter.

They met on Saturday mornings, established after that first Saturday in June after Rich had just endured his first three-mile slow jog around the Rice University track. It had been five months to the day since he had been the recipient of a barrage of bullets to his abdomen and chest. The TMC surgeons who had patched him together had warned him that he may never run again—that it was a miracle that he had lived.

But months of rehab and persistent work with weights by Rich had convinced them that he was ready. The docs had given him the green light just a day before.

The exercise served to fortify him for the meeting with Father John. He had deliberately not called the man but decided just to show up at his rectory office at 1600 Jefferson, the home of the four priests serving the Co-Cathedral of the Sacred Heart in downtown Houston. If he were there, great; if not well, he and Max would go and buy each other breakfast. Max had been unbelievably restrained that day—as if he could understand that any extra strain during the run around the Rice University track imposed by his almost one-hundred-pound body could cause re-injury to the still-healing musculature of his most favorite human. Rich had smiled through the physical pain of that first run, for he thought of Laura looking down on two of her three favorite boys. And of how happy she would be that he was going to see Father John. When Father John had opened the door of the rectory, he'd shown no surprise. He had smiled at Rich and Max and offered them both water.

After sitting in silence for quite some time, Rich had looked up at the priest and said the words he had never uttered in his life. "Father, I need help, I don't know what to do to feel better."

They had met every Saturday morning from then on.

Just over an hour later, he was in the town of Huntsville. As part of the recruitment package for Rich's position, Bell had given Rich two choices for living arrangements, and both were free. The first was the state-financed warden's house, recently vacated by Dorman, the man who Bell had fired, about a five-minute walk from the prison, or he could use an unoccupied cabin right on the edge of the Piney Woods that belonged to Bell's family, about a fifteen- or twenty-minute drive from the prison in an adjacent town.

Rich had accepted Bell's offer of his cabin, sight unseen. Bell had described the house, and since it sat right on the edge of the forest, Rich figured he and Max would have time for a quick three-mile run if they hurried. He turned the Mercedes south back down the old Highway 75, which ran parallel to the new freeway. After about ten or so miles, he was in the town of New Waverly, and after taking a number of wrong turns on Route 150, he found the house at the end of an unnamed and unmarked grass and dirt road. Bell had described the location of the road precisely, and now Jansen could see why; there was no way anyone could detect that the country home of the governor of Texas lay hidden there at the outskirts of the Sam Houston State Forest.

The house was stunning. It was a log frame house; a bit of a stretch calling it a cabin, Rich thought as he approached the wraparound porch of the huge home and walked up to the almost-all-glass door with Max padding softly behind him. Jansen had grabbed his single bag along with the three grocery bags he had filled at Randall's on the way out of town and now balanced them singlehandedly as he unlocked the front door. The entire floor plan was open. There was a great room with a cathedral ceiling, where one complete wall was a huge stone fireplace. The other three walls were mostly glass with stunning views of a seemingly endless expanse of densely packed pines and forest undergrowth. Jansen grinned when he opened what looked to be a Western antique and saw the Bose sound system complete with speakers discreetly placed throughout the first floor, and, sure enough, there was an XM Radio system.

The room was tastefully but sparsely furnished with brown leather furniture, glass and brass tables, and huge Navajo rugs covering the wood floor. Through the left side of the great room was a chef-sized kitchen with matching brown appliances and granite tops and extremely well-stocked cabinets. The iron stove and ovens were huge and looked as if they could easily handle meal preparation for one hundred people. Over to the far right was an island with several leather barstools serving as the kitchen table. There was nothing out of place and not a single dust mote that Jansen could see in the filtered light from the setting sun streaming through the western window.

The silence was deafening.

Jansen watched Max as he clicked up the broad wooden staircase at the rear of the kitchen and dining area to explore the five bedrooms.

He took the stairs two at a time and joined Max in the master bedroom, where he noted the same tasteful yet under-stated elegance. The king-size brass bed was covered with a quilt that looked simple yet very expensive. Laura had been interested in quilting and used to drag him through the hun-dreds of quilt shops in the Hill Country. He had been astonished at the price tags starting at seven hundred and continuing way up into the thousands. This one reminded him of some at the far end of that price range; the colors were vibrant and depicted familiar Western scenes.

The dresser was large and stocked with brand new under-wear and socks, all his size. In the remaining drawers were shirts and sweaters for both warm and cool weather—again, all his size and style. Amazed, he opened the door to the walk-in closet and found an entire wardrobe of sport coats, casual and dress pants, shoes, and shirts; of course, they looked per-fectly suited for Rich Jansen. Greg Bell had told Rich that he wouldn't need to bring anything because Bell would make sure the cabin was stocked. Jansen had no idea that Bell had meant an entirely brand-new wardrobe. As he looked quickly through the array of clothing, Rich wondered how on earth Gregory could select a collection of clothing that so perfectly fit Jansen's taste and style.

Clever, very clever, Greg, he thought.

Rich returned to his inspection of the master bedroom and saw that the whole south wall again was glass but with remotely controlled blinds, while the wall directly in front of the bed was covered with a plasma television that looked at least fifty inches; the remaining two walls were decorated with some excellent Western art, which Rich did not recognize. Sitting down in the leather recliner in front of the television, Jansen sat motionlessly as he absorbed all the changes that had taken place in what had been his calm, quiet, and admit-tedly isolated life. Max stood in front of him with a worried look; staring at his master, his eyebrows were growing closer together as the Doberman's amber eyes stared at Rich with greater and greater intensity. The scrutiny of the animal brought Rick out of his reverie, and he asked, "Hey, Max, what about a run?" At that signal, Max shot downstairs, prancing impatiently to get going.

Promptly at 8:00 a.m. the following day, Rich Jansen joined the seven Huntsville wardens in the conference center in the sprawling, red-brick building across from the Walls, the oldest prison of the seven. Rich had been at the prison since six that morning and had decided that there was no room in the Walls that was suitable for meeting with the group of wardens. Rich had never been to the Walls; he'd never had a reason to do so. Although Houston and Harris County Homicide police frequently attended the executions of criminals who were considered the worst of the worst, Rich had never joined any of his colleagues when they made the trek out to Huntsville. Watching a murderer die seemed barbaric to Rich although he kept that opinion to himself.

When Jansen had approached the Walls at sunrise, he was impressed by the ominous appearance of the prison. The prison itself was completely hidden behind a ten- or twelve-foot, dark, brick-walled enclosure with razor wire running between guard towers at each corner of the block wide enclosure. Rich had seen his share of prisons, but the Walls seemed to emanate menace. The rising sun did nothing to dispel this sense as Rich slowly drove around the block, seeking the entrance to the place.

Bell had covered very few details during their discussion following Jansen's acceptance of the job, but Rich recalled a mumbled comment about the warden's office at the Walls and a suggestion that he might want to keep the acting warden on site and set up his office either at the conference center or at Byrd Diagnostic Center. Staring up at the medieval look of the Walls, Jansen completely understood why Bell had made the suggestion.

Rich had read the résumés of the seven men the night before and had a fair amount of information to begin to evaluate their performance. The acting warden at the Walls had been serving in that role during the two weeks that had passed following the governor's request for and receipt of the former warden's resignation. Taking note of that, Rich realized that Bell had made that decision before he knew that Jansen would take the job. Looking around the room, he thought of another reason he liked the guy: *Balls, the guy had balls.*

Calling the meeting to order, Rich started it by telling these men about himself and his background. As he talked, he watched the faces in front of him. He was certain that the brighter members of the group—he applied that attribute to five out of the seven sitting before him—would have done the same thing he had done with them: done his homework by learning almost everything they could about him. But Jansen knew that 90 percent of leadership was acting and that the act, to be successful, had to convey confidence, knowledge, and control. All three could be faked—Rich had certainly worked under his share of idiots. Two of whom were consummate actors. But he figured that he had about five minutes to make an indelible impression by conveying what he considered the essential elements of a good leader. And so he played it.

Rich got his introduction over with and began to tell the group about himself. "I started out in the Marine Corps. The corps was kind enough to keep me alive through the fiasco in Lebanon so I could come home to Houston and go to law school at the University of Houston. Then I joined a friend in his private law practice as a criminal defense attorney. I hated it." Jansen intentionally omitted his four years at Harvard University, which preceded the Marine Corps.

With that comment, Rich noted a few suppressed grins around the table.

"I joined the Houston Police Department, much to the dismay of most of my family and many friends, and became a detective in homicide in the early nineties, then accepted chief of homicide for Harris County in ninety-eight."

Rich stopped and stared at the back of the room as he recalled that night that almost ended his life. He could "see" himself once more lying prone in the middle of the street in the fourth ward, one of Houston's most dangerous neighborhoods. He'd been positive that he was dying and remembered thinking that it wasn't so bad, that maybe he would see Laura. He could smell that coppery smell of blood—his blood—everywhere, until he passed out.

"Nine months ago, I answered a routine"—his mouth twisted as he uttered the word *routine*—"murder and robbery investigation and took a total of fourteen bullets in the chest and gut."

He watched a few expressions reflect surprise since some of what he had just told them about the shooting was most likely new information. Jansen knew that it would engender either admiration or jealousy in the group Jansen had revealed these details because he suspected that the grapevine had been buzzing with gossip about this new position being a political plum and therefore awarded to the most ingratiating member of the gubernatorial entourage. He didn't blame these guys, for they were often right. But he wanted them to be clear that in this case, they were dead wrong. Some of these men were military veterans; others had been in the police force. There was not a man in the room who did not know that most chiefs of homicide were desk jockeys. If they remembered nothing else from this soliloquy, Rich wanted each of these guys to know that he had not been only an administrator sitting at a desk.

For another ten minutes or so, he outlined his retirement and recovery months and ended with Bell's and his meetings over the last three months. Then he said, "My expectations of you are very simple—and they are non-negotiable. I have three. First, I want each and every one of you to understand that each inmate has been incarcerated at Huntsville *as* punishment. Not *for* punishment. I want you to think about that, and I expect that you will enforce that with all guards here at the Huntsville prisons. Second, I expect facts when I ask for them, your opinion when I ask for it. And last, I expect you to tell me the truth, no matter how bad or ugly it is. If I find that you have lied to me or that you have supported harassment of any prisoner, you will be fired."

That was when he went around the table and called each man by name, asking if he could agree to and enforce these simple rules. Each man did so until Jansen turned to the warden for the Ellis Unit where death row was located and asked a second time, "Roy, I cannot hear what you said, please answer me." It was said very softly; those who knew Jansen knew that the softer he spoke, the more you had to be wary of him.

Jansen was over six feet tall and muscular as he stood clad in a black T-shirt and trousers looking down at Roy Peterson. Peterson was no more than forty but looked closer to sixty, maybe fifty pounds overweight, and was not bright. However, he was smart enough to know that he had better reign in the condescending looks he had been making to his colleagues seated around the table and wipe off the sneer that had settled on his face when Jansen listed his expectations of them.

Head down and embarrassed to be singled out and not understanding that it was his own behavior that invariably got him into such types of humiliating situations, Peterson mumbled, "Yes, I agree."

Jansen heard the sharp intakes of breath when he kneeled down at a level close to Roy's face and whispered, "I cannot hear you, Roy, nor can anyone else in this room."

Peterson looked up and clearly stated a second time, "Yes, I understand and agree to run Ellis for punishment not as punishment."

Nodding, Jansen thanked them all for coming to the meeting and told them he would be scheduling meetings with each of them individually and then with all of their guards. There was silence among the seven men as Jansen walked out of the room and closed the door softly behind him.

We are made of wild and wonderful forces
—St. Francis

9

"Dr. McCall? Are you awake, Lindsey?"

The voice was familiar as Lindsey struggled to consciousness. Opening her eyes, she saw one of her favorite guards grinning in at her. Huge, black, and physically intimidating, Luke Preston had liked Dr. Lindsey McCall from the get go. Each had been a delightful surprise to the other. While Luke was a physical stereotype for a dumb, mean, Southern black man, he was one of the kindest and most intuitive men Lindsey had ever known. Although Luke had not been formally educated past high school, he could read people. Within a very few seconds of being in another's presence, he seemed to see the contents of his soul. Long ago, his family and friends learned to trust Luke's warnings and his insights. And the fact that Lindsey had saved the life of his youngest brother, Devon, cinched Luke's advocacy for Lindsey.

Luke had been born long after Texas integrated and had never seen the "Blacks Only" signs at toilets and water fountains and restaurants of his parents' days but Luke Preston had met his share of white racists. When he heard about the conviction of the Texas Medical Center cardiologist, he had immediately formed his own opinion of the newly convicted doctor. Therefore, when Luke had processed Lindsey during her first hours at Huntsville Prison, he'd expected condescension, defiance, and anger from the famous inmate. Instead, he was stunned by her humility. She had stood in a long line of about twelve prisoners waiting patiently while Luke and two other guards fingerprinted each prisoner and inventoried all their belongings. It was a dreary job, and he had mostly forgotten that the famous inmate was in the line until he saw a female right hand waiting in proper position to be printed. Startled, he had looked up from his seat at his table and had immediately recognized her. She had returned his gaze with a slight smile.

Lindsey had followed the directions by the jail to the letter, for she had nothing to declare: no rings, chains, watch, cash—no personal property of any kind. Most prisoners seemed to bring something with them to argue about; whether it was a book or a watch or cash, there was almost always something that they did not want to part with. This woman had nothing—nothing at all. Because this was so unusual, Lindsey had been subjected to a body search by one of the female guards. Luke had found himself apologizing to Dr. McCall as she was led away by the guard. Briefly, Lindsey had turned as if to say it's okay, but what Luke sensed in Lindsey McCall's green eyes shocked and saddened him. He could almost *feel* her profound sorrow and a world of weariness, which was much too great for such narrow shoulders to bear. And he vowed to help this lady, never dreaming how that help would come about.

Luke stood and waited patiently while Lindsey jumped out of her narrow bed, ran a brush through her hair, and turned to face him, smiling. *These days*, Luke thought, *her smile goes to her eyes.* And he said a quick prayer of gratitude for the changes that he saw in the lovely woman standing in front of him.

"So, another session with Valdoor?"

Unlocking the door of her cell with one hand, Luke balanced the cup of Starbucks as he opened the door and handed her the coffee.

"Luke, you're not supposed to bring me coffee; please don't get in any more trouble on my account. Valdoor has spies everywhere." Lindsey was whispering, for she had no way of knowing that Valdoor, her pet name for Warden Howard Dorman, had been fired by the governor two weeks before. Luke had attended a staff meeting early that morning to hear about the new chief warden and his expectations. Although he heard some murmuring from the minority of guards who had enjoyed abusing the prisoners when they could get away with it, the majority of the guards agreed with the expectations that had been laid out. After all, like Luke, many had family members here or in other prisons in the state and believed that simply being in prison was punishment enough.

Now, walking down the long corridor on the floor that Lindsey had all to herself, Lindsey prodded Luke with her hand and whispered, "Luke, please slow down. You went to all this trouble to bring me this coffee. Can you at least let me drink it please?" Lindsey was five foot eight, but next to Luke's six-foot-ten-inch, three-hundred-and-fifty-pound frame, Lindsey felt diminutive. She glanced up at the former Texas A&M tight end and noticed his smile for the first time.

"Okay, you look much too happy to be taking me to another session with Valdoor and man's best physician, so tell me, Luke, what is causing such smiles this morning?"

Just as she took another long and satisfying gulp of the strong coffee, Lindsey almost choked on the swallow when Luke replied, "He's gone, Lindsey. Bell fired him over two weeks ago now."

Lindsey caught her breath as the two reached the end of

the elevator.

"Luke, I could have sworn you just said that Valdoor has been fired?"

Because of Luke's deep East Texas accent, Lindsey sometimes had trouble understanding him. But as she stared, dumbfounded at the grin splitting the man's face, she knew she'd not heard him incorrectly. The two stood to wait for the elevator to take them down to the central corridor, which would take them out of the inmate cell blocks and into the administrative area. Dutifully, she held her hands out to be cuffed as was the practice when inmates were anywhere but in the exercise yard or in their work areas. Luke grinned again as he said that he had been instructed not to cuff Dr. McCall but just to bring her to Mr. Jansen's office at nine sharp that morning.

Rich had arrived at his office at six that morning and had already surprised the night shift with his appearance. His predecessor seldom had arrived at the prison before ten in the morning, so the night shift was buzzing with the early working hours of the new chief warden. He'd made quick rounds and had stopped to say a few words with each of the guards. By six thirty, he was back in his office calling Todd Kensington.

Todd and Rich had met at law school at the University of Houston. They had become and remained friends even though Todd was one of the many friends who had vehemently opposed Rich's decision to leave criminal defense and join the opposition. Todd had even gone so far as springing for dinner at Café Annie's, one of the more exclusive Houston restaurants, in his zeal to keep Rich on the defense side. Todd must have dropped several hundred dollars that night as the two men ate and drank their way through some of the best entrées and wines offered by the prestigious restaurant. Finally, Todd had said uncle and agreed to support Rich in his decision to quit the practice of law and become a cop.

While waiting for his friend to pick up, Rich had no doubt that he would find Todd in his office at six thirty on a Friday morning. Houston was a city with several prominent law firms; therefore, the competition was fierce. Ambitious partners like Todd routinely worked over eighty hours a week. Rich mulled over the events of the last twenty-four hours and was pleased as he reviewed an imaginary checklist in his head. He was also satisfied with the meeting yesterday and had received no surprises when he had made rounds just now.

He suspected, however, that he was enjoying a lull before the real action hit. Bell had told him that the physician who was suing everyone in Texas was a piece of work. Rich had read his personnel file last night, along with the records of all the wardens, and was surprised by the contents. Dr. Lance Pettigrew had been the physician for Huntsville Prisons for the last ten years. Rich had chuckled at the name as it sounded more Boston than Boston. Rich had gone to Harvard as an undergrad and was well aware of the Boston gestalt: Massachusetts Medical was the teaching hospital for Harvard Medical School and was considered by some to be the best hospital in the country. Pettigrew had gone to Harvard Med, then had done his residency at Mass Medical and four other teaching hospitals in the general Boston area. Then he had moved to Duke University in Durham, North Carolina, where he had worked as an internist for eight years. Then the record was blank for two years until he suddenly showed up in the Texas prison system and had worked there for the last decade.

With a background like that, the very first thing that Rich the cop suspected was drugs, maybe alcohol too; but there had to be an addiction in this man's past or present. Nothing else would explain settling for a job like this during what should have been the peak years of his career. There was no photo in the file, but Jansen calculated early- to mid-fifties for his age. If there had been a birth date recorded in the file, he had missed it.

"Hey, dude, what's this I hear about the ever-enterprising Jansen applying his magic touch to the infamous Texas prison system?" Kensington was chuckling as he spoke, but no one was proud of the twenty-year federal government oversight of the Texas judicial system, particularly native Texans like Jansen and Kensington.

Smiling into the phone, Rich replied, "Well, with the likes of your team out there defending every scumbag walking through the fourth ward, I decided I had better get in here and keep the streets safe for Mr. and Mrs. Houston. Hey, Todd, sorry for cutting to the chase so fast, but can we meet for dinner later this week so I can talk to you about this Dr. Lindsey McCall case?"

Rich heard the loud silence extend as the generally jovial and bantering Kensington finally sighed and, in a monotone, replied wearily that he was free that next Thursday night. Wondering at the startling change in the mood of their conversation, Rich could only agree to the time and place as Todd mumbled something like, "Looking forward to seeing you, bud, I but I gotta go and finish this brief. I'm due in court at nine today."

Rich understood that Lindsey's conviction had been a personal loss for Todd. Todd was considered to be one of the best defense lawyers in the city and had most likely expected this case to be a slam dunk. His specialty was medical malpractice, and Kensington routinely defended cases where the damages were claimed to be in the multimillions. Todd had to have been blindsided and badly. After all, Todd must have figured, doctors were never *indicted* never mind *convicted* of murder. One of Houston's best and brightest convicted of murder for the use of an experimental drug to try to save the life of her dying mother? No jury would convict and certainly not twelve Houstonians. That had to be what Todd had thought, going into the case. Yet they did. She was here doing two years for intentional homicide. Rich jotted a note to himself to get his hands on a copy of the transcript of the trial. As he sat and mused about it, the whole thing seemed more and more peculiar, and he began to understand why his friend Todd was reluctant to discuss the case with him. Glancing at his watch, Rich saw that he had less than ninety minutes to read through the voluminous folder of the events surrounding the bizarre lawsuit filed by Pettigrew against Lindsey McCall, Gregory Bell, and the entire Texas judicial system.

Thirty minutes later, having determined that the contents of the file were useless and misleading, as there was little substance there, Rich sat staring at the lone and tasteless painting hanging on the wall of the office of his predecessor. It was a poorly drawn watercolor of a coyote and a horse. Suddenly, he rose so quickly from the chair that it rolled noisily into the window in back of him. Crossing the small space in two long steps, Jansen grabbed the painting and leaned it on the floor with its paper backing facing him. Rich stared at the now-empty rectangle of clean wall, then gazed about the nine-hundred-square-foot office, and shook his head slowly as he whispered in wonder, "Man, and I thought the Harris County sheriff's offices were ugly."

The walls were painted a glossy gray over what looked like brick. His desk was gray metal. The brown swivel chair behind the desk was faded and cracked. And there were two huge file cabinets in each corner facing the door, also gray. In the corner on the right of the office was a small, round table with four chairs. Behind the table sat a little bookcase—also gray metal. The window behind the desk overlooked one of the exercise yards, and since it was forecasted to rain later, the view outside completed the bleakness of the atmosphere. Rich had never thought much about color, design, and their effect on the psyche, but the longer he looked around at the relentless lack of color, he realized that he couldn't stand this. He'd saved his scarred mahogany desk and wonderfully comfortable leather chair from his days as chief of the homicide department and decided to move them from the Montrose house when he could get some help.

Staring thoughtfully at the space around him, he quickly rearranged the sparse furnitureso that the desk and chair, now in a corner, still sat in the angle of the door. But was also next to the light of the large picture window on his right. Last night, as he and Max had wandered about the town of Huntsville, Rich had noticed an unusual plant shop. The owner was about to close but seemed happy to welcome Rich and Max into the store to browse. In the back of the store were some large plants, including a four-foot-plus Ficus tree he'd seen in a corner for one-third the price of what he would pay in Houston.

He glanced again at his watch and decided to chance it; he had enough time, if barely. Forty minutes later, the Ficus tree was standing in front of the empty square where the odious painting had been hanging, and Max lay on his bed to the left of his chair. He had felt terrible when he'd left their new house in New Waverly that morning, for Max was accustomed to going wherever Rich went. The drive to town was only ten minutes, so he had plenty of time to get both the plant and Max. There had been some amused expressions among the guards as Rich reappeared carrying a four-and-a-half-foot plant with Max padding his gunslinger walk at Rich's side.

Rich absently caressed the dog's ears as he thumbed

through the file to see if he had missed anything important in the few minutes he had remaining to him. According to the record, his predecessor had decided to place Lindsey McCall in solitary confinement and to rescind all privileges following the prison physician's allegation that McCall had practiced medicine without a license. The warden had refereed a meeting, if it could be called that, between Pettigrew and McCall, the substance of which had been transcribed by a court reporter. The transcript read like an old Cheech and Chong movie. Each time that McCall was asked a question, according to the transcript, the TMC physician was cut off by Pettigrew. There were over one hundred pages of transcribed conversation, but Jansen could see no reply of longer than three words by McCall before being interrupted by the Harvard-trained Pettigrew. That the fiasco had been allowed to continue for what looked like three hours was foolish; that his predecessor had decided in favor of Pettigrew with only his bombastic testimony as evidence was absurd. No wonder Bell had canned the guy. His decision was not only stupid but would also be expensive for the state. There would be a hearing, although Jansen was confident that the decision by the DA would be a no bill. Rich was sure that Houston's DA, Boyd Masters, already had his piece of flesh from McCall and would see the allegation by Pettigrew as frivolous. Sam, although ambitious, was a reasonable man, Jansen thought, and may even ask the judge for a contempt citation against Pettigrew for wasting the time and money of Houston.

Justice is what is established; and thus all our established laws will necessarily be regarded as just without examination, since they are established.

—BLAISE PASCAL, *PENSÉES*

10

Precisely at nine, at the tap on his door, Jansen looked up from his reading. Max sat up but stayed behind Rick's desk as he silently watched Rich open the door. Lindsey had hastily gulped the remainder of her coffee as the office door opened so that the radical changes in the scene appearing in front of her did not cause her to choke. But she was positive that her face conveyed the confusion and curiosity that she felt as she regarded this man, the new plant, and the pointed ears behind the desk that she was pretty sure belonged to a Doberman.

In appearance, Jansen was exactly 180 degrees from his predecessor, Harold Dorman, whom Lindsey had named Valdoor: an allusion to the enemy leader who fought against Luke Skywalker in the *Star Wars* films. While Dorman had been fairly short and squat, Jansen was about six feet one or two and lean. Rich Jansen wore his thick, mostly black but sprinkled with gray hair in a quasi-military cut leaving the front hair long enough to wedge down onto a high forehead Dorman was mostly bald with a little fringe of hair around his ears. And Dorman had never once met Lindsey's gaze the entire three hours that she had been in this office with Dorman and Dr. Pettigrew. Jansen seemed to have no problem frankly appraising her with the same attention she gave him; he had warm, brown eyes with laugh crinkles around them, and his mouth was full and looked accustomed to smiling. He was extremely good-looking, Lindsey thought, and a man who seemed to be at ease with himself. She was surprised to see a guy like Jansen here; he looked as if he belonged in an office in downtown Houston or at the medical center. He was dressed in a subtle rose-colored dress shirt with the first couple of buttons undone under a camel sport jacket and dark-brown khakis. Dorman had worn a three-piece suit that looked too small; the tie and starched collar of his white dress shirt had so tightly bound his neck that several folds of loose skin wobbled every time he had turned his head. Jansen's face was lean and craggy with a slight cleft in his square chin.

Rich Jansen was an expert at keeping his face devoid of any emotion, but he had to work at it as he nodded at this most unlikely pair. Extending his hand first to the enormous black guard, he smiled and said, "Hello, you must be Luke Preston. I'm Rich Jansen and the new chief warden." Although it was probably correct protocol to greet the guard first, Jansen honestly wasn't sure that this was true; he just needed to regain control of himself. The woman was drop-dead gorgeous. He sure wished that someone had warned him about this. Hell, maybe they had, but he'd not had a reaction to a female like this since, well, since Laura. Turning his attention back to Lindsey, he caught her just as her gaze completed a sweep of the room, including the plant and Max's head, for the dog had now adjusted his position so that he could see everything that was happening. Max would not get up to greet these people unless invited to do so by Jansen. And Rich was not about to extend the invitation.

"Hello, Dr. McCall. I've been reviewing the transcript of the meeting that you, Dr. Pettigrew, and my predecessor had about your interventions with Devon Preston, and I've got some questions. Please be seated." Pointing to one of the four ugly chairs around the table, Jansen chided himself for sounding like an ass. He sounded like the high school principal and hated it, but the woman made him really uncomfortable, and he really didn't know why. She certainly was saying or doing nothing to cause such stupid behavior on his part. He watched her as she walked over to the chair he had pointed to; she was fairly tall, about five feet eight he guessed. She moved with an athletic grace evident even in the prison-issued white cotton pants and T-shirt. She was fit; Rick guessed that she was a runner, and she looked comfortable in her skin. Rich caught himself as he realized he was using the phrase his mother had used when she had first met Laura.

Belatedly realizing that Luke Preston had been standing there, waiting, Rich said, "Luke, I wonder if you can come back in about an hour and join us. I know you were a witness to the doctor's intervention with your brother, and I would like to hear what you have to say. The record does not seem to include the accounts of the eyewitnesses."

Rich took a seat across the table from Lindsey and noted that she had not said a word nor did it look as if she intended to open her mouth. She sat at the table with her hands loosely clasped and resting on the table. Those remarkable green eyes were gazing somewhere to the left of his shoulder. Maybe she was searching for the coyote painting. If she spent over three hours in here only two weeks ago, she'd have had to look at something to occupy herself while listening to Pettigrew's harangue.

Rich caught himself as he recognized the bias for Lindsey and the prejudice against Pettigrew that were rapidly forming in his mind. That was unlike him, and he'd need to guard himself against becoming personally involved with this woman. His objectivity was essential in this new job, and Rich did not want to jeopardize the job; he realized that he had missed the rush of identifying and dealing with crisis. Whether with employees like Roy or this woman who was definitely trouble; he just didn't know yet what kind of trouble she was. Rich walked over to his desk, picked up the thick file, and brought it over to the table with him. He set it down and, spreading his hand over the document, said a quick prayer for guidance as he jumped in with both feet.

"Dr. McCall, I've reviewed the transcript of the three-hour meeting between Mr. Dorman, Dr. Pettigrew, and yourself, but I remain completely clueless about how you got involved with the knifing of Devon Preston and how you happened to be in the infirmary in the first place."

Nodding her understanding of both the question and Jansen's confusion, Lindsey replied, "Okay, why don't I start at the beginning?" Then for the first time since she had entered his office, Lindsey looked directly at Rich as she waited for his response. As she spoke, Rich had opened his sport jacket and retrieved a small tape recorder, which he placed on the table between himself and Lindsey. She watched him click the recorder to activate it but said nothing. Rich had not been sure that he needed to tape the woman's comments, for the case seemed fairly self-evident to him and to Bell, but it was looking as if nothing in this case was as it seemed. Recording the interview would permit him to concentrate on watching McCall's facial expressions and body language.

"Please, Dr. McCall, do start at the beginning." As he made the statement, Jansen realized that he had no idea of where the beginning was to Lindsey McCall: was it at the start of her trial or her arrest or her time in Huntsville? And he didn't really care because curiosity and compassion for the plight of this unusual woman were competing in equal measure.

Lindsey's eyes took on a thoughtful and focused expression as she frowned slightly, apparently concentrating on what she was going to say. Her gaze returned to that place over his left shoulder, and, as he followed it, he thought that he'd been right; she was looking at the empty space where that odious painting had hung. He waited while the woman collected her thoughts, intrigued by her self-possession. Rich Jansen had been in the presence of more criminals than he cared to remember, male and female alike. He could remember none who had been this reflective. From most of them flowed a torrent of words whether coherent or not; they talked instantly upon meeting with someone who may have some power or influence over the judicial system. Of course, he had never interrogated a physician with the scientific background this woman had either, so maybe it came with the territory. As the silence in the room extended, his memory dredged up a Texas Medical Center case he had been right smack in the middle of; it was about seven years ago, Rich recalled. A TMC doc had been accused of shooting his wife, and the media was all over it. Just as he was comparing the interview of that doctor with this one, he heard her voice. As his attention returned to the present, her gaze remained on the empty wall above the Ficus tree, but Rich would have bet money that she saw neither the wall nor the plant.

"There is a reason I am here," she said slowly and calmly in a soft and measured tone. After making the statement, she seemed to be jolted out of a reverie and then laughed self-consciously as her intense green gaze returned to Rich.

"Of course, I know that I was convicted of the murder of my mother, but I don't think that's why I'm here, Mr. Jansen. I don't know the reason, but I will before I leave Huntsville. I do know that Devon Preston is part of that reason."

Rich Jansen was speechless. He'd had no idea of what this woman would say to him, but he had never been as astonished in his life. It was clear that he was on new ground here. No prisoner *ever* started a conversation with any other statement but that he or she was innocent of the crime that had placed them in prison. Indeed, no prisoner ever said that she knew that there was a reason she was here. It simply didn't happen.

If he didn't know better, he would think she was speaking on metaphysical or even religious grounds, but that did not fit with what he knew of her background. He would bet that she was at least agnostic if not an atheist like many of the scientists and physicians he had known. His astonishment must have been clear, for her next comment brought them both out of the surreal and back into the purpose of their meeting.

Shaking her head as if to clear her thoughts, Lindsey next made a statement that got the conversation back on track. "I'm sorry, Mr. Jansen, I have no idea why I said that; let's both forget I said it." And as McCall looked sideways at Jansen, their gazes met, and both knew that neither of them would forget those words.

"I began to work in the infirmary my first week here at Huntsville." She looked at Rich thoughtfully and continued. "Yes, it was exactly two days after I was shown my cell up in the administrative segregation area, but I was on the third floor then, not the fourth." Lindsey was referring to the isolation that had been imposed on her by Dorman, where she had been moved to the mostly empty fourth floor as a concession to Pettigrew and his case against Lindsey.

Continuing, Lindsey said, "I was happy to get the job, as it would keep me busy, and I knew I needed that. The new assignment, along with the job I was given in the library, meant that at least sixteen hours of my day would be occupied and that was a relief." Her speech slowed as she concentrated. She did not seem frightened, Rich observed, for there were no manifestations of fear or of any anxiety at all. Her hands had not moved from their position in the entire time they had been sitting there. Her breathing was deep and slow, and her eyes were not dilated, nor did they dart around the room. She looked either at him or at the piece of empty wall where that painting had been hanging the last time she had been in this office. Lindsey knew that he was observing her and that he'd not made one note on the empty yellow legal pad sitting in front of him. But that did not rattle her, not at all. She was obviously using energy in an attempt to be as precise as possible in the way she told this story.

"In the first week, there wasn't much to do in the infirmary. I think there were only five patients in those first seven days until a bacterial infection caused by food poisoning came through, and Monica and I were able to handle the cases without any problem." There was a soft smile that suggested affection for Monica Bradbury, one of the registered nurses who had worked at Huntsville for over fifteen years. Just as Rich was about to ask Lindsey about that, she continued to speak, and he decided not to interrupt her.

"When we admitted the fourth patient, DPH came out and went through the Ellis Unit and the common areas with a fine-toothed comb. Monica told me there were over a hundred DPH employees out here investigating everything and everyone involved in the preparation and serving of food." There are two equally feared events in a prison: an escape and an infectious disease outbreak. The Texas Department of Public Health is the guardian against the latter and is scrupulous in its attempts to identify the source of a potential outbreak and to quell it immediately. Although an outbreak of four is not, by definition, an epidemic, four sick prisoners among a vulnerable population of over seven thousand is a red flag and would result in a massive response from the public health officials.

"I never saw Dr. Pettigrew that week. Monica said there was no way that he would come in while there was a GI epidemic, and he sure didn't. It was kind of fun, though, really. I had not done that type of patient care since I was a medical student. And certainly didn't do much of it then, just enough for the nurses to know that I didn't think I was above that kind of thing. And you know what?" The question was rhetorical, of course. By now, Rich figured that Dr. McCall had forgotten that he was even in the room, so again, he said nothing. The only sound in the room during Lindsey's frequent silences was an occasional very soft snore from Max, who had resigned himself to making do with sleeping on the hard floor under Rich's desk.

"Paula thought the same thing; she thought I believed I was above taking care of our mother. As much as Paula insisted that I refused to take my share for our mom's care and was an unnatural daughter, especially during the last few months of Mother's life, I did offer to take over for Paula. But she wouldn't leave Mom in anyone's hands other than her own or one of the nurses from the agency. Paula believed that she was the only one who knew how to take care of her. And maybe she was right. The few times that I did stay with our mother ended up in sheer frustration for both of us. It was always the same routine: I would try to explain ways that Mom could gain some control over her disease, having read some new study about nonmedical management of heart failure. Stanford, University of Wisconsin, and Cleveland Clinic all have shown the benefit of minimal exercise in patients with class IV heart failure. Consistent, simple exercises of the extremities for ten minutes per day could markedly reduce shortness of breath at rest, for example. The exercises are easy to do, practical, and require no equipment or technology. When I'd start to explain how she could help herself, without fail Mother would begin to cry and claim that I had no idea of how she suffered and how much pain she had. So I'd get annoyed as hell that she wouldn't lift a finger to help herself feel better. Paula would come in from wherever she had been and see our mother sobbing and me ready to bolt out the door as soon as I could. But it had nothing to do with my believing that I was above taking care of Mom, emptying her bedpan, or anything like that. I just got so angry at my mother's complete refusal to actively do anything that could help her."

Jansen was sure happy he was taping this narrative. For some reason, he was sure that Todd Kensington knew none of this and would be most interested in the tape when Rich produced it Thursday night at dinner in Houston. But then, remembering Todd's strange response to his introduction of the Dr. Lindsey McCall case, maybe he wouldn't be so happy to get the tape.

"The truth is that I was always so relieved when Paula told me that she could handle Mom and that I didn't need to worry about it. I hated being around there with my mother and my sister; it was depressing and maudlin. And Paula knew that, I'm sure.

"The truth was, Mr. Jansen, even in med school none of us wanted to take care of patients like Mom. They were sick and would get progressively sicker until they died. And there was nothing we could do about it. The female patients I saw in school frequently reminded me of my mother and how little I could do for her, no matter how hard I tried. The cure, the elusive cure that we went to school to learn didn't really exist for these people. That's why most of us go into the specialties like cardiology, pulmonary, GI. We get to go in for the consult and probably do the procedures we love to do and then leave. But none of us admit it, of course—how could we?"

Now the smile was sad and the expression grim. Rich had only a scant understanding of what this woman was talking about as he'd not had time to obtain, never mind read, the transcript of her trial. But if Jansen had harbored any reservations about whether he wanted to expend the time and energy to locate and plow through several hundred pages of court testimony, they were long gone. His curiosity had been piqued by these last remarks of Lindsey about her family; the introduction of a sister into this case shed an interesting new light. And the comments she'd made about doctors not liking to take care of sick people made sense as he thought about it. He wondered idly if the sister were a nurse, which would sort of figure.

He recalled what McCall had said when she had first begun to speak to him. She'd apologized for that somewhat mystical introductory statement by explaining that she had never talked to anyone about all of this. That sure would explain all the jumping around that she was doing in her narrative because he was sure that the woman was highly trained and expert in describing complex relationships clearly and coherently. So how long had it been since this woman had unloaded any of this personal baggage?

But when she began to speak again, her voice had lowered and softened slightly so that Rich had to concentrate to hear her. "Even though Monica never asked me anything about what had happened on the outside, she let me know that she heard a lot about me and about what I had done before all this …" Her voice trailed off, and she was staring at the same block of blank wall. Then she resumed, her voice stronger now, "So when all hell broke loose with the inmate who died in the infirmary of an acute MI, she must have expected that I would do something other than standing there while Pettigrew let the man die."

What the hell is she talking about? Jansen screamed in his head. *What patient who died of an MI?* He had finally jotted some notes on the large legal pad, writing slowly and deliberately while he calmed himself down. When he looked up, those spectacular green eyes were on him, not looking over his shoulder at the blank wall but directly as if she were challenging him to meet her gaze. Jansen could feel his jaw tighten as he began to suspect that he was being worked here, and he didn't like it. But just as he started to bark out some of what was in his head, Lindsey seemed to understand that she had lost him. She moved her left hand and very gently touched his right hand as it fiddled with the legal pad.

"Mr. Jansen, forgive me, I am sure I am confusing you, and that is not my intention, not at all. You see, I've not told any of this to anyone, and it is all fairly well jumbled up in my mind—ergo, my incoherence. I'm jumping around to associations which make sense only to me, and I am sorry for that. I probably should have written all this down, and I regret not having done that. From your reaction, I'll assume you were not aware of the inmate who died here at the infirmary seventy days ago?"

Rich had not taken his eyes from Lindsey's. He was responding to her on two levels. As an experienced cop, he sensed that the woman was genuine and that his earlier reaction about being played had to do with the response he was feeling as a man. He was both angry and frightened at the intensity of the physical attraction he felt for McCall—an attraction that Jansen considered dangerous for countless reasons. So he did what was always best in situations when you don't have a clue of what to say. He said nothing; he just nodded.

"Okay, I'll fill in the gaps with what took place when Dr. Pettigrew arrived in the infirmary. I had been there now about two weeks, I think. Since Monica has been there so long, she has a lot of influence over the others who work there: other nurses, physician assistants, and orderlies. Since Monica liked me, it was only natural that all the rest of them did as well. They all look to her in a lot of ways. But what I didn't know was that none of the infirmary staff likes Dr. Pettigrew. And that was the first problem I guess." Lindsey hesitated again here as she frowned, clearly focusing on what to say next.

"Once the infirmary had been cleared by DPH and the last patient was well enough to return to his cell, there was sort of a celebratory feeling among the group. And one of the orderlies, a prisoner, like me, had learned that it was Monica's birthday. Somehow, Pete, the inmate, managed to get this huge birthday cake into the infirmary. It was as beautiful as any cake you could buy at any of Houston's gourmet shops. It had three layers, all chocolate with German chocolate frosting that was the lightest you've ever tasted in your life. Usually, I never eat cakes and pies, figure that I'm just looking at four more miles to run. But this"—she was shaking her head in wonder at the memory—"tasted like chocolate air. And the best part, the very best was there was a miniature Monica on the top of the cake that really looked like her. Whoever baked that cake was an artist. It seems as if there is no end to the surprises that one can encounter in Huntsville Prison, Mr. Jansen."

This last comment was delivered with a grin. And it transformed her face, for a moment, into that of a child, alight with wonder and innocence and joy.

"Unfortunately, Dr. Pettigrew happened to appear just as were singing a loud rendition of 'Happy Birthday' to Monica." McCall's expression sobered, and the light vanished from her face as she continued, "In a word, he hated me on first sight. Naturally, he would have known that I had applied to work in the infirmary and most likely looked up my background. The information is certainly accessible, and I would have done that were I he." She paused again, her lips compressing into a grimace. "He would have learned about Digipro and a lot of people subscribe to *Time* magazine as if Digipro weren't enough." Lindsey interrupted herself but not before Rich began to track with her; she was talking about jealousy, he realized just as she quickly explained apologetically about her medical discovery. "I agreed to an interview with *Time* magazine because my boss at the med school and the CEO of Andrews, Sacks, and Levine, the drug company funding my research, insisted that the 'world needed to know me and understand the magnitude of the discovery.' *Time* decided that I would be their Woman of the Year. They had learned that I was a nominee for the Nobel Prize in Medicine for the discovery of Digipro." The last was said harshly, in a strident and bitter voice that Rick had not heard before. "*Of course, Pettigrew would despise me.*"

She fell silent, now staring at Max, who had padded over to her, sat down, and given her his paw.

Rich recalled a Scrabble game that he had lost to Laura early in their marriage. She had spelled out *flummoxed* and scored over a hundred points to win the game. Rich had argued there was no such word, and they had pulled out their worn copy of the *Random House* dictionary, and there it was: "*flummoxed*: confused, bewildered, bemused, stumped, perplexed, mystified, baffled." All of that, that's how he felt.

The doctor had apparently made one of the greatest medical and scientific discoveries of the century, and she said it as if she had won first prize for an apple pie she had made for the county fair. Further, Dr. Lindsey McCall was evidently so conditioned to people feeling jealous of her brains and accomplishments that she blamed herself when others disliked her.

Lindsey accepted the big dog's advances as if this was nothing out of the ordinary. She had not jumped nor gasped when Max got up and came over to her side. She'd just taken the dog's paw very gently as if she realized that Max was there to give comfort. Because he was, there was no doubt in Rich's mind that his dog had sensed the deep sadness of this woman and decided that she needed his comfort. This interview—if it could be called that—was the strangest he had ever conducted. And he confirmed with a surreptitious glance at his watch that they had another forty minutes before Luke Preston would arrive. Jansen felt as if they had been in this office together for twenty hours rather than twenty minutes.

Lindsey must have caught the not–so-surreptitious glance, though, because she picked up on her story, and had returned to her self-possessed state. And Max must have figured that he was no longer needed for he stood up and regarded Lindsey for just a moment, then turned to Rich for a quick pat before returning to his perch under Rich's desk.

"The party broke up right away. Dr. Pettigrew didn't have to say a word; but of course, he had a lot to say about the new technician, meaning me, and how low the mighty have fallen, stuff like that, but he was drunk, obviously plastered." Lindsey resumed, "I could smell the alcohol several feet away, but no one would look at me, even Monica. Everyone suddenly had lots of tasks to do that required their complete concentration, so I followed one of the orderlies into the equipment room to help him do some cleaning up in there. It seemed fairly obvious to me that these people had seen Pettigrew in this shape before. No one looked surprised. But then I heard some commotion outside in the hallway. And I heard Monica yell, 'Lindsey, get out here now, please.' Monica never yells, so I ran out just as Pettigrew came lurching out of his office, screaming at me to get back in my cell where I belonged, that this was his infirmary where only *real* doctors practiced, not unlicensed felons like Lindsey McCall. I got one look at the patient they now had hooked up to the monitor. He was in ventricular tachycardia, apparent to Monica and me but not to Pettigrew. Dr. Pettigrew decided to keep up his drunken rant at me. Meanwhile, the patient lost the low blood pressure he had come in with, and his cardiac rhythm devolved into ventricular fibrillation, then agonal rhythm, and then a straight line. He was dead. He was thirty-three years old, and he was dead because of a drunken, incompetent physician. Of course, I don't know if I could have saved him; no one ever knows, not even the pathologist who did the postmortem in this case; if they did one, that is. The look on Pettigrew's face when he pronounced the man dead was jubilant. There was no other word for it. Pettigrew *knew* I was in the equipment room, watching. There are security video cameras everywhere in the infirmary. When he pronounced the guy dead, he looked up at the camera and smiled at me. The egotistical, pompous fool is a disgrace to the medical profession; out of retaliation at me, he had stupidly let a young man die."

The words had poured out of her, tumbling over one another in a staccato torrent that seemed beyond her control; the expression on her face combined horror, incredulity, and rage as she relived an experience that had to have been pure torture. McCall's whole body was rigid, and her hands were no longer loosely on top of each other; each was curled into a fist. Those green eyes were flashing fire as she fought for control of herself, visibly working to calm down to escape from the awful helplessness she had felt when the man died, and return to the present.

What a nightmare this whole case was turning into; the whole thing seemed so unbelievable that Jansen wondered if he had actually heard all this. No longer did he feel indebted to the Texas governor for the use of his house and the new clothes. This story was worse than those TV shows about life in prison—much worse, and if this story got out? The warden could not imagine the feeding frenzy that would occur or the number of heads that would roll in the state government.

He couldn't decide who was more at fault, Dorman or Pettigrew, unless maybe the autopsy could shed some light. And then it hit him like a ton of bricks: Rich suddenly realized that Dorman most likely knew nothing about this because Pettigrew would have covered up his culpability by entering a bogus cause of death on the death certificate. And the Texas medical examiners were too overwhelmed by their workload in the four-million-plus Harris County civilian population to provide careful scrutiny of the sudden and unexplained death of a Huntsville Prison inmate. Pettigrew would have known this, of course; that had to be why the guy had decided to sue the state for Lindsey's actions in the Preston case. Pettigrew believed himself to be impervious to any authority. Jansen started to smile.

Lindsey had started to answer Rich's questions about the post and death certificate but was speaking more and more slowly and quizzically as she stared at the broad grin that had just taken residence on Rich's face. "Never mind all that, Dr. McCall. In your opinion, would Monica Bradbury back up your testimony about this patient who died without medical attention from Dr. Pettigrew?"

Lindsey was staring in fascination at the changes that had transformed Jansen's face; his brown eyes, formerly filled with anger, were now dancing with merriment, as if he were ten years old and had just received his first puppy.

"Dr. McCall, you have just handed me one of the best presents I've ever been given, ever, believe me, *if* Monica will back up your story. Will she?"

Rich began to worry as Lindsey frowned; if it were McCall's word against Pettigrew's, they were toast. But Lindsey was nodding slowly and then said, "Well, I can't speak for her, of course, but Monica cried that whole afternoon. She cried when she removed his electrodes, she cried when she bathed him, and she cried when she learned that there was no one to notify. He had no family, no one to mourn his death. But, Mr. Jansen, Monica is like all the others who work in the infirmary. She wants to keep this job, she is a single mother with four kids to feed, and she's afraid of Pettigrew. She'll need to be protected from the man."

A knock on the door, signaling that their hour was over. Preston had returned; Jansen sent for Monica and also asked his secretary to bring a larger tape recorder, because the tape on his mini-cassette was most likely filled with the conversation of the last hour. There was another soft knock on the door, and there stood his secretary, Wanda Miller. Clearly an East Texas girl from her accent, Wanda stood balancing a tray of coffees and chocolate-chip cookies with an enormous grin on her face.

"Hello, Dr. McCall, I thought y'all could use some refreshments and then"—Wanda turned to Rich—"that tape recorder I just gave you hasn't been used since we bought it; I'm sure there is no tape in it so let me get that set for you while you wait for Mrs. Bradbury."

All eyes were on the tall, heavy-set woman with the big Texas hair while she efficiently distributed the coffee and placed the chocolate-chip cookies in the middle of the table. Like the rest of the group, Rich watched this pleasant woman while reveling in his good fortune. Wanda seemed to be typical of the rural Texas females of her age and older: completely transparent, surprisingly tolerant, and extremely independent thinkers, with an ability to shoot, skin, and dress a buck deer should the need arise. Her deference to Lindsey pleased him, Rich realized; there had been no need to greet either Preston or himself because she'd just seen them moments before. That she took the time to greet Lindsey that way showed a lot of class, Rich thought.

As Wanda exited the office, Jansen nodded to Max, who had moved to sit next to Lindsey when Rich left to speak to Wanda; with a sigh, the dog reclaimed his space behind the desk. Rich looked at Lindsey, now calm and composed with those long, slender hands lying on the table one on top of the other. "Have some coffee and a cookie, Dr. McCall, while we wait for Monica to join us." Turning to Luke, he said, "Come on, big guy, you can do with a couple of home-made cookies, right?"

Rich took a sip of coffee, which tasted as good as Starbucks, then grabbed a cookie himself, thinking he would need to do three and a half miles tonight with Max, but the cookies smelled as if they had just come out of the oven. The three sat there comfortably, enjoying the civilized break.

Not five minutes later, Monica Bradbury joined them and Rich received confirmation of Lindsey's story. Jansen decided to confront it head-on: "Monica, you are not in any trouble here nor will you be. Dr. Pettigrew serves at Huntsville Prison at the pleasure of the warden. Right now, that's me. If Dr. Pettigrew decided to fire any member of his infirmary staff, I would need to approve that decision, and I would not do so." Instantly, Monica relaxed, her hands stilled, and her expression softened. *Good*, Rich thought, *she's with us*. "Based on what I have heard from Dr. McCall about Dr. Pettigrew's behavior and medical competence, I believe that Dr. Pettigrew and I can come to a meeting of the minds about this suit and his critique of Dr. McCall. Like you, I would like that resolution to come sooner not later, this week if possible. But first, Monica, I need to hear the facts of that patient's death as you recall the events. I also will need to record your testimony if I may?" Clearly, concisely and in less than fifteen minutes, the nurse corroborated every detail that Lindsey had provided. Bradbury also confirmed Rich's guess about the falsified death certificate. Pettigrew's arrogance apparently knew no bounds, for he routinely manufactured the cause of death for Huntsville inmates. This man, Monica opined, had not died of exsanguination resulting from a severed carotid artery as, Dr. Pettigrew had claimed, but rather from lethal arrhythmia from a myocardial infarction.

As Monica Bradbury was winding up the story that would place Lance Pettigrew in a hole that he would never be able to dig himself out of, Jansen was ecstatic. These were the kinds of cases that Rich Jansen excelled in: powerful personalities sprinkled with complex politics. Rich could feel the juices start to kick in and he felt more energized than he had in years. His eyes sparkling, he thanked Monica and invited her to stay if she would like but asked that Preston and McCall now describe what had happened with Devon. Monica surprised Jansen when she stated that she would like to stay because she had been on duty that day and had been involved in Devon's care.

Noting Rich's surprise, Monica explained that the nurse who regularly worked the evening shift had called in sick, and so Monica had worked sixteen hours that day.

Accustomed to actual events differing significantly from the files by now, Rich nodded in agreement and gestured an invitation for Preston to begin. That much had been in the record. Although the prison rules preclude a prison guard working in close proximity with an inmate who is a relative, there had been several sick calls that day, and no one noticed that Luke Preston's reassignment would place him in the same unit as his seventeen-year-old brother, Devon.

"I knew that La Emi was out to get Devon," Luke replied.

Rick nodded, "I got to know the Mexikanemi when I was

in the sheriff's office." The two were talking about one of the first prison gangs to develop in the United States, the Mexican Mafia.

"La Emi practically owns the high school where Devon was a senior; Devon's smart and doesn't have to study much, so the gang leader's girlfriend came to Devon for help with her algebra homework. The boyfriend saw Devon and his girl talking in the study hall, and that's all it took. The girl tried to explain what was going on, but that just made it worse, so they decided to get Devon away from the girl. Devon is at Huntsville because he was framed by La Emi," Preston claimed. "My brother was nowhere near that jewelry store they said he robbed at gunpoint. But La Emi intimidated three witnesses to the point that they identified Devon as the robber." The big man was shaking his head sadly as he resumed, "I couldn't protect him out there, but I am sure as hell going to do everything I can in here.

"It was late in the evening, maybe ten or so, when I heard Devon's whistle; we grew up near Galveston, and that kid could call seagulls to him by the time he was eight years old, so that was the signal we'd agreed on if he thought he was in trouble. I heard that call and ran. Devon was slumped over his bed and bleeding bad; the shiv was deep into his chest. The door of the cell was open, and I picked him up in my arms and ran. We got into the infirmary, and both Lindsey and Monica started to work on him." Luke looked over at the two women sitting side by side and grinned. "You two saved his life."

As if on cue, Lindsey picked up the conversation, "Devon would have died if you had removed that shiv, Luke. That knife was inside the lining of his heart; had you pulled it out, Devon would have bled out in less than three minutes."

Lindsey looked composed but solemn as she began to

relate the events of the case. "Monica and I thought we were alone," Lindsey explained. Jansen wondered for a moment what she meant, then realized that they assumed that Pettigrew was long gone since it was after ten at night. "We had to move fast, very fast, so we got Devon on the bed in the procedure room to verify my guess that he had a pericardial tamponade. While Monica was pumping intravenous fluid into him, hooking him up to the monitor, and getting his vital signs, I was checking his neck veins, blood pressure, and listening for distant heart sounds. I figured that the knife had penetrated Devon's left ventricle but only slightly so that with each contraction, blood was leaking out into Devon's pericardium. My plan was to withdraw as much of that pericardial blood as I could to buy us enough time to Life Flight Devon to Galveston and get him into surgery.

"Just as Monica handed me the cardiac needle to do the procedure, Pettigrew stormed in and began to scream and threaten Monica and me. As it happened, Luke was standing behind the open door of the procedure room and could not be seen by Dr. Pettigrew. Dr. Pettigrew was so worked up that he began to back up, and somehow he tripped over Luke's feet." The TMC doctor said this with a completely straight face; Rich was impressed, once again, at the seemingly ironclad self-control that Lindsey McCall possessed. Part of him wanted to laugh at the lugubriousness of this entire situation, but the tape recorder was running.

"With Dr. Pettigrew unconscious for the moment, I went ahead and did the pericardiocentesis, which restored Devon's blood pressure, and we had Devon on the helicopter within ten minutes. I call Devon my miracle patient."

Jansen saw that transformative smile on Lindsey's face for the second time. "I knew the helicopter pilot from my trauma call days at Houston General. I'm sure George knew that I was a prisoner here, but he acted just the way he always had and seemed to look past the prison clothing I wore."

"I accompanied Devon, and we had him in the Galveston OR within the hour." Lindsey's face shone as she completed her narrative.

The four were silent for a moment, the three looking at the grin on Lindsey McCall's face and each grinning back in return. Rich made a note to speak with Todd about Devon Preston's case; maybe one of Todd's associates could take a look at the case against the seventeen-year-old. The chief warden was impressed by the story that Luke had told about his kid brother, and it sounded like they needed to figure a way to get that kid out of Huntsville. From what Rich knew about La Emi, if the gang leaders had targeted the boy, they would figure out a way to get to him again if he remained here. Suddenly aware of the silence in the room, Rich stopped writing, looked up, stopped the tape recorder, and thanked them all.

The next day, Rich leaned back in his wonderfully worn, weathered, and therefore wonderfully comfortable leather chair and smiled as he surveyed the effects of the last day and a half. He had taken Wanda's advice and used the time to make this office habitable and civilized. He and Max had driven back to his Montrose house yesterday afternoon where one of his former detectives at the sheriff's office was more than happy to meet him to help move Rich's desk and chair to his Huntsville Prison office.

The Ficus tree remained, but now it sat in the corner to the right of the large picture window, overlooking the exercise yard. Rich had found three small upholstered antique chairs and table at the same store where he had bought the plant in downtown Huntsville. The chairs were comfortable, unlike most antiques that he'd sat in; the fabric in the upholstery was lovely, subtle variations of deep rose, green, and gold. The table was small but adequate, roomy enough to hold a few cups of coffee and a few files. The formerly gray office walls had been painted white, and on one of them hung two of Laura's favorite Boudin prints they had bought while in France on their honeymoon.

As Rich gazed at the impressionistic art that his wife had so loved, he smiled at the memories of their trip to Honfleur in northern France. Honfleur had been the favored site of many of the impressionists during the late eighteen hundreds based on the belief in a special filtered light that bathed the city in those shimmering and vibrant hues seen in Monet's, Gaugin's, and Seurat's paintings. The newlyweds had driven their rental car north from Mont St. Michelle. Rich chuckled as he recalled Laura's childlike insistence that he see and appreciate the unique light as they approached Honfleur. Laura had been so disappointed when he'd said that it looked just like the light in Texas that he'd relented and admitted that the light here may be more unusual than at home.

Laura had insisted on these two prints, Rich recalled, as he looked at the two Boudins hanging diagonally from one another. They had argued about the cost. He was just starting law school, and Laura made very little money as an art teacher, but his new wife had worn him down with her patient and relentless conviction that the couple needed a way to return to those magical two weeks.

"There will be times in our lives," Laura had predicted, "that we'll feel as if we'll never be happy again, but these clouds and this Honfleur light will dispel the darkness." Rich could sense her presence as he gratefully drank in the perfection of the clouds of Boudin's *Studies of the Sky* and his almost-unearthly *La Havre, 1989*, a lone sailboat in silhouette against spectacular yet subtle colors of a setting sun in the Honfleur harbor. Jansen realized suddenly that the memory of his dead wife no longer caused pain; that the memory of Laura now brought him joy, and he said a quick prayer of gratitude. "Maybe you really are right about the light in Honfleur," Rich whispered to Laura as he basked in the beauty of the two paintings.

At ten minutes to two, Pettigrew had still not shown up for his 1:30 appointment. Rich wasn't surprised because he was expecting the Harvard-trained prison physician to pull out all the stops in his arsenal of intimidating behaviors. The tardiness was a classical ploy intended to emphasize the importance of Pettigrew's time while minimizing Jansen's. Rich shook his head as he pondered what Wanda said about Harold Dorman, his predecessor. *The poor bastard*, he thought to himself about Dorman, *he was no match for this pompous bully. No wonder he couldn't wait to get out of here once Bell fired him. I'm really looking forward to meeting Pettigrew.* Just as the thought completed itself in his head, there was a loud rap at the door.

Sauntering over to open the door, Jansen was still looking at his watch, now registering that the Huntsville physician was exactly forty-five minutes late for his appointment. Rich stood blocking the doorway for an awkward moment, his only greeting a raised eyebrow as he stared wordlessly at Dr. Lance Pettigrew. Jansen watched as a series of expressions fleetingly altered the man's eyes and mouth: defiance, arrogance, anger, apparently settling on deference with evident difficulty.

"Mr. Jansen, I'm Dr. Lance Pettigrew, and I apologize for being late for our meeting. I got a late start leaving Galveston, and then there was an accident on I-45, which increased my delay, of course. You know how badly a wreck can back up traffic on the Gulf Freeway." Some hesitation and uncertainty had crept into the physician's voice as he stood in front of Jansen's office in the hallway of the administrative suite. At two in the afternoon, there was a lot of traffic along the hallways as inmates and guards walked to and from their work and the exercise yard. They all knew Pettigrew, and few had seen Dorman's replacement as yet, so most slowed down to stare at the two men standing there.

"Mr. Jansen, could we go into your office, please?" Pettigrew was eying a group of guards who were walking so slowly they had slowed to a crawl about twenty yards away. The physician was nervous, eyes darting around anxiously and licking his lips.

"Yes, Dr. Pettigrew, come in and sit down, please."

Rich had stood aside to let Dr. Pettigrew enter his office; upon closing the door, Jansen had to suppress the laughter that threatened to erupt. Apparently, his desire to disarm Pettigrew had worked almost too well. The prison physician was still standing in the middle of the room with his mouth partially open as he looked around Rich's office. Rich made no comment and just pointed in the direction of the chairs and table as he walked over to his desk to pick up his file and to signal Max to stay put.

Taking the seat across the table from the one the doctor had taken, Rich nodded to Pettigrew and thanked him for making the trip from Galveston, watching the prison physician carefully as he spoke. While Rich was making small talk, Pettigrew started to relax; he began to regain some control over himself: his hands stopped shaking, and the deferential manner began to fade. He may have an alcohol problem as well, but there was not a shred of doubt in Rich's mind that Lance Pettigrew was an addict, most likely to opiates. "Mr. Jansen, why did you ask to see me?" Having recovered most of his usual imperiousness, Pettigrew's tone was antagonistic when he interrupted Rich in his explanation of the authority vested in the position of chief warden at Huntsville Prisons. Rich realized that his silence and passivity to date had restored the confidence of the prison doctor; like most bullies, he respected only intimidation. Although not physically threatening, Pettigrew used the power of his profession and position to control those around him. That Rich had not behaved in the same way was at first confusing, but now Pettigrew had decided that Jansen was as weak as was his predecessor and could be bullied. The physician's facial expression was one of derision and contempt as he addressed Rich; both hands lay on the table with the fingers of the left hand drumming an impatient beat.

Good, thought Rich and decided to go for it. "Because I'd like to know why an inept and intoxicated doctor would sue a colleague for saving the life of a patient when he was clearly too intoxicated to do so."

The remark had the intended effect; Pettigrew jumped up, face now a dark red, and expression apoplectic, yelling, "How dare you talk to me like that, Jansen. I'm not staying for one minute to listen to your slanderous comments. The next time you hear from me, it'll be from my lawyer. I'll—"

"Sit down, Dr. Pettigrew, sit down *now*." Rich had stood as well and had grabbed the doctor's forearm, forcing him to take his seat. Simultaneously, he nodded at Max, who had stood up with the commotion but now turned away to disappear under Rich's desk. Rich's words had been said very quietly, but the grip on the physician's arm had been one of iron. Pettigrew sat and rubbed his arm as he repeated more quietly that he wanted his lawyer.

"Dr. Pettigrew, you cut me off earlier when I was explaining to you what Governor Bell has asked me to do here at

Huntsville. So perhaps you did not understand that I am your boss. Do you know what a boss is and what that means to you?" Pettigrew hissed, "Of course, I know what a boss is."

"Good, because I *am* your boss, Doctor, and we are conversing about your competence as the prison physician for Huntsville. As chief warden, I am vested with the authority to hire and to fire the doctor at Huntsville prisons." Jansen held out his hand to stop Pettigrew's angry response. "Doctor, I have not made up my mind. I am merely gathering the facts. And I would like you to answer my question, please."

"Boss or not, Jansen, you have no right calling me 'inept' or 'intoxicated.' You are not a doctor—even a nurse; therefore, you've no basis to make those allegations. I consider your comments slanderous and will pursue those spurious comments to the full extent of the Texas law." But Pettigrew was starting to get nervous again; his eyes began to dart around the room, and the fingers on his left hand had stopped drumming. The physician's hands were clasped together, tightly.

Rich sat motionlessly, staring at the man, waiting for him to answer the question he had asked. He had all afternoon to wait for the guy to talk, but he knew it wouldn't take long at all; Dr. Pettigrew was beginning to figure out that Harold Dorman was gone. In his place sat a new entity, one who was not easily intimidated. Rich's gaze never left Pettigrew's face. But he couldn't meet the doctor's eyes because they never stopped moving, and if they did meet Rich's, Pettigrew's eyes would widen then continue the frantic darting around the room. The silence in the room extended.

Pettigrew tried again. "I am not talking to you without my lawyer." And he started to push his chair back and get to his feet.

Jansen watched the physician stand and then very quietly commanded, "Sit down. For the third time, Doctor, why are you suing the State of Texas?"

Reluctantly, Pettigrew sat and finally glared at Jansen; trying and failing to regain control of the conversation, he sighed and looked at Jansen once more. "You have the files, Mr. Jansen; you know what has taken place here." But the physician's imperiousness was fading rapidly as he met Jansen's opaque gaze.

Nodding, Jansen got up and walked over to his desk to retrieve the tape recorder with both Monica Bradbury's and Luke Preston's testimonies recorded on the tape. Just as Jansen pulled out the tape recorder, Pettigrew stood abruptly and announced, "Mr. Jansen, I don't think there is any need to draw this meeting out. You will have my resignation on your desk by the end of the day, and you may tell the governor that I am withdrawing my lawsuit. I have only one request."

Breathing a sigh of relief, Rich left the tape recorder on his desk and strode rapidly back to take the chair opposite from Pettigrew to answer the unvoiced request. "Dr. Pettigrew, I have no intention of revealing the contents of those files or the audiotapes to any law enforcement agency or professional organization; you have my word on that."

Pettigrew stared at Rich and then said. "Thank you, Mr. Jansen, I appreciate your understanding." Upon rising from his seat, Dr. Pettigrew looked around the office, most likely seeing it for the first time. When his eyes rested on the two Boudin paintings, he murmured almost too softly to hear, "You'll make a difference here, Mr. Jansen, I wish you well." With that, Dr. Pettigrew quickly opened the door, closing it softly behind him.

Rich picked up his phone and dialed a familiar number. "I'd like to speak with Governor Bell, please. No, he is not expecting the call, but tell him it's Rich Jansen with good news."

❧

There's no better way of exercising the imagination than the study of law. No poet ever interpreted nature as freely as a lawyer interprets truth.

—Jean Giraudoux

11

It was another glorious early October afternoon as Rich headed south on I-45 in his Mercedes with his top down. Since restaurants generally objected to customers with four legs and big teeth, Rich had left Max home. But he didn't feel too guilty because he'd left work early enough to fit in a four-mile run with plenty of time left over to meet Todd at Amerika's in the Pavilion Mall on Post Oak Boulevard. Rich had left Max happily gnawing on a huge raw bone that would keep him busy for a couple of hours or so. Since Rich had not been going out to restaurants much in the last several years, he'd told Todd to just pick one, and he would meet him there. He didn't think he had ever been to Amerika's, but Todd said it was one of his favorite haunts.

Jansen had arrived at the restaurant first, so he took a seat at one of the inviting stools in front of the S-shaped bar and settled down to wait. As he remembered, Todd was generally late; Rich recalled that Todd seemed to set up his life so that he was constantly racing to the next appointment. Rich could care less; he was enjoying being out for the first time in months, maybe years. He was right; he had never been to this restaurant, he would have remembered the unusual decor and the unique layout of the place. The walls of the bar looked like some kind of black mosaic stone, and the glass chandeliers seemed to be

113

a facsimile of some exotic flowers. The bartender interrupted his examination of the bar to ask what Rich would like to drink. Sipping the merlot the bartender brought, he mused about the price of a glass of good wine; the last time he recalled ordering a glass of wine in a restaurant, it had been at least three dollars less. He smiled back at a very attractive woman seated at the far end of the bar who had been eying him for the last five minutes or so, surprised at the pleasure he felt in her evident interest.

"Hey, bud, sorry I'm late, hope you've not been waiting too long?" With a flourish, Todd Kensington descended onto the empty chair beside Rich and ordered from the bartender who had suddenly materialized, "Bombay gin martini please, straight up with onions." Turning to Rich, the defense lawyer looked him up and down. "My friend, you are looking great; if you were a girl, I would say *radiant!* This new job must agree with you, or could it be that some of the people you are meeting out there are responsible for this glow of yours?" The comments were accompanied by Todd's rapid raising and lowering of his eyebrows in an excellent imitation of a lascivious letch. This act was quickly followed by a broad grin, which displayed a set of perfectly even and perfectly white teeth suitable for an ad for cosmetic dentistry.

Todd Kensington was one of those rarest of people: a native Houstonian. Todd and Rich had met on their first day of law school at the University of Houston. The men had been drawn to each other for a number of reasons, but uppermost among them was that each had gone to one of the East Coast "mega schools" for their undergraduate work—Todd to Yale and Rich to Harvard. And each had turned down the offer of entry into their prestigious law schools because they wanted to come back home to Texas.

Todd scrutinized Rich. "Man, the last time I saw you, you

were in Houston Medical right after you were shot, I really thought ….” His voice drifted off, and the expression on the confident, handsome face dissolved into concern and discomfort.

“Todd, it’s okay, it really is. I thought I was going to die, too. Hell, the docs thought I didn’t have a chance, so don’t worry about what you were just thinking, man.” Rich smiled at his friend, appreciating the friendship and the opportunity to speak the shorthand that men used to convey their deep affection for one another.

Just then, their waiter appeared and set a plate of crispy, yellow objects with two brightly colored dips on the table as he simultaneously listed the specials of the evening; the list went on for a few minutes it seemed. Rich lost interest after the first five.

Todd glanced at Rich. “Does any of that sound good?”

And Todd grinned when he heard Jansen’s usual answer. “I’ll have whatever you’re having.”

Rich Jansen’s friends all knew that he was capable of throwing together gourmet meals in his own kitchen, which would challenge half the sous-chefs in the city of Houston. Todd turned to the waiter and ordered a New York steak rare for each of them with grilled portabella mushrooms and wild rice on the side. The waiter left, and Todd nodded at the unusual appetizer. “Plantains, dried bananas, very tasty … have one, Rich,” he said, reaching for the plate and nibbling on the end that had been dipped into the sauce.

Todd took a sip of his martini, chewed, swallowed his plantain, and then gazed levelly at his friend. “I laughed when Eleanor called me, Rich, I cracked up.” But there was no smile, nor was there any amusement in his friend’s expression. Todd Kensington’s dark eyes were somber, and his tone was one of pure chagrin as he stared into the clear liquid of the gracefully tall stemmed crystal martini glass.

"You're talking about Eleanor Philbin, the chair of the Houston Medical Board?" Although Rich did not travel in the same circle as one of the wealthiest women in Houston, he had met Eleanor through Father John Tobin, his priest at the Co-Cathedral of the Sacred Heart. There had been a dinner for the contributors of the new cathedral, and somehow Rich had found himself seated at the Philbins' table. He had thought her delightful, surprisingly so, and hoped that he would run into her again. "Why would Eleanor Philbin ask you to take the case of one of the doctors at the hospital, Todd?"

"Yes to your first question, and I don't know to your second. After I had stopped laughing my fool head off in Eleanor's ear, I asked that same question of her." Todd was silent for a minute then asked, "You've met Eleanor then?"

Noting Jansen's affirmative nod, Todd continued, "Then you know what a lady she is. I never use that word to describe a woman, but for Eleanor Philbin, there simply is no better noun. She never answered my question, Rich, and I realized that Eleanor believed that Dr. McCall was in deep trouble. When I tried to reassure her and tell her that I was certain the grand jury would not bill the case, she was very gracious as always, but I could hear her doubt and deep concern for this physician. I can still hear that conversation echoing back in my head. Eleanor was deeply troubled, and I had no idea why. But I sure found out ...." His voice trailed off.

Rich leaned forward so that he and Todd's heads were only a couple of feet apart and softly said, "Hey, Todd, I don't want you to talk about something that is so obviously causing megadoses of grief. I called you because we've luckily been able to sort out some of the latest weirdness surrounding this McCall woman, and I—"

"Jansen, I know you too well to believe that *luck* had anything to do with it." Todd was smiling, but his voice had an edge to it, making it evident that he neither needed nor wanted any sympathy. The air was suddenly charged and reminded Rich of the competition between the two back in law school; he remembered how angry Todd would get when Rich aced one of the many exams and Todd had not. Worse yet, Todd would never admit that he was angry, just like now.

Deciding that Kensington's ego had been seriously damaged and that Todd needed to chill for a bit, Rich laughed off Todd's last comment and related the whole sad story of Pettigrew's humiliation by the unlicensed Dr. Lindsey McCall to Todd, trusting that the story would remain a private matter between them. Rich knew the story was sufficiently compelling to educe a complete mood change in Todd if he was able to forget about himself for a few minutes. Sure enough, Todd's expression began to soften as Rich told him about the death of the first prisoner, his typical ebullience returning when he heard about Lindsey's determination to avoid a second unnecessary death at the prison.

"Has Pettigrew dropped the suit against the state then?" Without waiting for a response from Rich, Todd added rhetorically, "She is one remarkable woman, Lindsey McCall."

"His resignation was on my desk yesterday at the end of the day."

Letting out a long slow whistle, Todd shook his head as he exclaimed, "Man, Jansen, that was a hail of bullets you dodged. That's all Bell would need—one more fiasco at the Huntsville Prisons." Then, suddenly, he asked, "So what do you think of our Lindsey?"

Startled at the quick change of subject, Rich looked at Todd quizzically but saw only curiosity on the face of his friend. "Todd, I'm not sure what I think. I do wish that someone had told me how beautiful the woman is, though;

that sure took me a while to get past."

"At least you got past it, Jansen I think that was my biggest problem in that trial—those green eyes." The two men smiled at each other in acknowledgment of shared history, friendship, and appreciation of beautiful women.

Just as the waiter approached with two platters of steaming food, Todd reached into his briefcase and pulled out three very thick binders. "Here, Rich, see if you can make any sense out of this," he said as he handed Rich several thousand pages of the court transcripts from Lindsey McCall's murder trial.

"Hey, no way, my friend. Yes, I do want those transcripts but not on your dime!" Rich was stunned at the generosity of his friend knowing that Todd had obtained the transcripts by paying the court reporter for them, most likely at a dollar a page. From the size of the stack of the three volumes sitting in front of him, Rich figured that the purchase had to have set Todd back around four, maybe five, thousand dollars.

"Rich, look, man, I paid the reporter for these transcripts within days of the conviction so that I could beat myself up about all the minefields that I never saw until I was picking shrapnel out of my hair. And"—he made a rueful laugh—"preparing for the appeal, of course. I work on the appeal most nights and every weekend. Honestly, Rich, you would be doing me a favor by getting them out of my hands so that I could work on one of my other cases. Or maybe even have a night out on the town."

Gazing at his friend, at the bruised and weary expression in his eyes and at the fine lines that seemed more pronounced in his forehead and around his mouth, Rich reached over to grab the stack of volumes and placed them on the floor next to his briefcase. "In that case, Kensington, the only reasonable payment for this is a weekend out in the country at Bell's New Waverly cabin. We'll take Max and do five miles in the forest in the morning, drink all day, then do another five; then you can help me make dinner Saturday night."

"Bell's New Waverly cabin? What is that about?" Todd stared at Rich, then tapped his forehead, and exclaimed, "You're serious? You're living in Gregory Bell's place in New Waverly?" Rich just nodded and smiled at the enthusiastic reception his idea had received. Todd Kensington was wealthy several times over both through the success of his private law practice and the royalties he received from his grandfather's lucrative oil business. But there were few things Todd loved more than moving in the same circles of the movers and shakers of Houston and of Texas.

"You know what, Rich? That is the best offer I've had all month. Give me directions and I'll meet you there after I go home and grab some clothes for the weekend. Let's eat." And Todd proceeded to eat with gusto.

Saturday morning dawned gloriously clear and cool. Rich and Max quietly padded downstairs to check the sunrise in the forest, while Max attended to a couple of other necessities. Rich stood on the porch watching the soft light of the rising sun filter through the thick forest to the east. A deer and her fawn darted through the edge of the yard not ten yards away from where Max was exploring. The dog was on high alert, Rich could tell; he could see the trembling of the Doberman's rigid hind legs from where he stood. He wondered what Max would do because Rich was fairly sure he had never seen a deer before, but Max maintained his pose, watching while the deer and her baby leaped away. They looked as if they were on springs, Rich thought as he watched the wild animals taking impossibly high leaps into the air, and then they were gone.

The silence was impenetrable; there had been no sound at all. Max turned to stare at Rich as if to ask what's next and trotted back into the house when Rich turned to open the front door.

By the time Todd joined them, it was seven thirty. Rich already had the marinara sauce made for the coq au vin and had six potatoes set aside for the gnocchi in preparation for dinner later that night. Todd sniffed loudly and with gusto as he exclaimed, "You have indeed maintained your culinary skills, my friend; it smells like ambrosia in here." Pouring himself a cup of coffee, Todd exclaimed, "Even your coffee is excellent! Mine always tastes like dishwater, so I've given up and joined the rest of the lazy bastards in Houston to go stand in line and pay two dollars for a cup of coffee at Starbucks."

As he wandered around the great room and the kitchen where Rich stood sautéing garlic, green pepper, and onion for the red sauce, Todd said, "I think I'll move in here with you guys; there sure is plenty of room and"—looking down at the running shorts, shoes, and T-shirt that he'd taken from the master bedroom—"no way can you go through all these clothes by yourself, Jansen."

Rich smiled as he listened to the chatter of his friend, content to listen without feeling a need to contribute anything verbally. Once more, he was somewhat overwhelmed by the provisions in this "cabin." Neatly stored in the roomy birch cabinets were all the items required to feed three or thirty; he was pulling down a large slow cooker from one of the top shelves in a tall cabinet when he heard the *click* of the leather recliner extend. *Good,* he thought, *Todd is exhausted. He looks as if he hasn't slept more than three or four hours in the last several months.* In one of the adjacent cabinets sat a bread machine, which he also brought down for later.

In another ten minutes, he had transferred the parboiled chicken, now broken into its component parts without skin and bones, into the slow cooker and had carefully covered the meat with the red sauce, where it would simmer slowly throughout the day. He stood in the middle of the kitchen mentally reviewing his checklist for dinner and decided that there was nothing more to be done until that evening. He whistled softly to Max, knowing that the dog had been waiting patiently for this moment, and they left Todd sound asleep in the recliner.

Rich stood on the porch and did a few leg stretches while he wondered if he should wake Todd after all to go for the morning run they had discussed the night before. He turned back, reopened the door, and peered around the corner. Todd had not moved. Rich checked his watch and made a silent bet to himself that they could do five miles before Todd awoke. Back on the porch, Rich grinned at his prancing dog and murmured, "Okay, boy, which way should we go this morning?"

Max took off like a shot down the path where the deer had appeared with her fawn a couple hours before, and Rich followed at a slow jog. Running no longer came as easily, at least not during the first mile or so, and he knew that being forty-five years old plus six months out of major trauma meant that he still needed to take it slowly. Forcing slow and deep breathing, Rich felt his muscles eventually loosen; he could feel the strain around the three wounds in his abdomen and torso, but thankfully they were merely sore, not painful. Max suddenly appeared, racing around the corner of the forest path, tongue lolling, to make sure that Rich was where he should be. Grinning at his dog, Rich mumbled, "I'm coming, boy, you'll just have to give me a few minutes."

Assured that Rich was okay, the dog took off once more. Within another ten minutes, Rich had loosened up sufficiently to get close to his average speed as he and Max padded together along the pine-needle-carpeted path of the forest. The trees were densely packed together, permitting only filtered sunlight and protecting the man and the dog from the rising heat of the day.

☙

It was exactly an hour later when Rich opened the front door, figuring that they had done somewhere around six, maybe seven miles and was heading up the stairs to shower when he heard Todd stretching and yawning. "Hey, Rich, looks like I conked out on you and Max. Did you guys already go for our run this morning?"

Grabbing a towel from the downstairs bathroom, Rich came back down the stairs wiping the sweat off his head and face. "You were out like a light, Todd, so I didn't wake you; it looked to me as if you were in desperate need of more sleep." Coming around the corner into the great room, he smiled at a groggy Todd Kensington, who was still trying to wake up. "You got any plans for Sunday, Todd?" Noting the slow negative head shake of his friend, Rich explained, "I've been thinking about revising our plans for tomorrow. I really don't need to go into the cathedral for mass tomorrow; there's a pretty little church in the center of Waverly I'd like to see, and they have several masses in the morning." Now he was grinning at Todd. "If you can get your butt moving tomorrow morning, we can get in our run before or after I go to church and still have most of the day to relax around here. Then, I can drive you back to Houston either tomorrow night or, if you can get to the office late, Monday morning."

Nodding, Todd got up and said, "Sounds good, Rich. Yeah, I can get to my office later Monday morning, no problem." He was suppressing another yawn. "Got any more coffee?"

Rich gaped in astonishment at his friend as Todd slowly ambled into the kitchen. He could not recall having ever seen

Todd Kensington this mellow. "Sure, I'll make us a fresh pot, Todd. I think that half a pot I made earlier is mostly gone." Todd watched quietly while Rich grabbed three kinds of coffee beans from the freezer, spooned in a total of about eight tablespoons, added fresh water, and turned on the Cuisinart coffeemaker to grind the beans and make the coffee. He turned to Todd and said, "Let me show you some things about the house you should know."

To the right of the tall entertainment center was a closed, narrow door. Rich opened it and stepped aside so that Todd could see inside. There were four tall wooden bookcases standing parallel with one another. The room was surprisingly deep so that one could browse through the bookshelves to find one that was suitable. Todd picked up a Harlan Coben novel. "I think it's been five years since I've read a novel." He put the book under his arm as he followed Rich out the door and back into the kitchen where Rich took down a large mug, filled it with the aromatic coffee, and nodded toward the front of the house. Todd continued to dutifully follow Rich out the door and around the wraparound porch to the western side of the house, where Rich pointed to the hammock swaying invitingly in the breeze.

Rich took the coffee and the book from Todd and placed them on the small unpainted Adirondack table sitting next to the hammock. "Your office, my man, for the next several hours. Enjoy." Rich turned to return to the house and muttered an inaudible command to Max, who had followed them out the door; just then he felt a hand on his shoulder.

Todd looked Rich squarely in the eyes and swallowed the emotion he was feeling. Leaving his hand right where it lay on Rich's shoulder, he whispered softly, "You have no idea what this means to me, Rich. Taking the time to give a shit about the trials and tribulations of an old friend ...." Todd's voice broke and he laughed sardonically at the pun he'd just made.

Rich returned the intensity of Todd's gaze and replied quietly, "But see, Todd, I *do* know, believe me."

He said nothing else and stood, watching his friend until Todd turned away to murmur, "I feel as if I haven't taken a deep breath in months, maybe years." Then he collapsed into the hammock, reached for his coffee, and grinned up at Rich. "Hey, Dad, when's breakfast?"

Back in the house, Rich and Max trotted up the stairs one more time where Rich took the shower he had planned earlier. Glancing into the room that he was now using as his office, Jansen glanced at the thick volumes of court transcripts awaiting his perusal. If he was lucky, he figured that he could get through at least the pretrial motions and maybe the case for the prosecution by the time it was time to start getting appetizers together.

"Hey up there, it's gotta be cocktail time somewhere in the world, Jansen."

Rich looked at his watch and could not believe the time; it was quarter after four, and Todd was right: They needed a drink, and it was past time to get started on the appetizers and gnocchi for dinner. Suddenly the loud and raucous tones of Stevie Nicks filled the house, the vibration of the bass of Queen almost visible in the walls and palpable in the floor beneath his feet. Thankfully, Todd had instantly turned down the volume on the radio; the music from their college days was audible, but he and Max were in no danger of getting their eardrums blown out.

"Quite right, my good friend, it's cocktail time here! Thanks for the reminder; we'll be right down, Todd. Not Stevie Nicks though, Todd; somehow Queen seems disrespectful out here, don't you think?" Suddenly the strains of Sibelius's *Second Piano Concerto* filled the house. Max's breeder was a firm believer in the soothing effects of classical music on her dogs, and Rich had witnessed for himself the remarkable influence that beautiful music still had on Max.

Rick looked at Max and asked, "And you must be in the mood for some dinner too, right, Max? Let's go, boy."

Max bolted out the door, stopped at the top of the stairs, turned to look at Rich to make sure that he was coming, too, then took the stairs very cautiously. Going downstairs was new, and Max was taking his time to make sure that he didn't slip on the highly polished wooden stairs. Following slowly behind, Rich called out, "The bar has everything that you can think of, so help yourself, and the wine cooler is full. Why don't you open up a bottle of cabernet for us to drink with the coq au vin?"

"Got you covered, Rich. There's a Macallan on the rocks, sitting, waiting to reward he who has spent Saturday afternoon embracing *the State of Texas v. Lindsey McCall*." Handing the amber-colored scotch to Rich, and following him as Rich walked into the kitchen area of the great room, Todd queried, "I deduce that you still occasionally drink single malt scotch of the eighteen-year-old variety since I saw three bottles in the bar?" Rich gratefully accepted the drink, took a sip, and enjoyed the warmth of the scotch as it lit up his gut.

Todd glanced at Max, who sat in front of the island in the kitchen with an expectant look on his face. "And you must be looking for something to eat, too, boy? Rich, if you need to get cracking on dinner, let me know what to feed Max and what I can do to help."

Noting the pleased expression on Rich's face as he responded to the return of Todd's exuberance, Todd declared, "This country air is like the tonic my granddaddy always claimed it was; he hated the city and insisted it would shorten lives." He tapped the glass of Macallan to the Grolsch beer

Todd was drinking. "Let's toast hammocks and naps and Harlan Coben novels." Todd paused before gazing somberly at Rich. "I'm only going to say this once, but I have to get it off my chest, so you need to listen to me. I was afraid to have you look at the transcripts because I knew you'd see all the stupid oversights I made in McCall's trial, all the cues that I missed." Noting Rich's start at a verbal response, Todd placed his hand on the arm of his friend and very softly said, "No, Rich, I need to tell you this. Maybe I need to tell *myself* this. Off and on during this glorious day of reading fiction, then nodding off as I wished, I thought about last night and about the history between you and I for these last fifteen, or is it twenty years? And I realized that it's okay. I know I did the best I could do in that trial, the very best, and I could not do more than that. So when you uncover all the mistakes I made, and you will, if you haven't already, I'm not going to get all pissed off and sulk like I always did when you beat me; I'm going to thank you for being the man you are, for being my friend, and for not dying six months ago."

Rich said nothing. There was nothing he could say, so he took his glass, reached over, clinked Todd's bottle of beer, and said, "Let's toast to friendship, Todd."

With Todd washing potatoes for the gnocchi, Rich started to stuff the mushrooms for their appetizers with freshly sautéed onion, garlic, and gruyere cheese. Having gulped down his food, Max was standing at the door.

"Can he go outside without a leash, Rich?" Catching the affirmative nod, Todd walked with Max out onto the porch, then through the yard to one of the paths where Max made his rounds. Then Todd whistled to the big dog as he started to take off down the path. Max stopped instantly, turned around, and trotted back to Todd and stood in front of him as if to say, "Okay, here I am, what are we going to do now?" Before he met Max, Todd had never met a Doberman, and he fell in love with this one at first sight. Looking at the intent expression, the alert and beautiful golden eyes of the exquisite Doberman, Todd could appreciate the almost-human personality of the dog and the depth of the bond between Rich and him.

"Let's go see Rich, Max." The dog trotted up the stairs and stood at the front door as Todd came up behind him to open it. "Hey, Rich, this place smells wonderful."

"Want another beer or do you want a martini, Todd?"

"I had enough martinis last night to last me for a while, thanks; I think I'll have a glass of the cab I took out of the cooler. Can you work and tell me what you think so far, or do you want to wait until you've read the whole transcript?"

Rich took a few more sips of his scotch while he thought about the portions he had reviewed fairly thoroughly, the pre-trial motions and the case for the prosecution. Todd offered to freshen Rich's drink, but Rich declined as he'd decided to switch to wine as well. Nodding slowly, he smiled a thank you at Todd and accepted the wine. "Sure, Todd, we can do that if you'll help me with the salad."

With a flourish, Todd opened the refrigerator to reveal spinach salad already made earlier and chilling. "A few of your culinary skills have rubbed off; admittedly not many but a few."

"Great, then let's go sit down, and I'll let you know where I am to date. Plus you can answer some questions for me as well. First, let me go upstairs to grab my legal pad so I'll have the notes I made earlier. Meanwhile, if you want something livelier than classical, switch it but"—groaning—"please, no more Queen or rock or any of that. Max doesn't like it. Do you, boy?" At the sound of his name, the Doberman jumped up and followed Rich up the stairs.

Returning with pad in hand, Rich looked appreciatively at Todd as he noticed the classic strains of the Bill Evans Trio suffusing the living room with some of the finest piano jazz of the mid-last century.

"Okay." Rich was settled in one of the leather chairs. Max splayed out at his feet with Todd stretched out in the recliner near the window, listening. "Here's the O'Henry version of the case the prosecution made to the jury: Lindsey's mother had been a cardiac cripple for close to forty years. Out of the blue, she improves. Ann McCall's cardiac condition improves so much that her cardiac output is almost doubled, so says her cardiologist, Dr. Christine Stewart, who happens to also be Lindsey McCall's boss. What could account for such dramatic improvement in her condition? Dr. Stewart does not know but tells the state that a reasonable assumption would be that her patient had somehow received the drug now being marketed as Digipro, Lindsey McCall's modified digitalis drug. Following almost four weeks of almost normal activity, Mrs. McCall begins to go downhill. Stewart admits her to the ICU at Houston Medical where McCall worsens steadily until her death.

"A few days after McCall's death, the homicide department of the Houston police receives an anonymous tip that a TMC doctor, namely Lindsey McCall, has used her experimental drug on her mother and killed her. Masters gets the Grand Jury to indict for intentional murder. The cops dig up the body, perform an autopsy and find an expert witness to testify to the presence of the altered molecule of Digipro in the bloodstream of Ann McCall. Once Stewart is given that evidence, she claims that Ann McCall's death resulted from medical negligence and tells the DA that the effects of Digipro on Ann McCall's badly weakened heart would be tantamount to murder.

"McCall's motive, according to her older sister, Paula, was complicated. She had never felt the *normal*"—Rich rolled his eyes at Todd—"affection felt by a daughter for her mother; in fact, McCall had been interested in her mother only as a research subject from her early childhood. Clearly he had no case at all without the sister or Stewart: Why would the chair of medicine at Houston Medical, Dr. Christine Stewart, be the cardiologist for the McCall sisters' mother, and what kind of pathology would cause a sister to provide that kind of testimony? Paula Livingston *had* to know that she was providing the keys to lock up her sister. Oh, and there was also the questionable testimony of a forensic pathologist claiming the presence of an altered version of digitalis present in Mrs. McCall's tissue."

Glancing over at Todd from his notes, Rich observed, "He fell apart on your cross-examination when you got him to admit that the molecular structure distinctions between digitalis and Digipro were too subtle to be picked up by any available laboratory analysis and that he was inferring his conclusion on these subtleties."

Rich placed the legal pad in his lap, looked at Todd, and said, "I honestly see why you laughed your butt off when Eleanor Philbin first called you, Todd. This sounds like a plot out of *Grey's Anatomy*. Who could have ever thought a grand jury would indict?"

Meanwhile, Todd stared at Rich in silence, just shaking his head mutely and sighing deeply.

"What?"

"Jansen, it took me weeks to get that whole sequence down. You get it in, what, six hours? Unbelievable, freakin' unbelievable."

❧

Sunday morning was another unbelievably beautiful fall day. Todd had awakened before Rich and had attempted to descend the stairs quietly so as not to disturb either Rich or Max, but as he stood on the landing of the circular staircase, Todd looked back and up to see Max standing at the top of the stairs. "Hey, boy," Todd whispered, "let's let Rich sleep awhile; it was a late night." He smiled as he watched the dog turn around and walk back into the master bedroom to join the sleeping Rich.

Todd opened the door and softly closed the door behind him as he stepped outside into the early morning. Circling around the wraparound porch, he took in slow, deep breaths and tried to commit to memory the fragrance of the cool forest morning air and the gentle filtered rays of the rising sun. Finally, he stopped and stood there, thinking about nothing at all.

I smell coffee. And without opening his eyes, Todd extended his hand to where he thought Rich would be standing with the cup. "What a good guess!" Todd said and smiled as he accepted the cup of coffee from his friend. Two hours later, they sat in the kitchen finishing a huge guilt-free breakfast justified by a ten-mile run.

Taking note of the absence of shadows under Todd's eyes, the softening of the lines in his forehead and around his mouth, Rich commented, "You sure look a lot better than you did on Friday night, Todd. I think the Piney Woods agrees with you. But I wonder if you're getting anxious to get back to Houston, Todd. I'd be perfectly willing to take you back this afternoon if you'd prefer getting a head start on Monday."

"I need your help with this appeal for Lindsey, Rich." Chuckling at the stunned expression on his friend's face, Todd airily waved his hand in an attempt to make light of the magnitude of the change represented by that request. Todd was only too well aware of what Rich was thinking, for they had argued many times in the past about Todd's stubborn refusal to ask for help.

"I have wasted over six months coming up with an argument that will persuade the Court of Criminal Appeals to grant a new trial, and all I have done is to spin my wheels and wasted precious time. So, will you help me?"

Rich could only imagine how excruciating this request was for Todd; although he tried to mask his anxiety, Todd had jumped up and was pacing around the kitchen while he waited for Rich's response. It was not a trivial request as both men were deeply aware. As chief warden for the Huntsville Prisons, Rich stood a chance of an ethical violation with the Texas State Bar Association if he took on the defense of an inmate. At best, it could be considered a conflict of interest. At worst, as an employee of the Texas judicial system, he could be accused of negotiating with the opposite party and, therefore, risk disciplinary action, including the loss of his license to practice law. Although Jansen no longer practiced law, Todd knew that Rich may someday return to his first profession and was well aware of the risks to Jansen. He wisely let his friend think this request through while he paced through the house.

"Here's what I think, Todd. First"—grinning at Kensington in an attempt to lighten up the suddenly-leaden atmosphere— "I accept your offer to cook aioli for dinner tonight; that sounds like a winner. Second, my good friend, I commend you on your decision to make some changes in your life. Max and I look forward to having another running partner on weekends. Don't we, big guy?"

The Doberman had been lying down on the rug in the living room; when he heard his name, he sat up, tongue still lolling from the ten mile run, and grinned at Rich.

"And Lindsey's appeal? Yes, definitely, unequivocally, you have my help with her case. At this point though, for reasons that you know probably better than I do, we need to keep my assistance informal and between you and me. If we need to formalize it at some point in the future, I cannot do that without a long face-to-face talk with Greg Bell. I think our next—" Jansen stopped because Todd had stopped his pacing and returned to the kitchen area where he stood silently with a strange expression on his face.

"What?"

Kensington still had not moved and silently regarded Rich with an expectant look on his face.

Running both hands through his hair in frustration, Rich exhaled loudly and kicked back his chair as he, too, now stood, puzzling at what game Todd was playing.

Since Rich was up, Max trotted into the kitchen as well to make sure that he missed nothing. Absently, Rich stroked the underside of the dog's chin while he mumbled, "Do you know what Todd's up to, boy?" When suddenly, like a bolt of lightning, he got it. "You turkey!" Rich strode over and shoved Todd on the shoulder. "Café Annie, fifteen years ago when you gave up trying to talk me out of going to the sheriff's office. You said that it was all about timing and that one day we'd be back as partners—that we were too good together not to be …."

By now, Todd was glowing; he looked illuminated, Rich thought, as he looked at his friend, and the happiness was evident in the shining gray eyes. Rich could not remember the last time he had seen Todd happy before this weekend: excited, energetic, ebullient, sure—but never happy. Because he couldn't think of anything else to say, he growled, "I hate to break up these happy memories, but we need to get to work." Then looking at Todd, Rich adopted a thick drawl as he intoned, "Well, one of us has to work anyway, guess it's the junior partner."

"That's right, my man, I hear a James Rollins novel calling my name." With that, Todd walked out to his hammock perch, prepared to devour another of the novels from Bell's seemingly endless supply.

Rich returned to his upstairs office to reread what he considered the two most damning testimonies in the murder trial of Dr. Lindsey McCall: Christine Stewart and Paula Livingston. Both women had been extremely damaging to McCall, but the sister, Paula, had undoubtedly persuaded the jury of McCall's callous disregard for anything but her career and its advancement. She was articulate, coherent, and artfully managed to vilify her sister while claiming to excuse McCall's narcissism as a precondition of her younger sister's genius. Rich did not have the transcript of the voir dire, but he would affirm what he suspected tonight when he and Todd prepared their action plan for the appeal.

Rich whispered as he began to reread. "Who benefits from this, Paula? What are you getting out of sending your sister to jail?"

❧

Masters: Mrs. Livingston, good morning.

Livingston: Good morning.

Masters: Mrs. Livingston, could you please introduce yourself to the members of the jury. Tell them what you do for a living and a little background about your family.

Livingston: My name is Paula Livingston. I'm the nurse

manager of the cardiovascular intensive care unit at St. Michael's Hospital in the Texas Medical Center. I am also the single mother of three children.

Masters: Thank you. And, Mrs. Livingston, do you know the defendant, sitting over there? (*Points to the defendant.*) Dr. Lindsey McCall?

Livingston: Yes, Dr. McCall is my younger sister.

Masters: All right. Now, with you and Dr. McCall being sisters, was your mother Ann McCall?

Livingston: Yes.

Masters: Okay, please tell us briefly about your mom, how old she was, and a little about her as a person.

Livingston: Mom had just turned seventy-four on her last birthday when she died. She was a wife and mother. I think she had worked as an administrative secretary before she married my father. But she did not work outside the home after she had Lindsey—Dr. McCall and me. Before she became so ill, she was active in our church, and she loved to play bridge-and beat me at it—that was one of the only things she could do; she did that fairly often.

Masters: Please tell the jury about that, Mrs. Livingston.

Livingston: About beating me at bridge?

Masters: No, I'm sorry about confusing you, about her illness.

❧

Rich thought as he read through Paula Livingston's testimony for the second time that she had either been coached very well by Masters or she had testified before in court. One of the maxims of courtroom testimony was to answer only the question that was asked and then say nothing. Nervousness compelled most people to keep talking; inadvertently, they revealed more information than they intended, thereby giving the opposing counsel openings that would otherwise be closed. It didn't look as if Paula was either garrulous or naive.

❧

Livingston: Mother was diagnosed with cardiomyopathy a couple of years after I completed nursing school. So—

Masters: Excuse my interruption, Mrs. Livingston, but could you explain what that means so that the jury can understand?

Livingston: Sure. For some reason, perhaps because of a bacterial infection or a viral one, no one is really sure, some people develop an infection in their heart or myocarditis, which does not clear up. Instead, it becomes a chronic condition, causing weakening of the heart muscle, enlargement of the left ventricle, and failure of the heart to perform adequately. Eventually, over time, the person will die if they do not receive a heart transplant.

Masters: Thank you. Please continue with your explanation about your mother's illness and its effect on your family.

Livingston: Sure. I was calculating how old Mom would have been when she was diagnosed. She would have been just forty-two years old—about ten years younger than I am now. You asked about the effect on our family. In a word, it was disastrous. Everything changed and all at once. I was married with one child back then, but I knew that most of her care would naturally fall to me. Lindsey was barely thirteen, and our dad was a test pilot at NASA and had no idea of how to cope with an acutely ill and possibly dying, wife.

For the first time, Rich wished that he had been at this trial. Paula's testimony was extremely powerful; she spoke simply but eloquently, and with each word was undoubtedly gaining admiration and sympathy from the jury. He wondered what she was like in person, and the further he got into this testimony, the more confused he became about what actually had gone on in this case and was still going on. Jansen was more and more certain that the whole case revolved around the relationship between these two very different sisters.

Masters: Would it be fair to say that Lindsey had very little to do with her mother's day-to-day care then?

Kensington: Your Honor, I would object to obviously hearsay evidence; although they are sisters, Mrs. Livingston cannot know what kind of care her sister gave to Mrs. McCall when she was not present.

Although Rich understood why Todd had objected here, he thought it was a mistake. So far, Paula had not said anything critical of her younger sister. She was relating what sounded like a reasonable situation: older sister becomes caregiver by default because of younger sibling's youth and work demands. Todd's objection highlighted the nurturing, maternal traits of Paula, while drawing the attention of the jurors of the absence of those qualities in Lindsey; in effect, Todd was doing some of Masters' work for him. And the judged overruled it, anyway, and Paula was free to answer the question.

Livingston: As I said earlier, I developed a routine that was easy enough. I took a leave of absence from my work at the hospital. I was not a manager, so that was fairly easy to do, and I brought my baby over to Mom's while I did the basic stuff that Mom could no longer do.

Masters: By basic stuff, you mean what exactly?

Livingston: Oh, cooking, cleaning, making sure that Mom took her meds on time, that type of thing.

Masters: And you did that for a few months, a few years … about how long did you do those things for the family?

The Court: Mrs. Livingston, are you unable to answer the question?

Rich guessed that the judge had intervened because Paula

had not answered right away. In fact, Rich thought, she must have been silent for twenty to thirty seconds. A long time in a courtroom. Once more, Rich wondered about Paula Livingston; was the pause calculated, or was she honestly remaining silent because she was uncertain about how to answer Boyd's question? Rich's yellow marker was beginning to highlight more and more of Paula's testimony so that he and Todd could review Rich's observations and fill in the blanks about Paula's body language and other nonverbal cues. Rich was now sure that he had to figure out a way to get some information about Paula Livingston, and he suspected that Lindsey McCall would be of no assistance to him.

Livingston: I apologize, Your Honor, I was honestly lost in thought about Mom and how quickly thirty-two years went by. But to answer your question, Mr. Masters, I was Mom's caregiver the entire time she was ill, which amounts to thirty-two years. I had never stopped to add up the years before, that's all.

Masters: But I don't understand. What about your father and your younger sister? Didn't they help you with the care of your mother in all that time?

Kensington: Your Honor, I would object for relevance.

The Court: Yes, objection is sustained. Counselor, direct your examination of the witness to the question at hand.

Rich stood up, stretched, and walked over to where Max lay stretched out on the large Navajo rug in the bedroom that also doubled as an office. He sat down adjacent to the dog and began to stroke his body. Max stretched out even further as Rich's fingers slowly stroked up and down; when he stopped the movement of his hand, Max lifted his paw and plopped it on Rich's knee to signal that he wanted more.

"You always want more, Max, always." But he resumed the long strokes that the dog reveled in. Rich was bothered by this trial; it felt to him as if the case had been lost with this witness. He was bothered, too, by Paula. Either she was one of the dumbest witnesses that he'd ever been around, or she was one of the smartest—but not just smart. There was something else that was buzzing around his head that Lindsey had said during that strange soliloquy of hers when he'd first met her. Suddenly he remembered. He had the recording of their conversation, and he'd need to get it out and listen to it later, but he recalled Lindsey's comments along the lines of Paula had been right, that Lindsey didn't like taking care of sick people, that none of "them" did, meaning the other medical students because they preferred doing procedures like catheterizations to caring for people who would die regardless of treatment. Chronically ill people were boring and frustrating, she had said. At the time, he'd not thought much about it because he sort of agreed. But now, reading this testimony of Paula, the nurse sister made him wonder if Dr. Lindsey McCall hadn't said something like that to her sister.

Jansen heaved a big sigh and got up thinking, *So what, what if she did know her baby sister didn't like emptying bedpans and urinals? Why would that make her accuse her sister of murder?* Rich realized that was what he believed; the anonymous caller to the Houston Police Department had been Paula. He had no evidence, of course, but he was almost certain.

Mumbling to himself, Rich reluctantly returned to the transcript. It was painful to read; he was beginning to dislike Paula McCall Livingston intensely; ludicrous, but real.

❧

Masters: Mrs. Livingston, did you and your sister discuss your mother and her care over all those years of her illness?

Kensington: Your Honor, I would object for relevance.

The Court: Counselor, can you explain the relevance of this line of questioning?

Masters: Your Honor, the relationship of Dr. McCall to her mother is of critical importance in this case. This witness would have firsthand knowledge of that relationship.

The Court: Okay, objection overruled. Mrs. Livingston, please answer the question.

Livingston: Yes, we did, many times.

Masters: Can you tell us about some of the most recent conversations that the two of you had on the topic?

Livingston: Recent?

❧

Rich shook his head in incredulity as he considered this witness; she was perfect. If Masters asked too vague a question that could lead to an objection from opposing counsel, she led him to an out, like here when she asked for a specific time frame. It was eerie. What could Lindsey McCall have thought as she sat there listening to her sister impugn her so subtly, so deftly that he'd bet most of the jurors had thought nothing other than what a saint Paula McCall was; if it wasn't so unnerving, he'd call the woman a genius. And he knew what was coming next; it would be enough to bury Lindsey.

❧

Masters: Yes, say within the last two years or so.

Livingston: Okay, sure, let me think for a minute or two please. Over the last year or year and a half, we had several disagreements about hiring help for Mother. Lindsey told me that she felt guilty because she had not taken any time to take care of our mother and that it wasn't fair that all Mom's care had defaulted to me. Frankly, Lindsey surprised me, as she had never shown any interest in the mundane aspects of taking care of Mom. Lindsey had focused for so many years on her digitalis research that none of us questioned the fact that her research, along with her work as a cardiologist, left her no time for anything else; after all, I was the nurse and she the MD/Ph.D.. And I told her that many times. We disagreed because I didn't trust anyone other than me to care for Mom, and I think that was getting to Lindsey. But finally I agreed to hire round-the-clock nurses because I hoped it would ease Lindsey's guilt about not being there for Mom.

Kensington: Your Honor, I would object to the testimony as hearsay.

The Court: Sustained.

∾

Despite the fact that two of Todd's three objections had been upheld by the judge, Rich could not imagine a more toxic testimony to Lindsey McCall. Once more, Paula was able to maintain what Rich could only describe as a multilayered style of communication; on the surface, she was answering questions concisely and precisely while conveying a clear distinction between the sisters. Here is Paula, wife and mother of three who somehow manages her job and three kids to do the care for their desperately ill mother, while the scientist younger sister remains unsullied by the excretions of her dying mother. Once again, Rich thought this transcript read more like a screenplay for a *Grey's Anatomy* TV episode than it did court testimony. He wondered for the umpteenth time if Paula believed all this garbage she was spewing and if she could sleep at night. He was sure she was lying—positive; in fact, what he couldn't figure out was why. He thumbed through the pages and felt relief when he saw that the end of Paula's testimony was coming up.

∾

Masters: Okay, Mrs. Livingston, let's move up to the events of the last several days of your mother's life.

Livingston: Well, I was feeling hopeful about Mom because I knew that Lindsey had done it; she had developed a new molecule for digitalis that maximized the benefit of the drug and minimized the toxicity. I had talked Lindsey into asking the Institutional Ethics Committee at Houston

Medical—

Masters: Excuse me for interrupting you, but can you please explain what you mean by the Institutional Ethics Committee so that we can all understand?

Livingston: Of course. I wanted Lindsey to request that she be allowed to use Digipro on our mother under the compassionate review provision of the ethics committee. Such a provision exists for just such types of cases as our mother's.

Masters: And did the defendant request that the Committee consider such a request?

Livingston: She did not.

Masters: Did she tell you why?

Livingston: She did not.

Masters: I'll pass the witness.

Kensington: Good morning, Mrs. Livingston. I would like to ask a few questions about the last few weeks of your mother's life beginning with information provided by Dr. Stewart, her attending physician. Dr. Stewart reported that the clinical symptoms she observed in your mother had, and I quote here, improved dramatically and significantly. Dr. Stewart testified that your mother, who had been unable to walk a few steps, was able to walk the entire first floor of the medical school to see her in her office about three weeks before her death. As Mrs. McCall was accompanied by you, would you agree with that report by Dr. Stewart?

Livingston: Yes, I agree.

Kensington: Dr. Stewart attributed the dramatic improvement in Mrs. McCall to have resulted from a change in her treatment but that she had made no changes in the medications that your mother had been taking. Dr. Stewart concluded that your mother must have been given the new drug. Doesn't it seem strange the defendant refused to request permission to use her drug on her mother but then secretly changed her mind and administered the drug anyway, Mrs. Livingston?

Masters: Your Honor, I object; hearsay.

The Court: Overruled. Mrs. Livingston, please answer the question.

Livingston: Yes, it does seem strange for her to tell me that she would not ask for permission to give the drug and then turn around and give it to her anyway.

Kensington: You seem convinced that your sister did give the drug to you mother. Do you think that is what happened?

Masters: Your Honor, I object; hearsay.

The Court: Sustained. Counsel, please stick to areas of knowledge that the witness possesses. If we knew the answer to that question, we could all be out enjoying this beautiful spring day.

❧

Judge Roy Prentiss was tough but fair. Rich had been in his courtroom more times than he could recall over the years he was head of Homicide for Harris County. The guy seemed to be one of the few judges who could control his courtroom with a quiet dignity. Comments such as the one he made to Todd were rare, and Rich sat and considered why Todd had pushed Paula Livingston to the point that Masters had to object, forcing Prentiss to overrule and rebuke Todd for stepping out of legal bounds. Todd would have calculated those responses and decided to risk it because Todd figured she was lying, too. He must have wanted to push her that far to see how Paula would react to the pressure in hopes that she would reveal something.

❧

Kensington: Please tell the court about the last days of your mother's life.

Livingston: When Mother began to fail, Dr. Stewart admitted her to the ICU at Houston Medical. She had been there for several days and seemed to be getting worse. So I decided to stay in her room with her. The night before she died, Mom woke me up. She wanted my assurance that all of her affairs were in order, things like her estate and care of the house once she was gone. That was our last conversation because she lost consciousness and was dead by the end of the following day.

Kensington: That must have been extremely traumatic. I apologize for making you relive that night. Do you need a tissue, Mrs. Livingston?

Livingston: No, I'm fine, thank you.

❧

A couple hours later, the dinner dishes were washed, dried, and put away, and Rich stacked the books about the Big Bend Country and wilderness camping on the corner of the large glass coffee table so that there would be room for the volumes of the transcripts, his yellow markers, legal pads, and pens. Both men pulled the leather chairs closer to the coffee table so that each could easily view the materials there.

Todd began. "You're right; of course, Rich. Masters' whole case was made by Christine Stewart and Paula Livingston, in reverse order." Todd was referring to the comment Rich had made a couple hours earlier, before they had dinner. "I wondered why he had bothered to use the woman who was so angry—twenty-odd years later—at McCall being valedictorian of their medical school class, Lynn Wilcox. At the time, I thought that her testimony and the chair of the Animal Welfare Committee at Houston Medical were both over the top." Both men chuckled as they thought of the testimony of the chair of the committee, Dr. Martin Swanson. It was apparent that the veterinarian intensely disliked Dr. McCall for reasons that had seemed exceptionally trivial to both Todd and Rich. It looked to Rich that even Masters may have been wary of the bureaucratic veterinarian's effect on the jury because Boyd had truncated several of Swanson's protracted answers to his relatively simple questions. The bottom line seemed to be that

Lindsey did not show the appropriate deference to Swanson's committee made evident by her submission of incomplete research protocols and twice sending her research assistant to appear before the committee in her stead, apparently an unconscionably flagrant act of defiance.

"Boyd's order of his witnesses was obviously well orchestrated; he began with the most benign of the group and then escalated rapidly. But you know, Todd, I could use a brief review of voir dire and how that went so that I can get a picture of the composition of the jury. Do you remember well enough to tell me how that went?"

Todd's jaw tightened, and his eyes shifted rightward and down. "Oh yeah, Rich, I can remember all too well. There were two women I was ecstatic to see in the initial pool of twenty-four. One was a single professor of humanities at the University of Houston, and the second was a Ph.D. research scientist at the TMC. Masters struck both for cause. The twelve jurors who survived voir dire were a composite of Houston's average citizens: there were eight women and four men. All the women were married, and all had kids; ages ranged from late-forties to mid-sixties. Two worked part time outside the house as a nurse and teacher, two of the men were retired military, and two were thirty-something; one worked as a contractor and the other was in sales."

Rich nodded and mused, "Right, great for Boyd and lousy for us, but if either of us had been Masters, we'd have done exactly what he did. It's how we play the game: connive to assemble the most sympathetic jury we can then let the games begin." Rich's sarcasm was not lost on Todd, but he just nodded mutely and waited to hear Rich's take on Christine Stewart and Paula Livingston. But Rich's next comment surprised Todd. "Why was Lindsey's boss the attending physician for her mother? Hadn't she only been at the medical school for a couple years? And I know she's Chief of Internal Medicine at the school, but is she also a cardiologist?"

"I don't know, yes and yes. Stewart replaced a Dr. Simon Bayer, who had followed Ann McCall for years; I think he made the initial diagnosis of Mrs. McCall while Lindsey was in junior high school. I don't know how much time you've spent with Lindsey since you've been at Huntsville, but persuading that woman to answer questions about what happened, about her family, any of them—mother, father, or Paula—was an exercise in futility. I have never defended a more uncooperative client, Rich. See, I met her on the morning that the grand jury convened. McCall was sitting on the bench outside the courtroom alone. Apparently she was going to opt for a court-appointed attorney or something, I don't know, but when I introduced myself to her, she made all the right responses and all that, but it was as if she wasn't really there. To say her affect was blunted is putting it mildly. Initially, I put it off to exhaustion and shock and figured she would begin to talk to me once the indictment was in, but the facade never wore off." Todd's gray eyes were wide and staring out the glass wall at the now darkened forest. "The only answer she would ever give me when I asked if she had given her mother that drug was that she may as well have, whatever the hell that meant. At the trial, when I stood to enter the not guilty plea, I half expected her to stand up and tell the judge that she was guilty, but she didn't; she just sat there.

"And her sister, Paula, is a piece of work unlike any I've seen before. I knew she was a liar. I just could never tell why she was lying."

Rubbing his fingers through his hair as he thought, Rich murmured almost to himself, "There has to be someone who knew the McCall family, isn't there?"

"Yeah, Julie Grayson, but McCall wouldn't let her testify—

had a fit when I told her Julie had called, wanting to help her."

"And who is Julie Grayson?"

"Lindsey's best friend. They were like sisters the way Grayson tells it, practically grew up together and were roommates in college at Rice."

"And just what am I missing here?"

"I told you that this woman was the most uncooperative client I've ever had, Rich. I know how crazy this sounds, believe me!"

"Okay, but nothing says that I can't contact her, right?" At Todd's vigorous nod, Rich made more notes on his legal pad and then checked another page of notes as he asked, "This *Houston Tribune* reporter Townsend, did she ever talk with McCall for any of these articles?"

"Wait a minute, Rich," Todd was having some difficulty keeping up with Rich's lightning-quick subject changes and had to think for a moment to follow what Jansen was talking about as he peered over Jansen's shoulder to read Jansen's penciled notes regarding "Murder in the Texas Medical Center" and Kate Townsend's name. Todd had not included the copies of the articles because he knew Jansen's opinion of the press.

"Okay, now I'm with you. No, Lindsey refused to see her; big surprise, right?"

Todd was surprised at Jansen's mention of the *Houston Tribune* series. He doubted that Rich had read or seen any of the media hype about the series; but then Todd saw a copy of one page of Townsend's last article flutter to the pile around Rich's feet. Todd must have left a page in the stacks of materials by mistake. But he made a mental note to scan the entire series and send to Jansen's personal e-mail address; Todd knew that Rich would be interested and impressed by Kate Townsend's analysis of the McCall conviction.

Rich ignored Todd's last statement, completed a few more

notes before closing his legal pad, then stood, and stretched. "Okay with you if I do see Grayson and Townsend and see what I can dig up? Because these two seem like the best leads we have right now. I'd like to see Paula Livingston, too, but not before I've got something to talk with her about. Tomorrow's a school day, Todd, and if we're going to get you to the office before eleven, we'll need to leave here by six at the latest—what?"

Todd was shaking his head and laughing, "Nothing, Jansen. I'd just forgotten what a roller coaster ride it is to try to keep up with that brain of yours—nothing at all, my friend. Hold it though, not so fast, what are you thinking about the sister?"

"Yep, the oldest motive in the world," Rich grinned at Todd, waiting for him to catch up, his brown eyes dancing.

"I have no idea what the blazes you are talking about, Jansen." Todd was now pacing the room as he mumbled and repeated Rich's last few comments. Suddenly he stopped and stared at Rich as he gasped, "Oh my God, yes, older sister, nurse, married with kids to a husband she divorced, she's *jealous* of little sister, probably has been her whole life." Todd's long legs covered the distance between them; he grabbed Rich around the torso and squeezed. "I love you, I love you, my knight in shining armor." The last part was said in a fake falsetto.

"Get off me, you big lug. Come on, let's grab some sleep. We're going to need it."

The transition from tenseness, self-responsibility, and worry, to equanimity, receptivity, and peace, is the most wonderful of all those shiftings of inner equilibrium, those changes of the personal center of energy, which I have analyzed so often; and the chief wonder of it is that so often comes about, not by doing, but by simply relaxing and throwing the burden down.
—William James

12

Seven Months Earlier

Kate Townsend awoke with a start at the pilot's announcement over the intercom that they were approaching a final descent into Zurich. She glanced at her watch, which she'd set on Switzerland time before closing her eyes, and was surprised to see that she had slept for over six hours—a feat for her because she never could sleep on planes. Stretching, she rose to go into the ladies' room to repair the damage to hair and to her makeup. Although the light was dim in the small aircraft bathroom, she could see well enough to run a comb through her long, tousled, reddish-brown, curly hair, grateful for the curls she'd despised as a teenager but now appreciated. Checking her face, she studied the large, widely spaced brown eyes, high cheekbones, straight nose, and then slid some lip gloss onto her full lips.

"Not bad, Townsend. You'll do."

At thirty-five, Kate had dated a lot but had never been

interested enough to consider marriage or even living with a guy. She'd known from her freshman year at Stanford that she wanted to be a journalist and had always excelled in writing. The last fifteen years had brought her some success; she was certainly known in her industry and had an impressive résumé: five years at the *Los Angeles Chronicle,* four at the *Wall Street Journal,* then the last six with Jeff at the *Boston Times,* and now the *Houston Tribune.* But the top stories had eluded her, until now. Kate was sure this was it. And she knew she was ready for it—mostly because she had decided three years ago that working with Jeff was more important to her than staying with the prestigious *Wall Street Journal,* and she had known then that she may never get a chance at the prize, the Pulitzer.

Kate was a planner; little was spontaneous, neither in her life nor in her work. When Jeff had called her about the Boston job, she had been beginning to be noticed at the *Journal,* but just beginning. Moreover, her editor was an egomaniac or at the very least, a narcissist. The nephew of one of the board members of the *Wall Street Journal,* Rodney Stone was an incredibly poor writer, therefore a lousy editor. Worse than that, he thought his writing was superb although he hardly ever wrote anything. Kate knew that staying on at the *Journal* would mean another couple or more years of working under this idiot, and she didn't think she could stand it. Jeff's call could not have come at a better time, for she was sitting at her desk and staring at the article she'd submitted to Rodney, a perfect name, she had always thought, and wondering how she could make his changes without making them. So she did just that: resubmitted the article sans Stone's corrections along with her letter of resignation, effective immediately. Laughing out loud at her feeling of relief, she was still chuckling when Jeff had picked up his private line and heard a very happy

Kate Townsend asking if Monday morning would be too soon to start at the *Boston Times.*

Kate's sudden departure from the *Wall Street Journal* to the smaller and less prestigious *Boston Times* won her a lot of wisecracks from friends and associates across the country, but Kate took them good-naturedly because her twenty-ninth birthday had evoked a somewhat premature midlife crisis. Kate had just ended a several-year relationship with a really nice guy who only wanted a wife and family. They had planned a trip to Jamaica over Christmas, and Kate had a feeling that he would ask her to marry him on that vacation; so she took him to dinner at one of their favorite restaurants to explain that she would not be going on the trip. Although Kate had felt heartless, she knew that this was best for both of them in the long run. Kate had taken the planned five days and had gone alone to Cape Cod where she had spent the five days walking the cold and empty beach and thinking about what she wanted most in life. Among her conclusions from that five-day retreat was that her life would be fine if she never won a Pulitzer. She had realized that she loved writing and the detective work that accompanied a good story, but that she did not need to see her name in lights to live a happy life.

When she had first received the job offer from Jeff, Kate had listed the pros and cons of leaving the *Journal* to go with Jeff; she'd laughed at it because all the cons were under Jeff, and all the pros were under the *Journal:* money, prestige of the newspaper, financial security of the paper, while going with Jeff meant a drop in salary and a host of other risks. The only person she had shared her decision-making process with was her dad, who had joined her in her good-natured self-mockery; she smiled at the memory of his laughing response, "Katie, you're just like your old man. I turned down more offers to go in as a senior partner than I care to remember.

Most of those guys were making four times what I did at Stanford within five years of completing our fellowships." Kate's father was a retired cardiovascular surgeon who had chosen the far less lucrative path of academic medicine over that of private practice.

Quietly she had asked, "Did you ever regret your decision, Dad?"

She grinned as she recalled his response that sounded more like a bark. "Hell no, girl, how can you even ask that question with all the Saturdays you rounded with me and my residents?" There had been a few minutes of silence on the phone while Kate listened to her father breathe, then, "I loved the teaching, the research, and I was"—she knew he was cleaning up the adjectives—"one damn good surgeon. They were lucky to study under me."

Kate, too, had never looked back and was grateful on an almost-daily basis that she worked for Jeff. He was the complete opposite of Rodney: self-effacing and the old-type manager who really believed that you should never ask an employee to do what you are not willing to do yourself. Yet he was a risk taker. The move to Houston had been tough for Kate; it had taken a lot for her to get accustomed to the almost constant heat and humidity and the in-your-face chauvinism of Texans. Although Texans were light-hearted about their commitment to their love for all things Texan, Kate found it tiresome at times. Her evolving relationship with the Philbin sisters was changing that, and Kate knew better than to make precipitous judgments about the eccentricities of a place merely because they made no sense. Assuming that she was correct in her belief that this series would capture the attention of the journalistic world, then that time-worn adage was proving true one more time: once the desperate *need* for something or for some person was conquered, then it appeared. She had seen it over and over in her life.

The jouncing of the plane startled Kate; she'd been so deep in thought that she did not realize they were landing. Jeff had told her to take as much time as she could get with the powerful Reardon, but they both knew the first article needed to be in the Sunday *Trib*'s edition; that gave her exactly six days. And one, maybe two days, would be useless with jet lag, getting acquainted with Reardon, and then formulating a plan. Realistically, Kate figured she had Monday through Thursday night for research, period. Kate sighed deeply as she forced herself to focus on this opportunity rather than the intense time pressure she was under.

Rising when the all-clear signals were given by the hostess, Kate grabbed her well-travelled brown leather bag from under the seat, stood it upright so that she could roll it behind her, and smiled a thank you at the young man and woman from Swiss Air. First off the plane, Kate walked briskly up the ramp and thought about how great it felt to stretch out her legs as she headed toward baggage claim. Zurich Airport looked like all the airports in the world, packed with weary travelers speaking many different languages as they hurried to make connections or be the first in the taxi line. Kate arrived at the end of the concourse and was about to turn right to follow the signs to baggage claim and ground transportation when she heard a male voice, an American voice at that, yelling her name. Stopping and looking around to find the source, Kate turned to her left and saw a man waving and walking rapidly toward her. As the figure came closer, Kate's jaw dropped when she recognized Hank Reardon. He was almost upon her now, and there was no mistaking those electric-blue eyes and the broad, boyish grin filled with white teeth.

"Mr. Reardon, uh, what a … uh …." Kate was stammering and she knew it but could not coordinate her brain with her mouth, so she stood and stared stupidly at the billionaire CEO of Andrews, Sacks, and Levine, one of the top five pharmaceutical companies of the world.

Reardon reached over to grab her bag with his left hand, then took her arm with his right, and gently steered her in the opposite direction from baggage claim. "Kate, I'm assuming this is your only bag?"

Still speechless, she could only nod.

"Good, I'll bet you could use a cup of good coffee and some quick energy, and I know just the spot. Zurich has some great coffee shops and pastries." Glancing at his watch, Reardon observed, "We've got just enough time because the train to Lausanne leaves in a little over an hour." Hank regarded Kate closely with his brilliant blue eyes. "I decided that we both need some time at my lake house. This is a great excuse for me to go up there, and I assure you that you'll be a lot more comfortable at the house than at one of the Lausanne Hiltons."

Kate was beginning to adjust to the dizzying rate with which this man moved, thought, spoke, and changed subjects. Just as she opened her mouth to thank Reardon for taking the time to come and get her at the airport as well as accompany her to wherever the hell they were going, he slowed his rapid pace just a bit, gave her that scrutinizing look again, and declared, "Look, Kate, I'm in my office and on the phone, or on the plane and on the phone, or in a board meeting, explaining why I'm on the phone all the time, so when I get a chance to break away for some fun, then by gosh, I'm going to do it. And you, my dear Ms. Townsend, are classified as fun." Then he grinned at her in sheer exuberance.

Hank Reardon was a slight but wiry man, five- foot- eight give or take an inch or two, with thinning, light blond hair, and a long, lean, and boyishly expressive face with startlingly blue eyes. Dressed in jeans and a red flannel plaid shirt,

Reardon neither looked nor acted like what he was. He looked ordinary, Kate decided: a man most people would not look at twice—unless they caught that gaze of his.

Although he was in constant motion—his eyes, his mouth, and hands—he did not evoke anxiety in her; rather, Kate felt strangely comfortable in the presence of this man whom she had "met" once during a ten-minute webcam meeting last week in Dr. Christine Stewart's office and now for what, maybe five minutes? In many people, the movements of his hands, eyes, and eyes would look like fidgeting indicative of nervousness; but in Reardon, all that movement seemed like the dispersal of massive amounts of energy. Somehow she had the sense that the guy meant exactly what he was saying despite acting and sounding like a kid playing hooky from his high school Algebra class.

Kate had met and interviewed all kinds of people in the years she had been a journalist; most of them were successful in at least one part of their lives and some extremely so, but she'd never been in the presence of one of the top ten billionaires in the world. She'd had no preconceptions of this man, for Kate had long ago realized that the range of personalities among the rich and famous was just as widely variable as were those of more average folk. In reflecting back among the politicians, entertainers, and business types she had met, Kate could not think of a single one who would have taken the time to pick up a reporter at the airport. As Kate realized she had been deep in her own thoughts, she also saw Hank Reardon looking at her with genuine concern.

"Kate, I am sorry, you're exhausted, I know, but you'll feel better after we get some Café Henrici's coffee and a bowl of their muesli. It will fix you right up; then we'll get to the train where you can nap for the three-hour trip to Lausanne."

Kate was shaking her head and laughing at this most unusual man as she asked, "Hank, is this how you always treat journalists?"

Shaking his head, Reardon lost his jovial expression momentarily as he responded quite soberly. "Oh no, my dear Kate—only those with the potential to make my company several billion dollars over the next two to three years. And so far, you are the only one I've ever met with that kind of promise. With the others, I'm exactly what you would expect me to be, a pompous ass." He looked at her intently, then added, "I had a most interesting talk with Eleanor Philbin last Monday about your idea for your series of articles. She faxed over your proposal for 'Murder in the Texas Medical Center' right after we spoke and asked that I call her back once I'd read it. I called Eleanor back within the hour to tell her how intrigued I was by your approach. Ah, here we are." Reardon waved his arms expansively and bowed.

They had reached the café, and Kate, having accepted Reardon's suggestion about the muesli, consumed the hot, delicious mixture as she considered what she had learned about Reardon last week in preparation for this meeting. Hank Reardon was obviously brilliant. By the age of twenty-four, he had completed medical school and a doctorate in physiology. He had never practiced medicine but had done some basic science research when in medical school at Columbia Presbyterian Medical School in New York City. Following a failed attempt to start a pharmaceutical company, Reardon then had worked for one of the giants of the pharmaceutical industries for about ten years. Kate found very scarce information about Reardon's next decade other than a stint at Wharton to grab a master's degree in business administration and more failed attempts at financing private research companies of his own. Reardon reemerged in the mid-to-late eighties as the CEO of the company for whom he had worked the decade before. The company had been approaching bankruptcy, and Reardon had turned it around in less than five years. The subsequent next five to ten years were filled with four or five one-to-two-year stints with similar results, thus earning him the sobriquet "the Turn-Around Guy." Sometime during the late nineties, he retired to pursue his many hobbies full-time only to be talked into sprinkling his magic over the deeply troubled company Andrews, Sacks, and Levine after only two years of retirement. His worth was estimated to be in the double-digit billions.

As Kate enjoyed the muesli, outstanding Swiss bread, and coffee, she considered what Hank would have discovered while researching her background, and she understood why she was here. He would have seen that in the two years she had been at the *Houston Tribune,* she had written two series, one on the fundamentalist sects so prevalent in Texas and the second a series of features about the new Catholic cathedral with Texas's first Roman Catholic cardinal. Both pieces were examples of excellent journalism, but neither was the type of subject matter with mass appeal. Had he looked further at her stints in New York and in San Francisco, he would have seen the same pattern. Kate Townsend selected her material based upon an internal calibration of subject matter rather than choosing the prurient or salacious. Her series on the homeless in San Francisco had earned her paper a nomination for the Pulitzer. But a reporter for the *New York Times* had won it for his series on the Iraq war.

Wouldn't it be interesting, Kate mused, *if my annoying refusal to buckle under to the world of sound bites and stories aimed at the fourth-grade reading level has led me to one of the biggest stories of the decade.* She chuckled softly as she lifted her coffee cup to take another deep swallow. As she did, Kate looked across the table at Reardon. Predictably, his intense electric-blue gaze was on her.

"You're good, very good."

"What do you mean?" Kate was now enjoying herself because she was fairly certain she knew what Reardon was referring to.

"Kate, I've been around a few decades longer than you have and have never met another man nor woman who could remain silent in a conversation longer than I, until you, that is."

Kate nodded slowly, aware that Hank Reardon was probably not a man who showered others with praise; if indeed he considered his statement to be praise, then she did not know what to say, so she remained silent.

She considered the little she had been able to learn about his private life. Reardon had married a fellow medical student while in medical school; following the birth of their only child, a daughter, his wife had been diagnosed with cancer and was dead within six months of the diagnosis. Reardon had apparently raised the daughter alone while building his remarkable career, for he had not remarried until five years ago when he married a woman who had been his childhood sweetheart. Her name was Peggy, Kate recalled, and she was from the same small town in Oklahoma where Reardon had grown up.

"We have just enough time to make the train; it leaves at ten thirty, and I've got ten fifteen now. The Swiss are very punctual about the trains." They had rapidly crossed the broad thoroughfare and were now walking quickly toward the station about a block in front of them. "Have you enough material to read, or do you need to stop at a newsstand, Kate? It's about a three-hour ride."

Kate shrugged the shoulder that carried her briefcase that doubled as her purse and replied, "I'm finishing one of the books that you recommended, Hank; three to four hours should be enough time for me to finish it."

Reardon looked sharply at her and raised an eyebrow in surprise and appreciation. "Which one are you finishing?" Reardon had called Kate from Zurich late Thursday afternoon to give her the titles of several books that had been written about the pharmaceutical industry and their relationships with academic medical centers. He had indicated that many of them would be extremely critical of the pharmaceutical industry and academic medicine as well but would provide her excellent background for her first two articles.

"The one by the former editor of the *Annals of Internal Medicine*," she replied.

Kate knew why Hank was surprised. He had given her the titles of the three books only sixteen hours before she was scheduled to leave for Switzerland, and these were not books that could be found at the local bookstores. But since Kate had discovered the Jesse H. Jones Library at the Texas Medical Center the year before, she calculated that there would be several copies of these books at the library given the proximity of two medical schools and any number of medically related undergraduate and graduate programs located in or around the TMC.

Kate was delighted to find all four books in the health care section of the huge library; although Kate did not have a library card, the pleasant young woman took care of that detail in just a few minutes.

Because of the titles, Kate had expected to find the information prejudicial to the drug companies but was surprised at the depth of the acrimony she discovered as she scanned the books. Hank was obviously waiting to hear her opinion about what she had read, so Kate complied.

"Well, Hank, the title, *How Pharmaceutical Companies Exploit Americans and Their Doctors*, is a bit of a giveaway that the author is not intending to provide the reader with an objective look at the pharmaceutical industry. So I was expecting criticism; but honestly, reading between the lines, it sounds as if there is more at work in the mind of the author."

Hank stopped at Kate's comment, turning that intense laser-blue gaze on her. "What do you mean, Kate? That's an interesting comment."

Just as Kate began to answer him, Hank started as he looked at his watch. "Hold that thought, Katie girl, we've got to sprint to make this train."

Five minutes later, they were settled in a first-class cabin on the train to Lausanne. The seats were unbelievably comfortable, Kate thought, and she closed her eyes for just a minute. A couple minutes later, she stretched and looked out the window at the breathtaking view of a lake with snowcapped mountains. Slowly it dawned on her that she had not closed her eyes for simply a minute or two.

Reardon was grinning at her. "Hello, sleepyhead. You should feel better since you've been in a coma, but snoring, for the last three-and-a-half hours." Observant as always, Hank cut off her budding apology. "Kate, you've no need to feel embarrassed, no need at all. You've just flown twelve hours and had not stopped since you got off the plane. You needed the rest."

Kate smiled back appreciatively. "Well, I *am* sorry because we were starting to talk about that book I was … well, apparently did not finish on this train ride." The last was said ruefully. "Really, I normally don't do this. I had planned to complete the last two chapters so that we could dis—"

Explosive laughter cut her off; Kate could feel the heat rising in her cheeks as she now tried to avoid Reardon's gaze; despite his assurances, she was not only embarrassed, but also felt humiliated, and his mirth at her discomfort only highlighted her sense of having lost control of this critical interview.

"You and I have the whole week to discuss Dr. Johnston's book, as well as a wealth of other subjects that will help you understand the history and the politics of clinical research from the perspective of academic medicine, as well as the pharmaceutical industry. I am at your disposal for this entire week. But please, let's not turn an innocuous nap into a major journalistic catastrophe. Let it go, please. You were tired and you slept; so what?"

Kate looked up at the sincere, concerned, but slightly annoyed expression on Reardon's face and slowly nodded. "You sound just like my dad, Hank. That is exactly what he would tell me." She realized for the first time the similarity between the two men. Her father was slight, like Reardon, with the same long, lean, bony face.

"I'll take that as a compliment."

Kate cleared her throat. "Okay, Mr. Reardon, what is next on our agenda?"

The sharp, blue eyes were instantly examining her face for sarcasm or petulance; finding only a wide grin and open, clear, dark brown eyes gazing back at him, Reardon looked relieved and then glanced at his watch to reply, "We'll be in Lausanne within the next ten minutes, around three thirty. I need to introduce you to Peg and to my good friend Dom Perignon. We need to celebrate this week and this work. Then you, Peg, and I will walk down to the lake before dinner."

They smiled at each other, and Kate could sense the change in her and in the energy between the two of them. It felt good, really good.

Exactly ten minutes later, Kate and Reardon were standing in the Lausanne train station. The scent of coffee was irresistible to Kate, and she pointed to the source of the aroma. "Can I grab a cup of that wonderful-smelling brew for you, too?"

"Sure, sounds good, I'll wait here and watch your bag."

Kate walked rapidly to the kiosk of coffee and pastries and in French requested two cups of coffee-to-go to the smiling young girl.

"Comment allez vous?" Kate asked the girl. Hank had explained that Lausanne was in the French canton of Switzerland called Romandy, which was good for Kate since her French was fairly decent; the same was not true of her German, so in Zurich she had been forced to speak only English.

The young woman's smile broadened widely at the French greeting, and her dark eyes danced as she handed Kate the two cups of latte. "Bien, mademoiselle, tres bien. Vousez vous deux croissants?"

The croissants looked divine, and Kate was starving, but she declined the croissants, paid the girl, then retraced her steps to the train platform where she had left Hank and the bag. Stopping to sip her coffee every few steps and concentrating on not spilling Hank's cup consumed most of her attention, so Kate did not notice the woman standing beside Reardon until she was practically on top of the couple.

Her face was too long and angular to be classically beautiful, but Kate would have recognized those eyes anywhere. Handing Reardon's latte to him she then extended her now empty hand to the woman as she smiled. "You have got to be Hank Reardon's daughter, or I have completely humiliated myself yet again." A pair of laser blue eyes stared at her with no hint of a response long enough for Kate to begin to doubt herself.

Simultaneously both father and daughter gave up the game, laughing, while the woman took Kate's hand in both of her own as she said, "Yes, Kate, I'm Liisa Reardon." Grinning, she added, "That's *Liisa* with two '*i*'s. Welcome to Lausanne and to Switzerland; we're delighted to have you staying with us this week!"

Kate figured Liisa with two '*i*'s for about thirty-five or so, her own age. The resemblance to her father was uncanny as Kate glanced at the two of them standing side by side. Liisa's hair was shoulder length and blonde and she looked to be almost exactly Reardon's height. Like Reardon, Liisa was slim and dressed very casually in jeans and a sweater.

"Liisa and I weren't sure she would be able to be here this week, as she had a bunch of rescheduling to do. I didn't think it would work, so I didn't mention her to you. But I sure am happy to have my daughter around this week, and her presence is thanks to you, Kate."

Reardon was talking to Kate, but he had his arm around Liisa's waist as he hugged her and said, "It sure is good to see you, honey. It's been too long."

Liisa was hugging her dad while she explained to Kate, "My job has me in the air a lot, so we don't get much time together. You'd think that working in the same company would have us in each other's face 24/7, wouldn't you?"

Catching Kate's puzzlement, Reardon clarified, "As I mentioned earlier, my daughter, Liisa, is a research scientist and heads up the Digipro project at ASL. Liisa has been traveling back and forth to Houston for the last several years to work with Dr. McCall and had planned to fly out for a final trip but …." Reardon's voice trailed off, and he suddenly looked very sad, obviously thinking of Dr. Lindsey McCall, now in prison.

Kate was silent and somewhat uncomfortable as she realized that she knew next to nothing about Lindsey McCall other than that she planned to use the woman's story to catapult her name and newspaper into the big time. When she again looked up at the two Reardons, Hank's gaze was on her and seemed penetrating as he mused, "Kate, you would like

Lindsey. I hope this series of yours causes the two of you to meet." Looking sideways at his daughter, Reardon asked, "Don't you think they would click, Liisa?"

Without answering her father, Liisa swooped down to pick up Kate's bag and placed her arm in Kate's to lead her off the platform. "Your carriage awaits, Monsieur Reardon." Liisa looked back to tease her dad. Then she stopped to turn around and ask, "We *are* taking Kate to the house. Is that right, Dad?"

Kate loved watching the easy rapport between these two; once more, she was reminded of her dad and the way they teased each other. She was amazed at how comfortable these two made her feel.

Behind her she heard, "Right, honey, we'll go to the house for a cocktail and hors d'oeuvres. Then I thought Kate would like to take a hike down to the lake. What do you think? Has the weather been warm enough that we could do that about five or so?"

"It's starting to warm up a bit, but mornings and afternoon are still pretty chilly. I've got some warm clothes Kate can borrow for the week. We look about the same size, I think."

They were moving quickly through the imposing train station. Reardon was following the two women with his battered briefcase. Coming to the exit, Reardon asked Liisa which car she was driving.

"The Bentley, it's in the north parking lot."

Kate saw him nod then move even more rapidly to their left and down toward the rows and rows of parked cars.

Looking outside at the incline of the road ahead, Kate remarked, "Good grief, this looks like Russian Hill in San Francisco! We've been climbing steadily for the last five minutes. I'd sure hate to drive a stick shift in this town."

"We'll give you the grand tour of Lausanne later on in the week, Kate. But you know you are right with your comparison to San Francisco; many people consider the two to be sister cities. We'll see some of the shops and cafes in the next couple of days. Right now we're heading even higher into the Jorat forests where we'll get to the house. I would guess you could use a shower and change of clothes when we get home. Then we'll grab some drinks and appetizers on the patio and, if you're up for it, hike down to the lake before dinner. How does that sound, ladies?"

Liisa was smiling and nodding as her father had been talking; now she turned to Kate and raised an eyebrow while she awaited Kate's response.

"Wonderful, that sounds wonderful, thank you both so very much." Kate was gushing, and she knew it but could not stop herself so she continued on, "You know, Hank, if you and Liisa insist on treating me like royalty this whole week, I'm going to have to use vacation time for this trip. I am having too much fun for this to be work!"

"Katie girl, you don't understand, do you now, that work is supposed to be fun?" Reardon had affected an Irish accent, a good one at that, and once again he reminded her of her dad. She looked across at Liisa, but she was smiling back at her father and missed Kate's glance. Kate leaned back into the soft supple and luxurious leather seat and watched the beauty unfolding before her eyes as Reardon continued the climb out of Old Town and up into the heavily forested mountains. She reflected on the four hours or so she had spent with this eccentric billionaire and of the challenges he had presented to her in that very short time. Kate had never thought of herself as uptight and the other unattractive adjectives the word conjured up as she sat thinking about their conversation about her prolonged nap and the unfinished book. Nor had she ever thought of herself as humorless, but thinking back to her adolescent response to Reardon's simple understanding of what he considered normal fatigue, she'd have to judge herself as stupidly grim.

Liisa interrupted her reverie with a light touch to her arm. "Look, Kate, there is a super view of Lake Geneva. It's one of my very favorites." As his daughter was speaking, Reardon slowed the car and pulled off the two-lane road to a lookout point. As they all exited the car, Reardon elbowed Kate and innocently fixed his electric gaze on her as he queried. "So, are we homesick for Houston yet?"

Kate stared back with a half-smile and nodded as she looked at her watch to drawl, "Well, it must be rush hour in Texas about now, so the freeways are all back-to-back traffic. Well, sure, Hank, who wouldn't miss that?"

He isn't going to let it go, Kate thought and then, *well good, he's right, I need to loosen up.*

Reardon smiled at her then took both her hand and that of his daughter while he walked them out to the end of the lookout point. "Switzerland doesn't have the paternalistic fervor of the US yet, so you'll notice there are no guard rails, but feast your eyes."

The view was spectacular, like nothing Kate had ever seen in her life. The mid-afternoon sun shone on the snowcapped peaks of the jagged mountains on the far side, closer to where they were standing; the heavily forested land dropped so sharply that they could see the deep blue, sparkling lake. And the air was like a tonic; Kate had forgotten the exhilaration of breathing mountain air, the clarity of it, the sense of it being hyper-oxygenated when, in fact, just the opposite was true. They stood in silence for several minutes, all drinking in the beauty and the majesty of creation.

As the car cleared the gate, the enormous black gates closed noiselessly behind them. Materializing out of the forest were several buildings straight ahead of them. The main building looked to be a hexagonal structure with windows and corniced gables at each of the junctions of the house. The structure looked to be at least four levels, maybe five, as Kate glanced over the huge home. To the left of the house there were two much smaller buildings that appeared to be gatekeeper cottages, made of the same dark-and-heavy-wood-and-glass design as the main house. Surrounding the three buildings were some of the most beautiful flowers and shrubs that Kate had ever seen. The landscaping had been configured in islands of vegetation, yet the overall effect was natural and served to soften and lighten the harsh lines of the unusual house. Without realizing she was doing so, Kate breathed out softly, "These gardens are lovely, magnificent; what a feast for the eyes this is."

Reardon smiled widely as he proudly commented, "Our Peg is quite the gardener, isn't she, Liisa?"

Just then, the door opened, and a very slim figure with a scarf wrapped around her head stood beckoning them. Kate followed Reardon and Liisa, intentionally slowing her pace by taking in the splendor of the gardens. Watching out of the corner of her eye, she saw the very gentle embrace of Peg by her husband and the solicitous manner that Liisa had now adopted with her stepmother. As Kate drew closer to Hank Reardon's wife, her suspicions were confirmed; she now understood those times when Reardon had seemed to withdraw into himself and become very somber and reflective. Peg was smiling warmly at Kate and was dressed beautifully in white linen slacks and a cocoa-colored cashmere sweater accented by a Hermes leopard silk scarf around her neck. Peg's makeup discreetly accented her deep-set hazel eyes, and the scarf tied around her head had a certain rakish tilt to it, but nothing could disguise the signs that were obvious to Kate. Her face was gaunt with cheekbones that were unnaturally prominent. Under Peg's eyes were the tell-tale shadows of pain and sleeplessness. Although Peg Reardon's clothes were elegant and obviously very expensive, they could not hide her emaciated frame. Peg Reardon was battling cancer; from the map of suffering etched into her face, the cancer was winning.

It was an all too familiar war to Kate, and she was fighting to keep at bay the memories of watching her mother die from the ravages of ovarian cancer at. Walking beside Peg as they strolled down the beautifully appointed and light-filled hallway, Kate struggled to keep step with this Peg who was expending heroic energy to fulfill what she undoubtedly perceived as her obligation as hostess and wife of the multibillionaire, Hank Reardon. When Peg turned to Kate to continue their chat about Houston and her flight, Kate had to turn away quickly to exclaim about the beauty of the numerous impressionist oil and watercolor paintings that were scattered about the hallway and into a huge room where Reardon and Liisa were standing and talking quietly with an elderly couple whom Kate guessed to be Stella and George. It was an easy ruse because the paintings looked to be originals by Monet, Pissarro, and Millet, but the look that Peg had given Kate was so replete with the dignity and indomitable will of this woman that Kate had felt the sting of imminent tears. She remembered her mother behaving the exact same way, almost to the end, when her father would invite colleagues over for dinner, always at her mother's insistence.

Peg was too ill and thin to be pretty but the power of her presence seemed to fill the huge room. Clapping her hands,

Peg called out, "Let the games begin." Peg giggled at herself as the four turned to her and, as if on cue, all smiled at Kate and raised champagne glasses to her. The older woman, who had to be Stella, hurriedly scampered over with two glasses of champagne to where Peg and Kate. Peg introduced Kate to Stella and George then waved a hand to her right where there was a sumptuous banquet arrayed on a long antique sideboard. Peg took Kate by the hand and led her over to the table.

"Kate, you must be hungry. I'll bet Hank fed you muesli at Henrici's this morning, and although it is the best in Switzerland, it doesn't stick with you for long now, does it?"

Kate obediently picked up a cocktail plate, realizing that the few sips of champagne were going straight to her head, as she murmured grateful thanks for the delicious canapés. "Peg, this house is stunning. I love the way you have used the impressionists as a guide for your décor." Kate saw Peg's eyes widen in surprise and her face soften with pleasure at the insightful comment. By nature, training, and experience, Kate Townsend was an observer, but her observations were normally of people, not homes and their decorations. But Kate's comments were sincere. Peg had used the colors of the impressionists in her choice of window coverings, rugs, and in furniture. The mauves, roses, and greens could have been garish in a more conventional home; the eclectic mix of dark antique furniture and splashy upholstered chairs and sofas would look ridiculous in Kate's condominium; but these rooms were huge with ceilings that must have been over twenty-five feet high, so the bold colors and decorating schemes served to create warmth and invitation. Kate realized that she had unwittingly hit on the very best subject possible for Peg Reardon. The woman looked radiant as she walked Kate around the rooms and explained the provenance of selected paintings or pieces of interest.

When the tour was complete, the two women returned to the great room where Liisa and her father stood, still chatting with Stella and George. Noting the return of Kate and Peg, Hank strode over to the entrance of the room and smiled affectionately at his wife. "We're planning to hike down to the lake for an hour or so, honey. Stella isn't planning dinner until six thirty, so why don't you take a rest before then?"

Kate wondered if Peg would be upset at her husband's suggestion, but her expression revealed nothing but a suddenly tired smile as she agreed with Reardon's advice. Kate suspected that Hank Reardon had become quite attuned to the rapidly lowering ceiling of his wife's energy levels, just as her father had with Kate's mother in the months before her death.

~

It is like what we imagine knowledge to be:
dark, salt, clear, moving, utterly free,
drawn from the cold hard mouth
of the world, derived from the rocky breasts
forever, flowing and drawn, and since
our knowledge is historical, flowing, and
flown.
—ELIZABETH BISHOP

13

When Kate got to the breakfast table the next morning, she was surprised to see only Hank sitting there, sipping a cup of coffee and reading the latest issue of the *Economist*. Reardon got up as she approached and grinned in welcome as he pulled out a chair for her. "Small change in plans, Kate. Liisa wanted to get to her lab to set up some experiments for a new project she's working on; she said she would catch up with us later today. She also asked me to tell you that she's planning to go for a run before dinner in case you want to join her."

Breathing a sigh of relief, Kate responded with an enthusiastic, "Yes, I would love that. I slept like a stone last night and didn't awaken until seven thirty. I had intended to get a run in before breakfast but didn't wake up in time." Glancing up at Stella, who had just come into the room, Kate smiled at her and asked, "What dangerous, destructive, and delicious fare have you conjured up for breakfast, Ms. Stella?"

Grinning back at Kate, Stella replied in her thick Irish burr, "Well, Katie, we have Belgian waffles with fresh raspberries this morning; do you like Belgian waffles?"

Kate answered with sincerity, "Stella, if you served shoe leather, I am confident that I would love it, but yes, I love Belgian waffles; that sounds divine, thank you." Taking a sip of the coffee that Stella had poured, Kate exhaled an appreciative, "Wow, this coffee is better than Starbucks!"

Balancing what looked like a mountain of Belgian waffles on a platter, Stella huffed, "Well, I should hope my coffee is better than some American franchise."

Just then, Peg entered the room looking rested and relaxed. "What about an American franchise interests you, Stella?"

"I'm not interested in any franchise, Ms. Peg," the stout Irish woman replied, both hands on her more-than-ample hips. "I was just explaining to our guest here that I would hope that my coffee tasted far better than some Seattle whiz kid's."

Kate had emptied her cup and looked up at Stella sweetly to ask, "Stella, may I have about a gallon more of your incomparable brew, please?"

Stella's coarse features softened into first a frown and then a tentative smile as she decided that Kate's compliments were sincere. "Here, Dear." Stella produced an enormous cup of coffee filled to the brim and set it down. "Now, will that be suiting you?"

Peg and Hank were watching the repartee between Stella and Kate with amusement and commented that Kate had learned very quickly how to get on Stella's good side.

Kate protested, "I'm not trying to get on her good side, I'm just speaking the truth. This coffee is heavenly, and I am a connoisseur!"

Just then, Kate dug into her waffle and exclaimed, "Stella, this is the best, the very best waffle I have ever had, honestly!"

Stella looked at Peg and Hank as she patted Kate on the shoulder. "This one is a keeper; you two can invite her here anytime. I thought at first that she was just like all those other skinny females that Liisa brings here every once in a while, but this lass knows how to eat!"

Even Peg had two of the waffles, Kate was happy to see as she devoured her third and reluctantly pushed back her plate. "Stella, thank you for a most perfect breakfast."

Reardon, Kate noticed, had eaten only toast and boiled eggs. Catching Kate's survey of his breakfast fare, Hank patted his flat stomach and said, "Just watching the calories, right, Stella?"

He laughed at her return harrumph, "As if any of the lot of you had to worry about any calories." She shook her head as she poured Kate another half a cup of coffee.

Five minutes later, Kate and Reardon were seated in the library, and Reardon was explaining to Kate how he thought her week with them should be spent. Listening attentively, Kate realized how fired up she was about this assignment; of course, the gallons of coffee she had consumed were causing each of her millions of nerve ends to stand up and salute Reardon as he talked.

Reardon proposed a schedule for the week. He suggested that they spend their first day in the Reardon library where Hank would give Kate a mini-seminar on clinical research and the relationship between the pharmaceutical companies and medical schools. Then Reardon had accurately guessed that Kate would need to spend a day reading the reference materials she had brought with her and some that Reardon would give to her. The next day or two would be spent at ASL corporate headquarters in Liisa's departments to tour the animal research labs and speak with the ASL scientists who had worked on Digipro. That would bring them to Thursday, which Reardon thought should be a vacation day for all of them. They would do Old Town and spend some time seeing the sights of Lausanne. Then if time and weather permitted, they would have dinner on Reardon's yacht on Lake Geneva. Wisely, Reardon suggested that Kate spend Friday writing her story so that she would have most of Saturday to fill in any gaps of the article. Kate had arranged an 8:00 a.m. Saturday deadline to e-mail the article to Jeff; that was only two in the afternoon Houston time, so Jeff would have plenty of time to discuss any questions or suggested changes.

Kate happily concurred with the schedule for the week as she pulled out her tape recorder and grabbed her legal pad from her briefcase. Reardon's hands were tented as he sat deciding where to start with the "Digipro story." Taking a deep breath, Reardon began, "Okay, Kate, it was about ten years ago that Simon Bayer called me. Simon was chief of medicine at Houston Medical Center at that time; he and I had been friends since my doctoral studies in physiology at Columbia. Simon had been granted a sabbatical from the Houston School of Medicine, and he became one of my advisors for my research at Columbia during the last year of my studies there."

Reardon leaned his head back against the high back of the overstuffed leather chair he sat in and closed his eyes, remembering. "Simon was a cardiologist of the old school, Kate. The man was a brilliant diagnostician, and he had a passion for medicine. Had I met someone like him earlier in med school, maybe …?" Reardon shook his head as if to clear it and then chuckled, "Right, Reardon, a doc who detests taking care of sick people." The electric-blue gaze shone on Kate. "But then I think we've both met doctors who don't seem to like taking care of sick people, haven't we, Kate? So maybe it's not so unusual among our MD brethren."

Kate tilted her head at Reardon as she asked, "So how did the friendship between you and Bayer develop, if you didn't then utilize your medical degree?"

"I was in the MD/Ph.D. program at Columbia, and I rotated through Simon's research lab while I was doing the Ph.D.. In fact, we really became friends when I decided not to accept a cardiovascular surgical residency at Columbia. Bayer was curious about why a plum residency under the famed Bernie Levine at Columbia would be turned down by one of its best medical school graduates. When I told him that I couldn't stand being around sick people he laughed and told me to meet him at TJ's that night. TJ's is a bar right around the corner from Columbia and is a favorite of the med students and residents." Hank stopped, thinking for a moment, then added, "At least that's the story I tell the reporters. It's a little more complicated than that but now is not the time to get into it." He looked at Kate in an expectant way, almost as if he were challenging her to ask what the real story was but Kate knew better and said nothing.

Reardon's gaze then roved over his library and the stacks of books contained in the floor-to-ceiling shelves. Kate's gaze automatically followed his and she was startled to see some of the same cardiovascular textbooks that her Dad had in his library at home. For some people, Kate mused as she watched the man surveying the beautiful wood shelves made brilliantly light by an enormous window in the ceiling, their collection of books mapped their life and passion. This was certainly true for Hank Reardon.

Reardon and Kate were each seated on two of the six over-stuffed chairs and couches artfully arranged in the book-filled room, so it was fairly easy to survey the display subjects which composed the extensive Reardon library collection. The two predominant areas of interest were, quite naturally, physiology and business; but there were also extensive collections of biology-, chemistry-, and physics-related texts. There were even large fiction and decorating and gardening collections as well. Kate calculated that there must be over five thousand books surrounding them.

"Bayer tried really hard to convince me that an intolerance of chronically ill people could be an advantage in medicine. Simon believed that the hatred of disease could act as a catalyst for the relentless drive to discover the 'cure.' And maybe he's right, but getting out of medicine was the right move for me, and I have never looked back." Reardon's expression sobered, and Kate was certain he was thinking of Peg.

"Now, Simon Bayer as a physician? You couldn't find a man more compassionate or intuitive; his students had great respect and admiration for him. So when Simon called me about Lindsey McCall's research on digitalis, I listened to him even though the whole endeavor sounded somewhat quixotic to me."

Reardon's sharp gaze fixed on Kate and correctly read the questions in her eyes. "See, Kate, the drug digitalis has been used by physicians for the treatment of heart failure since the time of Hippocrates. An attempt to alter the molecular con-figuration of foxglove, the plant from which digitalis is derived, seemed implausible, even outlandish, to me." Reardon paused and smiled to himself as he recalled his conversation with Bayer. "Simon Bayer learned the most important axiom of any business: it's all about sales. And what a salesman Dr. Simon Bayer turned out to be!" Reardon chuckled. "So despite myself, I listened to this crazy saga of Bayer's star cardiologist, Dr. Lindsey McCall, and became intrigued."

"During the sixties and the seventies there was an unpar-alleled increase in medical technology and in pharmacology, much of it concentrating in cardiovascular medicine and surgery. What happened in the field of cardiovascular medicine and surgery could not have happened without the confluence of politics, medical genius, and the unique culture of competition and risk exhibited by Denton Cooley and Michael DeBakey on behalf of Baker College of Medicine.

"Lyndon Johnson had been a Texas politician for his entire life and was fully aware of the economic powerhouse known as the Texas Medical Center. When Johnson announced a War on Heart Disease, along with his Wars on Poverty and several other social ills of the late sixties, it was with full knowledge of what that war on heart disease could bring to his home state. Lyndon Johnson infused the National Institutes of Health with unprecedented funding and clout. By doing so, Johnson created the pathway for DeBakey and Cooley to compete successfully with the older and more established medical schools and their teaching hospitals. It was genius, real genius, and by the time anyone realized what had happened, these two physicians had a virtual monopoly on cardiovascular surgery in the country and, for a while, in the world.

"The very same explosion of knowledge was happening in the medical or cardiology side of the equation, a critical component because surgeons don't advertise for their patients; they rely on their medical brethren, the Simon Bayers of the world, for referrals.

"Initially, the new research was funded practically wholly by the government, Kate. The National Institutes of Health had been created by the federal government during the latter part of the nineteenth century but had little significant effect on the practice of medicine. That changed radically during the sixties when The Johnson administration expanded the physician manpower within the National Institutes of Health and made millions of research dollars available to medical schools to combat the chronic diseases responsible for the death of most Americans: heart disease and cancer. Beginning in those two decades, there flowed billions of federal—taxpayer—dollars to the major research medical schools like Harvard, Yale, Stanford, Cleveland Clinic, and Mayo Clinic each and every year. A natural partnership developed between the drug companies and the medical school researchers; the basic research was performed by doctors employed at the medical schools and then once approved, the new drugs were manufactured and distributed by the drug companies. The research developed at those centers was considered to be in the public domain and therefore not subject to patent law. Those early cardiovascular drugs had no patent: digitalis had no patent. The number one drug for treatment of heart failure in the world and no drug company made any real money for producing digitalis because the drug had been around forever; it never occurred to anyone to patent it. The same was true for the new antihypertensive agents that came on the market during the sixties and seventies.

"Everything changed when the politicians re-involved themselves in the late seventies and early eighties. The Bayh Dole Act authorized the NIH and academic medical centers to patent their discoveries and then grant exclusive licensing to drug companies for distribution of the drug. Many of those drugs were granted twenty-year patents for medications prescribed for millions of patients worldwide. And that's when the money started to really flow. For FDA approval of any new prescription drug, there must be clinical studies that demonstrate that the drug is more effective than no treatment at all. The FDA does not require the drug to be an improvement when compared with other like drugs on the market; only that appropriately targeted individuals will benefit from the drug when compared with no drug at all. The researcher, therefore, sets up clinical trials to demonstrate the efficacy of the drug as compared with standard treatment. You already know the purpose of a clinical trial: to assure the safety and effectiveness of a new drug when used in a population deemed appropriate for that drug. There are now a variety of purposes for clinical trials; there is one other type of clinical trial that is relevant to your series, Kate, and that's the compassionate use trial. It's a category specially developed for the use of experimental drugs for patients who have exhausted all other options." He was clearing his throat again, and Kate could only imagine how difficult this was for Hank Reardon, the man who had more money than practically anyone on the planet but not enough to save his wife.

Waiting a beat or two, Kate decided to interrupt and redirect his thoughts. "Dr. McCall had been seeking approval for use of her experimental drug on her mother, wasn't she?"

"Yes. McCall had applied for a compassionate use trial from the ethics committee at Houston Medical. That fact is one of the many that bother me about her conviction."

Reardon had stopped pacing and was looking expectantly toward the open door of the library. He was smiling, and his eyes were filled with light as he watched his wife enter the room and declare, "Liisa just came home, Kate; she is wondering if you'd like to go for that run with her."

Kate was stunned when she glanced at her watch showing the time to be after two in the afternoon; she and Hank had been at it for over five hours. Kate busied herself by stopping the tape recorder and packing up her legal pads into her briefcase as she asked, "I think I'll accept Liisa's offer if it's okay with you, Hank? I sure need to run off Stella's calories."

Two and a half hours later, Kate and Liisa were racing each other back up the path toward the house. Kate grinned at Liisa. "I thank you for this, Liisa, it was a wonderful run, and I feel as if I've had another three gallons of Stella's remarkable coffee."

"Are you and Dad finished for the day?"

"I don't know. Peg came to tell me you were home, and then they went off together. I would think they could use some time alone together. Why, do you have something in mind?"

"Do you like quirky, funky bars?" Liisa had her head tipped, and her expressive blue eyes were dancing as she awaited Kate's answer.

Kate laughed, "There is nothing I like better—and I'll let you know how well the Swiss version of funk compares to Houston's."

Precisely at nine the next morning, Reardon met Kate in the library. Standing in the doorway in his signature jeans and sweater, sipping a cup of coffee, Hank asked Kate what she had thought of Pierre's.

"Interesting bar, Hank, very international."

Grunting, Reardon said, "I don't like the place either, but Liisa loves it." Reardon changed the subject before Kate could deny her dislike of Pierre's with, "We stopped at the compassionate use trials and the ethics committee, right?"

Reardon paused to take a drink of his coffee. "Patents for prescription drugs are awarded for up to twenty years to a specific drug company for a substance or chemical composition for a specific condition in a particular form—either liquid or a capsule—and manufactured by a specific process. For a new patent to be approved, a new molecule or new molecular entity was not required. Instead, three criteria must be met: the drug must demonstrate benefit to the target population, the drug must be significantly different from its earlier iterations, and the use must be 'nonobvious' or demonstrative of a conceptual leap.

"These criteria are ambiguous and arguably much too

vague, but because the intent of the legislation was to support and promote new drugs to eradicate the major causes of death in the civilized world, there was wisdom in leaving adequate wiggle room for researchers to test new ideas. But it didn't take long to see that companies could legally be granted new patents for the same drug if the drug were found to be effective for another condition or at a higher dose."

Then Reardon began to explain how much medicine had really changed in the past few decades because of research on new drugs. "In less than fifty years, doctors went from being perceived as inferior to merchants and soldiers to being accorded more power over individuals than any other occupation in our history." Reardon paused and glanced out the window again as if to seek his wife, but the garden was empty. "Dangerous, maybe the most dangerous force in the human psyche: power. A few of us can accept power like that with grace—all too aware of our limitations—but others? We begin to believe that we *are* extraordinary and therefore capable of anything and of understanding everything."

Again, Kate saw that quick smile that wasn't a smile at all; with a start, Kate realized that Reardon was not talking theory and philosophy here. He was talking about himself here, which made sense.

"Some are immune to it. Certainly Simon Bayer was. The man was unarguably brilliant, but he was grounded in a way that few of his contemporaries were; maybe that grounding came from working in his parents' retail store, or maybe it was the fact of his Jewishness and the prejudices associated with being a Jew, but Simon was never seduced into the power of it all. But Lindsey McCall?" He stopped for a moment, thinking. "I know Lindsey, and I believe that she bought the ideal and was eaten alive by those stronger and more strategic. Lindsey never saw it coming."

At that moment, Peg walked into the library with a tray of wine, canapés, and a huge smile. Reardon's face glowed as he looked at his wife, then looking at Kate, said, "I think we're done for the day, Kate, don't you?" He reached for two glasses of wine, handed one to Kate, and then clinked his glass to hers as he toasted, "To men like Scott Townsend and women like his daughter, Kate, may they be blessed, and may they prosper—always."

Kate walked into the Reardon dining hall exactly thirty minutes later, feeling great. She was smiling to herself as she approached the Reardons, feeling proud of herself for having done that entire punishing run. Stella strode in just then and, with broad sweeping gestures, herded them all over to the table where over ten mouthwatering appetizers sat displayed amid a spectacular floral arrangement that Kate was certain Peg had made. The four of them stood there for a moment, appreciating the aroma and presentation of the canapés. Finally, Kate reached for a plate and grinned at Stella while she began to load up her plate.

Three hours later, Liisa walked Kate back to the guest house as she explained when they would leave for the ASL labs and gave her an idea of what to expect for the day. Once inside and alone, Kate changed into pajamas and got to work on her notes from the past two days.

❧

An active field of science is like an immense anthill; the individual almost vanishes into the mass of minds tumbling over each other, carrying information from place to place, passing it around at the speed of light.

—LEWIS THOMAS, *THE LIVES OF A CELL: NOTES OF A BIOLOGY WATCHER*

14

Kate stood at the door of the guest house waiting for Liisa to come and pick her up. When Liisa got there, she explained about the day ahead of them, "Dad has invited a group of venture capitalists to visit the lab, and he wants me to do a dog-and-pony show on Digipro for them and then attend a luncheon he has planned for them at the Astoria Hotel downtown. They are French, so Dad thinks that my presentation and presence at the luncheon will persuade them to invest in us." She laughed lightly. "Fine with me, the more venture capitalists we bring in, the more secure we are in funding new projects."

"But I thought that Digipro is ready to go to market. Isn't it?"

"It's absolutely ready; in fact, we plan to have it in doctors' offices before the end of this month. We like to use the Digipro story as an example of the research done at our labs. Digipro is also a great way to demonstrate the mechanics of our collaboration with medical schools for our research; in this case, of course, it was Houston Medical School." Liisa took her eyes off the road to quickly glance at Kate to predict, "Profits from this drug will turn my department into a profit center within six months. The folks at Houston Medical are happy campers since Dad decided to share the profits on a fifty-fifty basis with the school. No other drug company had ever offered an even split, but Dad determined that deal from the beginning.

"I'm sorry, Kate, as this means that I'll be not available for most of the morning and early afternoon; but Eric and the team know Digipro and its history almost as well as I do. None of them has ever been to Houston though, so why don't you keep any questions you have about Lindsey or Houston for me or Dad?"

Kate nodded absently but could not stop wondering why a multibillion-dollar corporation such as ASL needed to worry about venture capital. Liisa noticed her lack of response and concern, and then she asked, "Are you disappointed that I can't be with you in the lab today, Kate?"

"No, no, Liisa, I trust your judgment. I'm sure that your team can teach me the basics of clinical laboratory research. I just wonder why a company the size of yours has to worry about attracting venture capitalists."

Relieved, Liisa laughed and said, "Ask me that question again after you've spent the day in the labs, Kate." Then she sighed deeply. "Dad told me that you'd read Dr. Johnston's book about our business. Right, Kate?"

Kate turned to look at Liisa as she was expertly down-shifting and guiding the Jaguar to hug the hairpin curves of the back road into Lausanne, noted the long, slender fingers of Liisa's hands as her left tightly held the steering wheel while the right deftly switched gears from drive down to first, then back. Idly, Kate thought they looked more like the hands of a pianist than those of a scientist.

"Yes, that's right, Liisa, I finished Johnston's book last night along with most of another that your dad had suggested."

"Do you recall the cost that Johnston estimated for the research and development of an average new drug?"

"It was something like one hundred million after taxes, wasn't it?"

"Yes, that's right; I think that's exactly what he quoted." Liisa was braking now and turning onto a wide two-lane highway with huge aspens and birch trees lining the road.

"Care to take a guess at the research and development costs to ASL for Digipro, Kate?"

"Half a billion." Kate had turned back to gaze at Liisa as she threw out a number that seemed about right, given what she had read so far, and was rewarded with one of Liisa's megawatt grins.

"Hey, girl, you are almost exactly right! Our costs were close to six hundred million by the time we received FDA approval for Digipro, not bad at all! So now you have answered your question about why a company like ASL seeks venture capital funds so vigorously, right?"

Once more, Kate was nodding, but she was distracted by the now obvious explanation to the unusual beauty of this highway and the trees lining the road: straight ahead lay the gleaming corporate headquarters of Andrews, Sacks, and Levine. Transfixed by the immensity of the place, Kate could only gape at the ten, maybe fifteen, sculpted steel buildings of various sizes and shapes arrayed in front of them. Liisa maneuvered her Jaguar to the huge parking lot next to the building in the foreground and parked the car. Glancing at her watch, Liisa stepped up her pace. "Sorry, Kate, but I've got a bit of work to do before I meet this group of men from France. I'm going to assign you to Eric for the day; he and our team are working on another NME—which is a 'new molecular entity'—with a researcher from the States. So you'll enjoy working with them this morning. Dad said that he'll come to get you early this afternoon because he wants to take you to out for a late lunch. Dad said that you and he had a lot to discuss."

Kate was nearly jogging to keep up with Liisa, who was moving as rapidly as if she had on running shoes. Kate had heels as well, but knew better than to wear the stiletto heels that adorned Liisa's long, toned, and shapely legs. How the woman could walk so quickly in those shoes was a complete mystery to Kate, but Liisa looked entirely comfortable as she raced along the pavement in her four-inch heels. The grounds of ASL were beautifully landscaped; they were passing innumerable beds of flowers and plants that were artfully arranged around the walkways crisscrossing the ASL campus. Suddenly they were entering the building foyer where a uniformed security guard addressed Liisa by name and rapidly produced a guest pass at Liisa's direction.

Liisa took the stairs very quickly with Kate following closely behind her. When they arrived on the second floor, Liisa turned into an enormous open space with at least twenty, maybe thirty, men and women sitting or standing in groups of twos and threes among a variety of cubicles. Liisa looked quickly around and then waved to a young man who immediately waved at them and then leaned down to say something to a young woman seated next to him. As he left to meet Kate and Liisa at the doorway, she stood and took the young man's place at the whiteboard. All were dressed in jeans but with long white coats reaching just past their mid-calves.

When the young man reached Liisa and Kate, Liisa smiled a greeting and introduced Eric to Kate. "Hey, thanks for helping us out, Eric. I've got to run if I'm going to make that ten o'clock presentation." And she took off, those long, slender legs striding as naturally in those stiletto heels as if she were barefoot.

Kate chuckled when Eric caught her staring at Liisa's rapidly disappearing figure. "I would give my right hand to be able to move like that on four-inch heels, but I've learned to stop trying". Kate continued, "She's a remarkable woman, so simple and seemingly down to earth. I've only known her for four days, and I feel as if I've known her forever. Does she have that effect on everyone? What do you think, Eric?" Her question was rhetorical: Kate really did not expect a response and was unsurprised when Eric just nodded. Turning away from Liisa's departing form, he gestured with his right hand as if to guide Kate back into the long lab and toward the group of team members assembled at the whiteboard.

As they approached the group, Eric murmured, "I'm not going to introduce you, Kate; they know who you are and why you're here. So if you'll take a seat, we'll continue our work; we're a bit under the gun here." With that, he pointed to a chair somewhat outside of the five scientists and ambled over to join them.

Kate took the seat as Eric suggested, amazed that not one of the three women and two men even glanced over at her, so absorbed were they in their work. As quietly as possible, she pulled out her legal pad and began to jot down observations about this place. The mathematical formulas they were writing and then erasing on the whiteboard meant nothing to Kate; if the scientists had been speaking Swahili, the conversation would have made more sense than the formulas did. At least she could have grasped the syntax and the emotional content, even if in a foreign language.

Looking around at the almost football-field-sized lab, Kate was struck by the brilliance of the stark white walls on one side with the external wall composed almost entirely of glass, which permitted the brilliant early spring sun to diffuse throughout the cavernous room. Without standing up, Kate could see the artfully landscaped grounds ablaze with marigolds, geraniums, impatiens, and a profusion of blooming plants she did not recognize. Kate had been inside only one basic science laboratory before, and that was Dr. Lindsey McCall's lab at the medical school in Houston. Reflecting back to the hour or so she had spent there with Dr. Steve Cooper, the chief of cardiology at Houston Medical, Kate was struck by the contrast. Lindsey's lab had seemed bleak, austere; the two rooms had been windowless, and the walls had been painted an indeterminate color—perhaps long ago they were pale yellow—while the ASL laboratory, though stark, was filled with light and with shining chrome everywhere. According to Steve Cooper, Lindsey McCall had spent thousands, maybe hundreds of thousands, of hours in those austere rooms, alone. Kate remembered Cooper stating that because McCall had many responsibilities at the medical school, Lindsey's primary research times had been weekends and nights when few people were around at the medical school. She wondered how the woman had stood the surroundings for so many years; Kate had been there for less than an hour and had begun to feel claustrophobic in the small rooms. McCall, Kate mused, probably never stopped to take notice of her surroundings; to attain her accomplishments the woman must have had superhuman focus and persistence. Kate recalled Reardon saying that McCall had begun to work on Digipro when she was in junior high school, so it had taken her over thirty years to accomplish her dream—unimaginable, Kate thought. She considered herself extremely disciplined and persistent but knew that Lindsey McCall was an entirely different species from anyone she had encountered before.

Her ruminations were interrupted by a flurry of activity among Eric's group.

Eric and his team of scientists had remained utterly

engaged in their project as one or another of them jumped up to stand at the whiteboard waiting for the chance to brainstorm with his or her colleagues. It looked like orderly chaos; more importantly, these youthful scientists looked as if they were having the time of their lives. Kate couldn't help but wonder how much fun it had been for Lindsey McCall laboring alone in her dreary lab. Quietly, Kate slipped out of her chair and, as she stood up, saw Eric's inquisitive look; Kate signaled him to stay put, that she was fine, and stepped away from the cubicle.

Slowly, Kate ambled through the series of work areas where between two and sometimes three scientists worked. Amazingly, no one looked up from their microscope or laptops as she wandered by. The work areas were designed for maximum utility, Kate decided. Although there must have been thirty or so cubicles in the large space, there was absolutely no sense of crowding; each work area was spatially defined by S-shaped counters that appeared to be black marble, with a scientist at each of the openings of the S. There were wide rows between the counters, giving an airy open feel to the place, and Kate noted extremely large steel sinks at the beginning of each work area.

As she walked the length of the room, Kate was struck by the near silence of the lab; she could hear an undercurrent of conversation as she passed, but the voices were all muted. Looking up at the ceiling, she wondered if there had been some insulating materials used to so effectively dampen the ordinary conversation of men and women actively engaged in their research. Glancing at her watch, Kate figured that she had about five hours before Reardon was to meet her for lunch. Thinking that she could get a start on the beginning of her article, Kate decided to go look for a place where she could sit and write.

Simultaneously, she felt a gentle hand on her arm and

heard Eric whispered, "Sorry, Kate, I'm taking you to the animal labs now. There will be a whole lot more activity there for you to see."

Quickly looking up at Eric's dark brown eyes, Kate thought that he must be at least six foot six as she demurred. "Eric, please, I really don't want to interrupt your work here, please go back to your team. I'll be fine for a few hours. I need the time to start writing anyway."

Shaking his head, Eric directed Kate out of the lab as he replied with a grin, "I've got my orders from the boss. I am to give you a tour of the Andrews, Sacks, and Levine corporate headquarters. Thanks for your concern about the team, Kate, but my team will probably be more productive in my absence, truth be told."

Kate saw that there was no point in debating the point any further and willingly followed the tall, dark German scientist out of the lab, into the main corridor, and out the door. The tall German extended his hand to the first of the constellation of buildings they had reached. There were no signs on the door, and heavy wiring covered all the windows, Kate noted.

"Kate, we've reached the animal labs. Liisa wanted me to show you all of them but spend the most time in the labs where we did the Digipro research." They had reached the door of the first building where Eric stepped up to the unmarked, black metal door, took off his name tag, which hung on a lanyard around his neck, and slid it though a small, black object at the right side of the door that looked similar to the lock on the door of most hotels. The lock flashed green, and there was an audible click. Eric grasped the steel handle and opened the door, then stood aside to let Kate precede him.

"We have almost twenty-five thousand animals at ASL."

Nodding at Kate's gasp, Eric continued, now comfortably ensconced in his role of ASL tour guide. "Over seventy-five hundred of those are white mice and rats because all animal research begins with mice or rats. This building is mostly mice and rats and—"

Suddenly a slight figure emerged from a doorway to Eric's right. They were standing in a very small vestibule with a plain wooden table and chair serving as the sole furnishings. The newcomer was dressed in blue scrubs that read TMC in large block letters on the top and bottom. Until she smiled, Kate realized that her gender was indeterminate given the surgical paper hat covering her hair and booties covering her shoes.

Extending her hand, she simultaneously handed Kate a pile of similar clothing while also shaking Kate's hand. "Hi, Kate, my name is Ariana. I'm the senior tech for the animal labs here at ASL." Kate smiled back and shook the young woman's hand as she calculated that Ariana must be about twelve years old and to weigh no more than eighty pounds. Kate did not think she had ever met such a diminutive person. Ariana was French but spoke English perfectly with just the right amount of accent to fit an Edith Piaf impersonator. Ariana turned to Eric, smiled, and went through the same routine, handing him the pile of scrubs, booties, and hat, but the two looked comical as Eric bent nearly double to accept Ariana's offering.

"She may be tiny, Kate, but no one comes in here without Ariana's okay. She runs the best animal labs in all of Europe, maybe even including the States. Before Ariana was hired— Liisa's decision by the way—we lost hundreds of thousands of dollars caused by frequent epidemics among the animals."

Ariana was leading Kate and Eric through the same door that she had emerged from and pointed right for Kate and left for Eric. Joining Kate in the women's locker room, Ariana picked up Eric's tutorial on animal research. "When I got here, no one changed clothes when coming into the labs unless they were going into the surgical suites. Of course, everyone knew to use sterile procedures in the operating suites."

Kate was struggling to get her form-fitting sweater off without messing up her hair too badly. Ariana deftly stepped in back of her, unbuttoned the two top buttons, and then lifted the top over Kate's head.

"Thanks, Ariana, I would have been here for another thirty minutes struggling to get out of that top." Kate felt like a giant as she grinned down at this French elf. With tight, curly brown hair that flew in an unruly halo around her small head, amber eyes, and a cupid bow of a mouth, that is exactly what Ariana resembled, Kate thought—an elf.

The chief tech nodded in response to Kate's grateful comment, then asked, "Is there an order in which you would like to see the labs, or are you comfortable with us following Liisa's instructions?"

Kate understood that this was a subtle method of communicating the hierarchy of ASL and replied, "Ariana, I am grateful for the time and energy you all are taking with me, so whatever you would like to show me is fine with me, and the order is irrelevant."

Looking at Ariana's expression soften very slightly, Kate realized that she had passed some type of test with this young woman and wondered what this was all about. But then, Kate realized that the chief tech must regularly be touring potential investors through the research labs—investors infused with the power of megamillions. Turning to follow Ariana as she left the women's locker room, Kate was so absorbed in her musing about the politics of money that she didn't see Eric coming out of the men's locker room until she had nearly collided with the German scientist.

Eric was grinning as he extended his hand to steady Kate as the two proceeded quickly down the main corridor to catch up with Ariana, who was turning left at an intersection of three broad corridors. Raising his voice, Eric called out, "We heading into the lilliputian labs, Ariana?"

Answering with an unmistakably Gallic gesture with her left hand, Ariana managed to convey both affirmation and a rather peremptory invitation without slowing her pace.

"Lilliputian labs refers to the rats and mice, I take it, Eric?"

"Right. Rodents compose the bulk of our animal experiments here at ASL; we must have tens of thousands at any one time. Hank is a big Jonathan Swift fan, ergo the use of *Gulliver's Travels'* nomenclature."

Kate and Eric had followed Ariana into an enormous open room where thousands of white mice in steel cages scurried around and through a variety of mazes and miniature toys. Ariana stood in the center of the room, gesturing to all the cages and explained, "Kate, this is the intake room. We breed our mice in another facility, then bring them in here at about three weeks of age to assure normal growth and development for another two to three weeks. There are fifteen thousand white mice here at any given time."

Kate was staring in fascination at the busy little white bodies engaged in what looked like normal mouse behavior to her untrained eye. There were three or four to a cage; each cage was meticulously clean, and surprisingly, the only odor Kate could detect was a slight whiff of disinfectant.

"Once we've ascertained normal weights and development, the mice are available to the scientists for experimentation." Ariana raised an eyebrow as if to ask if Kate had any questions, then nodded briskly in response to Kate's negative shake of her head, and opened the door while she stood back to permit Eric and Kate to pass through and back into the hallway.

"Onward to Laputa," Eric intoned.

"Laputa? You must be kidding, aren't you?"

Ariana had joined them and replied, "No, he's not kidding at all, Kate. It's Mr. Reardon's not-too-subtle message to his scientists." But the tech was looking at Kate in surprise and turned to Eric to remark, "The first in two years."

"The first in two years to do what?"

Smiling at each other, Eric and Ariana chorused, "Laputa. No one ever comments on the name, ever!"

"Leave it to an American journalist," Ariana mumbled as she led them back down the same corridor and back to the intersection, now taking the right-hand hallway.

"Is that a compliment or an insult, Ariana?" Kate asked the question lightly, but she was not at all sure of this unconventional French elf.

Deliberately thickening her accent, Ariana turned to give Kate the first genuine smile of the morning. "Kate, anyone who decodes Laputa deserves a compliment, even if she is an American." The chief tech's expression was impassive, but those amber eyes were alive with merriment.

Kate smiled back and commented, "Stanford University freshman English; it was the flunk-out course, and believe me, lots of kids did. But *Gulliver's Travels* stuck with me, obviously." She stood in reflection for a moment and asked, "But isn't Hank concerned that one of the venture capitalists may react negatively to his whimsy? I'm sure these folks are unbelievably serious about the decision involving millions of investment dollars."

Ariana's and Eric's expressions were sober, and Ariana turned to the tall German scientist in an unspoken request for assistance.

"Kate, you're right, of course. After lunch today, Liisa will bring over the group whom she is now addressing for a tour.

This company is considering a $1.5 billion investment with ASL for a drug still in preclinical trial. It's a drug for treatment of drug-resistant tuberculosis; both the World Health Organization and your own Center for Disease Control in Atlanta are very quietly calling drug-resistant TB the next potential for a worldwide epidemic. Liisa told us to be very free with you, Kate, and that you would know where we would need to be off the record, but the effects of such an epidemic would be catastrophic—obviously.

"See, Hank Reardon's 'whimsical' naming of our basic science research labs serves as a grim metaphor for our work here at ASL. Either Hank or Liisa personally interviews each and every scientist and postdoctoral fellow employed or studying here at ASL. In that interview is a review of the extensive battery of psychological tests required for employment. The Reardons do everything in their power to avoid hiring cowboys and to assure that each is committed to the high road of drug research.

"They meet with us all at the end of each quarter to report on the financial state of ASL and update us on all ongoing projects. And the ASL bonus program is the best in the industry; with the FDA approval of Digipro, we all received a 20 percent bonus check, which will increase to 30 percent annually when the drug is available for prescription sometime this fall."

Ariana had been standing motionless while listening to Eric. With his last comment, she nodded vigorously and stated emphatically, "My tech turnover is less than 10 percent; most research labs lose 50 percent of their techs each year. Here, they leave because we fire them for cause or because they decide to move elsewhere. No other research lab pays bonus checks for their techs—that I know of anyway.

"Our low turnover has a significant effect on the health of the research animals and therefore on the cost and quality of the animal experiments here at ASL."

The trio had been walking down the corridor and reached the Laputa labs; once more, Ariana stood aside to permit Eric's and Kate's entrance. Another vast room lay in front of them but was radically different from the lab where the mice had been happily chasing about in their cages. The design was somewhat similar to Eric's suite of lab facilities, in that the S-shaped design was continued here but with twice the space to accommodate the equipment necessary for the tiny research subjects.

Kate blinked several times because the busyness of the scene before her took her breath away. She was guessing, of course, but there looked to be 30 to 40 white-coated people attending to one or two rats in his or her open cubicles. Upon entering the door marked with a huge sign "Silence! Live Experiments Under Way," Kate had not needed Ariana's non-verbal finger to her lips, but suppressing her gasp of astonishment was not easy. The silence in the lab was a tangible thing, yet it was not the silence invoked by a cathedral or the majesty of a sunrise; rather, it felt alive. Kate could feel the energy in that room pulsing through every nerve in her body. Crazily, Kate wondered if her energy had somehow tuned into the frequency of the miniature monitors and other machines that most of the mice were attached to.

After a few moments, Kate realized that Ariana and Eric were waiting for her to nod her okay to leave this hushed hive of busyness. As with Eric's team earlier that morning, these folks were so focused on their small charges that none seemed to take note of the trio's presence. Ariana was standing slightly in front of Kate and Eric, her feet intentionally—Kate was sure—just short of a bright-red stop sign on the floor. Kate gently tapped Ariana on her right shoulder to get her attention; when the chief tech turned back around to face her, Kate silently held up two fingers to signify two minutes and raised her eyebrows to sign a question. Ariana smiled and nodded but held up the flat of her hand in front of the reporter in a clear communication to stay put.

Quickly, Kate surveyed the large space and the people within it. Some were making notes on small desktop computers while seated in front of mice that appeared asleep, while others were standing and working on the mice. Kate was too far away to see any details of any experiments, but there were a few cubicles right in front of her that she could see a bit better than the rest. While scanning the room, Kate was surprised to see that many of these technicians were older and multiethnic; some appeared to be in their forties and fifties, considerably older than their elfish boss.

The construction of the room was ingenious acoustically because while there had to be several hundred machines in the room, the electronic noise was almost subliminal. Again, the entire side of the lab was tinted glass, permitting the bright, warm sun to spill throughout the lab and affording anyone who gazed out an incredible view of spectacular flowers, shrubs, and fountains, while providing privacy to those inside the lab. Again, Kate wondered about the design of ASL and who had been behind the artful and ergonomic layout of the place.

She looked up to find Ariana's gaze on her and drew her finger across her throat and grinned.

Raising an eyebrow to Ariana, Eric stood and glanced at his watch—an obvious suggestion that they move on through the remainder of the labs.

❧

Bolstered by genuine advances in science and technology, the claims of the professions to competent authority became even more plausible, even when they were not yet objectively true; for science worked even greater changes on the imagination than it worked on the processes of disease.

—Paul Starr, *Social Transformation of American Medicine*

15

Kate sat next to Hank and was silenced by the view displayed through the window to her right. They were seated at the Chateau d'Ouchy's trendy, pure white bar, each of them sipping a glass of Pouilly-Fuisse and gazing in awe at the splendor of Lake Geneva backed by snowcapped mountains. Kate sensed Reardon's attention and returned his smile and silent toast by raising her glass and gently touching his. The bar could have been anywhere in the world: an immense pure white marble *S*-shaped bar dominated the room which cleverly gave up its fifteenth-century origin with its concrete walls and small windows at the ends of the bar. Hank had selected chairs at the end of the bar so that Kate could easily see the stunning view.

Ouchy had been a fishing village but was now primarily used by tourists and some natives for strolling along the waterfront or lounging in one of the many café's. About two thirty, Reardon had met Kate just as Eric and Ari had completed the tour of the ASL research labs. Kate's gaze met Reardon's intense blue one, and she answered his unspoken question, "My mind is spinning, Hank. I feel as if about a month's worth of critical information about ASL has been stuffed into my head."

Reardon merely nodded in response, saying nothing as he waited for Kate to continue.

"I really don't know what I expected, but it certainly wasn't what I saw in Ariana's labs." Kate toyed with the stem of her wineglass, twisting it around and around. Now looking back at Reardon, she exclaimed, "That woman is amazing, Hank. What a rare find she must have been for you and Liisa." Toying with the wineglass again, Kate suddenly became aware that she was nervous and it surprised her; she could feel Reardon's scrutiny and the heat beginning to rise in her face. But when she looked sideways at Reardon, he was beckoning the waiter.

Realizing that they were moving into the restaurant, Kate followed Reardon and their waiter as they walked down the narrow aisle to a sparkling white table with plush upholstered, white leather booths. The waiter seated them at their table and was refilling their wine glasses while listing the many specialties of the day. Completing the long list, the young man regarded Kate expectantly. "Hank, I wonder if you'd order for us both please? My brain is on overload, and I could devour any or all of those dishes." Smiling at the waiter, Kate asked in French where the ladies' room was, nodded at Hank, and left the table to wash her hands and collect her thoughts.

Smiling at Kate when she returned, Reardon said, "Why don't you tell me what you're thinking?"

"Hank, this story is *huge*; the subject matter is complex and rife with politics and emotion, as well as potentially serious—maybe catastrophic—consequences for you and your family, for Lindsey McCall, and for a host of people I'm not even aware of yet. This is bigger than anything I've ever tackled, and frankly, I'm not sure that I can do the story justice."

Kate's voice had softened to the point that Reardon was forced to lean forward across the table so that he could hear her last few murmured words; she was staring out the window on her left, but Reardon suspected that she was seeing neither the beauty of the lake nor the snowcapped mountains. He sat quietly and waited, figuring there was more she had to say.

When Kate looked back over at Hank, he was surprised when he saw her huge dark brown eyes glistening, "But most of all, Hank Reardon, I am afraid that I'll disappoint you; you've been so generous with me this week in welcoming me into your family and in opening up ASL in ways that I know you would never do to for most journalists." Annoyed by the emotion she heard in her voice, Kate's lips compressed into a quasi-grimace, and she took a shaky breath, planning to continue her confession when she felt Reardon's hand cover her right hand as it reached for her wineglass.

"Katie girl." This time, Kate delighted in the familiar and endearing sobriquet and cast a watery smile at this man who was beginning to seem like a second father.

Reardon continued without removing his hand from Kate's, "Of course, you're anxious, Kate; you'd be ignorant not to be and" —grinning quickly—"ignorant, you are not."

Reardon squeezed Kate's hand then picked up his wine glass to take a sip. "Quite honestly, I'm a bit nervous myself about how all this will play out, and I don't mind admitting that to you."

They finished their meal in companionable conversation and left the restaurant to go for a walk. Reverting back to her journalistic curiosity, Kate returned to the subject that had direct relevance to her writing. "Okay, so what is your take on Lindsey McCall, her indictment, and her conviction? And what role do you think Christine Stewart plays in all this?"

Reardon sobered and nodded as he repeated her question, "What's my take on Lindsey McCall?" Kate and Reardon had been ambling along the boardwalk but picked up their pace a bit as a sudden breeze from the lake cooled the air. "I liked

Lindsey the first time I met her at that luncheon with Simon. That would have been around –'95 or '96, I think. Simon had been telling me a great deal about Lindsey McCall for years." Reardon hesitated for a second then continued, "Lindsey was a daughter to Simon, not *like* a daughter but *was* his daughter. The Bayers had never been able to have children, and I think that was a great sorrow to them both.

"I don't *know* this, but I'd guess that the feeling was reciprocal. Lindsey's dad had been killed when she was in college, and her mother had become ill when she was a young teen, so I think the arrangement suited everybody just fine." Although it was getting colder by the minute, Kate was enjoying their walk along the lake and had no trouble hearing Reardon because the crowds had thinned out.

"From what I've been told by others at the school and the hospital, Simon's opinion of McCall was pretty much everyone else's; she was that rare combination of clinician, researcher, and teacher. Simon told me that he had never seen a doctor with her skills.

"I was biased in favor of Dr. McCall before I ever met her, but it was fairly easy to admire what she had already accomplished as well as her persistent conviction that she would figure out a molecular reconfiguration of digitalis, which would lack the toxic effects of the drug but retain its powerful beneficial effect on the failing heart. When I met Lindsey at that first luncheon, she had been working on this problem for over twenty years." Reardon had slowed the pace of his strides down and now regarded Kate with widened eyes. "I'm a really bright guy, Kate—most likely brighter than most—so I've never doubted my ability to do whatever I set my mind to; however, the single-minded focus of that woman to create Digipro exceeds any ability I have—or anyone I've ever met, for that matter. For some of us, that kind of unparalleled dedication is insanity; to others, like me, it's genius. But then of course, I have the benefit of knowing that she did it."

Kate was listening for differences of opinion about McCall. So far, what Reardon was saying fit the picture Steve Cooper had painted of his friend and colleague. She decided to move the conversation along. "Okay, Hank, so you and Lindsey McCall became instant friends and all was smooth sailing from then on?"

Reardon was laughing so hard that he had to stop walking; he tried to talk but couldn't get the words out.

Finally, she could make out his remark. "I know you weren't trying to be funny, Kate. That's what makes you so refreshing."

Reardon had stopped on the sidewalk so suddenly that a young couple holding hands and strolling behind them had stumbled into Kate and him; they had looked very strangely at Reardon and then at Kate as they ambled on past. Turning once more to Kate, he explained, "I went to Houston that first time because I owed my friend Simon Bayer. I would have done anything he asked of me. But honestly, I'd only half-listened to Simon explain what McCall was doing when he had called me in Lausanne. I was buried with all the minutiae of ASL; I'd only been there six months or so I think, and I was wondering why on earth I had agreed to back and attempt yet another turnaround of a giant pharmaceutical about to go under. Anyway, I'd planned a turnaround trip: fly to Houston for the luncheon to appease Simon and then get back on the plane that same day to be in the office in Lausanne by the next morning." Reardon had once more picked up the pace of their walk to counteract the oncoming chill of dusk.

"I was not prepared for Lindsey McCall. In no way was she what I had expected." He looked askance at Kate to say, "I have worked with enough bright—even brilliant—women to

know that beauty and brains are not mutually exclusive but—
" Reardon interrupted himself to ask, "Have you seen pictures of McCall, Kate?"

Nodding at Kate's negative shake of her head, Reardon declared, "The woman is stunning: more beautiful than any movie star I have ever seen."

Kate found this comment quite interesting; she'd not stopped to consider what McCall looked like, but she knew that Hank Reardon was not given to the casual use of superlatives; if Reardon said she was stunning, Kate had no doubt of the truth of his judgment. Cooper hadn't mentioned McCall's looks, but Steve had made it fairly clear that he and Lindsey had been good friends without any romantic or sexual entanglements. Kate had known plenty of women whose jealousy of a more beautiful competitor knew no bounds—including women who arguably should *know better* or to rise above such petty considerations. She wondered if Christine Stewart were among the group who incorrectly perceived themselves to be above that level of pettiness, and decided that she definitely could see Stewart despising a smarter, more accomplished woman who just happened to be spectacularly beautiful. Kate's musings were interrupted by the sound of Reardon's voice.

"At the luncheon, I gave McCall a hard time, a *really* hard time; by then I'd had close to thirty years in the drug research business, and I had either experienced or had heard about all the disasters that could take a company down. Yet there was no question that I asked of Lindsey that she wasn't able to answer clearly and simply. I kept expecting Simon to jump in and bail out his protégé, but he never did. Bayer just sat back and watched us do verbal battle. And when I threw her a curve now and then, as in asking a question that was unanswerable, Lindsey had the grace to laugh. She was never defensive, nor was she arrogant; she had every right to be both because she lost me on her first schematic of the molecular configurations she had tried."

Kate attempted to picture Stewart responding to a similar grilling by Hank Reardon; the two responses that popped into her head were defensive and arrogant. In fairness to Christine Stewart, Kate felt that she could understand her somewhat, only because they had some similar characteristics: namely, maintaining a sense of personal distance, which kept most people at arm's length. Kate had recognized that behavior in herself when she had felt intimidated by Hank Reardon. Like Stewart, some of the distance could be attributed to the reality of their respective careers; medicine and journalism continued to be male dominated professions even in the twenty-first century. That fact affected relationships with male colleagues as well as subordinates. It's peculiar, Kate thought, not for the first time, how the presence in others of disagreeable aspects of her own personality caused an immediate visceral reaction. Kate's self-analysis was interrupted by the sound of Reardon's voice.

"After a couple hours with McCall, I cancelled my plane reservation that night, and Lindsey and I went to her lab at the medical school." Reardon looked at Kate appraisingly. "Cooper took you there last week, right? So you've seen where McCall spent most of her academic life?"

Kate's mind took her back for the second time that day to those two dreary rooms. Still observing Kate's expression, Reardon commented sardonically, "Right, wonderful place to work—really gotta love the way that medical schools treat their star faculty members.

"By the time I got back on the plane to come home, I figured we had a fifty-fifty chance of making this happen. Lindsey would be both fifty percent of the problem and fifty percent of the solution, and yes, McCall had named her baby

Digipro by the time of her first animal experiments while she was completing her Ph.D. at Houston Medical University."

This time, it was Kate who stopped suddenly. "Why did you think Lindsey would be fifty percent of the problem?"

Reardon stopped alongside Kate and looked thoughtfully back at her. "I don't really have a good answer for you; it was more a prediction that I based on that weekend I had spent with Simon and her. I'll give you a couple examples. Like most researchers I've known, Lindsey McCall was a loner, but most of the guys I knew were so focused on getting their drug approved that they were willing to compromise. I remember guessing that compromise was not in McCall's nature. She couldn't or wouldn't do that; it was just a hunch, but it proved to be correct.

"That weekend, Lindsey and I had discussed at length her methodology; in her animal studies, she was comparing a control group on Digipro with one on digitalis and—"

Kate interrupted to ask, "Isn't that the logical thing to do?"

Reardon smiled in agreement because Kate was quite right, of course. "Yes, it is the logical thing to do, but the FDA requires only that a new drug show benefit over those treated with a placebo; there is no requirement to show benefit over drugs already existing in the marketplace."

Again Kate interjected, "And Lindsey insisted that the Digipro clinical trials be pure—compare the benefit of Digipro with digitalis, didn't she?"

Reardon turned quickly toward Kate and commented, "You don't miss much, do you, Ms. Lane?"

Laughing, Kate thought back to Ariana and Eric calling her Lois Lane that morning. "I sure try not to, but why would that type of a study be a problem? Wouldn't that add to the rigor of the test of the new drug? Assuming that it performed better than digitalis?"

"The last time I checked there were more than twenty-five drugs being used for treatment of heart failure. Limiting the control population to only patients on digitalis would make recruiting patients for the study much more difficult and therefore would quadruple the cost of the trial."

Nodding her understanding, Kate asked, "So who won? What was the final methodology?" A gust of wind suddenly burst from the mountains, over the lake, and roared past them. Kate knew Reardon had answered her but she couldn't hear anything but the wind.

But then Reardon looked at Kate and exclaimed, "Your lips are getting blue, and we'd best get you back to the car." Reardon shrugged off his light wool sport coat and held it out for Kate to slip into. In no mood to argue, Kate accepted the coat, still warm from the heat of Reardon's torso, and began the ten-minute walk back to the hopefully warm Bentley.

Walking very quickly now, for the wind was indeed picking up, Kate could feel the edge of the coming winter in the clear, clean air. "Hank, I didn't hear your answer about the design of McCall's clinical trials. Did she persuade you to do it her way?"

He answered with a shrug and, "There was no way that she would listen to me—or to anyone, for that matter."

Kate waited for additional explanation, happy that she didn't have to speak now that her teeth were practically chattering.

"McCall's boss, Christine Stewart, is a relatively straightforward woman; she is an extremely aggressive businesswoman and is after power and money—in that order. Christine is unlike any physician I've ever known: Most of the docs I know at least dabble in clinical research and at least voice their commitment to bench science. Stewart is a different breed entirely:

Christine makes no pretense about her interest in money." Smiling now, Reardon said, "And who am I to judge her for that?

"McCall and Stewart are two entirely different species, in my opinion, so a comparison between them is a bit of a futile exercise. I don't think Lindsey McCall cares about money; Lindsey is—or was—as driven as is Stewart, but for entirely different reasons. I think Dr. McCall had always believed that her research would save countless lives and reduce suffering in millions of others." Reardon smiled sadly. "And she's right: Her drug will have an incalculable impact on the treatment of heart failure.

"While Lindsey is an idealist and perfectionist, Stewart is practical and a realist. Stewart did not like McCall, and I think McCall all but ignored Stewart, never realizing how badly Stewart could hurt her if she chose to do so." Reardon stopped to briskly rub his hands together and kiddingly ask Kate if she could see the car yet.

"But do I believe that Stewart is responsible for McCall's arrest? Not for a second can I conceive of Christine calling the police to report Lindsey for using her new drug on her mother. From what I was told, that's how the Houston police got involved; someone made an anonymous call about Lindsey using her mother as a guinea pig for her unapproved research drug." Reardon slowly shook his head as they walked and he repeated, "That just doesn't fit with the Christine Stewart that I know. I don't believe she would make that call for the simple reason that McCall was no great threat to her." Reardon fell silent for a few minutes and took Kate's arm to keep her from getting jostled by a group of loud Italian tourists.

"Both Stewart and McCall are controlling people but for very different reasons; Lindsey's was about her inability to trust anyone but herself, and Stewart just expected people to do what she told them to do. Stewart was frequently annoyed with the controls over the data that Lindsey imposed once we got into multiple animal studies on Digipro in Houston and Lausanne. Several times a month, we'd be on the phone with Stewart to work out some way to reconcile Lindsey's unwillingness to adjust certain parameters of the study she made her frustration with McCall quite evident each time this occurred. I think Lindsey was so accustomed to the unconditional support of Simon Bayer that she had no clue of how to work for a real boss."

Kate interrupted to ask Reardon, "But Dr. Stewart wasn't the principal investigator on the study. Why would she have even been involved?"

"Stewart clearly understood the potential of McCall's research; she may not be a clinical researcher but she was well aware of the contribution to her bottom line." Reardon took note of the surprised and confused expression on Kate's face and explained, "Sorry, that's another piece to the story that I need to back up and explain."

Reardon reflected for a moment or two, then answered, "Although I've known McCall for over ten years, I certainly can't say that I understand what makes her tick. I don't think anyone ever knew Lindsey very well except Simon, and I'd wager that he understood her better than she did herself." Reardon watched a thoughtful smile appear on Kate's face.

"Simon was the best friend anyone could ever have. You knew beyond a shadow of a doubt that anything he knew about you would never be revealed to another, and I'm sure that Lindsey had opened up to Simon over the years But he never talked about her in any other way than as a professional colleague. When the three of us met, our subject was always Digipro; that was Lindsey's sole interest, and it was certainly mine."

Reluctantly lifting her face into the now-constant wind, Kate asked, "What about men in McCall's life? Weren't there guys she dated even for short periods of time over the years?"

"I know of no romantic interest in her life; there were a number of black-tie events that the medical school orchestrated for fund-raising during those ten years, and I saw McCall attend them. A few were held in honor of her. She never brought a date with her, not even one time. Lindsey would show up as late as she possibly could without being unconscionably rude and would leave as soon as she could get away with."

"Lindsey is not that much older than Liisa,"—Reardon stopped for a second as he considered— "and like Lindsey, Liisa is bright. She is not only intelligent but ambitious and personally confident. But I pushed Liisa into sports and extracurricular activities when she was in school because I didn't want her to isolate herself by marrying a career." Reardon slowed his pace because they were almost at the car and he turned to face Kate as he added so softly that she had to strain to hear him, "At least Liisa had one parent who knew the dangers of raising a teenaged genius; Lindsey had none."

Listening attentively, Kate wondered what Lindsey's friend, and Kate's friend, Steve Cooper would have to say about Reardon's analysis of McCall.

"Working with Lindsey was tough for all of my people and Liisa usually can get along with anyone. A few months before Simon announced his retirement, I flew to Houston to see if Simon had any ideas about a glitch in the Digipro project back when we were still in the stage of creating the new molecule. Liisa's team could get no help from Houston with the problems they were having. ASL was paying the UT Department of Medicine about a million a year, so that Simon could fund Lindsey's lab with three or four post-docs as well as with the equipment she needed, and I knew that Simon's successor would change the rules; so I spent several days in Lindsey's labs and talked with her and her team.

"After a couple of days, I figured it out: Lindsey didn't *want* our help. She wanted to do this all by herself, so she was creating all kinds of silly obstacles for everyone, including the folks on her own team. When I went to tell Simon my revelation, he just nodded sadly and defended her the same way he'd been defending her to me and, I guess, everyone else for years. So I went back to Lausanne and told the CFO to stop our payments to Houston Medical. Lindsey lost her team, but she managed to do the work anyway—it just took twice as long.

"By then, Simon had gone, and Stewart had replaced him; I was one of her first appointments. I think she'd been in Houston for a week or so and I appeared in her office. After about five minutes with the new chair of internal medicine, I knew how to assure Digipro for ASL: money. I offered Christine half a million a year for consulting with us along with an annual two million to the Department of Medicine. Christine was happy, and so was I. Two and a half million brought into the medical school by the newest chairman would make the Chancellor of Health Sciences a jubilant man—a win-win all around."

Reardon turned to look at Kate and saw that she had stopped a few yards back, her face a study in shock and disgust.

Reardon walked back, grabbed her arm, and pulled her along the street. "Come on, Katie girl, you can be angry at me in the warm car, but you'll freeze standing here."

Finally seated in the Bentley where she was warm, Kate sputtered, "So you're buying off the doctors just as Johnston claims that 'big pharma' does in her book, Hank! How on earth can you be so nonchalant about buying off doctors?

And how is paying Christine Stewart a gazillion a year fair to Lindsey McCall? This was her invention, right? And she gets nothing at all?"

Reardon was absorbed in avoiding pedestrians who were walking along the waterfront, some obviously inebriated as they swayed along the road, weaving in and out of the street.

Sarcastically, Kate answered her own question, "Oh right, excuse me. Lindsey gets indicted for murder for this multibillion-dollar invention. How could I forget that?" Kate was exasperated more at herself because she knew she was acting like a child who had just been told that there was no Santa Claus. Reardon had been very open with Kate; more than once he had claimed that his aim in life had been—and assumedly still was—making money and lots of it. But something in her took deep offense at the blasé way he had cut McCall off and then coldly struck a deal with Stewart who had done nothing to earn the money—only taken over as the chair.

Finally free of the crowded wharf area, Reardon picked up speed and headed up the sharp grade. Kate could hear the low growl of the transmission as the powerful engine downshifted to accommodate the steep grade of the road up to Old Town. The road was fairly narrow with several *s*-shaped curves requiring Reardon's full concentration as he drove the large car; he kept his gaze on the road while he calmly inquired, "What are your plans for this evening and tomorrow? I know you want some explanation from me about the financial arrangements with Houston Medical, and that's easy. We can do this later tonight or tomorrow; it depends on you, Kate. Do you need to go back to the labs tomorrow or do you even know yet?"

Kate had to chuckle; he wasn't even going to dignify her outburst with an acknowledgment. Thinking about the answer to Reardon's question, Kate replied, "I'd like to go back in the morning to just tie up some loose ends, and then I'll need to get to work. I'd like to have at least an outline sketched out by the end of the day tomorrow. Then, if you're still up for a day of play on Thursday, I'll have all day Friday to flush out the article and get it to Houston by my deadline."

Just hearing herself speak her plan out loud to Reardon helped Kate feel less anxious about this first critical piece. She could feel herself regaining her confidence and was really quite eager to get to work. She was surprised to see that they were almost back to Reardon's home and decided that he must be looking forward to some time alone with his wife.

"Hank, why don't you drop me off at the guesthouse now? With the late lunch we just had, I'm good to go for the evening, and I'd really like to get to work, if that's okay?"

Fifteen minutes later, Kate was sitting cross-legged on the floral couch in the sitting room of the Reardon guesthouse and was listening to the Swiss version of NPR as she opened up her laptop to start jotting down her thoughts.

By three in the morning, nine hours later, Kate was happy with the first draft of her article; she stood, stretched, and then walked outside to gaze at the brilliant fall sky before returning to her laptop to reread what she'd done so far. It was hard for her to believe that it had been only five nights ago that she had stood out here gazing at these same stars with Reardon. Kate felt as if she had been in Lausanne for years rather than days.

The wind of the earlier evening had stopped; only a gentle breeze stirred the evergreens, aspens and ash as Kate stood under the magnificent sky of northern Switzerland. There was no sound at all; the silence was total. Kate was aware that she had never experienced such immense silence nor could she remember ever standing motionless and alone under the majestic night sky, and she wondered why.

In only two days she would return to Houston to resume her hectic urban life, but Kate knew that the Kate Townsend who would arrive at the Houston Intercontinental Airport was not the same woman who had left. She felt profoundly altered by the experience of this trip, and Kate stood in silent gratitude.

Deciding that it was time to read what she'd written, Kate took several huge deep breaths in hopes that these clear mountain molecules would remain with her when she returned to Texas. Turning her back on the night, Kate walked slowly back to the inviting cottage, wondering if Steve Cooper ever went camping, and smiling at the thought. Pulling her thoughts back to her work, she began to proof her first article for "Murder in the Texas Medical Center."

Murder in the TMC

On January 29 of this year, Dr. Lindsey McCall, internationally acclaimed cardiologist, researcher, and a 2002 nominee for the Nobel Prize for Medicine, was convicted of murdering her mother through the use of McCall's non-FDA-approved drug, Digipro.

Dr. McCall is currently serving a two year sentence as an inmate at Huntsville Prison in Huntsville, Texas.

The bald facts are surprising and perplexing. Criminal indictment of medical doctors for mistakes, errors of judgments, and/or accidental deaths by physicians has been so rare as to be nonexistent. Historically, the medical profession by nature of the authority of its status has been granted immunity from oversight by the criminal arm of the state. In situations where the patient or family has suffered a bad outcome while under the care of a doctor, the traditional method for seeking judicial redress has been through accusations of medical malpractice or medical negligence. The University of Houston's Law School employs some of the finest health law professors in the country, many of whom came to teaching after successful careers as prosecuting or defense attorneys in the rapidly growing specialty field of health care law. Watkins and Peterson, one of Houston's most prestigious law firms, employs more than thirty attorneys who specialize in the defense of the ten thousand or so doctors and hospitals accused of malpractice annually in this city. More than 95 percent of these cases never reach the courtroom because the plaintiff and prosecuting attorneys are able to reach a financial settlement acceptable to the defendant(s).

There are three questions which beg for answers:

Why did the Houston district attorney decide to involve the state in an area of the law which it has historically treated as sacrosanct: that of medical decision-making?

Second, why did the DA decide to charge McCall with *murder* rather than criminal negligence in a civil court?

And last, in a city where the Texas Medical Center reigns as one of the top employers in Houston and houses over three thousand medical researchers making the news with new pharmaceutical discoveries almost daily, why did twelve Houstonians unanimously decide to convict Dr. McCall for intentional murder following her trial?

According to the Texas Penal Code, a charge of intentional murder is defined as intent to murder while in the course of committing or attempting to commit a felony such as burglary, robbery, arson, sexual assault, obstruction, or retaliation or terroristic threat. To achieve a bill to indict from the grand jury, Masters must have persuaded the jury that Dr. McCall had a premeditated plan for murder. Her decision to use her new cardiac drug as a prelude to the death of her mother was assuredly the claim by the state that justified the indictment but this makes no sense as the practice of medicine is immersed in the use of last-minute attempts to save lives. There had to be other persuasive facts which convinced a jury to convict this physician. One must ask then, what happened here? How did the measures taken by a highly trained specialist to save a life become interpreted by the state as murder?

Several days of research and investigation brought no answers to these initial questions; in fact the case became more puzzling. It seemed as if each new piece of this story served to obfuscate rather than clarify the answers to the questions; eventually the innocuous list of facts suggested that the conviction of Dr. Lindsey McCall encompassed contextual factors that were completely beyond her control.

This four-week series, "Murder in the Texas Medical Center," is the result of an intense investigation of Dr. Lindsey McCall's murder conviction. What has become clear is that this very curious case can be understood only by placing it in the context of existing social and cultural changes that are restructuring the American medical and health care system and concurrently eroding public confidence in both the system and in doctors themselves. To understand the present, however, we must make a quick visit back to the past, the beginnings of what has been called the most successful corporation in history: American medicine.

The twentieth century saw the professions of law and medicine enjoying an extended alliance where medical decision-making was awarded with more and more autonomy by the state and federal governments, such that the profession of medicine was infused with more self-rule than had ever before been granted. This new alliance was deserving of a new concept and new language by the sociologists studying the dizzying speed with which medicine was gaining political and cultural power. The word profession describes a group of individuals whose knowledge, education, vocabulary, decision-making and yes, even poor outcomes, could be evaluated only by one another. Individuals who lacked specialized training could not reasonably judge the practice of the physician. Doctors were individuals who were above the common law because their specialized knowledge and expertise placed them outside of the usual human foibles of greed, immorality, corruption and ignorance; only other doctors were permitted to testify for or against physicians accused of malpractice or negligence. Such was the agreement between medicine and law for much of the last century.

But the rules have changed. And suddenly. Investigation reveals no cases of criminal prosecution until the 80s, during which there are a few, with slightly more in the 90s; but an increase of over 20 percent with the new millennium. A complete cultural turnaround in fewer than thirty years has resulted in what one physician has called *The Criminalization of American Medicine: America's War on Doctors*.

Why?

"The rise of reason did not take power into account." Starting with his first sentence, Nobel Prize-winning author Paul Starr debunks the attributes given to medical professionals by the sociologists of the mid-twentieth century and instead characterized physicians as mere mortals subject to the same flaws and foibles of all of us. Starr then describes the complex factors which coalesced in the last century to create this illusion of a category of persons thought to fly higher than most of us.

The Social Transformation of American Medicine portrays the culture of the early twentieth-century American as one who was fiercely independent of the influence of any authority over his health and that of his family. Americans were born at home, had their babies at home, and died at home. Midwives were widely available throughout the country and knowledge of the beneficial effects of herbs and other foods for the treatment of flus, colds, and pneumonias was understood and practiced by average Americans. Education about basic hygiene had been assimilated by most of us; therefore, death from infectious disease had dropped significantly in this country— prior to the introduction of the use of widespread antibiotics; a fact that has been widely ignored by the public as well as by mainstream medicine.

Yet by the late 1930s, these very same independent American men and women handed over their personal authority for health and well-being for themselves and their families to the physician. There was a myriad of factors explaining the shift from independence to dependence, of course: the moves from the country to the city following the advent of the industrial revolution foremost among them.

Starr methodically and persuasively explains how the independent American of old ceded authority over birth, death, and many interim events through the alliance of medicine and the law. By 1950, a medical doctor was required by law as the authority to pronounce a person dead, and a medical doctor brought most of us into the world and was present when we left it. Where once midwives had performed the task of birthing, the partnership of law and medicine in legislating credentialing invariably favored the medical doctor, midwives and homeopaths became a relic of the past. Where only a few decades before, women were instructed about the care and feeding of infants and children by mothers and grandmothers, pediatricians were now required to write prescriptions for baby formulas. As a society, it seemed, we were quite content to turn over the responsibility for our health to the medical profession by the middle of the twentieth century. This radical cultural change provided the ingredients for the growth of the largest corporation the world has ever seen: American medicine.

In a prescient statement regarding the 21st century medical doctor Starr writes: "Bolstered by genuine advances in science and technology, the claims of the professions to competent authority became even more plausible, even when they were not yet objectively true; for science worked even greater changes on the imagination than it worked on the processes of disease." In simpler words, medicine over-promised and under-delivered.

At the time his landmark book received the Nobel Prize, Paul Starr was on the faculty of Harvard University. But Dr. Starr was denied tenure at Harvard despite a Nobel Prize winning book. Harvard Medical School is one of the most influential in the country; one can deduce readily that the revelations in Starr's book were not received well by the physicians in power at Harvard University.

One of the more critical attributes of the professional model as defined by the sociologists is independence from any profit motive. The professional provides her services because of the moral obligation to do so; financial gains are not a motive in her decision making.

A review of the available literature shows the fallacy of these ideas. The following list is merely a partial listing of the vast available research.

- Over 16 percent of the gross national product of the United States is spent on Medicare, over 90 percent of these monies occurring during the last year of life.

- Despite numerous studies suggesting that high cholesterol is not a risk factor for cardiovascular disease, both the American Heart Association and American College of Cardiology maintain cholesterol as a top risk factor, disregarding mounting evidence of the dangers of low cholesterol.

- The AHA and College of Cardiology recently have broadened their standards for the prescription of statins in the name of prevention to include just about every American over the age of twenty-one.

- Financial relationships between Cardiologists and Cardiovascular Surgeons writing the standards and the pharmaceutical manufacturers of the statin drugs have been demonstrated repeatedly.

- Multiple researchers have empirically demonstrated the inverse ratio between medical treatment and mortality. There is a point at which more medical treatment increases morbidity and mortality. In other words, there comes a point where increasing medical treatment kills, consistently.

- Population studies have repeatedly shown the lack of correlation between health, hospital bed, medical providers, and health. In fact, these studies have shown increased mortality and morbidity rates as directly proportional to presence of specialized physicians and the accoutrements of modern medicine.

- The cost of the United States medical system exceeds that of any other Western country by several margins, with medical outcomes that are far inferior to other Western nations.

- Data have existed for decades showing that salaried physicians order significantly fewer costly procedures and medications than do those in private practices with significantly higher quality outcomes in those patients. Yet in the 21st century, salaried physicians remain a small minority of the whole, most remain of a fee for service payment system.

- Pharmaceutical companies are rivaled only by oil companies in their profits and dividends paid to shareholders.

- For decades, epidemiological studies have revealed that over 80 percent of the illnesses for which Americans seek medical intervention will resolve on their own and yet a majority of us increasingly seek a doctor's treatment for colds, flus, and the myriad of aches and pains that accompany healthy people and children.

- As a consequence, death from taking prescription drugs as they are prescribed is now the fourth leading cause of death in this country: Annually, more than one hundred thousand people die from the side effects of taking prescription medications in the manner in which they were prescribed. Small wonder, too, that the abuse of antibiotics has caused new and frighteningly virulent strains of bacteria which are resistant to most antibiotics.

These are but a small percentage of the data available to the public objectively illustrating grave ineffectiveness in many areas of medical practice. Among these sterile data and numbers live individuals and their families—persons who have stories to tell about their experience and disillusionment with the unfulfilled promise of medicine and its technologies.

It's possible the information in this article has surprised and may even have frightened you. But I know that most Americans, prefer to know the facts even if they do not support long-held beliefs.

In light of such numerous examples of the existence of inconsistency, error, and greed in the practice of American doctors, isn't it reasonable to conclude that the perceptions of some Americans toward physicians are no longer trusting but have become skeptical—even suspicious? And that this erosion of trust is now being seen in the courtroom, specifically, the courtroom trying Dr. Lindsey McCall? Further, is it not conceivable that the actions of an individual physician under scrutiny could be judged as criminal, given the proclivity of jurors to believe guilt merely because one has been accused, when there has been no harm done at all?

There are two kinds of truth, small truth and great truth. You can recognize a small truth because its opposite is a falsehood. The opposite of a great truth is another great truth.

—Niels Bohr

16

Present Time

Kate arrived at the quirky little bar before Steve. Although it had been close to nine months since she had met Steve for a drink at Marfreless, nothing had changed, and for that, Kate was grateful because it seemed that everything else had. She glanced at her watch, surprised to see that it was only five thirty; she had left the office at five, expecting there to be a lot more traffic and had made it here in about twenty minutes. Forcing her over-stimulated mind to focus on only one thing, Kate sat, deliberating about ordering. She'd had little to nothing to eat today, and a martini would go straight to her head; on the other hand, had she allowed herself no alcohol last night at the award dinner.

Interrupting Kate's mental argument about the pros and cons of starting to drink before Steve arrived, the very same tall, thin young woman who had served them last year stood towering over Kate.

"Hi, what can I get for you?" the cocktail waitress asked pleasantly.

Kate studied the woman in the dim light to make sure that she was the one and suddenly wasn't sure.

"Hi, I'd like a vodka martini on the rocks with plenty of

olives, please." Overnight, she had become a celebrity in Houston and maybe in the country if the requests for her appearances on talk shows continued to pour into the *Tribune*'s public relations office. Although Kate had expected some reaction from the medical community, the volume of letters to the editor from physicians both locally and nationally stunned Kate and her colleagues at the *Tribune*. Strangely, there were more letters congratulating Kate and the newspaper for "opening the black box" of clinical research and exposing the growing crisis in medicine than there were critical ones.

She sighed, thinking of her initial insistence to Jeff and the Philbins that she could handle the correspondence. Gratefully accepting the martini from the waitress, Kate took a healthy swallow and then realized she had better order some snacks, or she would be drunk before Cooper even arrived. When the waitress walked over with an enormous bowl of popcorn that smelled freshly made, Kate smiled in gratitude. When the waitress told her it was on the house and congratulated her on the receipt of the Pulitzer last night, Kate was not disturbed that she had recognized her. Of course, her sudden nonchalance may derive from the straight vodka that now marinated her brain; Kate was surprised to see that she had consumed over half the martini. The young woman was classy; she simply walked over with the bowl to congratulate Kate and then walked back to the bar even though there was only one other couple there. The waitress seemed to understand and respect Kate's need for solitude and privacy.

Kate had received mail from fans and critics after each of her series; the one about the plight of the homeless in San Francisco had drawn volumes of reaction, both very positive and blisteringly negative. And so, Kate had not thought much about the response of readers to this series. But when Kate's surgeon father had e-mailed the draft of her first article without one single correction just a typewritten note which had been extremely complimentary but a prediction of a storm of letters to the editor, she had been surprised at his comment but relieved that he had approved of her material. She'd asked her dad a couple of weeks ago how he had known that her series would ignite such a furor; he had just smiled and advised her to hold on tight because the ride could get very bumpy.

Kate picked up her drink to stare at the olives lying on the bottom of the crystal goblet, thinking about the metaphor her father had used and how aptly it fit a few letters she had received from the institutional side of medicine. One had been from someone high up in the FDA, another from the president of the AMA, and a third from members of the board of the American College of Cardiology. Kate winced as she recalled the barely suppressed condemnation, anger, and condescension of the language in each document. Thankfully, those were in the minority.

Now, with the news of the Pulitzer award, the letters, e-mails, and requests for Kate to speak locally numbered in the hundreds. The paper had hired two new assistants for Kate just to handle the voluminous correspondence, and they were already working twelve-hour days.

Grateful for this time to sit alone and reflect, Kate realized that she had not a clue about how to handle this notoriety; the interest in Kate Townsend had begun slowly, and the first few requests had been flattering and fun. But by the end of her series, she realized that this was only the beginning; she had already been contacted by three publishers about a book and nationwide speaking tours. She closed her eyes as she reflected on the unpleasant conversation with the first book offer, the one she had sitting on her desk at home. It was dizzy-ing and she wondered just what had been the impetus for such acclaim. Sure the research was good, but Kate's research was always good. She thought of the series on the homeless and the one on the ethics committees; nothing she had ever done even came close to what was happening here.

Kate sighed again thinking of Lindsey McCall, the ostensible subject of her series, and felt the now-familiar sadness at this woman's incarceration and Kate's inability to do anything about it. Kate felt as if she now had an interject, because she thought of McCall so often and had imagined such a clear picture of the woman.

Suddenly she was startled at the force of the physical response caused by the presence of Steve Cooper. Kate was uncomfortably aware that her heart was racing so fast that her chest hurt and her palms were suddenly damp with perspiration. Pushing back her chair to rise, she felt two strong hands push her shoulders down and that soft drawl instruct her to remain in her seat.

"I believe this lady is the famous Kate Townsend, winner of three Pulitzer Prizes—not one, mind you, but three. You will not rise for this country boy." Kate felt the warmth and strength of those hands on her shoulders right down to her toes. Happily, she remained seated because her legs felt rubbery, as if they may not hold her if she stood. Marfreless was a small bar, and although Steve had not spoken too loudly, the only other couple in the bar was looking over at them curiously.

Cooper was commenting on an unprecedented decision by the Pulitzer Prize board which had been announced to an already electrified audience at that evening's awards ceremony in River Oaks. Nate Parker, president of the Pulitzer board who had introduced Jeff at the start of the ceremony, had returned to the podium with a strange expression on his face. The man looked the part: tall, fit with a shock of white hair, and rimless glasses. Dr. Parker also happened to be the provost of Columbia University, the dignitary responsible for the proceeding since the endowment had rested at Columbia from the very first award in the early part of the last century.

As Dr. Parker had adjusted the microphone to fit his six-foot-plus height, Kate had wondered for the first time that evening just why the ceremony was being held in Houston. She was reasonably sure that the awards were generally held in New York City and hosted by Columbia University; this evening was not the norm. Kate had glanced across the table to find Reardon's gaze on her; just as she had been about to lean across the table to ask him about the change in venue, she heard Parker call her back to the stage.

"Because Ms. Townsend broke precedence earlier this evening with her acceptance speech, which wasn't a speech at all and left us with a good twenty minutes of unfilled time, I'm going to use my authority to explain to this august group why the spring luncheon at Columbia's Law Library is instead being held on this glorious fall evening in Houston, Texas, at the beautiful River Oaks Country Club; I'm going to do that while our guest of honor returns to the stage." Parker had been looking expectantly and somewhat impatiently at Kate as she sat motionless at the table.

Kate had felt a sharp elbow in her ribs and heard Eleanor's whispered, "Go up there, Kate, now, and please don't keep the man waiting, Dear."

Parker had smiled back at Kate and loudly enough for the entire room to hear, had commanded, "This time, we request that Ms. Townsend stay right here, don't we, folks?"

With those words, the urbane New Yorker had suddenly developed a Texas drawl. Kate had stood, transfixed by the transformation of this genteel academic into an urban cowboy. Parker had glanced sideways at Kate, taking in her somewhat dazed countenance as she headed toward the stage, and then directed his full attention back to the crowd.

"By now, y'all have figured out that this entire ceremony is quite unorthodox. The Pulitzer Prize board had thought that we were aware of the many unconventional aspects of this dinner in deciding the location. But Ms. Townsend added some of her own when she decided to include the owners of the Houston Tribune and Mr. Hank Reardon in her acceptance speech."

Turning half around to Kate, Parker had then addressed both her and the audience. "I've been on this board for over thirty years, and I have never seen a Pulitzer Prize recipient deny themselves this once-in-a-lifetime chance to address an audience that seldom listens to anyone's but their own words—and you did this with such grace, Ms. Townsend!"

By now, Kate had been squirming as she stood beside Parker; she had smiled at him and at the audience but felt extremely uncomfortable. She had realized there was more the man had to say, and she had no clue what it might be. She had accepted that she had no choice but to stand, smile sweetly, and wait for the other shoe to drop.

Dr. Parker had continued in his normal speech, dropping the Texas drawl, "I really am from Texas, you know, folks. I was born right here in Houston, too many years ago to count, so I decided to see if I could get my accent back for a minute or two tonight. I hope I did okay?"

Cutting off the smatter of applause, Parker had continued to speak, now adopting a serious manner. "The Pulitzer Prize board decided on this dinner to be held here this evening for three very special reasons. For the first time in our history, we are awarding the Prize to Kate Townsend and to the Houston Tribune for three category definitions of excellence in journalism: for distinguished investigative reporting by Kate Townsend, for a distinguished example of explanatory reporting illuminating a significant and complex subject by this reporter, and for a distinguished example of local breaking news by the Houston Tribune. For these three awards, I have been authorized to grant Ms. Kate Townsend a check for one hundred and fifty thousand dollars and the Houston Tribune our gold medal for excellence in public service. Would the owners and editor-in-chief of the Houston Tribune return to the stage, please?"

If there had been chaos before, there was now bedlam that accompanied Eleanor, Marguerite, and Jeff's return back to the stage. Kate had stood alongside her bosses and allowed the thunderous acclaim to wash over her; stunned, she had tried to assimilate the heady fact that she had just been awarded three Pulitzers for her series, *Murder in the Texas Medical Center.* The board had never made a multiple award to a single individual before; she was the first. She had wondered idly if her old boss at the Journal were there, attending the dinner. Kate had heard that he'd accepted a post one of the prestigious Pulitzer Prize nominating juries.

Cooper pulled out his chair, sat, and then reached over to take the last swallow of Kate's martini. Then with a broad grin, he said, "Thank you for that, I've not had a Marfreless martini since you and I were here last fall."

Kate smiled back and heard herself saying, "Steve, it's really, *really* good to see you. Thanks for coming last night." Kate could hear the emotion in her voice, the giveaway tremor. This openness was unlike her; in the past, Kate had always been so driven by an assignment or a deadline that a phrase like this was just never spoken. Kate was surprised at herself, but her words and feelings were deeply felt, and she could tell that Cooper could sense the sincerity and depth of feeling behind her words.

Steve had been about to joke with her when Kate's words took them both somewhat off guard. Cooper's eyes widened slightly, and then he took her hand very gently in both of his to say, "I've missed you, too, Kate, and I would not have missed that dinner for anything." Shaking his head a couple times, he gave Kate a rueful smile to add, "But there are some folks at Stanford who aren't incredibly happy with me."

Kate's response was immediate and apologetic because she had not thought to ask him about his new position as Chief of Cardiology at Stanford, but Cooper waved her off and insisted that they talk about her. "Your series was brilliant. You know that, right?"

His deep and warm dark eyes seemed to bathe her with light as he sat across from her waiting for a response. A few times Kate started to speak then stopped, and then, laughing nervously, she said, "I'm stammering. Why is it so much harder to accept praise than criticism?"

Just then their waitress appeared to ask Steve what he wanted to drink, and the moment was gone. Cooper looked up at her to say, "I've been in San Francisco for the last few months, and no one in San Francisco can make a martini that even approaches the ones you guys make here. So please, a dry vodka martini, neat with plenty of olives."

The waitress winked at him as she headed back to the bar. "Coming right up and welcome home!"

Steve reached over to drink some more of Kate's martini, realized that her glass was now empty, and hollered to the retreating figure, "And another for my friend here, please?" Cooper smiled widely at Kate as he took the last olive from her martini and popped it into his mouth.

"I'll echo your sentiment, Kate, and tell you that you are a sight for sore eyes, and so is Houston!"

"When did you get in, Steve?" Smiling at the waitress who had appeared now with their drinks and a refill of the popcorn bowl, Kate was more than happy to get the subject of their conversation off her series. She felt as if she had been living and breathing the material for a year. The four-article series had stretched out over one month since each article had been the Sunday headline of the *Tribune*; the last piece had run just a month ago. But because of the series' widespread exposure by the national press and her first two appearances on local talk shows, and now the Pulitzers, Kate had not been able to get distance from her work; on the contrary, she felt as if she were on a train that was rapidly gaining speed and heading toward an unknown destination.

"My plane landed at seven thirty, and I got a fast cab from Hobby to River Oaks Country Club, so I only missed your boss's opening remarks."

Kate did not know how to ask this next question, so she played with her drink while she thought about how to ask Steve how he had learned about the award and this event. She certainly had not told him; their communication over the last year had been by e-mail and had been very superficial. But now Kate wished that she had invited him; she was more than embarrassed that someone else had done it for her.

"What is it about that martini that has you so engrossed? You've been staring down into your glass as if it held the secrets of the universe."

"I'm really sorry that I didn't have the presence of mind to tell you about last night, the award, and the dinner weeks ago. I feel terrible that you didn't hear about all this from me, Steve." Kate stopped herself from fumbling any further to instead study the long angular planes of Steve's face and those expressive brown eyes and saw no evidence of resentment or offense there—merely warmth and affection. "But wait, you're not upset with me at all, are you?"

Lifting an eyebrow, Cooper half smiled and replied, "Why on earth should I be upset with you, and why do you think you need to apologize to me for not letting me know about last night, Kate?

"Look, if anything, I'm the one who barged in on your parade, so I'm the one who should say that I'm sorry, but that's a problem, Kate, because I'm not in the slightest bit sorry; in fact, I was ecstatic when I got the call from Todd Kensington." Part of Kate's brain registered the name Todd Kensington as Lindsey McCall's attorney and wondered how and why Kensington would take sufficient notice of the dinner to not only attend but to call Cooper. Very briefly, Kate's reporter's instincts were aroused, but she had no interest in redirecting this conversation; in fact, she was quite content to surrender the lead to Steve. Kate laughed at this new and perhaps improved Kate Townsend.

Cooper took note of Kate's smile and laughed. "We sound like a couple of teenagers, don't we?" Just as Kate was about to laughingly say something appropriately sophomoric, the intensity of Cooper's stare suddenly deepened, and both of them lost their smiles. Kate could feel the force of Steve's gaze like an arrow piercing through her very center right down to her toes. She *did* feel exactly like she used to with her first high school boyfriend: She was breathing fast, her heart was racing again, and her stomach was all fluttery.

Without breaking eye contact with her, Cooper reached for his drink and took a long swallow. "It's getting pretty warm in here, Kate. Drink up."

"Good idea, Dr. Cooper, I'll do that." Kate hoped he didn't notice the crack in her voice but was exceedingly grateful to have somewhere to put her hands; she picked up the glass and finished half the drink in two deep swallows.

"You know—" They each burst out laughing because they had each spoken the same words. Kate motioned to Steve to speak first.

Cooper looked directly at Kate, this time without sensual energy, and placed one of his hands on her right one as it lay on the table next to her empty glass. "I like you, Kate; I like you a whole lot, more than any woman I've met in a very long time. And you feel the same about me. I know you do. But there's a good reason that we've reached our respective ages without ever getting married, and that's because neither of us rushes into anything but our work."

Steve smiled at the riot of expressions on Kate's face and in her eyes, but his eyes now seemed to probe her. "You're not the only researcher in this family, Ms. Townsend, not by a long shot.

"You're much too important to me to do anything but take this *real* slow, so we're going to pretend that the only thing we want from each other right now is a friendship. I'll get back to Houston as often as I can, and you'll come to San Francisco as often as I can persuade you to leave the *Tribune*. But we're going to see movies, eat dinner, walk on the beach, and tell each other about the things we love the most and the things we fear the most. And then, when it's time, we'll get back to what just happened between us."

He stopped for a second to finish his martini and to signal to the waitress standing by the bar for two more. Dismissing Kate's whispered protest, "Good Lord, Steve, that will be my third martini."

Steve directed his gaze back at Kate, again with that piercing, probing intensity. "On that four-hour flight from San Francisco, I did a lot of thinking about us, Kate. Todd only gave me a day's notice, so as I mentioned earlier, I'll owe some people when I get back to Stanford; I had to call in a lot of favors to clear my schedule for two days, but there was no way I could miss getting here to see you receive the award." Cooper grinned, and quickly corrected himself, "Sorry, *awards!*" Then the smile faded, and the intensity reappeared. "On the plane, I thought of all the reasons that I feel this way." Steve reached over to touch Kate's cheek very lightly; his hand felt cool and gentle. Just then their waitress returned to set their drinks in front of them and to take the empty glasses away.

"Would you two like some more popcorn? We're just making some fresh now."

Steve and Kate chorused, "Yes, that would be great, thanks!"

Steve's eyes suddenly widened, and he frowned. "Kate, I am sorry, I'll bet you've not eaten all day; I didn't even ask you if you wanted that second martini. I've been so focused on my little *speech*." Kate realized that the man had been so nervous that he had not heard her protest about the *third*, not the second, martini and was delighted with herself for having not the slightest desire to correct him.

Kate reached across the table to grab the hand that had so gently touched her and squeezed it, hard. "Steve, I'm fine, we'll get dinner later. Please continue; I want to hear what you have to tell me. Truly I do, don't stop." Kate forced her herself to stop there; it was hard, very hard, for she wanted to tell him how courageous she thought he was, how honest, how *real*, and how rare; but none of those words was enough, and she did not want to control Steve's way of sorting out and expressing all kinds of conflicting thoughts and emotions. Kate smiled as she recognized this new behavior of hers, enjoying the memory of all the many lessons that she had learned at the feet of Hank Reardon.

Misinterpreting her smile, Cooper tensed and quickly studied Kate to see if she was being facetious, but Kate could feel the tension bleed back out of him through the hand she still held when Steve saw the genuine sincerity and openness in Kate's face and the obvious affection in her soft, dark brown eyes. She slowly and deliberately reached into the huge popcorn bowl that had been placed in front of them and offered him a handful, then took and ate some herself as she watched Cooper recollect his thoughts.

Taking a deep breath, Steve nodded and continued, "On the plane, I decided that this is a chance that doesn't come around too often—at least not for me; I always intended to marry and have kids, but somehow the right woman never showed up, or maybe she did, and I didn't recognize her." Cooper picked up his drink and took a deep swallow, then put it back down precisely in the middle of the dampening cocktail napkin, slowly twisting the glass. Lifting his eyes back to Kate, Cooper said very slowly and deliberately, "But I recognized you—that first day in Christine's office."

Kate was as still as she had ever been in her life, barely breathing as she listened to this man methodically discard every layer of himself—one by one until he was completely and totally vulnerable to her.

"The beginning of something new is a magical time; it's a time to converse and explore each other's hopes and dreams and hear about what each of us thinks *really* matters in this life we are living. You and I have each been successful. We've worked hard, taken risks, and we've enjoyed the benefits of all the sacrifices; but now, we're wondering what else there is other than work." Cooper stopped and with a gentle, loving smile, let his eyes caress Kate's face, and interpret her astonished expression. "Kate, I am no mind reader; truly I am not. But no thinking person receives the adulation that is being showered on you right now without wondering how you got here at this moment for *this* story rather than any of the others you have written, which may have been just as good."

Kate was speechless, for Steve was putting into words exactly what she was feeling right now and had expressed her emotions just as she was starting to be capable of feeling them. She was grateful that Cooper seemed to expect no comment from her, which was a very good thing because she was starting to feel a little bit drunk—and vulnerable. For some really weird reason, Kate realized that the emotions she was experiencing right now were flooding her system so thoroughly that she wanted to cry. Kind enough to appear as if he did not notice the emotional wreck that Kate was becoming, Cooper continued to speak in a relatively matter-of-fact way. "We are both pretty much at the top of our game right now. I had wanted to make chairman of cardiology by the time I was forty. I'll be thirty-eight next month, so I made it a couple years early." Cooper's gaze was on Kate, but in the darkened bar, she hoped that he had missed the wetness in her eyes. Kate refocused on Steve and this conversation that was unlike any other she had ever had with a man in her entire life. "And you, Ms. Townsend, are caught up in a hurricane that seems to be heading toward a category eight."

Steve leaned toward her and said, "Neither of us will have much time over the next year or so." Cooper's voice suddenly dropped a few decibels, and he murmured so low that Kate had to strain to hear it. "And believe me, there is nothing I would like better than ..." His eyes were suddenly black with longing, and Kate could feel the heat from Cooper's body even though they were not touching. With remarkable effort, Steve regained control of himself, once more taking her hand and predicted, "And if we don't take that time, if we let ourselves be overpowered by the desire we both feel, we can never recapture the innocence and the wonder of exploring each other in the ways that are most profound and lasting, and we'll never know what we could have become."

Cooper grabbed a large handful of popcorn and turned Kate's hand over to place a handful of kernels into it. "Eat," he ordered.

"I liked you the minute I met you last year." Steve paused for to take a few swallows of the fresh martini and consider what to say next. His gaze fixed on Kate's when he confessed, "But I was disappointed in you when you told me what you were going to call this series. We were sitting at this table last year when you told me the title. I thought 'Murder in the Texas Medical Center' sounded like an Agatha Christie novel, and I thought I'd misjudged you—that you were simply after a sensational story, after all, like any ambitious reporter would be. I tried to convince myself that no one could resist the salacious combination of medicine and murder. But then I read your articles." Cooper's eyes danced and his mouth widened into a huge grin as he continued to talk; his enthusiasm was infectious. Kate knew where he was headed in this conversation, but was surprised at the pleasure she felt in hearing Steve's observations and praise.

"You just used the title to reel in your reader, didn't you—yellow journalism without the stains? You never had any intention of dragging Lindsey McCall and the medical school through a media frenzy." Now Cooper's grin was back, and he was clearly delighted with himself and with *her*.

Listening, Kate wondered if Steve was right. From the very moment Kate had found the small piece about the incarceration of a famous cardiologist for the use of her experimental drug on her dying mother, Kate had wondered. She recalled her nagging sense that there had to be something more here—something to warrant an arrest and indictment of this doctor. Most people who knew Lindsey felt the same way. Cooper had made no secret about his feelings about the case; Eleanor Philbin had dropped some subtle hints as well. Then when she got to know Reardon and began to assimilate all of the information he was giving her, Kate realized that the Lindsey

McCall indictment and conviction was only a very small part of a much bigger story, one that has affected, or will in the future, every American.

At one point, she had called Reardon in Lausanne. The first two articles had been printed, and she was working on the third. Somehow, Kate had assimilated and been able to write about Reardon's complicated love of medicine with all its promise and all its heroes without being blinded to the dark side of power and greed. She had been struggling, though, with this third article that needed to relate to her title and to the facts: Lindsey McCall had been convicted of intentional murder and was in prison in Huntsville, Texas. But McCall would not see her; Kate tried every inducement she could think of, but nothing moved the physician. She would not see her.

Kate did meet with Lindsey's sister, Paula, quite a number of times. Paula was more than willing to talk about her sister and to answer any question about the McCall family, Ann McCall's illness, Tom McCall's early and dramatic death in a NASA test plane, or anything else, it seemed. Kate had two audiotapes completely filled with her questions and Paula's answers. Paula was a puzzle to Kate—very attractive, a shapely petite brunette looking ten years younger than her stated age of forty-seven; Kate thought Paula must have been a compelling witness for the district attorney against her sister, for she had remarkable recall and was quite articulate, with a distinct presence.

Kate and Paula first met at a Starbucks halfway between Houston and Clear Lake since Paula now resided in Clear Lake. Following the trial, Paula had resigned her cardiac care head nurse position in the medical center and had sold her family home in the Heights and lived in Clear Lake in the house where she had grown up. The moves had been gradual,

Paula had explained, when Kate asked why Paula had retired at the relatively young age of fifty. During the last several months of Ann McCall's life, Paula had been granted a leave of absence from her job and had spent most of her time in Clear Lake, caring for her mother. Paula was divorced, her children were grown, and she couldn't expect Lindsey to leave her job to care for their mother, so it fell to her.

When Paula explained all this to Kate, she revealed no emotion about these decisions and the sacrifices she was making. When she spoke to Kate, Paula's eye contact was excellent, and she had a very pleasant speaking voice; further, she seemed to have been coached very well by someone or was naturally a perfect witness. When answering a question, Paula gave only the information necessary to completely answer, unlike most people who feel a need to explain or justify. Kate was aware that Paula had to have told this story multiple times before and during the trial, so that may have been the reason for the smoothness of Paula's responses. Kate was impressed by her apparent sincerity and seeming absence of any resentment toward her famous sister and the matter-of-fact way she seemed to have viewed the situation—someone had to care for the mother, so it made sense for her to do it.

Paula had huge, expressive, blue eyes, which had an almost-hypnotic effect on Kate. She blinked rarely and seemed to have endless patience in answering questions about the events leading up to her sister's arrest and then her trial. Yet when Paula talked about Lindsey, she sounded as if she were speaking about someone whom she didn't know very well; it was subtle, but definitely there. A sense of estrangement was evident between the two sisters—at least in Paula's mind. However, Paula was very detailed about her mother and the onset of her debilitating illness; she even explained it to Kate in a way that helped Kate understand the pathology and progression of Ann McCall's disease. When talking about Lindsey, however, Paula answered very quickly even when it seemed that the question required some thought and recall.

Kate had decided to make the call to Reardon for some advice when she played the tape of her third meeting with Paula, and listened to Paula's voice and a couple of Paula's odd responses.

"Paula, I want to thank you for spending all this time with me, and I think we can wrap this up for today with only a few more questions." Kate recalled that Paula had nodded her curly, dark head and murmured a soft assent that the machine had not picked up. "I'm just trying to get a sense of your family when you were growing up, Paula. Would you say that you and Lindsey were close?"

Kate recalled those huge, blue eyes staring back at Kate when Paula replied, "I would say that Lindsey and I were not close."

Kate had waited, expecting Paula to add something explanatory like the fact that there was a ten-year age difference, that the two had very different interests as kids. Paula had said nothing at all; she had only continued to sit there, regarding Kate with a sort of distant air about her. Listening to the tape, Kate had timed the silence before Kate asked the next question: two minutes and thirty seconds.

Hoping to break this eerie self-control of Paula's, Kate had asked about the last few weeks of her mother's life and how Paula had coped with the impending loss of this woman for whom she'd provided care during most of her adult life.

"Paula, your mother was weakening every day; you're a cardiac nurse, so you could see the end approaching better than most. How did you cope with the stress of the constant care for your mom?"

Once more Paula's reply came instantly. "Well, I was

begging Lindsey to get approval for use of her new drug. I thought if we could get a compassionate care exception for Lindsey's new drug, Mother could live another year or two or, at the very least be more comfortable the last weeks of her life." Here Kate could hear a lot of emotion in Paula's voice—maybe tension or anger. Kate did not know, for Paula's expression had revealed nothing.

"You sound very sure that Lindsey's drug would work. Yet it hadn't been tested on humans, so how were you so sure that it would help?"

"My sister had been working on that drug for most of her life; of course, it would work."

Kate remembered Paula's expression when she had made that comment; her mouth was turned down almost in a condescending manner, while her large, blue eyes were wide and guileless. Kate had found the response odd—even disturbing—so she pressed.

"What do you mean, Paula? I'm a little confused. I can think of a few people—some, say, geniuses really—who work on projects their whole lives and are never successful. Like Tesla, the man who was treated so badly by Thomas Edison." Kate had realized that she may have overstepped her bounds so she had backed off by adding a more conciliatory comment, "You sound so confident, Paula. I'm just trying to understand why you had so much faith in the drug and in your sister, really …." She had let her voice soften and trail off to tone down her question in hopes that Paula would not get defensive. Kate had deliberately avoided Paula's gaze while she waited for her response; there was something about the woman that belied her calm facade, and Kate did not want to provoke her. This time, Paula's reply had not been immediate.

After a minute or two, Kate looked up to see Paula smiling at her, but the smile did not reach her eyes. "Yes, Edward Tesla, my sister read all kinds of biographies about him. When she began working on the drug, she was in the seventh grade, and she started to get interested in nuclear magnetic resonance to learn about molecules and their crystalline structures—" Paula interrupted herself with an exclamation and a laugh. "Gosh, listen to me, I sound as if I know what I'm talking about!" Once again, though, the humor was not reflected in Paula's eyes.

Paula had no intention of answering the question, Kate realized. And when Kate's gaze met Paula's, there was a flash of something like triumph in those wide, blue eyes; but it was gone so quickly, Kate wondered if she had imagined it. Kate had decided to end their conversation for that day, and so the remainder of the interview centered on safer ground. Sitting in her home office, Kate had not been able to make sense of it all. There was something off about Paula; her evasion to answering Kate's question about Digipro seemed strange as well, Kate had thought as she began to arrive at her decision to consult Hank Reardon.

⁓

When she placed the call to Hank, the sound of his voice provoked a grin on Kate's face as she delightedly filled him in with answers to his many questions, and she basked in his praise of her first two articles. Kate knew that Reardon was not a man to lavish praise on anyone, so she was certain that she'd exceeded his expectations, and that delighted her.

She suspected that Hank had limited time, so she tackled her problem right away. "I'm calling you because I've got an issue with this third article, and I don't know how to handle it. I'll quickly explain. I need to get back to my subject—at least according to my title—and this 'murder' thing feels like

I'm trying to grab a handful of water." Kate had heard Reardon's deep chuckle at her last comment, but Kate couldn't see a lot of humor here; she didn't have a lot of time—as usual—and felt frustrated. "As you had predicted, Hank, Lindsey refused to meet with me. I wrote, called, and at Eleanor's suggestion, asked McCall's lawyer, Todd Kensington, to intervene. Nothing worked. So Todd very generously set up a meeting with her sister, Paula, and I've met with her." Kate paused, considering. "We've met three, maybe four times, and … there's something not right here, Hank. The more I talked with Paula, the stranger she seemed."

"Strange, how?"

"It's really hard to explain; she just seems *too* good, too rehearsed, too controlled, too *everything* to be real. I understand that she has told her story hundreds of times, and I tried to convince myself that was all it was, but I think there's more to it—to her. And it's not good; there's a robotic quality to the woman that is unnerving. I suppose the flat affect could be caused by medications like antidepressants, and she's certainly had a plateful of misery handed to her to justify pills; but I get the distinct feeling that it's all an act. There's someone else behind the mask. Just once in hours of interviews, I was able to provoke a response." Kate explained quickly what she had done and that distinct flash of anger or triumph that Kate had seen so briefly.

"What do you want to do then? It sounds as if you're questioning this whole case or at least the truthfulness of the state's primary witness?"

Kate let out a long, slow sigh of relief. That was *exactly* how she felt. She had not read the court transcripts, she had not taken the time to find the court reporter and ask for the transcripts, plus she didn't know if a journalist had legal access to court transcripts in a criminal case. Now she wished she had taken the time to research all that, but she had only a few days before her deadline.

Reardon spoke again thoughtfully. "Look, Kate, I told you when you were here that I was puzzled about how this whole thing came down; even if Lindsey had used the drug on her mom, a charge of intentional murder seems like quite a stretch for a new molecular configuration of a two-thousand-plus-year-old drug; but the Houston DA got a grand jury to indict, so I just figured there were additional facts that I was not aware of ...." As his voice trailed off, Kate could practically hear Reardon thinking; she guessed he was in the library because when he was home that was where he worked, and by now he was most likely pacing around the room as he pondered Kate's dilemma. She waited.

Kate could hear pages turning, and then Reardon suggested, "Kate, I've just found your first two articles; let me reread them, make a phone call, then I'll call you back within the hour." With that, he was gone. While she waited for Hank's return call, Kate did the same thing he was doing—found and reread the articles so that she would have both pieces fresh in her mind when Reardon called her back.

Forty minutes later, Reardon was on her line. "I think you've answered your own question in your first article, Kate." Reardon read her words to her: "After several days of research and investigation, I was no closer to answers for the questions I began with; in fact, I was even more puzzled. It seemed as if each new piece of this story served to obfuscate rather than clarify the answers to my questions; my curiosity deepened as I studied this fairly innocuous list of facts, and I began to wonder if the conviction of Dr. Lindsey McCall encompassed contextual factors that were completely beyond her control."

"The way I see it, Kate, you've got three options. I think you're right in realizing that you need to address Lindsey. In your first article, you mapped out what you were doing and why; then you provided background about the context of your subject. Then in the second you explain, and very lucidly I might add, the complexities of medical school financing, the diminishing role of the government with the exception of the FDA, and the rise of an alliance between the pharmaceuticals and academic medical centers.

"Yes, you need to return to Lindsey, but what if you do that tangentially? Instead of digging into the courtroom morass that I think is unexplainable, why not return to McCall but with a twist: delve deeply into the life of a clinical researcher and use Lindsey McCall as your prototype. You understand the mind-numbing work that she went through as well as any of us in creating that molecule, and you know the animal and the clinical trials that were done. You also understand the significance of her insistence of testing the new drug against the old drug."

Reardon chuckled, "After all, you initially placed a question mark at the end of your title, right?"

❧

Kate had done exactly that. Thinking about the conversation with Reardon made Kate realize that Steve was right: From almost the very beginning, Kate had sympathized with McCall and had formed her own conclusion about the state's charge against McCall. The title *had* been intentionally provocative. Staring at Cooper, Kate silently nodded her agreement with his statement. *He's right*, she thought silently.

"I read every word of your series and thought each was better than the last. But you know what I liked the most, Kate Townsend?"

Kate returned Cooper's question very somberly. "No."

"You don't believe that she did anything wrong, even if she did use Digipro on her mother."

Cooper made the statement as a statement; he was not asking her. And then Steve jumped back to their personal relationship by adding, his eyes glowing, "There's one more reason that I think this can go somewhere, Kate." Steve's gaze had dropped the intensity, and he was scrutinizing Kate with those expressive, deep brown eyes. With another quick grin, he said, "You're tall enough for me; we'll look good dancing.

"I think we have a choice here; we can do what most men and women of our generation do next. I've certainly done it as I'd guess you have. Or we can decide this may be special and choose to protect it and see where we can go." Cooper paused to take a healthy swallow of his martini. "I choose the latter but you need to know, my dear, that I *want* you." Steve's voice became husky and tremulous at those last few words; Kate's response was involuntary, immediate, and physiological. She conjured up a fake cough to recover.

Steve sat quietly, done. But Kate could read the hope and concern in his eyes that couldn't be masked by his slightly nervous smile.

Kate cleared her throat while she collected her thoughts.

"At the risk of echoing you, Steve, I liked you from the get-go too." Grinning, she said, "You're tall enough for me." Her smile faded, and she stared back at Cooper somberly. "I'll bet I've interviewed hundreds of men—and women too, of course—but I can count on both hands those who can handle change in leadership and factions with the grace that you do, Dr. Cooper."

"I suspect the last year has been the same for both of us: no time for anything. But honestly, that's the way I've set up my life, Steve." She was smiling wryly. "It's safer that way." Kate held up a restraining hand to Steve as he started to interrupt her. "If I don't get this said now, I'll lose my nerve—truly I will." With a somewhat tremulous smile, Kate explained, "You are a whole lot gutsier than I am, but I will follow your lead.

"The week I spent with Hank Reardon was precious to me, for so many reasons. Strangely, all the information he gave me about clinical research and academic medicine land is at the end of a very long list.

"His wife, Peg, was dying, from the very same illness that took my mother when I was just a kid. But being there with them—two people who were so much in love—made me see something I'd been too young and selfish to see when I watched my mother and dad behave the very same way. Back then, I thought my parents were liars and cowards. That week that I spent with Hank and Peg taught me that my parents were just the opposite: courageous and truthful.

"Reardon works hard, as hard as anyone I've ever seen, but he makes the time to *be* with his wife and daughter. When they're together, Hank is *there*. Forgive me for sounding like a half-baked Buddhist, but when I watched this family for the week that I lived with them, I realized that I had never done what Reardon did so naturally. I've always made sure that work was always the priority so that my relationships with men had no place in my life except as hobbies: a way to give myself a break between assignments—diversions, nothing more, nothing less." Kate scanned Cooper's attractive, masculine face, which was completely focused on her, noting the way he cocked his head very slightly to his left as if to hear her better. Drawing a very deep breath, Kate whispered, "And I have decided that I no longer want to be that way." Watching him start to relax, Kate's racing heart began to slow, and she basked in this new and foreign feeling of surrender.

"You're right, Steve—in everything you have said. You never mentioned the word *sex* but you haven't needed to; we're very attracted to each other. You know it, and I know it. Very frankly, I'm relieved that we'll not end up in bed tonight. I can't believe I'm saying that, but it's true." Kate stopped and swallowed, then said, "What you've said about getting to know one another? It's scary, Steve, *really* scary—much more frightening than hopping into the sack."

Kate was quiet for a long moment, and then continued, "How warped is that? I'm quite comfortable in jumping into bed with you but afraid of getting to know you … and probably more so—you getting to know me." Her words were tumbling out in the effort to get all of this said, to be honest, more honest than she had been in a very long time.

"I am not sure what I want next. I've been so focused for the last fifteen years on achieving the goal that every reporter has: the Pulitzer … and now ….?" Kate's voice trailed off, and she sighed deeply. Cooper had not taken his eyes off Kate, and she could see as well as *feel* his understanding.

In a deliberate attempt to lighten her mood, Kate joked, "So this takes a lot of pressure off both of us, doesn't it?"

Kate sat back in her chair, quite content to enjoy the easing of pressure, along with more than a little happiness. *No*, she thought, *it's joy.* She grinned broadly and gaily at Steve. "What now, my friend?"

Cooper had listened without interruption, his expression a mixture of concentration and affection. Now he nodded and smiled widely at her. "First, we need to discuss food, to be sought after we finish the martinis, of course. Tell me what you're in the mood to eat, and I'll tell you about the next phase ahead for Dr. Lindsey McCall." Laughing at the astonished expression on Kate's face, Cooper commanded, "Drink up! The sooner we finish the drinks and get to a restaurant, the sooner I'll tell you about what Todd Kensington has in mind."

Fifteen minutes later, Kate and Steve sat at a table for two at one of the dozens of trendy restaurants that dotted the River Oaks area. The décor was chrome and black, which was a little dated Kate thought, but the black leather chairs were wonderfully comfortable, wide and lushly upholstered; Kate wished for a chair like this in her condo, but she knew she'd fall asleep in it. Sitting there, relaxing, pretending to read the menu and feeling the effects of the vodka, Kate realized how tired she was; bone tired. When she looked up, she saw Steve's warm and affectionate deep brown eyes on her.

Smiling at her, Cooper said, "You're really beat, aren't you, Kate?"

"Yes, and I didn't know it until this very minute. You know how you just keep going and going, getting maybe four or five hours of sleep. You think this is good, everyone works like this; I'm young and love my job. And then all of a sudden, it hits you like a ton of bricks. You need to slow down, or you're going to be sick."

Steve was nodding vigorously. "Yep, you're describing my life correctly, Kate." Continuing to study her, Cooper suggested with a smile, "The best treatment for exhaustion is about twelve hours of sleep and"—glancing at his watch—"we'll have you in dreamland by ten, I promise. Meanwhile, I think a dose of some heavy protein is in order." And he proceeded to order two New York Strip sirloin steaks, with Caesar salads and baked potatoes, for them both.

Fifteen minutes later, Kate was relishing the taste of the perfectly grilled steak as she listened to Steve explain Kensington's plan to overturn McCall's conviction. Now that the food was dampening the effects of all the vodka she had consumed, Kate's head had cleared, and she felt renewed energy.

When their entrées had arrived, the servings looked enormous, but both Cooper and Kate were dispatching their dinners with ease. Between mouthfuls, Steve had explained that he had testified for Kensington during Lindsey's trial, and that following the conviction, Todd had called to ask Steve if he would be willing to testify if the appeal was granted.

Steve explained, "I checked him out once I learned the verdict; the guy has lost only three cases in over twenty years of defending doctors." Steve was having trouble with his steak; the knife was sawing the piece of meat quite ineffectively. But before either Kate or Cooper could ask for another, the sharp young Hispanic waiter was on it: delivered a new knife, then stood to wait while Steve used it. The new knife cut through the meat as if it were butter. Cooper smiled at the young man in appreciation.

Cooper looked at Kate to get himself back on track. "Lindsey's case was the third; Kensington was really devastated." Steve stopped to cut chew and swallow several chunks of the meat then glanced at Kate's plate to make sure that she was eating, which she was, with gusto.

"Todd thinks he made a number of mistakes. He blamed himself for taking the case in the first place because he was not trained in criminal law and this was obviously a criminal case, the seriousness of which he underestimated. And then he completely misread the jury. The first times we met, Todd exuded confidence and told me that he thought the case would be wrapped up in less than a week. But the last time was an entirely different story."

"He'd met Paula."

"What did you say, Kate? Who's Paula?" Steve was gaping at Kate in an effort to understand.

Kate was sympathizing with Lindsey's lawyer; she could only imagine the devastating impact of Lindsey's sister in that courtroom and on the jury. She was sure that Paula Livingston had confounded Kensington's entire case.

"Lindsey's older sister, Paula Livingston, head nurse of St. Michael's cardiac care until she had to take early retirement to care for their dying mother."

Kate's tone was phlegmatic, but the impact of her comments on Steve was explosive. Looking as he'd been struck by a thunderbolt, Cooper's eyes widened, and he breathed out a long low whispered expletive before asking Kate, "Of course. I remember how much her testimony damaged Lindsey's case. And now you've interviewed her, haven't you?"

Kate nodded slowly and sadly. Kate stared at her plate and the half-eaten steak, realizing that she had lost her appetite. Looking over at Steve, she noted that he looked as if he had quit as well

Their waiter reappeared, one hand raised to carry something flaming on a relatively large platter. The young man was slim and dark, and Kate could see his teeth flashing as he smiled, aware of the attention he was getting as he carried the flaming concoction over to their table. With a flourish, he set down what looked like a chocolate cake, but as Kate stared at it, she realized that it was chocolate … something; she had no idea what it was. When she looked up, she saw that Steve, the waiter as well as most of the other customers in the restaurant, were watching her.

The aroma coming from the exotic dessert was seductive, so Kate decided that someone had to do it; she took her spoon and dipped it into the gooey mess to scoop up a liberal serving. "Oh my gosh," Kate exclaimed. "This is to die for. What is in this?" She thought she could taste cherry, as well as orange along with the dark, sweet chocolate.

Kate grinned at Steve, shrugged, and challenged, "Best you get your spoon out, Doctor, or this whole thing will disappear."

Steve laughed and then, eyebrows high, exclaimed, "Lord save me from getting between this woman and her chocolate." Then he took his turn and swallowed a big spoonful of the dessert.

"This really is superb, Steve. What is it?"

"I have no idea. It's called the Chef's Special dessert on the menu. I'd had it a couple times before and remembered how great it was." Steve looked at Kate as he licked his spoon. "But it's a lot more fun eating it with you." Steve thought about his last girlfriend, a ballerina named Briana with the Houston Ballet. They had dated for over a year; their relationship had worked mostly because her schedule was as demanding as his but on a lark, Cooper had brought her here to this restaurant. In a celebratory mood after the Stanford Medical School had selected him for chief of cardiology, Steve had wanted some company. Briana picked at her salad, mostly lettuce leaves and without any dressing, a few vegetables, and had eaten maybe an eighth of a teaspoon of this dessert. Steve had been ravenous; he'd not had the time for anything other than coffee the whole day but felt like a glutton with every bite he had had eaten. They had very amicably decided that this simply wasn't working for either of them. Cooper had not dated anyone since then.

Steve grinned in appreciation as he watched Kate unabashedly chow down on the dessert; she was so much more fun, he thought—more fun than anyone he could remember dating in many years.

Our life is an apprenticeship to the truth that around every circle another can be drawn; that there is no end in nature, but every end is a beginning; that there is always another dawn risen on the mid-noon, and under every deep a lower deep opens.
—Henry David Thoreau, Essays

17

Following the Dr. Steve Cooper-prescribed twelve hours of sleep, Kate felt like a new person; lying on her bed grinning like the proverbial Cheshire cat, Kate considered all that had transpired during the last several days. Kate stretched luxuriously as she delighted in the knowledge that for once, there was no deadline she had to make, that she was sure Steve Cooper could be a fixture in her life, and that Kensington and Cooper wanted her help with Lindsey McCall. Kate pondered that last thought.

Thinking back to the Pulitzer award ceremony at the River Oaks Country Club, Kate recalled Eleanor Philbin's enigmatic comments about McCall to Kate and her suggestion that Kate meet with her and Marguerite this weekend. Eleanor had said something about "us all getting together" to talk. Steve had explained something about a meeting when he had driven her home last night, but Kate remembered little of his conversation, as he had to wake her up when they arrived at her condo. She'd been too exhausted to be embarrassed or to apologize; Kate realized that she'd only walked into her bedroom and fallen into bed, not bothering to kiss Cooper good night or even lock her door. Jumping out of bed, she ran out to the hallway to make sure that the door was locked and it was.

For the first time, Kate noticed the sunlight streaming through her sheer, white drapes in the living room and wondered just how late it was because she was always up by six to fit in her run at Rice or at Memorial. As she wandered into the kitchen to make some coffee, Kate noticed the time. The kitchen clock read ten thirty, but that couldn't be right; she went back to her bedroom to check her alarm clock, which she kept set at six. That clock, too, read ten thirty; puzzled, Kate picked up the clock and saw that her alarm had been turned off. Quickly deciding that she must have forgotten that she'd turned off the alarm, Kate raced to the bathroom to brush her teeth and wash her face so that she could get a quick three miles in before the blistering heat of another tropical Houston day. As Kate was pulling on her jogging shorts, she suddenly stopped still, remembering that Steve had driven her home last night. "Good thing, too," Kate muttered to herself because the combination of alcohol and exhaustion could have been lethal; but that meant her car was still in the Marfreless parking lot, a good twenty-minute drive from her place in Montrose.

Just as Kate was about to pick up the phone to call a cab to take her to get her car, the phone rang.

"How about a run in Memorial then breakfast at the La Madeleine in River Oaks and then I'll drop you by Marfreless to get your car?" Cooper sounded cheery and wide awake.

"Super, I'm just tying up my running shoes now so—"

"That's good because I'm right outside your door."

Sure enough when Kate went to the door, there he was holding his cell phone while he grinned at her. *My goodness,* Kate thought as she motioned for him to come in while she searched for her purse. *He gets better and better looking.* Slinging her purse over her shoulder, Kate took a band to tie her hair back and then lifted her head to kiss Cooper's cheek. Unfortunately, Steve was turning toward Kate as she did this, causing their lips to meet briefly. Somewhat shakily, Kate led the way through her front door, then shut, and locked it. Reaching behind her, Kate grabbed Steve's large warm hand. "Come on, I'll race you out to the car."

Ninety minutes later, Kate was sitting across from Steve at La Madeleine's. Immediately upon their arrival, Kate had thrown water on herself, finger combed her hair in the bathroom, and sniffed under her arms to make sure that she didn't look or smell too bad so that she could sit fairly comfortably while Steve's gaze scrutinized her every feature. Kate was dark, which meant that she really didn't need makeup; her eyebrows and lashes were very dark, and her olive complexion took on a golden cast when she was exposed to the sun. Cocking her head to her left, she lifted an eyebrow to ask, "So you like the sweaty, smelly type of girl, Dr. Cooper?"

Steve had been comparing Brianna to Kate again as he sat enjoying the natural good looks of Kate Townsend. He and Brianna had spent several weekends out of town together, and he had forced himself to endure patiently the hours Brianna spent with her hair, makeup, and dress. Brianna was a beautiful woman but did not feel fully dressed without her mask of makeup and a perfectly coiffured hairstyle. Initially Steve had hoped that their relationship would develop into something other than occasional weekend sex but then realized that he didn't really want more than that.

Cooper smiled back at Kate's flushed face, still glowing with a light sheen of perspiration. "No, Ms. Townsend, I *love* the sweaty, smelly type of girl." And he enjoyed seeing the color heighten in her cheeks. "Damn good thing, you're on a plane back to San Francisco tomorrow, Cooper," he murmured to himself under his breath. Steve caught the flash of those deep brown eyes and knew that Kate had heard him. He grabbed her hand, "Come on, sweaty one, let's go get some coffee and breakfast."

Over coffee, Steve decided to bring Kate up to speed about the meeting that night. He had explained the whole plan but wondered just how much Kate had remembered from their conversation at dinner; her first question confirmed his suspicion that she recalled next to nothing. He was certainly not surprised, given the intensity of their conversation about the two of them and of her work over the last several months.

"Sorry, but the name Rich Jansen means nothing at all to me." Kate had dropped her eyes to grab the enormous cup of coffee, but she glanced back at Steve and saw the laughter on his face and in his eyes. "That's funny?"

Steve could literally watch her processing and waited while she figured it out. "You know, when I woke up this morning, I wondered how much of what you told me last night had penetrated." Laughing, Kate shrugged and admitted frankly, "Guess the vodka, wine, and fatigue ate up some brain cells. Thanks for driving me home, Steve." Kate marveled at how comfortable she felt with this man, warts and all. "I think you'd better start at the beginning."

"I'll cut to the chase, Kate. Rich Jansen is the new chief warden at Huntsville Prison. I've not met him yet, but Jansen and Kensington apparently go back to their law school days. After law school, the two of them went into practice together until Jansen decided to join the police force. He was captain of the Harris County Homicide Department until he was critically wounded in a robbery." Cooper waited until he saw the recognition appear on Kate's face because the media had been all over that case for weeks. He was sure that she had done at least one story on Jansen.

"Oh my gosh, I'm slipping. I did the first couple of articles on him; then Jeff took me off that story while Jansen was still critical." Kate remembered now and was stunned that the man had not only recovered but was also working again. From the sounds of the initial reports, the guy was dying; it was only a matter of time.

Nodding his agreement, Steve continued to speak, "Well apparently, Jansen is fully recovered and has decided to help Todd with Lindsey McCall's appeal." Interpreting Kate's quizzical expression correctly, Steve said, "There's a story that Rich will tell us tonight—you, if you agree to keep it off the record. And yes, everybody agrees that this is highly unorthodox, maybe even unethical for a warden, even a chief warden to be actively working to help an inmate win an appeal—everyone that is, except Jansen and Governor Greg Bell."

Kate thought back to her waking ruminations about the absence of deadlines and sighed.

Cooper was watching Kate carefully. Although he had been around her less than twenty-four hours since meeting her, he honestly felt as if he knew her as well as she knew herself, maybe even better. It was strange, even eerie, but Cooper didn't doubt the sense. He understood that Kate was doing battle; the series had taken everything she had to complete it. Now she was being asked to give more. Yet she had opened the door to this next step by writing an extraordinary analysis of the Lindsey McCall case in her clear and convincing prose, suggesting that maybe there was an injustice here: Maybe the perpetrator was actually the victim.

And Kate had to know that it wasn't over. It was far from over. More than anything, Steve wanted to take Kate Townsend in his arms and tell her that she had worked hard enough and that she could relax and enjoy the life of a Pulitzer Prize-winning reporter. But he couldn't; Lindsey had done nothing wrong, and he'd known that at the time but had never really processed it until he met Kate. So Steve waited and said nothing.

At least two, maybe three, minutes had passed while Kate had silently said good-bye to leisure. But when she looked over at Steve, her face had lost the softened feminine contours, and the decisive angular journalist regarded Steve intently. "So Eleanor Philbin has arranged all of this, right?"

"Kate, I've met the Philbins maybe once or twice; I don't really know who arranged it all, but you have to know that you set it up in your series, don't you?"

"Yes and no, Steve. Once I began to think about Lindsey and guess at what she was like—"

"What do you mean, *guess* at what she's like? You interviewed her, didn't you?"

"No, she refused to see me. I asked Hank and Todd to call her for me, but she would not speak to them either."

Cooper had wondered why Kate hadn't written directly about Lindsey. Kate started to explain, "I imagine that Lindsey McCall evoked a good deal of jealousy in most of the women she came in contact with. Hank Reardon called her the most stunning woman he had ever met and Hank is not given to hyperbole." She waited for a response from Cooper and was gratified to hear his agreement with Reardon's assessment of McCall's looks. She was grateful, too, that Steve did not add some insipid and ingratiating attempt to assert that Kate was more beautiful than McCall.

"And I also met with a bunch of the nurses who had taken care of Ann McCall. I tried six ICUs at Houston Medical before I found the one that Ann McCall had been in; that was the tough part. But when I got to the CICU, they were having a really slow day, and four of the nurses on duty that day had taken care of Mrs. McCall and were willing to talk with me provided that I didn't print their names—that was easy."

Steve regarded her carefully, realizing that this lady was deadly in so many ways.

The humor now gone from Kate's eyes, she said softly, "These folks had figured out that some 'crackpot' had called the police to accuse Lindsey of murder. One nurse said that it wasn't all that unusual to pull out all the stops on a dying patient." Lindsey stopped herself as she realized that she was repeating information that she had written in the articles.

"To answer your question, finally, yes, I knew I was openly challenging the indictment and the conviction. That certainly wasn't my intention when I started this whole investigation. But you know you begin these things, and they actually take you over." Kate picked up the fresh hot coffee and took a deep swallow. "When this all started, I figured that it was unusual and could be of interest to the public simply because of the drama of a mother-daughter relationship gone south. Then once I spent that afternoon with you and saw Lindsey's lonely, ugly lab, something began to whisper to me." Kate stared at Steve contemplatively. "I tried to make a case to myself about a crazy researcher Lindsey, who was so obsessed with proving that her new drug could work that she was willing to risk her mother's life to do it. But could not do it.

"I've never read the court transcripts of this case. For a while, I kicked myself for not taking the time to get them, but I'm confident that Masters' case rested on the argument that Lindsey McCall had worked her entire adult life on her drug and had become obsessed with proving to the world and to herself that she could do it. So Lindsey grabbed the opportunity to test her drug on her mother, treating her own mother as if she were one of her research animals. Her sister, Paula, was only too happy to provide the context: herself as the martyred daughter who gave up everything for her mother, while her genius female Frankenstein of a sister labored in her laboratory caring for nothing or no one."

Kate smiled sardonically and lifted a dark, sculpted

eyebrow, still holding Cooper's gaze. "And the strange thing, Steve, the really bizarre thing is that I think that's a fairly accurate description of Dr. Lindsey McCall, don't you?"

Steve didn't bother to respond to her; it was apparent that Kate was inside McCall's head. Kate was right, of course: that *was* a fairly accurate depiction of Lindsey, albeit somewhat dramatically phrased. He had never thought about her that way, but then he'd not spent the time analyzing Lindsey that Kate had—nowhere near as much. But Kate was heading somewhere, and he was curious to know where.

Kate was now taking apart the half of the baguette that sat on her plate. Unconsciously, Kate was tearing off a small piece as if to chew and swallow it, but then she placed the little piece of bread back on the plate. She did this three times before she realized that both she and Cooper were watching the steadily accumulating pile of uneaten pieces of bread.

"You could say that about any one of us, Steve."

Kate's expression was tense, and she stared at Steve expectantly. When Cooper just knit his eyebrows together and opened his mouth to express his confusion, Kate cut him off, sighing. "You and I are where we are because we have worked like Lindsey—obsessively. Maybe not to the degree that she did, but it's only a matter of scale. We've both sacrificed our personal lives and even our family obligations because of our work. Most people will not do that. They choose wives, husbands, and kids, along with all that come with those responsibilities.

"Paula is the norm. People can see themselves in Paula, but a Lindsey? Your average person here in Houston or anywhere else in this country cannot identify with a woman who purposefully cuts herself off from everyone and everything to work on a dream.

"Worse yet? She succeeds at this quixotic, seemingly impossible task; she creates an improvement on a centuries-old cardiac drug; one that will bring relief and maybe life to millions suffering from heart disease." Kate picked up the remaining small piece of the baguette, buttered, and ate it. Swallowing, she took a swallow of her coffee and then placed it carefully down on the small, wooden table. "So Masters really had an easy job. All he had to do was to point out the differences between these two sisters: here is wife, mother, nurse who gives up her *job* for heaven's sake to care for her dying mother. And well, here is Lindsey: stunning, brilliant, successful beyond the wildest dreams of anyone in that courtroom and totally unlikeable. *Of course*, someone with all those gifts must be evil."

Cooper could only stare at Kate, enthralled and speechless upon hearing Kate's rigorous analysis of a woman he'd known for over twenty years. Her ability to assimilate information from diverse and disparate sources and then apply them to the practicalities of a problem exceeded that of anyone Steve had encountered previously. Suspecting that Kate was looking for some feedback from him, he glanced at her, expecting to see those deep brown eyes boring into his psyche. Instead, she was staring somewhere to the left of the long bar where La Madeleine displayed their breads and baked goods. Cooper turned his head in the same direction as Kate's gaze but could see only the door to the parking lot. He doubted that she was seeing anything in front of her eyes; instead, she was quite clearly very deep in thought.

Without changing the direction of her gaze, Kate quietly said, "I think Paula gave the mother that drug, and I'll bet Lindsey knows that Paula did it." Then she closed her eyes and took several deep breaths, looking to Cooper as if she were praying or meditating. When Kate opened her eyes again, she turned to Steve and smiled. "Of course, I have no proof of what I just said, and I have not said those words before, even to myself, Steve; but it's the only thing that makes sense. I think Paula hates her sister, is jealous of her, and probably has been for most of their lives. And I think Paula is happy as hell that Lindsey is sitting in Huntsville prison."

Steve was thinking about the meeting tonight at the Philbins'; he wondered if Kate planned to inform the group that would be gathered there of her conjecture. Todd Kensington would most certainly be interested in hearing what Kate had to say, and he knew that Kate would be fascinated by the tale of McCall's medical exploits while in prison. Tonight would be a most intriguing evening, he had no doubt. Feeling Kate's gaze on him, he smiled at her and commanded, "Eat and drink, you need nourishment. I think tonight may answer many questions for both of us."

Now is my way clear, now is the meaning plain:
Temptation shall not come in this kind again.
The last temptation is the greatest treason:
To do the right thing for the wrong reason.
—T. S. Eliot, *Murder in the Cathedral*

18

Rich Jansen rolled back the leather chair of his desk, put his feet up on it, and closed his eyes. The past week had been a bear, and Rich was a lot more concerned than he had admitted when he had assured Todd that he wanted to help write the brief for McCall's appeal. As the newly appointed commissioner and chief warden of the Huntsville Prisons, he had no business working on behalf of an inmate. There were a thousand reasons why this was not smart; foremost among them were small matters such as conflict of interest, numerous ethics violations with the Texas bar, and placing the governor in an untenable position if the media learned of his involvement with one of the inmates in the prison where Jansen was in charge. The risk to the governor had bothered him so much that Rich had called Bell the day before to inform him that he had agreed to assist Todd Kensington in writing the brief to appeal the conviction of Dr. McCall. Jansen had called Bell from his cell phone, chuckling about the mounting level of his paranoia now that he was back working in government.

Still euphoric about Jansen's efficient, effective, and unobtrusive disposal of Dr. Lance Pettigrew's lawsuit against the State of Texas, Governor Greg Bell took Jansen's call immediately. "Hey, Warden, how are things down in Huntsville on this gorgeous October day?"

Despite his unease, Rich had to smile. The Texas governor could wear his Texas accent like a favorite shirt; when it suited him, Greg Bell could speak deep East Texas with the best of them; but when necessary, he was also fluent in East Coast Ivy League. Today was East Texas.

When Jansen replied formally, "Governor, there is something I need to speak with you about; I'll need about fifteen minutes of your time." Bell answered with a request to give him ten minutes and to wait for a callback.

Rich sat waiting for Bell to clear his office and call him back on his private line. Bell had given Rich the number of his private line to use for emergencies, but Rich saw no need to use it for anything but an emergency. This was no emergency—yet.

Twenty minutes later, Jansen had related to Bell all the relevant details he had learned about McCall during his first week on the job, the highlights of his interview with Julie Grayson, and his intention to speak with the now-famous Kate Townsend to see if she would be willing to partner with Jansen—initially off the record—on McCall's behalf; the benefit to Townsend would be a firsthand account of the events that had transpired in the Huntsville infirmary. When Rich stopped talking, the silence at the other end was complete—so complete that he wondered if the connection had been severed. Forcing himself to remain silent, Jansen counted the seconds to pass the time until Bell replied.

Speaking pure East Texas, Bell said, "Thanks for letting me know this, Rich. This could be awkward." Bell's pronunciation and use of the understated adverb would have been comical if Rich were feeling humorous. "Awkward if you and I were called to explain this, and I believe in guessing at the temperature of the water at which I'll be parboiled"—there were a few more seconds where Rich could hear clearly the sound of Bell's fingers drumming his desk—"but I think the benefits stack up a lot higher than the risks, Jansen ... if you're right and this lady is innocent ..." More silence. "And if we can get that Kate Townsend to continue asking the right questions and if she agrees to our timetable, then maybe no one will notice all the ethics violations you are committing and all the responsibility I'm shirking as governor. Those are some big *ifs* there, aren't they?"

Rich remained silent, recognizing Bell's habit of thinking out loud when confronted with a new problem.

"Go for it, Rich. But keep me posted, and next time you need me, use the private line. If I'm not in the office, this line automatically switches over to my cell, and it's live 24/7. Oh, and call me after ya'll meet at Eleanor Philbin's house tomorrow night."

Jansen was sitting at his desk in the home office of Bell's New Waverly cabin that Rich now called home and wondered for the one hundredth time since their conversation how much of what he had told Bell the night before had been already told to him by Eleanor Philbin. The guy was a consummate politician; although he must have known some of what Rich had talked about, Bell never intimated that any of this was old news. Nor had he asked any questions. Bell had simply listened.

Rich had not known what to expect; he'd been ready for Bell to tell him to drop it, and he'd also been ready for a typical political response: If you decide to continue with this, do it, but know that you're on your own. And Jansen had been crystal clear about what he would do if he'd been ordered by Bell to extricate himself from the McCall case now; he would have resigned immediately. There was no way that he could walk away from this woman and the bizarre circumstances surrounding her indictment and conviction. Truthfully, Jansen had been captivated by Lindsey McCall from the first moment he laid eyes on her early Monday morning.

Rich believed that he may have been able to maintain the suitable professional distance and detachment from the TMC physician, which was required by his position, had he not become entangled with Lance Pettigrew, former medical director of Huntsville Prisons. Knowing what McCall had risked to save the life of a young inmate precluded any sense of detachment from this woman—at least until Jansen had satisfied himself that Lindsey McCall deserved to be in prison.

That Bell had given him a green light despite the risky business they were now both embroiled in should have relieved Jansen, but it didn't. Strangely, he would have preferred the standard political response of plausible deniability to Bell's surprising unqualified support. He didn't mind placing his own career at risk. But he surely didn't relish incriminating anyone else in this endeavor, particularly the governor of the state of Texas who just happened to be on the short list for president.

Startled at the feel of a cold nose pressing into the hand that had held his cell phone and now was hanging by his side, Jansen decided that Max was right; a run in the woods was exactly what the doctor ordered. Five minutes later, Jansen and his Doberman were jogging slowly through the trees of the forest behind Bell's log home. They had left at six, and the shadows were lengthening in the forest, but there was adequate light for them to do about four miles. The only sounds were Max's panting breath and the rhythmic sound of Jansen's feet pounding the cushioned forest floor.

"This beats running on pavement back in the city, doesn't it, boy?" Rich asked Max as he began to drop down to a fast walk heading back home. Max, about half a yard ahead, turned back at the sound of Rich's voice and stood in the center of the path, tongue lolling and grinning to display his affirmation about the superiority of the forest over pavement.

The fog in his brain now cleared. Rich grabbed a towel in the downstairs bathroom to mop the sweat off of his face and hair, turned on XM's symphony station, and grabbed Max's bowl to feed him some kibble and raw hamburger. The dog watched Jansen's every move; when Rich talked to him, he cocked his head, seeming to understand every word. When Rich placed the bowl on the elevated stand, the dog stared at it, but waited until Rich released him from his stay.

Rich decided it was cool enough for some scotch, so he filled a glass with crushed ice and poured a couple of fingers of Macallan over the ice. Jansen had made vegetable lasagna for a dinner that he had prepared for the acting warden at the Walls the night before and decided to reheat the dish and then mixed a green salad together. Slowly, the aroma of the marinara sauce, cooking vegetables, and cheese began to fill the great room and kitchen. Rich stood in the great room and looked out at the darkening shadows of evening, watching the individual pine trees slowly begin to blur, and then retreat into the density of the forest as night claimed the Piney Woods.

Smiling as the strains of Dvorak's "New World Symphony" filled the house, Jansen closed his eyes and let the music wash over him to fill him with some of the beauty, the innocence, and the grandeur that had inspired the young Czech to create his ode to America.

An hour later, Rich was again at his desk, figuring that he had about four hours before he would need to knock off and get to sleep. Deciding to get the work related to his real job done first, he reached into his briefcase and removed the thick stack of paperwork that Wanda had prepared for him before he left for the weekend. On the top was the personnel action form approving Bob Cleary for warden at the Walls. Rich leaned back in his chair to think about Cleary, freely admitting to himself his bias for the kid based on his six-year stint in the corps. Rich reviewed his list of pros and cons one last time. The con list was short consisting of two facts only: youth and inexperience. Jansen had noticed Cleary immediately upon walking into the conference center last Monday. Was it truly only ten days ago that he had turned his life completely upside down?

Cleary had stood out: the patently military physique, posture, hair, and dress starkly separated him from the rest of the group. With Cleary being a good ten years younger, at twenty-eight, than the next youngest warden, Rich was certain that the kid had taken his share of harassment from his colleagues; but the subject had never came up at his dinner with Cleary the night before. Jansen had learned that his most profitable interviewing technique was to invite his prospective candidate for dinner and drinks to see how they performed when he was relaxed; with a few glasses of wine, the fundamental nature of a person rose quickly to the surface.

The dinner last evening had confirmed Jansen's impression of a man young in years but old in experience; combat tends to age a person. But the kid wasn't cynical; he had talked with genuine relief about Jansen's Monday meeting list of expectations at the prison. Cleary had no interest in playing bully to those unable to defend themselves. Rich had seen his files from the marines and knew that Bob Cleary had seen more combat than Rich Jansen had ever dreamed of, but somehow the trauma of war had not seemed to damage him.

Rich had deliberately opened up their conversation in ways that Cleary could talk "in private" about what the warden at Ellis was doing or Byrd, but Cleary never bit. The last time Jansen brought up the name of one of the other wardens to

Cleary, the kid had simply fixed his gaze on Jansen and asked, "Sir, are you asking me a question?" Jansen had laughed. Rich had learned, the hard way, that one of the most toxic characteristics of members of a group was splitting: the irresistible urge of one person to prove himself superior to the rest. Jansen had seen the effects of a master when he was in the sheriff's office; he would never again underestimate the ability of a single individual to destroy an entire group through gossip. The last name Rich had brought up to Cleary had been that of Roy Jenkins. Roy was a fool, and Rich wasn't sure if *he* could have kept his mouth shut if his and Cleary's roles were reversed. But Cleary did; he never said a critical word. Jansen happily signed the authorization for a twenty percent raise and promotion.

Next on the pile were several pages clipped together: Dr. Lance Pettigrew's resignation, his accrued vacation and sick time converted into dollars for his final check, the check, and a new form authorizing the state to search for a new medical director for the Huntsville Prisons. Briefly, Jansen mused about Pettigrew, about what had gone wrong in his life and had caused him to hand himself over to the whims of drugs and alcohol. He signed the forms.

Glancing at his watch, Rich saw that he had about two hours left to get to sleep by midnight. Standing and stretching, he then dropped to the floor to sit cross-legged in front of Max, who was splayed across the length of the bed. The dog's eyes immediately opened, but he lay still, waiting for his favorite part of the day. Rich leaned over and began to scratch the dog's chest and abdomen; at his touch, Max stretched his body as much as possible to expose the most skin possible to the hands of the person he loved most in this world.

Rising from his crouch, Rich quieted the dog and returned to his desk where he reached into his briefcase to remove the tape recorder. Placing it squarely in the center of the desk, he pushed play and began listening to Julie Grayson's voice. Jansen had reached Julie on Tuesday after leaving messages on her cell, home phone, and. She had returned his calls late Monday afternoon, apologizing profusely for not getting back to him sooner. Between coaching her high school soccer, tennis, and basketball teams, teaching high school math Julie somehow managed to co-parent along with her husband, Ted, three girls and a small boy. After listening to the woman think out loud about her schedule that week, Rich was exhausted. The two finally agreed that Rich should come to Julie and Ted's Friendswood house with Rich reassuring Julie that the one-way two-hour drive was no big deal. A typical math teacher, Julie gave Rich precise directions to her rambling ranch home.

When Jansen arrived at the house, he realized how nervous he was; he had not yet talked with Bell to get his okay for this venture, and he was all too aware that he had no legitimate reason to interview Mrs. Grayson. Deciding that he and Max needed a walk around the block, he had barely started a rapid pace with Max at his side when he heard a woman's voice.

"Mr. Jansen? Come on in and bring your dog with you, please; we have a large fenced backyard, and the girls have wanted a Doberman for years." With that, Julie Grayson crouched down and called with both palms extended in front of her, a treat in each palm. "Hey, boy, want a treat?"

Immediately, Max pivoted to Rich, begging for permission.

"Okay, Max, you can go."

With that, the Doberman walked back to the house and sat in front of Julie, craning his head to look back at Rich, while restraining himself from taking the treats, which were right in front of his nose. Charmed by Max, Julie exclaimed, "What an amazing dog, Mr. Jansen; he is not only gorgeous but polite as well!"

By then Rich had caught up to his Doberman to give him permission to gently take the treats from her hands. Standing, Julie extended her hand and fixed him with two warm, brown eyes, with deep laugh lines at the corners. "Welcome, Mr. Rich Jansen. Thank you for coming all this way to help Lindsey; please do come in." Her voice was low, pleasant with a slight Texas accent.

Following this tall, slim woman with an athletic gait, Rich felt himself begin to relax. This was apparently the best friend that Lindsey McCall had ever had, and Jansen looked forward to learning more about his infamous inmate. Upon entrance into the house, three girls stood at the top of a long stairway looking down at their mother, Jansen, and Max. They looked to be around fourteen, ten, and maybe eight. But when Rich heard the question, none of the girls' mouths had moved.

"Mom, can we come down to see the dog?"

Rich couldn't figure out where that little voice had come from until Julie answered, "Okay, Charley, but you'll need to be careful with Max; he's not used to little people."

Like a small tornado, a little boy of five or six catapulted down the stairs with his three older sisters more or less sedately following. While the kids were coming down, Julie crouched down in front of Max again but stayed about three feet from him when she asked, "Would you like some kid company, Max?"

Watching as Max gave her his paw, Jansen thought, *This lady must be one great teacher and coach.*

Now standing, Julie held her right hand out as a barrier between Charley and Max and looked at Rich to ask, "Is he okay with kids, Mr. Jansen?"

"I honestly don't know; he hasn't been around small children."

Max was sitting but looked extremely alert, not anxious but not relaxed either. The dog was looking quickly back and forth to the little boy and then to Rich. Just as Jansen was about to suggest that he take Max out to the car, Julie told Charley to go to the pantry to get some dog biscuits. The kid raced out of the room and was back in thirty seconds with his little fist filled with small dog biscuits. Julie reached for one of the biscuits, then flattened out her hand as she had outside, and instructed Charley to do as she was doing. Max looked to Rich for permission to get up and, getting the nod, walked over to take the biscuit from Julie. Charley was standing behind his mom and had his palm outstretched as well. Max walked to the right of Julie and stood in front of the kid, and gently placed his muzzle in the tiny hand to take the biscuit. Charley's eyes were shining, and so were everyone else's. With that, the three younger kids went outside into the fenced backyard to play ball with Max. The oldest of Julie's four kids returned upstairs without saying a word.

Inviting Rich to take a seat on one of the brightly patterned chairs and matching couch, Julie asked, "How about a glass of wine? I opened a red for dinner but didn't finish the bottle."

"Sure, thanks, and please call me Rich."

Julie smiled, revealing a dimple on either side of her mouth. "Okay, Rich, I'll be right back with our wine." Returning with a tray of cheese and crackers and the two glasses of wine balanced precariously, Julie quipped, "Can you tell that I worked my way through school as a waitress?"

Rich took the wine and sipped it, a good quality merlot, and watched Julie as she spread some cheese on some crackers and then spread them out. She was pretty, Rich thought as he watched her; not as beautiful as Lindsey but very attractive in a wholesome all-American way. Her brown eyes had flecks of amber in them and danced when she smiled. She looked like someone who kids would like but would respect and listen to; she looked happy.

Julie turned and caught Rich staring at her. She smiled as if she were used to being scrutinized. Then she said, "I want to thank you again for making the trek out here from Huntsville; it's a long drive, and you've still got to get back home, so I'd suggest that we get started." Her eyes darted outside as she did what looked like a quick body count of kids and turned back to Rich, fixing two slightly down-turned almond-shaped brown eyes on Rich. Smiling again, Julie suggested in her lilting Texas drawl, "Why don't I tell you about Lindsey and me?"

Thirty minutes later, Julie had covered her close friendship with Lindsey since first grade, a relationship that had continued through college at Rice but began to fade when Lindsey entered medical school. Julie seemed matter of fact about the way that the two had drifted apart as life took them in different directions, but she made it obvious that Lindsey McCall had always been important in her life. Julie picked up a large, thick leather-bound book and handed it to Jansen. "I started this when Linds and I graduated from Rice. I followed everything she did in med school and everything else I could find, which as you could see was a whole lot." The grin could not have been more genuine nor more full of love had she been talking about one of her children. "Lindsey McCall is a remarkable woman, and I am—" the soft voice choked for a moment and Julie Grayson swallowed then took a sip of her wine to swallow the tidal surge of love and sorrow she felt for her best friend"—*proud* to be Lindsey's friend."

Julie smiled sadly and then gave Jansen a watery glance. "You can take this and keep it as long as you would like, but of course, I would like it back when you no longer need it." There was a slight shudder in the narrow shoulders at the last phrase.

Taking the book, Jansen leafed through it quickly and saw that it was packed with newspaper clippings, professional articles by McCall, as well as a few hastily scrawled messages and letters. There were also printed copies of e-mail messages between Julie and Lindsey. The very last inclusions were the four *Houston Tribune* articles. Todd had scanned them to his home e-mail address, suggesting that he read them, but Rich had not yet taken the time to read Townsend's series.

Rich glanced over at Julie to see if she had recovered; she was standing at the glass door that led outside to the backyard, watching Charley and Max splayed out together with her two younger daughters looking on. "I wish I had a camera to witness Charley being still … awake but still …." Julie's voice trailed off, and she stood motionless for a few more seconds and then turned back to face Rich.

"Julie, thank you very much for lending me this material; I cannot imagine the hours that you must have spent finding and copying these." Jansen was overwhelmed by the span of years that were covered in the book; Julie Grayson had been maintaining this tribute to her friend for almost twenty-five years. Each page was protected by plastic page covers and was numbered. Looking up again, Jansen met Julie's gaze; she was openly scrutinizing him. Rich had been waiting for the question; he was just surprised that it had taken Julie over an hour to ask it.

"Why are you doing this, Rich?" Julie's soft brown eyes were darker, and the expression on her face was one of deep concentration, the way she must look when she was grading her calculus finals or deciding if one of her kids was lying.

Jansen nodded slowly, taking his time before answering because he had known she would ask why; however, he wasn't sure that he understood his reasons himself, completely anyway. Jansen took a deep breath to start to reply when Julie continued speaking to him.

Still staring at him, Julie sat down on the couch next to the chair where he was sitting, picked up her glass of wine, frowned, and said, "It isn't as if you haven't given enough of yourself, Rich Jansen. Only six months ago, you were very nearly dead."

Rich blinked at the blunt statement.

"After I got your messages, I called a few people, including Todd Kensington, and I also looked you up on the Internet." Julie's gaze became softer and lighter as she expressed her curiosity about the motives of the man sitting in her living room. "And now you've decided to take on Huntsville Prisons and, not so incidentally, the curious case of Dr. Lindsey McCall."

Grayson crossed her long slender legs, sat back on the couch, and sipped the red wine from the earthenware goblet in her hand, clearly content to wait while Rich came up with an answer to the incisive questions now hanging in the air of the darkening living room.

Jansen nodded once more and looked carefully at Julie Grayson—this time seeing much more than a wife, mother, math teacher, and longtime friend of Lindsey McCall. Rich had missed the subtle shadows under the almond eyes, and the rare combination of sorrow, peace, and weariness reflected there.

Deciding that he could trust Julie, Jansen shocked himself by telling her exactly what had happened this week, beginning with his first meeting with Lindsey, her peculiar mystical statement that she knew why she was in prison, and ending with Pettigrew's suit against the State of Texas resulting from McCall's dramatic intervention to save Luke Preston's life.

Julie sat motionless through the ten-minute-or-so account of the events of the week; eyes now shining and with a slight smile, she softly repeated her question, "But why are you doing *this?*"

Rich laughed. Julie Grayson would be one hell of a lawyer, he thought fleetingly, and felt exactly as he did at the age of eight when he had taken the dare of his friend Timmy to dive off the high diving board. The water of the sparkling blue swimming pool had looked as if it were twenty miles down.

"Because I can't let Lindsey McCall remain in prison." This was the first time that Jansen had admitted that he believed that Lindsey was not guilty—even to himself; his legal training plus his years as a cop had shaped a man who believed in the rule of law and therefore was loath to push its boundaries. Of course, there were countless situations where Jansen had been forced to think outside the box; that was implicit in any life, but particularly in the one of a soldier, a cop, or a lawyer. The difference was that almost all of those were circumstances where lives were in danger, both his own and those for whom he was responsible.

This situation was unique in the experience of Rich Jansen. There was no time crisis here, no imperative to *act*; the crises were over, and the judicial system had been followed. An imperfect system, Rich knew, but arguably the best one in the world. This was dangerous territory for Jansen—dangerous at many levels. Rich's gaze engaged Julie Grayson's as he calmly and quietly stated, "I am sure that she did nothing to warrant an indictment for murder."

Julie's reaction was almost comical in the riot of emotions that competed for first place in her eyes and on her face. The joyful one won out when she whispered, "Ah, thank you my sweet Jesus," and closed her eyes for a moment.

Suddenly, the patio door slammed open with Charley entering first, then Max, and the two girls in tow, and the quiet room was alive with excited chatter. Max came straight to Rich with a grin on his face, sat directly in front of Rich, and gave him his paw, for all the world as if the dog was thanking Rich for this really cool playtime with Julie's kids.

"Okay, girls and Charley, time to get ready for bed, tomorrow's a school day, and it's almost ten o'clock."

Rich smiled at the expected chorus of objections from all three children but noticed that Julie didn't need to tell them again. She only looked at each of the kids and pointed in the direction of the upstairs.

"Say good night to Mr. Jansen and thank him for bringing Max before you go up now."

Dutifully and shyly, the two girls who looked like small facsimiles of their mother came over to Rich and politely shook his hand to say good night. Not Charley. He barreled over to Max first and hugged him so tightly, Rich thought he had to be choking the Doberman, but Max looked over to Rich with the expression that Rich always interpreted to mean, "See how much they all love me?" When Charley turned away from Max, Rich was startled to see tears coursing down the boy's face. Seeing this, Julie immediately swept up her little boy into her arms and said, "Come on, my little man, let's get you upstairs and into bed." As she climbed the stairs with her child, Julie mouthed to Rich that she would be right back.

Rich stroked Max absently as he glanced at his watch to see that Julie was right on: it was close to ten, and he would be lucky to make it home by midnight. Standing up, Rich stretched and yawned, his movements causing Max to stand, too, eager for the next phase in this adventure. As Rich was checking his BlackBerry to see if he had an early meeting, Julie came back down the stairs and suggested, "Rich, why don't you and Max crash here for the night? There is an alarm clock in the spare bedroom. But if you don't need to leave at the crack of dawn, I'll be fixing breakfast for five in the morning around six thirty. I'd be happy to have you and Max as well.

"We have plenty of dog food, too," Julie added but her face looked suddenly strained and tired as she explained. "My husband and I reluctantly agreed to buy a dog for the kids six months ago; this is a very busy street, and we had held out for years because we were afraid the dog would get hit by a car." She took a deep breath and sighed; Rich could see tears standing in her eyes which Julie impatiently rubbed away. "She was a really wonderful dog, a shepherd and golden retriever mix rescue that we found at the Friendswood pound. Last Sunday night, Charley forgot to latch the gate in the backyard, and she got out. Charley raced out through the front door just in time to see the car coming around the corner slam into her as she was running back to Charley. Of course, Charley blames himself. The driver of the car who hit her never even stopped, just kept going." Julie took another shaky breath and walked over to where Max still sat to crouch down beside him and murmured, "So that's why we have food for you, Mr. Max."

Standing again, Julie still didn't leave the dog's side. "It's really nice for us to have a dog in the house; we really miss Ginger."

At that, Rich was sold; besides, he really didn't have it in him to drive for another two hours. He looked at Max and asked, "What do you say, boy? Shall we get some sleep before we drive back home tomorrow?" Julie walked over to the closet and pulled out a dog bed. "This was Ginger's, and I haven't had the heart to throw it out." Max and Rich followed Julie through a closed door, to the left of the patio door, into a spacious guest room complete with a queen bed and bath. Placing the dog bed fairly close to the queen, Julie turned to Max and asked, "Well, does that suit you, boy?"

In answer, Max climbed onto the bed, turned around twice, and then curled up on the bed and went to sleep. "Rich, there are towels, a new toothbrush, and all the necessities in the shower and bath; there are even razors and shaving cream. Ted's brother frequently stays with us, so it's decked out for men." Eying him, Julie added, "You're about the same size as Ted. I'll bring down one of his dress shirts for you to have in the morning." Brushing aside Rich's objections, she added, "Believe me, it's no trouble at all. Ted's in California on business and won't be home until a week from Friday; he won't miss one dress shirt."

Julie cocked her head and regarded Rich with curiosity. "Why haven't you asked me about Paula?"

Jansen was tired, and his mind was scattered, but his gaze snapped to meet Julie's and answered honestly, "I figured when you were ready to talk about Paula, you would."

Julie smiled and nodded approvingly at him, touched his arm, patted Max's head, and said, "Good night, boys, I'll see you in the morning." The door was almost closed when she knocked softly and reopened the door. "Forgot to ask you: Is there anything you can't or won't eat for breakfast?"

Rich grinned at her before he replied, "Quiche?"

Laughing now, Julie shut the door.

❧

You will see every sparrow fall
You will see each dying blade of grass
You will hear every child's cry and every father's despairing sigh
The terrified screams and hungry moans will be woven into the song
Of who you are and your heart will be broken and broken again
And then you will know a heart of flesh and not a heart of stone.
You will be alive.
—DESMOND TUTU, *MADE FOR GOODNESS*

19

With Max around, Rich Jansen never needed an alarm clock. Max's system was programmed to awaken at five thirty in the morning. Generally when he felt the thud of the heavy paw on the bed, Rich was dreaming; but not today. He'd been lying awake thinking about Julie Grayson, her friendliness, hospitality, and the sorrow that he sensed not far beneath her serene exterior. Rich wondered about that; it could be a result of the death of the family dog happening in such a horrid way and right in front of her six-year-old who was calling the animal to him. To be sure, Rich thought, that was pretty awful, but he decided there was something else. Maybe it was her friend Lindsey; but no, he immediately discarded that thought and decided it was something close, something in her family. He hoped there weren't problems between Julie and her absent husband.

Max had been sitting impatiently at the side of Rich's bed for a minute or two, expecting Rich to get up; when he didn't, the paw thudded the side of the bed again.

"Okay, Max, I get it." Rich hopped out of bed feeling surprisingly refreshed, and opened the door of the guest bedroom just a crack to see if anyone in the house was up. There were no sounds of any activity, but when he looked down to see the pile of clothes, Jansen grinned at the sight of running shoes that were close enough to his size, and the socks, shorts, and a T-shirt with a note that read, "You look like a runner, and so is Ted; feel free but remember breakfast is at seven sharp. Have a good run. Okay to leave the patio door unlocked when you go out the back."

"PS: In back of the house, you'll find a path through the woods. You might want to keep Max on the leash, though, because a lot of people in the neighborhood run there in the early mornings."

Rich estimated that they could do four or maybe five miles and still leave time for a shower, so he dressed quickly and quietly left the house.

Julie was right: the running path was perfect. The air was cool and crisp, the hint of fall in central Texas in the air. After about ten minutes of a slow jog with Max on the leash, Rich decided they were alone and unclipped the leash so that Max could explore the rich smells of a new forest. It had taken a few weeks, but Rich and Max had regained the rhythm of the runs they used to do before Rich was hurt.

About ninety minutes later, Jansen and Max walked into Julie's kitchen where simultaneously, Max was accosted by Charley, and Rich's senses were assaulted by the smell of coffee, bacon, and buckwheat pancakes. Standing at the griddle of the island in the middle of her large country kitchen, Julie smiled her greeting.

"Good morning, I hope you slept well and enjoyed your run?" Without waiting for an answer, Julie said, "Take a cup off the place setting nearest me and pour yourself some coffee,

Rich. Half and half is on the table, and if you need sugar, it's on that counter over there." She was pointing with her free hand to the bar to the right of the huge refrigerator.

The table was huge, wooden, and right out of Country Kitchen, but didn't dominate the room because the room was so well designed. The walls were painted bright yellow, and the window coverings were pale yellow with bright daisy fabric above them. The island, stove, and spacious cupboards with glass doors dominated the room. Precisely designed for a busy cook, the room was functional yet warm and inviting. On the far side of the room were two casual couches, three comfortable-looking chairs, and a plasma television; this must be where the Sunday sports shows were watched. Scanning the scores of plaques and trophies on a bookcase beside the television, Rich figured this was a family who took their sports very seriously. Dressed in a khaki skirt with a light pullover, striped, sweater, Julie looked as if she could be a college student at A&M herself.

Noting Rich's inspection of her kitchen, Julie smiled and offered, "This is my dream kitchen. I designed it, and ten years later, I still love it—wouldn't alter a thing." Once more, she pointed, this time with her spatula, and at the bookcase of trophies; she laughed, and said, "The Grayson wall of honor. Any of us who competes in any sport ends up there even if we only get an honorable mention, like me when I ran in the forty-kilometer marathon in San Antonio last year." Those captivating brown eyes drew down with her pretend grimace. "Honorable mention for my age group." Noticing that her spatula was now dripping pancake batter on her tile floor, Julie exclaimed, "Oops, pay attention to what you're doing, Grayson. That's what I tell the kids, and just look at me."

One by one, the girls wandered into the kitchen and took their places, looking expectantly at their mother. Other than

Julie's, there was one empty seat. "Go ahead and get started, y'all." None of them needed any prompting, for the serving plates were stacked with pancakes, biscuits, and scrambled eggs. Charley sat right next to Rich where he could almost reach Max to pat him. Just as Charley slid off his stool to go over to the dog, Julie, without turning around, commanded, "Charley, get back up to the table and eat your breakfast. You can pat Max later." Charley rolled his eyes dramatically at Rich, but did as his mother had bid him.

Satisfied that her charges were all eating, she turned to Rich and asked, "I've got kibble and canned meat; which do you give Max?"

At the sound of his name, the dog's ears stood up, and he looked at Rich, who was starting to get up. "Julie, I can feed him, really. Why don't you eat some of your delicious vittles here and just tell me where the food is? Max will eat either canned or dry food, thanks."

At that, Charley had raced into the walk-in pantry and was standing in the door with a dog dish and a huge grin on his face. "Here, Max. Here, boy. Can I feed him, Mom, please?" Shaking her head when she looked at the uneaten food on the boy's plate, Julie sighed and raised an eyebrow at Rich.

Jansen nodded at Julie and rose to help Charley with the dog food; Rich also wanted to stay close to Max because the dog had not been around small children at all before last night; so Rich stood close by as the little hands piled kibble into the metal bowl. Max was sitting very patiently while he watched Charley slowly fill the bowl with the dry food. Finally when there were about two cups in there, Rich told the boy he could set the bowl down so that Max could eat.

While Charley and Rich had been absorbed with feeding Max, Julie's oldest daughter had joined the family and sat picking at her food. Walking back to finish his breakfast, Rich heard Julie quietly speaking to her, "Lindsey, your Dad and I said no. That decision will not change regardless of how many times you repeat the question or how cleverly you rephrase it."

Startled to hear the name Lindsey, Rich walked over to the large glass coffee pot and refilled his cup; then he walked back to the table with the carafe and filled Julie's and Lindsey's cups as well. The teen looked up at him to smile a "thanks" before reclaiming the sullen expression she'd had while arguing with her mother. While Julie's two younger girls looked enough like her to be small clones of Julie's tall, lean athletic frame, Lindsey was petite with curly dark hair and big intensely green eyes with long thick eyelashes.

Ignoring her oldest daughter's sullenness, Julie offered, "Rich, if you can spend the morning here, I've got most of the day available because my first class isn't until three this afternoon. I just need to drop the kids off at school, and then you and I can finish up where we left off last night."

Julie was standing by the sink as she rinsed dishes and began stacking the plates in the dishwasher. The kids each brought their plates over to the sink and then raced out of the kitchen, telling their mother they would be back with their backpacks. Only Lindsey remained seated, still picking at her food.

Rich replied into the suddenly uncomfortable silence. "That would work well for me, Julie; I'll plan to head back this afternoon then, thanks for taking the time." Rich rose from the table, brought his empty plate over to Julie, and smiled at her. "I'm really good with dishes, ma'am," he drawled. "I'd be happy to finish cleaning up while you get the kids to school."

Julie looked surprised at his offer but readily accepted, "You know what, Rich, I'll accept your offer. Thanks a lot, be back in a half hour."

Rich could hear Julie's whispered voice, gentle and very loving, "Come on, Linds, it's time to go."

Another whisper and then, "Goodbye, Mr. Jansen, it was nice meeting you." Rich turned around to acknowledge the girl's greeting, but she was gone; five minutes later, the slam of the front door announced that he and Max were alone in the house.

As Rich cleared the remaining dishes and platters off the table and stacked them into the dishwasher, he thought about the Grayson family, about how much more complicated were our lives than what they seemed to the casual observer. Clearly Julie and Ted Grayson worked hard at their jobs and with their kids; Julie more than Ted, Jansen suspected, for it seemed to him that the women he knew who were mothers in addition to their demanding careers just worked twice as hard as their husbands. Regardless of how hard our culture worked to equalize roles and responsibilities between men and women, the reality was that women seemed hard-wired to see and attend to the needs of home and children, many of which most men simply missed.

After watching the interaction between Julie and her oldest child, Rich was sure that the source of the sorrow he sensed in Julie Grayson lay with her daughter Lindsey. He had been touched by Julie's patience and compassion in dealing with behaviors that seemed to Rich to be normal teenage rebellion. Jansen wondered about the girl and about her name; he wondered at the striking difference in Lindsey's looks from that of her mother and her two younger sisters, and Rich ruminated about what problem of Lindsey's could cause the deep sadness in her mother. Julie Grayson did not strike Jansen as someone who could be shaken by the developmental challenges of teenagers as they pushed at the boundaries of parental restraint.

Just as Jansen was finishing his kitchen duty, he heard Max scramble to his feet and stand, facing the door. Rich figured Julie was home.

"You can stay at the Grayson house any ole time you wish, Rich Jansen. This kitchen sparkles—thanks a lot for cleaning up!" Julie was leaning against the door of the large refrigerator, watching Rich wipe down the counters, her brown eyes full of amber light and her heart-shaped face wreathed in a broad grin. "Can you drink more coffee if I make a fresh pot, Rich? I could use another cup or two; I don't think I had more than a sip or two of the one I poured for myself when I started cooking breakfast."

"Sure, sounds good, I can drink a couple of cups, Julie." Rich was a bit of a coffee snob; he would rather forego it than suffer the watery, tea-like concoction that passes for coffee in most homes and restaurants. But Julie's was excellent, full-bodied and bursting with flavor. Like Julie, Rich had been focused on making sure that Max didn't mistake Charley for one of his fleece chewies to drink more than half a cup.

Within moments, the scent of freshly ground coffee beans filled the room. Julie had moved over the far end of the kitchen and was now seated on a somewhat garish upholstered chair with matching ottoman. The fabric was floral, wildly so, with enormous lime green, fuchsia, yellow, and orange blossoms on a navy-blue background. Placing her feet on the ottoman, Julie said, "This chair is universally hated in this house, but I cannot bring myself to get rid of it. Lindsey and I found it in an antique store on West Alabama when we were in the dorm at Rice together." Smiling happily at the memory, Julie recalled, "It sat in the very back of the shop amid a lot of other junk." She looked sharply at Rich. "I hope you're not into antiques, Rich. I think most of that stuff is *ugly*." She was drawing out the word for emphasis.

Rich did like antiques, but Julie was right; most of the stuff in stores *was* junk, though not all of it. You had to be willing to examine a lot of useless discards to find the occasional diamond; he and Laura had loved browsing through antique stores, but rather than explaining all that, Jansen simply smiled, encouraging Julie to continue with her story.

Julie started at the sound of the beep signifying that the coffee was done, but Rich, still standing, motioned for her to stay seated and brought over the coffeepot, two fresh mugs, and coffee cream. With a flourish, he set it all on the small glass coffee table, smiling at Julie's exaggerated expression of gratitude.

"Thanks, I could get used to service like this, I'm afraid." Taking a sip of the hot brew, Julie laughed. "The owner of that store initially quoted a price of two hundred dollars for this." Her left hand was stroking the worn arm affectionately as if it were a pet. "Lindsey and I burst into laughter when he said that and told him we'd give him fifty dollars for both pieces, and they had to be delivered to the Rice University dorm because we didn't have a car big enough for it. The owner fussed and fumed about the price but finally agreed to do it. I wrote many a paper in this chair, and studied for I don't know how many exams ...."

Blinking, Julie snapped out of her reverie, glanced at her watch, gazed at Rich soberly, then did a double-take as she noticed the tape recorder that Jansen had placed there early this morning that was sitting next to the coffee and creamer.

The brown eyes suddenly clouded, and just the touch of a frown appeared on Julie's mouth as she asked, "Are you planning to tape our conversation today?" Pausing for a few seconds, she said unconvincingly, "I guess it's okay to do that." But Julie's wary expression revealed that it wasn't okay, not in the least.

Rich leaned over the side table separating him from Julie and lightly touched her arm. "A recording would help me, Julie, simply because it captures the nuances of your phrases much more accurately than my memory, but it is not essential. If taping this conversation disturbs you at all, I'll get along fine without doing that." Jansen paused then and wondered if this next decision would come back to bite him but decided to do it for the simple reason that if he couldn't trust Julie Grayson with this information, then he couldn't trust her with anything.

"There's another reason I brought the tape recorder, Julie." He paused while he stared at Julie Grayson. She had collected herself once more and sat in her whimsical chair calmly holding Jansen's gaze and waited for his explanation.

"This is the recording of my first meeting with Lindsey McCall on Monday of this past week." Jansen had expected a reaction, and he got one as he held up the two audiotapes.

Julie's eyes seemed to double in size, and she took a huge deep breath and held it as if she were going to dive a long way underwater. The arm Jansen had touched flew to her heart in that universal expression of stunned surprise, but Julie only stared at the tape recorder as if it were alive and had sprouted wings and was about to fly away, saying nothing.

Rich decided to wait as well. This lady was extremely self-possessed; Julie seemed to Rich as if there were nothing that could confound her. Her response to his revelation of what was on the tape was, Jansen believed, the equivalent of another's hysterics. Rich liked Julie Grayson; he could easily see why she and Lindsey McCall had been best friends since childhood, and he had no interest in causing Julie any more pain in her life. So he sat there in silence to see what Julie would do or say next.

Rich was intentionally looking away from Julie and around the pleasant sitting room and taking in the details of the subtle shades of pastel yellows and greens that upholstered the two small couches and other chair. He was careful not to smile because he suspected that Julie may be watching him, but the colors in her garish chair *almost* worked in the room—well … almost.

Jansen also inspected the Grayson wall of honor to avoid Julie's face while she struggled with her memories, her demons, or maybe both. From where he sat, he could read some of the Grayson names; although it was difficult to read the small print of some of the plaques and trophies, it seemed that all sports were represented there: tennis, baseball, volleyball, basketball, football, soccer, and even golf. Each of the six Graysons was displayed on the wall or in the bookcase or both; there was even a baseball trophy for little Charley.

Suddenly, Julie reached over to the tape recorder and pushed play; together, they sat listening to the first hour of the two-hour interview that Jansen had conducted last week with Lindsey. This time Jansen kept his eyes on Julie as she listened; Julie was so engrossed in listening to the audio that she seemed unaware of Rich at all. When Lindsey made that peculiar statement about there being a reason she was there in Huntsville and then quickly retracted her statement by claiming that she hadn't meant to say that, of course, she understood that she was there because she had been convicted of murdering her mother, Julie began to cry. Actually she was sobbing as if her heart were breaking into a million pieces.

Rich leaned over to stop the tape and apologize when somehow, through what looked like a herculean effort of will, Julie was able to get herself under control. She placed a slender hand over Rich's and said shakily, "It's okay, Rich. Really. It's just that it's been so long since I've heard Lindsey's voice. I want to hear the whole thing, please."

Reluctantly, Jansen settled back and let the sound of his questions and Lindsey's responses fill the room. Jansen had listened to this tape at least three times this week, but he heard something new with each additional review. This time it was the clarity of McCall's speech and the pleasant, low-pitched timbre of her voice. When he glanced over at Julie to see how she was doing during the grim recitation of the facts of the suit by Pettigrew against the state, he was surprised to see her staring at him. This time he did pause the recorder to pursue the unasked question on Julie's face.

"What is it, Julie?" Jansen asked. Her mascara was smudged under her eyes, and there were tear streaks down each cheek, but Julie Grayson looked remarkably composed for someone who had been sobbing not ten minutes ago.

Still gazing at Rich, Julie answered, "You're taking quite some risks being here with me and allowing me to hear this interview." It wasn't a question, it was a statement, and Rich saw no need to confirm the obvious, so he nodded and turned the recorder back on. The tale was fascinating, Rich thought, as he listened once more to the infirmary nurse, Monica, backing up Lindsey's account of the inmate who had died from a lethal arrhythmia and the boy who would have died had Lindsey McCall not taken charge.

Julie's attention to the tape was total; so when Rich's cell phone rang and he saw that it was Wanda, Rich decided to take the call out on Julie's patio. Max eyed Jansen as he quietly closed the patio door, but the dog stayed stretched out on Julie's Oriental rug in the sitting room. Briefly, Jansen conferred with Wanda about moving appointments to Monday since he'd not get back to Huntsville until early evening. Then he silently walked back into the sitting room where Julie sat unmoving, transfixed by the interview.

Another thirty minutes and the tape ended.

The sound of the tape clicking off to signal the end of the interview was loud in the suddenly quiet room. Julie sat staring at the tape recorder as if willing it to give her more. And then, still sitting as still as a statue, she whispered, "The last time that I saw Lindsey was at a Starbucks in Houston when she was pregnant with our little girl, Lindsey."

Rich had walked back over to the kitchen side of the large room to discard the coffee that Julie had hardly touched and refill both of their mugs a minute or so before the tape ended.

Unfortunately, by the time that Julie spoke, Jansen was carefully walking the two newly filled cups back to the sitting area; Julie's disclosure was so astounding that both cups slipped out of his hands and onto the porcelain tile floor to smash into what looked like hundreds of tiny and large ragged shards. Thankfully, the spill missed Julie's Oriental rug.

Max jumped up at the clatter and started to come to Rich but stopped when he saw Jansen's restraining hand. Meanwhile, Julie stood and then said, "Here, Rich, I'll get some stuff to clean up that mess; those were Houston Oiler mugs, so that gives you an indication of how old they were."

Ten minutes later, a third pot of coffee was brewing, and the floor was clean. While Jansen and Julie were standing near the pot waiting for a cup of fresh coffee that they could actually finish, Julie smiled grimly and said, "I don't have a lot of practice in talking about any of this; only three people know it: Lindsey, Ted, and I. My daughter Lindsey knows that we adopted her, but she doesn't know that Lindsey McCall is her mother."

Rich Jansen had been delighted to have something to do while he attempted to process this latest piece of electrifying information. Using his dog's soft pads as an excuse, Rich had insisted that he, rather than Julie, get down on his hands and knees to make sure that all the sharp pieces of smashed ceramic mugs had been discovered and picked up. The simple cleanup gave Jansen some time to get his bearings and to surrender the notion that nothing could surprise him after his years in the corps, as a criminal defense attorney, and as a cop.

As he searched Julie's floor with a flashlight looking for telltale glints of pottery, Jansen pondered the mystery and complexity of the human heart—in this case, Julie Grayson's. He could guess at the outline of the story: best friends who work out an impossible solution to an impossible crisis. Rich had noticed the crucifix that hung on Julie's neck; she seemed never to be without it. The two of them would have been in their mid-twenties then, which would have placed McCall in the middle of a demanding cardiology residency program. Too demanding for a baby and seemingly impossible while pregnant; yet somehow McCall had managed it. And somehow, Julie must have talked Lindsey out of the abortion, which would have been the easiest solution for everyone—except for the baby. He wondered how she had done it and why Lindsey had listened to her. On a more practical level, Jansen recalled those intense green eyes of Julie's adopted daughter. He had seen an eye color like that only one other time in his life: Lindsey McCall.

This time, Julie poured the coffee for them both and reached into her cupboard to retrieve a box of Trader Joe chocolate hazelnut biscotti. Placing several on a large plate, Julie gave the plate to Rich and carefully stepped over Max to return to her chair. All business now, Julie resembled a teacher as she declared, "We don't have a lot of time, and I have a lot I need to tell you, Rich, so let's get cracking." Attempting a smile at Rich, she gave it up and took a deep breath to warn him as he leaned over to pick up his mug. "Not yet, Rich, there's more."

Realizing that Julie meant that there were more surprises in store, Rich kept his hand suspended in midair and looked into the brown eyes now darkened with the weight of their burdens. "My daughter Lindsey—Lindsey's daughter—looks enough like Paula Livingston to be Paula's daughter." Julie took a huge, deep breath and gulped as if she were trying to ingest an egg—whole. "And Lindsey is an alcoholic, at fifteen. My daughter is an alcoholic, exactly like Paula." The tears flowed once more but this time soundlessly; it was if they traversed a familiar route, a map of pain and suffering traveled time and time again.

"Of course," Rich replied sardonically.

Rich knew that many of his closest friends, Todd Kensington for one, would attribute this ironic consequence of Julie's selfless decision to the weirdness of the genetic lottery. She adopts her best friend's baby, and the child grows up looking just like the best friend's sister and is an alcoholic at that. Jansen wasn't surprised to hear this about Paula; he had figured there was something off with the woman when he'd read over the court transcript of McCall's trial, but alcoholism hadn't entered his mind.

Of the many alcoholics Jansen had worked with in his life, a majority had been bright and quite adept at balancing demanding careers while hiding their need for alcohol. He thought of the man who had been the captain of the homicide department when Jansen had first joined the Harris County Police force. Matt Peterson had been a model cop, husband, and father. Over the three years that Rich had worked for Matt, Rich had attended many departmental functions with him, had joined Matt and other members of the force on Friday nights to celebrate a difficult collar or simply that a hard week had ended, and Rich had never considered alcoholism to be an issue with his boss. The guy had reminded

Jansen of his friend Todd Kensington; he liked to drink but was never affected by the alcohol he drank, even on nights when he drank his bourbon and beer for hours on end. It was only after Matt's sudden death from a heart attack that Jansen had learned of Peterson's alcoholism; Rich had been stunned.

Jansen had no idea what could have prompted Julie to adopt Lindsey's daughter, nor why Ted Grayson had gone along with it, but these two sure didn't need this as the consequence of such unselfishness. Rich said nothing to Julie because there was nothing that *could* be said. So he remained quiet until Julie surprised him again by removing the tape of Lindsey's interview and replacing it with a new tape that had been sitting next to it on the coffee table.

Surprised, Rich looked questioningly at Julie.

"I figure that you've trusted me with enough information to get you at least disbarred if not fired from your job, so I think I can trust you with this story that needs to be told." Taking a deep breath, Julie glanced at Jansen's untouched coffee and said, "Drink your coffee before it gets cold." The tone of her voice sounded exactly like Jansen's marine drill instructor at Paris Island; immediately, Julie realized how her command had sounded and added a perfunctory, "Please?"

Jansen was still looking at Julie's face, surprised at how their conversation had drained her of color and energy; she looked weary and dispirited—yet resolved.

Glancing at her watch again, Julie looked over at Rich as she asked, "You weren't surprised when I told you that my daughter was an alcoholic exactly like her aunt, Paula. Had you figured Paula out when you met with her?"

"I have not met with Paula yet; I figured I would do so once I spent some time with you." He regarded Julie soberly as he disclosed, "I've only read the transcript of her testimony at Lindsey's trial, but I read it three, maybe four, times because

Paula seemed unnaturally controlled—almost expert in her testimony."

Julie's eyes and facial expression hardened at Jansen's comment, but she said nothing.

"But no, I'm not surprised to hear that she's an alcoholic; her testimony was remarkable in a number of ways, Julie. I read it several times because she didn't make any of the mistakes that most people with little to no prior courtroom experience make, such as answering questions that were not asked and generally giving too much information in their responses."

Rich interrupted himself with a grin and ordered, "Eat your biscotti, Julie."

The jibe dissipated the tension in the room, and Rich was happy to see Julie laughing. When she laughed, ten years came off her face and were erased from her eyes. Obediently, she picked up the biscotti and broke it in half, placing one-half next to her coffee mug and eating the other.

"These are good; you should try one, Rich."

For a few minutes they sat in companionable silence; the only sounds in the room were Max's snoring and their chewing of the crunchy biscuits.

Checking the tape recorder to make sure that the recorder was on, Julie sat back in her funny chair, put her feet up on the footstool, and began. "Ted and I had been married for about a month; we were still living in Houston because both of us were finishing graduate school at Rice." Julie took a bite out of the remaining half of the biscotti, swallowed, and then drank more coffee. Glancing at Rich, Julie continued, "I hadn't seen Lindsey since our wedding and not much before that, not to really talk anyway because we'd both been so busy. I was cramming for my one of my theology finals, so I ignored the ringing of the phone and was surprised when Ted came into the spare bedroom we both used as an office. We had an agreement that when one of us was studying for exams, the other would cover. Ted had the phone in his hand and whispered Lindsey's name; Ted looked worried." Julie smiled fleetingly. "Ted and Lindsey had liked each other instantly when they had first met back in undergraduate school, and back before the wedding we'd double-dated a few times with Lindsey and a surgical resident she'd been seeing.

"When I took the phone and heard her sobbing like that, I could not imagine what was wrong; I just waited until she could get enough control to be able to tell me. Finally, she managed to tell me that she was pregnant and was scheduled to get an abortion in the morning at the Planned Parenthood Clinic. I asked her if she could reschedule it, but before I could explain why, she'd started screaming at me, accusing me of wanting to fuck up her life because she knew I'd want to talk her out of killing the baby—those were *her* words, not mine."

Julie's eyes were filled with the pain of that conversation; there were no tears any longer, but the expression on her face was desolate. Rich preferred her tears to those haunted and tormented brown eyes. Her voice was now a dull monotone— devoid of her regular slightly Texan cadence. "When she finally let me say something, I told her that I just wanted to be with her when she went to the clinic, and that I wasn't trying to do anything but love her and be a friend to her. But I had two finals the next day that I obviously couldn't reschedule." Sighing deeply, Julie's right hand absently toyed with the last quarter of the biscotti, standing it on one end and then the other. "But of course, Rich, Lindsey was right. That is *exactly* what I wanted to do: I *absolutely* wanted to talk her out of having an abortion." Her mouth now a grimace, and her right hand dropped the piece of biscotti on the table and began to finger the small gold crucifix on a gold chain around her neck;

Rich watched those long fingers turning the crucifix over and over in a gesture, which looked unconscious but maybe wasn't at all.

"I must have convinced Lindsey with my lies because she started to thank me for being willing to go with her. She was grateful because she really didn't think that she could do this alone; she agreed to postpone her appointment, and we agreed to meet her the following afternoon at the Starbucks that was right around the corner from the clinic. It was miraculous that I made it through and passed my exams that next day because Ted and I stayed up most of the night talking and praying. I did no more studying that night." For the first time that morning, Jansen saw a genuine smile on her face as she looked up from the tape recorder and beamed at Jansen. "I couldn't have done any of this without Ted, and no way could I have driven off to meet Lindsey that next afternoon if we had not reached the decision we did that night."

"You knew that you two would adopt Lindsey's baby before you even went to meet with her." Rich was spellbound. And he thought, not for the first time, of the quiet and unsung heroes in this world; those rare people who when faced with the completely unexpected, perhaps the calamitous, choose the high road; with eyes wide open, they choose to risk everything, motivated by sheer goodness. Jansen was certain that Julie and Ted Grayson were ill-prepared to be parents after only one month of marriage and still completing their graduate school educations. He was certain they were frightened of the enormous and unknown consequences of adopting someone else's baby, but they did it anyway. Jansen was very sorry that he had missed meeting Ted Grayson; he must be one hell of a man. And he was also relieved to know that Julie had a partner: not just a husband, but a partner on the rocky road she seemed to be traveling.

Lifting an eyebrow in surprise at Jansen's insight while nodding her agreement, Julie looked again at Rich and declared, "We knew that Lindsey would agree to have the baby and let us raise her as ours." Fingering the crucifix once more, Julie whispered, "What we didn't know was that Lindsey would never speak to us again." Pausing to swallow visibly, Julie said, "I hardly remember our conversation at Starbucks, Rich. I don't know what I said other than how much I loved Lindsey and how devastated I was that she had to go through this alone. Luckily, there were very few people in the coffee shop at the time, and those who were there seemed to take in stride the sight of a couple of girls crying. We talked, and we cried, and we talked, and we cried until I looked at my watch in shock to tell Lindsey that she'd missed her appointment; we'd been sitting there for three hours. She just nodded, and then I will never forget what Lindsey said next.

"She was so clear, so determined, so … *Lindsey*.

"'I'm going to have this baby, Julie. I know how you feel about abortions, and I can't say I disagree with you, not really. Every once in a while, I can feel her move, and, Julie, it is the *weirdest* sensation!'

"She almost laughed then, almost. Then she reached into her backpack and pulled out a piece of paper and handed it to me. She said, 'The baby is Matt's.'

"Matt was the surgeon she'd been seeing for a couple years off and on, and I had figured that he was the father of her child. Lindsey told me to read what was on the paper; it was a notarized statement signed by Dr. Matt Carlisle surrendering all rights and claims to the child named Lindsey or, in the event that the baby was male, Luke.

"I was so shocked that I couldn't speak. I just sat there, staring at Lindsey, who by now was calm and completely in control."

Rich had no problem visualizing this conversation between Lindsey and Julie, and he felt as if he could literally *see* McCall discussing this child and its future as if it were one of her laboratory rats; Jansen understood Lindsey McCall in a profound and unfathomable way. Although it made no sense to him at all, Rich knew that he understood Julie's best friend in a way that Julie never could.

"I *never* asked her not to have the abortion, Rich, and I never told her that Ted and I wanted to adopt her baby; somehow, she just knew."

Jansen kept his musing to himself and just nodded at Julie while he fabricated an expression of astonishment.

"Then she took out a second sheet of paper from a notebook in her backpack. But this time, she had started to cry, hard, really hard. I reached for the paper, and she stopped me by squeezing my hand so hard that it hurt. She said that this would have to be the last time we saw each other. I started to argue, and Lindsey managed to tell me that she couldn't do this any other way and begged me to understand. This second document was a list of stipulations surrounding the adoption of her daughter beginning with Ted's and my agreement to name the child Lindsey and ending with our agreement to cease any contact with Dr. Lindsey McCall from this day forward. We would be notified of the baby's birth by Lindsey's attorney, and that was it. She had two copies of Matt's document and of hers; I signed them both, and she walked out.

"And that is the last time I talked with Lindsey.

"Just six months later, Ted and I got a call from Lindsey's attorney to come and pick up our baby girl. When we went to St. Mark's to pick up baby Lindsey, we arrived just as Lindsey was leaving. She looked right through me as if she never saw me. Through the years, I did call her and left messages. When Lindsey was indicted for her mother's murder, I begged her to call me, leaving messages on her voice mail, but she never returned the calls; I've tried to get permission to see her at Huntsville, but she refuses to see me."

Suddenly Julie stood, stretched, and asked, "Don't you think we need a walk in the woods, Rich? I'll take you on my favorite path back there; it's about four miles, so we can do it in an hour or so."

At the sound of his favorite word, Max had jumped up and stood staring at Julie and Jansen as they collected their mugs and dishes and walked them over to the sink. Then the big dog had pranced over to nose the leash that Rich had left hanging on the doorknob of Julie's pantry door, and within minutes, all three were in the midst of Julie's backyard hideaway.

"I try to get down here several times a week; it's amazing what an hour in the woods can do for the psyche," she was speaking loudly over her shoulder, but her words were being tossed about by the wind, making Rich hear only partial phrases as the three strode along the narrow forest path— Max in front of course, followed by Julie, and then by Rich. Squinting at the sky, which could be seen only through the densely packed firs, he could see the rapidly moving clouds and guessed that a norther was quickly approaching. The cool temperatures were fine with Jansen, but northers sometimes brought torrential rains, which would mean that he and Max could have a grueling ride back to Huntsville. Glancing at his watch, he was startled to see that it was already noon, and he and Julie still had many verbal miles to walk. Briefly, Jansen toyed with cutting his visit short; if he left within the next thirty minutes or so, he might stay ahead of the storm and would most likely be home in time to get some office work done, but abandoned that thought almost as soon as it had taken form in his mind.

He could only guess what this conversation was costing Julie Grayson. The serendipity of her decision to reveal intensely private aspects of her own life and that of her family to a virtual outsider on this day did not escape him. Rich knew that any attempt to rekindle the remainder of their conversation on a more convenient day was risky, not only because of his and Julie's schedules, but he also doubted that the intimate connection that had developed between Julie and him could be turned on and off at will.

Jansen smiled at their small parade, momentarily relieved to clear his mind of the overwhelming content of the morning; Max was loping along at a slow trot, checking back frequently to make sure his charges were following. Julie had unclipped his leash after receiving an okay from Jansen, and she carried the long leather strap in her right hand. Her left was busy holding thick branches back so that Rich could walk without being walloped by them. After Julie's failed first attempt to converse, she grew silent; the two walked amid the increasing wind. There was no rain as yet, but they could smell it in the air and almost taste the ozone.

Rich thought again about how much he liked Julie Grayson and of the strange but irrevocable bond between Lindsey and her. As he walked behind Julie's lithe athletic form, occasionally laughing with her when a branch slipped from her hand and into his torso, Rich considered the superficial differences between the two women and decided they were insignificant. Somehow, he felt confident that all this would be resolved and all would be well; the thought was bizarre, Rich thought, but the conviction was familiar to him, and he had learned not to doubt it when it came.

What does it matter if you do not make it right?
What does it matter if your efforts move no mountains?
It matters not at all.
It only matters that you live the truth of you.
It only matters that you push back the veil to let your goodness
shine
through.
It only matters that you live as I have made you.
It only matters that you are made for me.
Made like me,
Made for goodness.
—Desmond Tutu, *Made for Goodness*

20

Max, Julie, and Rich raced into Julie's kitchen in a mad dash; predictably, the norther had arrived along with sheets of icy driving rain. Misjudging the arrival of the rain by about ten minutes, the three had sprinted back through the forest as soon as the rains began, but were soaked through and shivering by the time they reached the house. While Max stood shaking himself repeatedly in a futile attempt to dry and warm himself, Jansen and Julie stood panting and dripping on her porcelain tile floor. First to recover, Julie spun into action and grabbed huge towels from the downstairs guest room. As she threw two at Rich, she asked Rich to use one for Max while she ran upstairs for dry clothes for them both.

Julie and Jansen, now reseated in the chairs they had occupied earlier, all breathed a contented sigh simultaneously now that they were warm and dry. Julie and Rich laughed as they glanced over at Max stretched out in front of the woodstove in the Grayson sitting room. The stove blended so well with the colors in the room that Rich had not noticed it earlier in the day, but the pale rose stove was burning brightly and pouring out heat into the large room.

"I called Ted while I was upstairs getting warm." Julie's color was back to normal, and she had regained her vitality and, what Jansen now assumed, her natural ebullience. Rich was delighted to see the amber lights back in her dark brown eyes. "I wanted Ted to know how much I appreciate your remarkable decision to assist Todd Kensington in Lindsey's appeal process." Julie took a hunk of hair and stuck it behind her ear. "I also wanted Ted to know that I had decided to tell you everything—the *whole* story." Her hand was absently twisting her hair as she spoke. "I guess I needed to know that Ted was okay with that decision." She was now glancing at Rich. "We've not told anyone about Lindsey's alcoholism—not our friends—and even our parents don't even know, Rich.

"But it's good to say the words … to get them out; it's strange, but once I started to talk to you this morning, it felt as if an enormous dam that I didn't even know was there had burst wide open." Her voice trailed off as she shifted in her favorite chair and folded her long legs underneath her. Staring at the microphone on the table, Julie nodded as if to herself and said, "Please turn it back on, but know that I don't need to leave for my three o'clock class. I called my TA, and he can distribute and monitor the tests that the students need to take, so we have all afternoon, Rich. Lindsey has soccer practice until six tonight, and I told the younger girls they could go to a birthday party after school so long as they brought Charley with them. They are both amazingly patient with Charley."

Julie smiled and then said, "Ted asked me to tell you that he was sorry he wasn't here to thank you for doing what you're doing for us and that he really looked forward to meeting you soon—if not now, then hopefully to celebrate Lindsey's release from jail."

Startled and humbled by the depth of Ted and Julie Grayson's trust and faith in him and his ability to unravel the convoluted mess that was the state's case against Lindsey, Jansen found that he could not meet Julie's gaze. Instead, he busied himself with the tape recorder while he prayed that their confidence was warranted.

Watching Jansen turn over the tape in the recorder and click the "Play" button, Julie began, "I know you need to understand Lindsey's sister, Paula Livingston, to build a plausible scenario of what actually happened with Lindsey's drug, Digipro. And believe me, Rich, I've been eager to blow Paula's cover for over thirty years." The amber brown eyes regarded Jansen gravely. "But the truth about another person, specifically a person we dislike intensely, is never as simple as we would wish, is it?"

Jansen was listening to Julie with keen interest for a host of reasons; primarily because she was right, he needed a whole lot more information about Paula Livingston before he arrived at her doorstep. Interviewing Paula, Rich knew, would be the biggest risk he would take among this cast of characters. It seemed that there was little left for Paula to lose, and he suspected that she was shrewdly capable of anything, like most of the alcoholics he'd known in his life. Deciding to notify the media, the Texas bar, or a Texas midlevel bureaucrat of Jansen's ethical violations was an act that seemed very consistent with what he was learning about Paula Livingston. But on a far deeper level, Rich suspected that Julie had reached an understanding of Paula through much more arduous means than the simple knowledge gained by being the best friend of Paula's younger sister.

"Lindsey and I met in nursery school and were best friends

at first sight." Julie's eyes were soft and warm at the memory. "That's never changed; I still consider Lindsey McCall to be my best friend even though we've not spoken for almost sixteen years." Rich watched Julie's face as she reminisced about her childhood and that of Lindsey; the weariness and dispiritedness of earlier had been erased. Julie seemed solemn, but the deep sorrow that he had sensed since meeting her was mitigated; she seemed lighter somehow. "I am the only child of parents who lacked the burdens and blessings of the McCall family." Rich was struck by Julie's oddly academic way of distinguishing between her family and Lindsey's.

"My mother was a high school math teacher," Julie smiled, "—like mother, like daughter—and my dad worked at NASA like Lindsey's father but as an engineer, not a test pilot. And both my folks have always been blessed with good health. We didn't have the money that Lindsey's folks did, but I often thought that all their wealth hardly compensated for all the trouble that family suffered—still suffers." Julie unfolded her legs and stretched them out on the ottoman of her favorite chair, wiggling her toes in the heavy warm gray socks that were on her shoeless feet.

"Because my mother worked during the day, I spent most of my childhood at Lindsey's. Mrs. McCall did not work outside the home, and she thought it was great for Lindsey to have a quasi, live-in friend, so I was more or less a third daughter to the McCall's and another baby sister to Paula.

"Tom McCall was a remarkable man. He was loved by everyone who ever knew him; my dad still speaks of Tom as one of the last great pilots that NASA produced before the pilots were reduced to technicians." Julie grinned sideways at Jansen. "That's what Dad

calls the astronauts—technicians." She frowned slightly. "Dad respects the skills of the new breed, but he insists that the NASA test pilots were the real heroes of the space program because they had to fly the prototypes of the machines that ended up in space. And some of them died doing just that—and no one knows their names; no one has ever heard of Tom McCall."

Julie answered Jansen's unspoken question, "Yes, Lindsey's father died in a crash when we were freshmen at Rice." Recognizing the stricken expression on Rich's face, Julie gazed at him and nodded very slowly. "Lindsey and her dad were unbelievably close. I love my dad, but we're normally on pretty different wavelengths; I'm closer to my mother and always have been. We just have more in common, I guess."

Julie paused to take a sip of her cup of tepid coffee, wrinkled her nose in distaste, and put the mug back down on the coffee table. Closing her eyes momentarily, Julie continued, "Paula's interests were typical teenaged girl stuff—our daughter Lindsey looks exactly like Paula did; they both developed early and liked boys—a lot.

"Ann McCall loved the fact that Paula was so popular. From about thirteen on, Paula had a long line of boys after her; she was constantly going from one party to another dance; her weekends were always busy with whomever she dated at the time. Lindsey and I used to roll our eyes when Mrs. McCall would answer the phone and holler up to Paula the name of the boy who was on the phone for Paula. Sometimes she seemed more excited than Paula did. I think all that flurry of dating and activity must have brought her back to her own teenage years—" Julie frowned "—to simpler times, maybe.

"Mrs. McCall was so incredibly proud when Paula became a cheerleader. Paula had tried out for the Clear Lake Cheerleader Squad when she was only fourteen and made it; I think she was the first freshman girl to make the squad." Julie closed her eyes and smiled wistfully, lost in the memories of her childhood. Then opening her eyes and looking at Jansen, she continued. "I can still see Paula doing her gymnastic routines for her cheerleader practices over and over again; she was really quite good, but five-year-old kids and fourteen-year-old teens tend to live on different planets, so Lindsey and I had no appreciation of an accomplishment like that. But Mrs. McCall sure loved to watch her Paula practice her routines." Julie watched the tape rotating slowly for a moment, and then she whispered, "How *different* Lindsey and Paula were." Her voice trailing off, Julie blinked a few times and then looked at Rich as if startled out of a reverie.

"I always knew I was smart but not at Lindsey's level. We were both pretty ambitious kids, but again, Lindsey much more so than I." Looking again at Rich, Julie eyed him and said, "Lindsey decided to be a doctor—a cardiologist—when she was seven years old, Rich. Seven!

"I think most folks thought that a seven-year-old kid talking about becoming a cardiologist at the age of seven was 'cute.' Certainly Mrs. McCall did. She'd comment about her little genius frequently to her friends but seemed convinced that Lindsey would 'grow out' of the doctor dream and have goals like Paula and me—husband, kids, the whole nine yards." Julie waved her hands expansively as if she were the conductor of the large house and all its inhabitants.

"But Lindsey's father knew better, and so did I. When Lindsey said something, you just knew you weren't listening to a child; she was never like any of my other friends who were going to be astronauts one day and veterinarians the next. Lindsey never wavered. And the chasm between the dyads of Lindsey and her dad, and Paula with her mom, widened with each passing year."

Just as Julie had closed her eyes, Rich heard the click of the recorder, signaling that the tape was full. He reached into the briefcase that sat next to the couch he was on and retrieved a clean tape. As he did so, he wondered why Julie was suddenly having trouble staying on point. She had intended to give him some background information about Paula Livingston almost forty-five minutes ago, yet her story seemed to wander all over the place. He couldn't understand the reason for Julie's sudden spurt of disorganized thinking and was happy to have the recordings because there was no way he could make sense of the details of the McCall family as Julie was now relating them. He could only hope that listening a few more times would help him assimilate all the detail and apply the information to Paula.

As if she had read his mind, Julie stood up and walked over to the large Oriental rug that had been appropriated by Max's splayed-out body, crouched down beside the dog's head, and then began to rub his velvety ears. The big dog stretched out his long, lean body in appreciation and offered her a front paw without opening his eyes.

After a minute or so, Julie wisely stood up and, away from those huge paws, walked over to the couch where Jansen sat, and took a seat at the far end of the couch; turning her dark brown eyes on him, she said evenly. "If you'd come to see me six months ago, I'd have had no problem in explaining Paula Livingston to you in one sentence: Paula's an alcoholic and a drug addict who manipulates everyone to her advantage, whether family, friend, or acquaintance. I would have also told you that she was the most accomplished liar that I've ever met. And that is all true; she is all of those things and more." The pitch of Julie's voice had dropped to a point that Jansen could barely hear her. "But I never stopped to wonder how she got there—how it *felt* being the much older sister of a genius and how deeply Tom McCall's obvious preference for Lindsey had to have *hurt*; I never tried to understand her pathological jealousy of Lindsey and her patent manipulation of their mother to side with her against Lindsey. By the time I was old enough to recognize Paula's alcoholism, I just thought it fit with everything I knew about the woman; she was weak, amoral, and she disgusted me." Julie grimaced. "Paula made it easy for others to dislike her; when Lindsey and I were little kids, she'd laugh at us, of the clothes we wore, and of the cartoon characters we liked. When she would lean over to speak to us, her breath always smelled funny. Lindsey and I would joke about it. Now I know what that funny smell was. I am sure she had started her drinking really early, just like my Lindsey, and I'll bet my house that it was for the same reasons that Lindsey did."

Jansen was surprised to see the sheen of tears in Julie's eyes; she didn't look upset, and she looked and sounded calm—almost peaceful yet sad, a combination of emotions that was pure paradox. He waited, making sure he kept his face expressionless, fascinated by the ruthless honesty this woman possessed. In that way, Julie Grayson reminded him of his wife, Laura, always examining herself and her beliefs for consistency and conformance with her faith.

"Almost exactly six months ago, Ted and I came home early from a party at Ted's boss's house; Lindsey was babysitting for us. She'd started doing that when she turned fourteen, and we paid her the going rate. It was an arrangement that seemed to suit all of us and had been working just fine—or so we thought. We had given her permission to have her girlfriends over while she was sitting, but no boys. Lindsey wasn't expecting us home until after midnight as it was a Saturday night, but we got home at ten. The kids were all upstairs asleep, but Lindsey and her best friend were so stoned and drunk that they couldn't stand up. I called my mother to come to stay with the younger kids, while Ted and I took Lindsey and

Brittany to the emergency room to get their stomachs pumped out. Little by little the whole story came out over the next few weeks." Julie took a deep breath, expelled it, shook her arms and hands as if to discard negative emotion, and stood and glanced at her watch. "Hey, Rich it's after two. How about some lunch? I could use some calories about now; how about you?"

She was smiling, but the smile didn't quite make it up to those dark brown eyes.

"Sure, Julie, sounds good. How can I help?"

When Rich stood up, Max did as well; he stood watching Julie and Jansen, both ears standing straight up but with a very slight curve at the tips and his golden eyes fixed on Jansen.

Julie had started over to the kitchen section of the great room but had stopped when Max had stirred. "You know, I've never known any Dobermans, Max, but after meeting you, I can see you are one extraordinary creature, aren't you?" The big dog had turned his attention to Julie at the sound of his name and had cocked his head while he regarded her. "Can he have a couple of bones, Rich? I was planning to send you and Max home with all this dog food we no longer need, but now I think we'll spend this weekend looking for a rescue dog. Who knows, maybe a Doberman."

Without waiting for Rich's answer, Julie had gone to the pantry and returned with a couple of good-sized bones. She extended her arm toward Max, held the two bones out on the flat of her hand, and said, "Come get 'em, boy."

Max was *very* interested; he loved his food but stood to look at Jansen, waiting for an okay to take the treats.

Rich smiled at the dog. "Good boy, Max, it's okay, get the bones."

In a flash the dog sat down in front of Julie, eyes fixed on the dog bones. Julie crouched down so that the dog could take the treats, and in another flash they were gone. "My gosh, Rich; this dog is well trained. Did you do the training?"

Jansen smiled. "I wish I could take the credit, but my wife, Laura, was the one who trained this guy. Laura was friendly with a breeder in Pearland who had been breeding Dobermans for over thirty years; Candace sold Max to us when he was a little guy at twenty-six pounds." Both Julie and Rich looked at the eighty-five-pound mass of muscle and bone and tried to imagine him as a little puppy. "Candace gave Laura a bunch of puppy training books to read, which she devoured and introduced her to the Doberman Whisperer of Houston, Kirk Kendell. Laura spent hundreds of hours with Max at this Kendell's classes. All I had to do was show up at a class once a week to learn what they were learning." Jansen smiled again at his dog. "There have been many times in the last year, Julie, that I don't know what I would have done without him."

Julie had begun chopping and then sautéing mushrooms and onions for a quick marinara sauce and directed Jansen to get a pot boiling for the spaghetti while they talked. Pointing to a wine cooler that Jansen had not noticed, tucked away in a corner beside the refrigerator, Julie suggested, "Why don't you select a pinot that suits you, Rich? I could use a glass or two of wine. How about you?"

Jansen was bending down, looking at the contents of the cooler; the shelves were arranged by whites starting with several types of Pinots and Chardonnays, then four shelves of various brands of cabernets, and merlots. The reds predominated; apparently the Graysons preferred red over white wine. Soon the kitchen was suffused with the intoxicating fragrance of sautéed garlic. Jansen selected a Rutherford Cabernet, found an opener, and set it on the top of the cooler to breathe. Glancing over from the stove, Julie chuckled when she saw the bottle, "I take it you don't care for the pinots, Rich?"

"Actually I do, but spaghetti begs for a heartier wine. Do you mind?"

"Not at all, we keep the pinots for hot days and for friends who really don't like the reds, so that's great." Smiling, she accepted a glass from him, and they clinked their glasses. Rich lifted his glass and gazed into Julie's pretty face. "To a superb hostess, loyal friend, and all-around classy lady. Julie, it's a privilege to be invited into your life like this. I thank you." Rich watched the blush invade Julie's neck and cheeks, but she stood there gamely, returning his gaze and bowing her head in acceptance of the compliments.

Places now set and the steaming bowls of spaghetti sauce and garlic bread in front of them, Julie sipped her wine. "Please, Rich, help yourself." Watching as Jansen loaded his plate with food, Julie sipped her wine and said, "It's only been in the last couple of months that I've allowed myself to drink again." Then she laughed as Rich placed the loaded plate on Julie's place mat and grabbed her empty plate to serve himself. Softly, Julie murmured a thank you and what sounded like a quick grace and began to eat. Suddenly her eyes widened, and Julie exclaimed, "I didn't even ask you, you do like garlic I hope?"

Jansen laughed quietly. "No worry here, Julie, all my friends know that they'll be eating plenty of garlic whenever they come to my house to eat. This is delicious marinara sauce by the way; you must have a tomato garden?" The sauce was too delicate to be canned, and Rich had not recalled Julie opening a can, so he figured that she must have frozen the summer's crop.

Nodding, Julie commented, "You sound like a cook."

"Cooking relaxes me, but I find that I'm a tough critic when I go out to restaurants. Todd hates going out to dinner with me. Speaking of Todd, why didn't he have you testify at Lindsey's trial? You would have made a great witness and may have mitigated some of Paula's power over the jury."

Julie took a big slice of the steamy and aromatic garlic bread, placed it on her plate, broke off a piece, soaked it in the sauce, then brought it to her mouth, and ate it. "My favorite part of a spaghetti dinner." Wiping her mouth with a large napkin, she took a swallow of her wine, then set the glass down very deliberately, and replied to Rich, "I wanted to testify *very* badly, Rich. And you're right, I think I'd have made an impression on the jury; whether my testimony would have altered the verdict will never be known, but it was academic because Lindsey would not permit Todd to call me as a witness. In fact, she made it explicitly clear that she did not want me in the courtroom. I ignored her of course."

Taking another sip of her wine, Julie laughed. "Man, I could get used to this life: good food, conversation, and wine rather than a sandwich on the run." But then she added opaquely, "I'm so grateful that I didn't testify, Rich, despite the possibility that it might have helped Lindsey. I'd have done more damage to Paula with my testimony than she has done to herself, and she doesn't need more pain inflicted on her; she torments herself more than adequately."

Rich started to clear off the dishes, but Julie placed her hand on his arm and said that she would have plenty of time to clean up later. She took the bottle of wine, her glass, and the plate of garlic bread back to the sitting room side of the great room and resumed her claim of the ugly chair. Rich followed her with his half-filled glass of cabernet and settled down on the couch once again.

He had just switched the tape recorder back on when Julie said, "C. S. Lewis called experience 'that most brutal of teachers but you learn by God, you learn.'" She closed her eyes for a few seconds. "Lindsey's trial ended on a Friday in January, and we discovered that our daughter Lindsey was an alcoholic that next weekend. Interesting coincidence, wouldn't you say, Rich? But I have never believed in coincidence, have you?"

He didn't but saw no need to say so; Julie was lost in her story.

"This all started as a dare when they were eleven. There are three of them who are alcoholics along with Lindsey: Brittany, Sarah, and Lisa. Each of the girls says it was someone else's dare, someone they won't name. Lindsey says it was her idea and has insisted that to be the case from the beginning. When they were at each other's houses, they would drink whatever liquor was in their parents' liquor cabinet, carefully replacing what they had taken with water.

"None of us ever noticed. When we all discovered what was happening, we hospitalized the whole group, and cut off their supply, and these kids went into DTs! That's how much booze they had been drinking for the last five *years* ... and we had no clue that it was happening."

Julie opened her eyes, and they were haunted. "How can you not notice that your kid is a drunk? How is that possible? Lindsey has told us that she started each day with straight vodka and mixed it with whatever drugs the others could get from home. Her words were never slurred, her grades were excellent, and the last two years she's been captain of her soccer team."

Rich felt nailed to the couch as he tried to imagine the guilt; the burden of the guilt was unimaginable to Jansen, incomprehensible. He could feel it like a presence in the room: heavy, dark, oppressive.

Julie continued speaking despite the cracked voice, signaling swallowed sobs, and the silent tears coursing down her face. "I think back of my facile analysis of Paula, my disgust at her addictions, my frustration with Mr. and Mrs. McCall for never dealing with Paula, and my complete exasperation with

Lindsey for her refusal to deal with her older sister." Julie was shaking her head as she whispered, "And it's myself that I'm disgusted with … I knew *nothing*." She practically spit out the word as she glanced briefly at Jansen and then quickly looked away as if she couldn't bear to meet his eyes. Rich started to reach across the couch to touch her arm and offer the meager consolation of his touch when she suddenly met his eyes to declare, "I bet I've read fifteen books on drug addiction and alcoholism in the last six months. And do you know what I've learned?"

Rich could not take his eyes away from hers, now filled with deep pain, and shook his head while she continued, "The psychiatrists believe that addiction is biochemically based; clinical psychologists that it's rooted in poor self-esteem; and the non-Ph.D. counselors that it's a combination along with family history." Julie sighed deeply. "Alcoholics Anonymous claims that there is no way to know why one person can drink a couple of drinks and stop while another cannot stop at three or five or an entire bottle. The first step toward the cure AA teaches is to accept that there *is no cure*." Julie held up her wine glass and said, "I could not drink anything for the first three months after we found out about Lindsey. Ted and I tortured ourselves with the what-if scenarios: what if we'd decided to keep no alcohol in the house, what if Lindsey had never seen us drinking, what if we'd sent her to Catholic school rather than public school? It went on and on for weeks; we could not stop.

"One night about four months ago, Ted and I were down here in the living room talking and crying when suddenly I said that I *really* wanted a glass of wine right then. I couldn't believe that I had said it, but after the words had come out, I realized that I would not be a bad mother, an irresponsible parent if I had some wine." Julie pointed to the wine cooler.

"We had packed up the cooler and were going to give it away, and all the wine bottles had been packed away in boxes ready for donation somewhere; we just hadn't figured out where yet."

"But when I said that, the strangest expression came over my husband's face. Ted jumped up and told me he'd be right back. A few minutes later, he came in wheeling the cooler, told me not to move just as I was getting up to help him, disappeared for ten more minutes and came back loaded down with three really heavy crates of the wine that we were going to give away. By now, I was trying not to laugh; it was after midnight, after all, and we didn't want to wake the kids, so the harder I tried to suppress my giggles, the harder I was laughing." Julie's smile was warm and genuine, remembering. "We had not *smiled* in weeks, and we both understood without saying it that we could not let this destroy us. We had to get our life back. But you know what, Rich?" Her eyes drifted around the sitting room, scanned the wall of awards and ribbons, then her gaze shifted back to him.

"I couldn't have done it without Ted. I couldn't have made the jump." Jansen felt as if her eyes were boring into him, and very quietly, she said, "'No one ever told me that grief felt so like fear.' Ever read C. S. Lewis's *The Problem of Pain*, Rich?"

This time she looked as if she were expecting a response, so he answered, "No, but my wife Laura did and also *Mere Christianity* and *The Divorce*." He smiled, thinking of Laura and the surprising similarities between his beloved art teacher, Laura, and this calculus professor, Julie, who had a master's degree in theology and mathematics. They smiled at each other until he prompted her, "'No one ever told me that grief felt so much like fear.'"

Julie stared at him. "What does that phrase mean to you, Rich?"

Rich had simply parroted Julie in an attempt to help her recall where she was in her story; he was unprepared for the cascade of emotion that suffused him when he took a few seconds to consider Lewis's words. Suddenly he was awash in memory.

Saturday after Saturday, Rich and Max had gone to see Father John at the rectory of the Co-Cathedral of the Sacred Heart in downtown Houston where Rich had gone when he could no longer anesthetize, through nonstop work, the gut-wrenching sorrow at the sudden death of Laura. The drive to the Co-Cathedral that first Saturday was one of the harder things he had done in his life. He'd been a lifelong Catholic and had attended daily mass for years, but his relationship with priests was bounded by the sacraments: confession, mass, baptism. The idea of seeking a personal relationship with a priest was alien. But from the time Rich had known Laura and they began to speak of such things, he had been aware that Laura had met monthly with a priest in their own parish or a nearby parish. Through the years, Laura would periodically bring up a subject that she and her current director had discussed. Although Rich had tried to understand the point of spiritual direction, it made no sense to him. And Laura had never pushed it. When he and Laura had started going to mass downtown at the Cathedral, she had asked Father Tobin to be her spiritual director and had gone to see him more or less monthly during the last five years of her life.

About a month before she was killed, Jansen had taken Laura out for dinner to one of their favorite restaurants to celebrate her birthday. Everything had been perfect at the restaurant, and the two had lingered over their meal, discussing all kinds of things that they had not taken the time to talk about in years. Rich asked Laura that night why she thought she needed formal direction in her spiritual life; what was it that made her keep going to this priest then that priest, month after month, year after year?

Her lovely, violet eyes had been filled with deep love and understanding when she smiled at him and replied, "It's hard being a Catholic, Rich, and I simply cannot do it alone."

Rich and Laura had been married for over twelve years, but with that comment, Jansen realized there were parts of his wife that he knew nothing about and that maybe he never would. Her answer bewildered him, and he began to apply her response to some lack in him and in their marriage, but before he'd been able to travel too far down that road, Laura had placed her hand on his and squeezed very tightly to get his attention. When she had it, Laura said, "Rich, this has nothing to do with you or with our marriage. It's not about *you*, Rich." She had stopped speaking and was staring at him, fiercely.

Reading him like an open book, Laura had laughed. Rich had always loved the sound of her laughter; it was like bells. "I envy your faith, honey. You don't have the questions I do; you just believe." Her expression sobering, she added, "You're still a Marine; the rules fit you like a glove."

Julie's face was concerned, her forehead furrowed in a frown; she leaned forward and grabbed Jansen's arm as she apologized, her voice quiet and measured, "I am so very sorry, Rich. I don't know where you went just now, but I sure did not want to be the person who sent you there." Julie sat on the couch, her body turned toward his and her hand on his in what had to be an extremely uncomfortable position. Jansen realized that she was giving him the chance to speak about what he had just been thinking about. He shook his head.

Julie nodded her understanding; they needed to stay on point. "By one that morning, Ted had opened one of our favorite reds, and we were toasting each other when we heard a stifled cough; we both jumped at the sound as if we'd been caught necking and turned around to see Lindsey standing on the stairs watching us. She was crying. Of course, we assumed that she was upset by the fact that her parents were sitting up and sneakily drinking, but that was far from the case. Lindsey came downstairs, sat between us, hugged us both, and managed to explain the reason for her tears."

Julie blinked at Rich, laughed wryly, and said, "She told us that she was happy to see that our life had a chance of getting back to normal … that maybe she hadn't ruined everything by being born and adopted by us.

"The three of us talked until four in the morning: no counselor, no psychiatrist—just us. We had not talked with our daughter alone like that since we'd found out about her alcoholism." Julie looked sadly at Jansen, "We'd forgotten that *we* were her parents and we had allowed all of our actions, behaviors, and even our words with Lindsey to be directed by the professionals. The psychiatrist had suggested getting rid of all the alcohol in the house, so of course we thought we must. We were so afraid that we let strangers take over the parenting of our own child; we figured we had to be incapable. If we were good parents, how could our daughter have become an alcoholic right under our very noses? That is why I keep Lewis's thought about grief and fear in my head. He's right: the two are inseparable."

They both heard the telltale click of the tape recorder; while Jansen dug into his briefcase for another cassette, Julie watched the rain coursing down the patio doors and puddling on the concrete. When the tape began to play, she continued speaking.

"Rich, I don't *know* that any of what I am going to tell you about Paula is fact, but I believe Paula never had a chance at a 'normal'—" Julie's fingers spread in the air as she made the quotation marks "—life; Lindsey never wanted one, but that's all Paula wanted—to be a wife and a mother along with a part-time job as a nurse. And she desperately wanted her father's love and respect, but she never had it. After that dreadful scene about Paula's prom dress, Mr. McCall hardly spoke to her, and I am positive that Paula's drinking kept increasing to deal with the awful pain she felt."

Julie picked up her wineglass, cradled it in her hand, and placed her chin on the lip of the glass as she stared out at the rain. "Can you guess the reason Lindsey gave us for having made the dare to the other three girls?" It took Jansen a second to track back to Julie's daughter, Lindsey. Julie's gaze remained fixed on the rain as she answered her own question. "She was *lonely.*" Only then did Julie turn back to look at Jansen. They sat on her couch listening to the rain and to the gentle rhythmic sound of Max's breathing.

"One of the main reasons that Lindsey and I, as young children, became so close so quickly is that we *recognized* each other. Even when they are very young, kids can be remarkably sensitive; Lindsey and I were well aware of the differences between us and other kids—different from them for entirely different reasons of course. Although I was a bit more 'average' than Lindsey in terms of career choice, my interest in the church," she was fingering the crucifix around her neck unconsciously while she spoke, "set me as far apart from most people as did Lindsey's drive to become a doctor. I heard my mother talking to my dad and to Lindsey's mom on several occasions about her fear that I'd become a nun." Julie sat with her feet curled up under as her as she twisted the crucifix on the delicate gold chain. Glancing over at Jansen, she continued, "Lindsey and I used to laugh that we'd look normal if we'd just keep our mouths shut; if we never talked about what we were really interested in, then no one could guess how weird we really were.

"As I listened to our daughter explain what she meant by loneliness, I realized she had not felt she fit into the family the same way her younger sisters and brother did. When she was younger, we had explained to her that she was adopted, and she had somehow developed a sense of separateness because of it. Lindsey told us that it really wasn't the taste or even the high of the liquor or the drugs that she'd been addicted to, it was the feeling of *belonging* that she felt when she'd drink because she knew the others were doing the same thing as she was.

"Lindsey accused me that night, as the three of us talked, of not understanding how lonely she had felt, and I'd explained to her that she was wrong—so very wrong. I know very well what loneliness is and how it feels. But that I'd learned when very young, no one could understand my increasing devotion to and curiosity about my faith, the saints, and all things religious, not even my best friend, Lindsey McCall. That loneliness must be *embraced*. That's what kept us talking until four in the morning with her. Ted and I talked about the blessing of being created a unique and irreplaceable human being, one that carries with it the obligation to *bear* that exclusivity. And of learning to look inward for direction rather than outside, to other people and things who will usually confuse and distract." Julie sat quietly, sipping her wine.

Rich understood why Julie reminded him so much of Laura; these could have been her words to him in many conversations through the years. Although he had tried to follow those conversations, he'd frequently been distracted by the thousands of details of the Harris County Homicide Department. These two could have been soul sisters, he thought, and was grateful that the thoughts of his dead wife were unaccompanied by guilt or by sadness. Noticing his silence, Julie lifted an eyebrow at him, a silent invitation to comment. Again, he shook his head.

After a minute or two, Julie nodded as if in satisfaction. "I cannot imagine how lonely Paula must have been, still is, I am sure. I'd guess that she started to drink around the same age that Lindsey did although we were too young to know. And I'd guess that she was hoping that she'd be caught, just like Lindsey was but her parents either never saw what was happening or maybe they simply closed their eyes to it."

Very softly, Julie said, "But Lindsey, as the little sister, knew about Paula's drinking; she believed she caused Paula's alcoholism, at least in part."

"How do you know that, Julie?" His tone was more abrupt than he intended. It wasn't that her comment surprised Jansen; in fact, in thinking back to his first meeting with Lindsey McCall and her inexplicably unguarded narrative about Paula, Julie's insight made perfect sense. And if that were so, then Paula would have used her younger sister's guilt to her advantage in a myriad of ways.

Julie didn't reply right away. She still held her half-filled wine glass in her hand, and she was twirling the deep red cabernet around in the goblet, watching the viscous legs left by the alcohol trace down the glass. Strangely, she was smiling when she looked over at Jansen; both eyebrows were raised in a look that was expectant. *Of course*, he thought. *Julie had listened to the recording of his interview of Lindsey and knew what he had heard*; Julie was waiting for him to arrive at the same conclusion as she had. Thinking hard, Jansen nodded slowly.

"By the time Tom McCall was killed, Paula more or less had taken total control of her mother's care. We were only sophomores at Rice, but I think Lindsey understood as much or more than most of her mother's pathology—more than most of the doctors caring for her, certainly more than Paula did. Lindsey stayed away because she saw that Paula got great satisfaction from the dependence her mother had on her. When she did visit, Lindsey attempted to explain Mrs. McCall's need for exercise. Within certain parameters, the function of her heart could get stronger; that working the body would improve oxygenation throughout the musculature and body. Lindsey was a born teacher; she could explain this stuff so that you could really understand.

"I went with Lindsey once when she had decided to go to Clear Lake to see her mother. Paula had hired sitters by then, and we drove down to see Mrs. McCall when we thought Paula would be at work." Julie was sitting up, her legs crossed, with one leg swaying back and forth to some internal rhythm. "Lindsey had her mother walking slowly from her bed, in the room that had been Lindsey's, to the foyer. They looked almost like any mother and daughter, both tall and slim with blonde hair. Ann McCall had been a beautiful woman and at that time was still pretty, even with the cost that her disease had taken on her body. Lindsey had told the sitter to take a break and to come back in an hour. Things were progressing along very well when Paula blew in, and all hell blew loose. It was obvious that she'd been drinking ... although her words slurred only slightly.

"On the way back to school, I tried to get Lindsey to talk about what had happened, even to admit that she knew Paula was drinking and was most likely an alcoholic. I was ranting because I was so angry at Paula for her behavior and her unbelievable selfishness. Lindsey was driving and had not said one word. When I started to turn on her, too, I saw the tears. Lindsey never cries, *never*.

"So I knew. She felt responsible for the whole mess, for Paula's jealousy and for her mother's slow deterioration. I think Lindsey knew that she'd never develop that drug in time to help her mother; at some level she knew. That's why I am sure that Lindsey did not give her mother that drug; she would have known that it was too late to help her.

"I went to Lindsey's trial—managed a leave of absence without pay to do it—and was *riveted* by Paula's performance." The corners of Julie's mouth turned down with her last word. "That was what it was really; it was the best performance I've ever seen, and you know the strange thing? I'm sure that everything she said was fundamentally the truth." Julie's voice trailed off as she sat staring at Jansen, her mind clearly back at the trial. "The minute that Paula took the stand and opened her mouth, I knew that Lindsey didn't have a chance. Paula would *bury* her and not with a direct attack, never that: but with inference, implication, and omission." Julie took an enormous deep breath and let it out very slowly. "Lindsey could never see how dangerous Paula could be to her, so I am confident that the comments Paula quoted Lindsey as having said were literally right. I could easily imagine Lindsey telling Paula that she hated taking care of their mother." Julie paused, reflecting. "Lindsey and Paula didn't like each other; they were far too different to be able to communicate, but Lindsey *trusted* Paula." Julie nodded at Jansen's raised eyebrow. "I know … but if Paula asked Lindsey what she thought or felt about anything, Lindsey would tell her. The thought would never have crossed Lindsey's mind that Paula could hurt her … would even *think* of hurting her until she sat and listened to Paula's testimony over those two days."

❧

A man would do nothing if he waited
until he could do it so well that no
one could find fault with what he
has done.
—John Cardinal Newman

21

Jansen had made it home from Julie Grayson's with enough time to shower, shave, and change into something he thought acceptable for a dinner with the Philbin sisters, the reporter from the *Houston Tribune,* and some others who Todd had said would be attending but whose names now Rich could not recall. Thankfully, the monsoon that had erupted over Friendswood had cleared by the time he hit I-45, allowing him to carve almost an hour off his drive time.

Appraising his reflection in the mirrored closet doors, Rich turned to check the crease in the dark-brown dress trousers and critically evaluated the mahogany-striped white shirt, pastel Hermes tie, and the camel's hair sport jacket. Deciding it would do, he turned to see if Max needed to go out before he left and smiled as he looked at the big guy sound asleep on his bed. They certainly had gotten plenty of exercise on the turn-around trip to Friendswood, and he knew the dog would be exhausted after sleeping in a strange house the previous night. Like all of us, the Doberman liked his routine, and Bell's country house had become home for Max; Schubert playing in the background helped, too. If he hadn't been so wired from the events of the last week, the meeting with Julie Grayson and her family, and the anticipation of this dinner,

Rich would have been more than happy to curl up on the king-sized bed with a novel.

Jansen crouched down next to Max, then murmured, "Watch the house, boy." And he took the stairs two at a time. Checking his watch, he saw that he had about ninety minutes to get to the Philbin house, barring accidents along the way. The chill in the air felt great; he was happy he'd selected the camel jacket, too warm for many Houston nights but perfect when the October norther blew in, to drive the temperature down into the low fifties.

Jansen smiled as he drove out the unmarked dirt road that led to Bell's house on Route 150; no one would ever find the home without careful and precise directions. He had overshot the road several times before he became familiar with the copse of pines that was the solitary identifying mark of the way.

Although it was a Friday night, there was surprisingly little traffic on the road, so he decided to take I-45. Jansen thought about the invaluable time he had spent with Julie Grayson. It was so strange, he thought. Laura had been dead for five years; in those five years, he had not encountered one woman who interested him in the slightest. A couple of his buddies at work had devised some awkward dinners, which he had suffered through before finally giving up, and Kensington had talked with him several times about Jansen's isolation from everything but work. And then in just one week, he met not one but two women who not only interested, but fascinated him.

Julie Grayson was not beautiful, but there was a presence about the woman that was almost electric. His interest in her was not at all sexual; she was married, and even if she were not, the chemistry between them was not an erotic one, but … he pondered just what it was about the woman as he slowed the car to turn onto 610, the loop that circled downtown

Houston. And he kept thinking and discarding adjectives to describe Julie Grayson and then decided that he had it: wisdom, the woman was wise; she emanated it. Although the word felt alien, he decided that this was his attraction to her; but his attraction to her best friend, Lindsey? Jansen took a deep breath as he decided not to go there tonight.

The Philbins lived in South Hampton, an exclusive small community just past the Texas Medical Center, identifiable by the gates that had cloistered these mansions long before the notion of gated communities came into vogue. Jansen drove down Fannin Street slowly, looking to his right at the lights of the enormous Texas Medical Center complex, thinking of Lindsey McCall and the decades she had spent there struggling to save the lives of those entrusted to her care.

Leaving the medical center behind, Rich drove toward the brightly lit Mecom Fountains, which were disgorging ten-foot columns of illuminated geysers into the air. He turned left onto Sunset Boulevard where he slowed down to look for a gate that matched the description Todd had given to him. Sunset Boulevard is one of the lovelier streets in Houston, with huge hundred-year-old cypress trees lining both sides of the residential street. The Rice University campus borders the northern side of the street, while a ten-foot, red brick wall runs continuously along the south side of Sunset to provide total privacy behind the wall for the residents in the mansions from curious onlookers. The address of the Philbin house was 5 Sunset Drive, but of course, there were no numbers to be seen. Jansen slowed his car to a crawl as he searched for the black metal gates Todd had described, when suddenly they appeared in the night. Jansen stopped his Mercedes, pulled into the driveway, and looked up at the securely closed imposing gates, wondering how one announced his arrival, when magically the doors swung inward to reveal a massive, white stucco antebellum mansion with four columns brightly lit by floodlights, and several cars parked in a circular drive in the front of the house. Just as Rich drew up the car to the front, a grinning and extremely fit middle-aged man, looking like a cross between Morgan Freeman and Danny Glover, walked rapidly over to his car, opened the door, and said in a resonant baritone, "Let me take and park your car for you, Mr. Jansen. Ms. Eleanor and Ms. Marguerite are in the drawing room straight through the foyer."

Did he say drawing room? Rich thought as he swung his long legs out of the convertible, stood, and smiled back at the dignified handsome features of the man standing in a distinctly military posture behind the opened door of the car. "*Semper fi*," Rich said as he handed over his keys.

The grin widened, and the man replied, "Hoorah." He extended his hand to Rich, took the car keys, and silently watched him climb the stairs, cross the porch, turn the door knob of the large mahogany door, and enter the house.

The moment Jansen entered the mansion, a tall female version of the ex-military butler appeared; in a soft and almost melodious voice, she said, "Hello, Mr. Jansen, please follow me. Ms. Marguerite and Ms. Eleanor are in the drawing room."

The woman looked to be in her mid-sixties but was slender and carried herself with grace and poise. Jansen guessed the man who had parked his car was her husband; he followed her through the spacious foyer with what looked to be twenty-foot ceilings, hearing their heels clicking on the wide-planked, dark-stained hardwood floors. Following the woman into a room he assumed was the drawing room, Jansen saw a group of people collected around an enormous embroidered tapestry. They were standing with wine glasses in their hands deeply absorbed in their examination of the fabric when a small white-haired woman spotted her assistant.

Moving more quickly across the large room than a woman of her years should, Eleanor Philbin extended her hands; one reached out and up to the tall woman as she said, "Thank you, Sophia, I didn't even hear you come in." The other went to Rich, and she said, "Thank you so much for coming, Mr. Jansen, what a pleasure it is to meet you." Sophia smiled at both Eleanor and Jansen as she glided out of the room. Rich was charmed by the diminutive, little person before him; she looked to be less than five feet tall, yet carried herself with the presence of a much taller person. Her eyes were bright blue and filled with warmth and kindness. Jansen took the tiny hand and held it in his large one, gazed back into the face of one of the wealthiest women in the state of Texas, and replied, "Thank you for the invitation, Ms. Philbin. It's a privilege to meet you and to be invited to your home."

The members of the group that was assembled around the tapestry were all moving slowly across the room to join Eleanor and Jansen. Although he was not close enough to see the details of the fabric, the color, dimensions, and overall theme of the exquisite piece were reminiscent of the Bayreuth tapestry in Holland; the dominant figure of a white unicorn surrounded by forest and hunting scenes were visible even from Jansen's more than twenty-foot distance from the piece. Quickly scanning the group approaching him, the only one he knew was Todd Kensington. But then he looked again and was surprised to see Julie Grayson directing a smile his way. The elderly woman leading the group had to be Marguerite Philbin, Eleanor's sister: the same beautiful soft white hair, sky blue eyes and diminutive stature. As Marguerite made the introductions, Jansen was rapidly assimilating the names of the group as he was introduced: the tall, slender, dark-haired Kate Townsend stood next to Steve Cooper, smiling as Rich congratulated her on her journalistic triumph with her series on McCall, the Texas Medical Center, and academic research.

Todd had e-mailed the series to Rich early in the week and had advised him to take the time to read the lengthy and extraordinary series of articles. Jansen had not wanted to take the time to read them but was enthralled by the first paragraph. Smiling back at this attractive reporter, Rich found himself gushing as he described his reaction to Townsend's series. Finally stopping the litany of complimentary remarks, Jansen declared, "Sorry, I didn't mean to be so effusive; you must get pretty tired of hearing this." Rich was somewhat embarrassed and looked it.

Townsend graciously laughed in reply, "Are you kidding? I love it! I dust off my awards every night before I go to bed." Her eyes were almost black and seemed to dance as she responded to him; watching her glance at Cooper, he wondered if there might be something between the two of them. Just then Jeff Simmons walked over to introduce himself as the editor of the *Houston Tribune*. Rich was in the middle of explaining his new job to Jeff when he noticed Sophia back in the midst of the room and leaning down to hear what Marguerite was whispering in her ear. Sophia clapped her hands, and in the ensuing silence, Marguerite asked that the group move to the dining room, extending a thin arm in the direction of the rear of the room as she spoke.

Simmons walked along with Rich on the short journey into the next room where an elegant dining room table sat gleaming with crystal, silver, and china under an enormous chandelier. Noting the small name cards in front of each plate, Jansen saw his name between Simmons and Eleanor Philbin. He followed Jeff's lead, as the newspaper editor seemed to know the protocols, and stood behind the chair that sat at the place marked with his name. In a surprisingly powerful voice, Eleanor asked the group to be seated and began to pull out her chair, then smiled engagingly at Jansen when he took over to pull the large English Tudor chair away from the table and help her bring the heavy chair back in, so that she could reach her food comfortably.

Looking around the table as Rich took his seat, he noted the journalist and Cooper, the cardiologist, seated next to her, directly across the table from him. Interestingly, Todd sat at one end of the long table and Marguerite at the other. Todd seemed preoccupied, his attention on Marguerite Philbin who smiled at him and began to speak. "Eleanor and I thank you for taking the time out of your busy schedules to join us for dinner here at our home and to assist Todd and Rick Jansen in devising a strategy to reveal the truth about Dr. McCall." Her blue gaze surveyed the six people who sat listening and eventually lingered on Jansen. The lights from the chandelier shone on Marguerite in such a way that her soft white hair seemed to float about her head like a halo; that sort of fit, Rich mused, because the face below the pure-white hair was cherubic. There was no other word to describe the clarity and depth of the almost sapphire gaze that now rested on him.

Interrupting his musings, Marguerite declared, "But it is you, Mr. Jansen, whom I thank most of all; we all understand the extent of the risks you have shouldered with your decision to assist Dr. McCall, and I assure you that such a sacrifice will not go unnoticed. You are in my prayers each and every day."

Suddenly supremely discomfited, Jansen shifted in his seat, aware that all eyes were on him; he was relieved when he saw Sophia appear at Marguerite's left side, leaning over to speak softly. Marguerite nodded vigorously in agreement with what-ever Sophia had said, then announced with a merry smile, "Let's table our weighty subjects for the next hour or so and enjoy the feast that Sophia and Samuel have prepared for us." Immediately on the heels of that statement, out walked the ex-marine who had parked Jansen's car, this time balancing three bottles of wine and a tray of wineglasses.

Samuel moved quickly along both sides of the table as he poured either white or red wine; arriving at Jansen's place, Rich murmured, "Thank you, brother, merlot, please." And he caught the lightning-quick grin on the chiseled features as Samuel poured from a 1990 of Stags Leap Private Reserve. Just as Rich had lifted the crystal goblet to his lips, he heard Eleanor Philbin speaking, "Todd, would you be so kind as to say the blessing, please?"

Although it was difficult, Rich managed to suppress the laughter that was threatening to burst from his mouth; unfortunately, he happened to catch Julie Grayson's eyes and was forced to cover his mouth and fake a cough. When he looked up, Eleanor Philbin was looking directly at him, blue eyes twinkling and a small smile playing at her lips. Kensington was a Catholic but hadn't been to church since college as far as Jansen knew; he wondered if Todd remembered how to say grace when suddenly he heard Todd's clear baritone.

"Bless these gifts we are to receive, Lord; we ask your blessing on those who prepared this food and on all those here at this table. In Christ's name we pray."

It was a variation of the traditional Catholic grace, Jansen thought, but it sure worked well. He began to raise his eyes to send Kensington an approving nod when he heard Eleanor once again, "Lord, forgive please a small addendum to this grace. We ask you to send the gifts of the Holy Spirit upon us this evening as we work on your behalf to build a case for the appeal and acquittal of Lindsey McCall; we ask for wisdom, counsel, knowledge, fortitude, prudence, and piety in this work. We trust in you, Lord, for we know that we would not be here without your mercy and your love."

Her words seemed to hang in the air in the total silence

that followed. Samuel and Sophia stood at the left side of Marguerite's chair; the most senior member of their small group sat completely still with both hands folded in her lap with her eyes closed. Jansen had opened his eyes and was now looking at those sitting around the table, expecting to see discomfort or at least unease with these very Catholic prayers; instead, as he scanned the room, all were seated in an approximation of Marguerite's pose: eyes closed and heads lowered in prayer. *Amazing*, he thought. Just as he thought the word, Julie Grayson opened her eyes, and smiling at Jansen, she serenely said, "Amen."

"Thank you, Dear." Marguerite was smiling at Julie; with a nod to Sophia, the meal began: appetizers, then soup, followed by a veal dish that Rich could not name, but that was outstanding. About nine or so, Marguerite suggested that coffee and dessert be served in the library in about fifteen minutes and gave directions to the restrooms and to the patio for those who would like a breath of air before convening in the library.

Jansen walked out the patio doors onto a large flagstone patio with an assortment of chairs arranged invitingly; there was also a narrow flagstone path leading into the grounds that he decided to explore.

"Have you spoken to Paula Livingston yet, Rich?"

It was the attractive reporter who had silently followed him along the path. Although the patio was well lit, the path was dark, permitting Jansen to clearly see only the outlines of Kate Townsend. She was a few inches shorter than he, had dark hair loosely hanging about her face, and was dressed in a fitted pants suit; her eyes were hidden in the darkness. Jansen stopped and turned toward her.

"No, I haven't. Why do you ask?"

"I'm sure this will come across as meddling on my part;

in fact, I have been trying to talk myself out of talking with you all evening about this, but I feel compelled to—" Something large and furry ran across the path, and they were both startled. Kate laughed somewhat nervously.

"Let's move back into the light; that was probably a raccoon or a skunk, and I don't think either of us needs a skunk shower tonight." Jansen took hold of the reporter's elbow and gently steered her around so that they were facing the brightly lit patio and mansion. "*Compelled* is a strong word, Kate."

They were walking slowly back to the patio; Jansen was surprised to see how far they had walked away from the house. Like many of these old gated mansions, the Philbin property was quite large, most likely four or five acres. But they were now close enough to the lights that Rich could see Kate's face. She was attractive, with high cheekbones and large, wide-set, deep brown eyes, which were now drawn together in a frown of concentration.

"Yes, I know. It's not a feeling I've often had, and I'm not very comfortable bursting into your quiet walk with my compulsion but—"

Jansen could see that she was unsettled, so he placed his hand on her arm and applied enough pressure to slow her down. When Kate had stopped walking, Jansen turned his body so that the light would reveal his eyes to her. "Look, Kate, not two hours ago you had to listen to my meaningless patter about how great your series was, so this is good; turnabout is fair play, right?"

Kate was charmed and calmed by Jansen's touch and kindness. This was a guy who could take care of himself, she thought, as she regarded the military-style haircut, strong features, and cleft in his wide, masculine chin. His eyes were piercing; she couldn't tell if they were brown, hazel, or amber.

It looked as if they could be all three colors. He looked like a cop, she thought, or maybe a marine; she guessed him to be in his mid- or late-forties, but he had the build of a much younger man. Idly she scanned his lean body and surmised that he was a runner. Taking only a few seconds for this assessment, Kate gazed back into his eyes—hazel, she decided—took a deep breath, and said, "Todd told me that you were planning to see Paula early this next week, and I'm asking that you not do that."

Of all the things this reporter could have said to Jansen, this comment would never have made even his tenth list. He was dumbfounded and only stared at her.

Kate nodded her head vigorously, tossing her long, dark, curly mane in the process and fixed her gaze on Jansen. "I've spent many hours with Paula Livingston—" she cast her big, brown eyes up and to the right, clearly estimating "—over twenty hours give or take." Now she looked soberly at Rich. "I've never met with a more dangerous person. I am afraid that Paula could do you serious harm."

Oddly, now that Rich had heard her out, he was no longer surprised. In a peculiar way, he had almost been expecting this and was relieved to hear Kate say it out loud; but he had no idea of what to do with her information, not a clue. Paula Livingston held the key to her sister's prison cell; he was sure of it.

Kate was watching him, expecting some kind of response he was sure; but he had none, so he just said, "We'd better join the others in the library. They must be waiting for us."

Nodding, Kate asked, "Please consider very seriously what I have said, Rich. If you do go to see Paula, I beg you to be extremely careful with your explanation of why you are there."

Together they rapidly covered the remaining distance on the flagstone path, walked up the stone steps to the patio, and entered the house. None of the others was in the dining room, but Sophia waited there to show them into the library. Quickly she led them back into the long wood-planked hallway and took a left turn into an enormous wood-paneled library. To Kate, the beautiful room was somewhat reminiscent of Hank Reardon's library office at his Zurich home. Like Reardon's, the Philbin library was composed of floor-to-ceiling stacks with moveable ladders in each separate stack. Hank's house was suffused with light from the huge windows on three walls of the room and was built with very light oak. Lacking the views of Lake Geneva and the mountains overlooking the lake, there was only one window in this library, which looked over the gardens where she and Rich had just been walking. To the left of the window was a floor-to-ceiling stone fireplace, now pleasantly emitting a golden glow from a roaring fire. Kate walked over to the fireplace to warm her hands, grateful for the heat. The group was assembled on chairs and couches artfully arranged in a group so that they could be near the fire and one another. Steve extended a hand to her and pulled her down beside him on the soft, weathered, brown leather couch where he sat.

Glancing around the corner of the room, Kate scanned what looked like first volumes of familiar literary works as well as volumes of bound business journals: *Harvard Business Review*, *Wharton Monthly*, she could see clearly. Smiling to herself, she thought of the prejudicial attitudes that she used to hold against the really wealthy and was interrupted in her private musings by Eleanor.

"Please help yourself to dessert and coffee while Todd and Rich bring us up to date with their actions." Eleanor was dressed in a long, black skirt with a white silk blouse and looked elegant, as always. When no one moved to survey the dessert and coffee cart, Eleanor smiled sweetly and asked,

"Would you rather I serve you?" That elicited a rustling of activity as everyone rose rather than presume to have Eleanor Philbin serve them.

Now sitting, each with a dessert from the beautiful array, and a hot, steaming cup of coffee in front of them, the group was pronounced by Eleanor to be ready to begin. Todd began by reviewing the major issues of the case, mostly surrounding Paula's testimony and added a brief report on Rich's success in persuading the former medical director of Huntsville Prisons to drop his suit against Lindsey McCall and the State of Texas.

Kate, who had been half-listening to Todd—lulled by the wine she'd had at dinner, the food, and the fire—suddenly snapped to attention. "Excuse me, Todd, what did you just say about a medical director dropping a suit against Lindsey and the State of Texas?"

Everyone in the room began to laugh; Steve was laughing uproariously. Looking around at the amused faces laughing at her expense, Kate began to feel the old flush of anger at being the butt of a joke she hadn't heard, stopped herself, and began to laugh just as hard as everyone else.

❧

I believe you did not have a happy life.
I believe you were cheated.
I believe your best friends were loneliness and misery.
I believe your best enemies were anger and depression.
I believe joy was a game you could never play without stumbling.
I believe comfort, though you craved it, was forever a stranger.
I believe music had to be melancholy or not at all.
I believe no trinket, no precious metal, shone so bright as
your bitterness.
I believe you lay down in your coffin none the wiser and
unassuaged.
Oh, cold and dreamless under the wild, amoral, reckless, peaceful
flowers of the hillsides.
—MARY OLIVER

22

Paula Livingston paced the floor of her mother's empty house, smoking one cigarette after another and drinking her fourth vodka of the day, phone cradled between her right ear and shoulder as she listened to the litany of her oldest daughter's financial woes.

"Yes, Amy, I am still here. I'm just listening." She stood in the living room of the huge home in Clear Lake that she had inherited upon her mother's death. It was a beautiful room. Paula's mother had possessed impeccable taste; the house reflected Ann McCall's refined elegance in every chair, window covering, and mirror. Right now, Paula watched her reflection in the gilded six-foot-long mirror, which Ann had positioned perfectly to reflect the beauty of her rose garden. When Ann had been able to tend the garden, it had been breathtaking. Now the few roses that managed to force their way into the world seemed to do so by defiance; Paula had not paid attention to the growing problems with the irrigation system that Ann had cared for with vigilance. Ann had died in January, and the summer that was ending had been one of the hottest in the history of Houston. Had Paula noticed, she would have seen several of Ann's most-prized rose bushes dying from lack of water, but all Paula saw was her own reflection staring back at her as she examined herself from several angles.

Still looking good, kid, she thought as she inspected her body from the side, front, and back. She was on a portable phone, so she walked closer to the mirror to examine her forty-seven-year-old face for sags and wrinkles. Paula had enormous blue eyes with long lashes and lips that naturally looked as if they had been plumped up with collagen; most people assumed her to be in her mid to late thirties. Dressed in a form-fitting, white linen pantsuit with a black-and-white turtleneck sweater, Paula was a striking woman. She was checking her profile to see how much the turtleneck caused the skin under her chin to sag when she heard, "Mother, have you heard a word I've said?"

In fact, Paula had not heard a word her oldest daughter had said. But she sighed deeply and dramatically before lying, "Of course, I have heard every word you have said, Amy. I've been listening to you cry for thirty minutes now."

"Okay, then what was I saying before I asked if you were listening?"

Paula had expected this question and, with disgust dripping from each word, answered her daughter, "Amy, you were complaining about Bobby and Sarah's lousy performance in school."

"I was *not* talking about the kids, Mom, I was—"

"Well, Amy, you should have been. I'll bet their grades are still awful." Amy had shown her mother the report cards of her ten-year-old and her eight-year-old over two years ago, and Amy was still paying for that adolescent attempt to confide in her mother.

Of Paula's three children, Amy was the only one who maintained a relationship with her mother. Although she was now over thirty years old, Amy kept hoping that one day she would call her mother and have a "normal" conversation with her, like her friends said they had with their mothers. Her younger brother and sister had moved to California years ago, but Amy could not bring herself to leave Houston and her mother. Unfortunately, Amy was the least likely of Paula's three children to receive consistent affection from their mother.

Paula had married the father of her three children during her senior year of nursing school; her marriage had been one of the biggest mistakes of her young life. But by the age of twenty, Paula had developed a pattern of behavior that defined her character, motives, and actions. She had become unwilling and eventually incapable of accepting responsibility for the consequences of her wrong decisions. Tony and Paula had dated off and on since she'd been sixteen, and he had been twenty-one. The way Paula saw things, this marriage had ruined her life: Against her will, she married a man she did not love and was stuck with her infant daughter, Amy, before her twenty-first birthday. Paula never forgave Amy.

When a twenty-one-year-old man had arrived at the door to pick up his sixteen-year-old daughter to take her to her junior prom, Tom McCall had been infuriated. Although he had stormed out of the McCall house because of his anger about the exorbitant cost of Paula's junior prom dress and the deception of his wife and daughter in purchasing the dress against his wishes, McCall had felt badly about his outburst and had arrived back at home in time to see Tony and his daughter walking down the walkway of the house. McCall had been smiling when he jumped out of his Porsche in time to see the couple off to the prom, but that good cheer had quickly evaporated when he met Tony, saw his navy tattoos, and realized that Tony was no high school kid. Anne McCall had quickly intercepted her husband and successfully avoided another scene by coaxing her husband to leave the young couple and return to the house.

Upon Paula's return home that night, however, Tom McCall had the first of what would be many contentious conversations with Paula about his objections to her dating Tony. Perhaps because Paula finally had the attention of her father in a way that her younger sister Lindsey could not or because she enjoyed rebelling against her father, she refused to stop seeing Tony and further augmented the tension among the four members of the family through her open disdain for her father's authority. Ann McCall tended to sympathize with her older daughter, both because her husband's preference for Lindsey had hurt and angered her for years, and because Lindsey was becoming a complete mystery to her mother. Paula, although difficult, was a person Ann could understand, while Lindsey seemed stranger and stranger to Ann the older she got. Ideally, families can grow to form a cohesive unit during times of stress and crisis, but the disunity in the McCall family had horrific results for Paula. Although Ann McCall agreed with her husband's conviction that Tony was all wrong for Paula, she found herself unable to resist Paula's aggressive inveigling and stopped supporting her husband's ultimatums regarding dating the ex-sailor. The end result was another conspiracy between mother and older daughter, which was aimed at keeping Tom McCall in the dark about Paula's continuing relationship with a man that neither parent thought was suitable for their daughter; furthermore, Paula was being schooled by her mother in the art of lying and in deceit. Most assuredly, Ann McCall had no such intent in mind; she was just supporting a daughter who was being denied love and affection from her father, and hoping to compensate for his inaccessibility.

Oddly, Paula confided to her friends and to her mother that she really wasn't all that interested in Tony in light of the many differences in their goals and their outlooks on life. Consequently, Paula broke off their relationship several times over the next four years. When Paula announced to the McCalls that she and Tony wanted to marry, everyone was stunned. Paula claimed to her father that she and Tony had met at a wedding after not seeing each other for years and realized that they were "madly in love." This time, both Ann and Tom had tried to talk her out of the wedding; but Paula was insistent that she wanted to marry Tony, until the morning of her wedding day.

She awoke screaming at her parents and pleading with them not to make her marry Tony; sobbing and crying, she begged them not to "force" her to go through with the wedding. By that time, Tom McCall had lost any vestige of respect for his daughter and was completely fed up with her subterfuge and considered this outburst just another example of his older daughter's histrionics. Adamantly refusing both his wife's and daughter's pleas, McCall refused to cancel the wedding; Paula fulfilled the expectations of the 250 guests; she looked lovely in her white bridal gown. But the animosity between Paula and her father would never be reconciled, and Paula's drinking escalated day by day, year by year, matched only by her bitterness.

Julie Grayson's speculations to Jansen about the early onset of Paula's alcoholism had been dead on. Paula's popularity with, and acceptance by, her peers had been unusually important to her as a young teenager, most likely resulting from the loneliness caused by the sudden changes in her life and her relationship with her father. For the first ten years of her life, Paula was an only child and enjoyed the total attention of her mother and father. The small family moved around the country as military families are required to do. In those early years of Paula's life, McCall had a lot more time at home than he did later when he went to work at NASA. McCall had quit college to join the air force right after the Korean War and had become an officer after successfully completing flight school. Having found his great passion in life, flying, Tom McCall became one of the most versatile pilots in the air force; he could fly anything. Life on military bases suited Paula and her mother just fine, as neither Ann nor Paula had any difficulty meeting new people and making new friends.

As a little girl, Paula had been an extremely verbal, imaginative, and beautiful child; she had created several imaginary friends, ranging from fairies to small animals, and would entertain her parents with wildly imaginative stories of her exploits with her imaginary friends. In her elementary and junior high school years, her natural vivacity and charm endeared her to her teachers and to her parents. She was a happy, chatty, and outgoing child who seldom sat still. While early photographs of Lindsey reveal a somber and contemplative little girl, Paula's photos were studies in activity, play, and joy. Perhaps because of the sheer life force of his older daughter, Tom McCall was as charmed by the young Paula as were the rest of those in her small world. The father and his daughter were often stopped by passersby, asking if they could take their pictures because Paula was so clearly his daughter with her dark, curly hair, brilliant blue eyes, upturned button nose, and small stature.

For Tom and Ann McCall, the NASA offer came at just the right time. In the twelve years of their marriage, the McCalls had moved six times and had enrolled Paula in four different schools by the time she was nine. There were small lies that either Tom or Ann would hear from Paula about inconsequential things; both of Paula's parents thought that the lying could stem from all the moves, the many changes in schools, and the loss of friends that Paula had endured in her young life.

The idea of settling down in one place seemed ideal for the family. Although neither Ann nor Tom had ever lived in Houston, both were natives of Texas; Ann was from Dallas, and Tom had been born in Austin, and so the lure of going home to Texas was powerful. They had been living in Washington for the previous two years and were both eager to make the change to civilian life, to adopting what they both hoped would be a more stable lifestyle for Paula. The first few months in Clear Lake, Texas, were a whirlwind of activity for the McCall family; arriving in late summer, they had little time to decide on schools and to get Paula enrolled. Since the move from the military to the private sector meant that Tom nearly doubled his income, he decided to buy one of the first homes they had looked at when they had been invited by NASA to attend a family recruitment weekend. All three had celebrated their new home by dedicating their first shopping trip to Paula. They had gone to one of Clear Lake's nicer furniture stores to buy a bedroom suite for their little girl, a beautiful pink and white set that Ann later had given to Paula for her daughter Amy's room, now many years ago.

Paula was pacing the length of the house now, listening to her older daughter's explanations of the poor academic performance of her two children. Paula sighed finally. "Amy, enough already with the excuses. It doesn't matter whether they can read or not; the teachers will pass them anyway just to get them out of their hair."

Laughing at her daughter's stunned insistence that of course her kids could read, Paula shocked herself by interrupting her daughter to invite her and the kids out to the house for the weekend. "Look, honey, why don't you bring the kids over for the weekend after you pick them up from school? I'll go get some food for the weekend at Randall's now, okay?"

On the other end of the line, Amy had taken the phone away from her ear and was shaking it as she wondered if somehow she'd been connected to a different mother in another dimension.

"Amy, are you still there? What do you think? It's supposed to be hot this weekend; we can take the kids to Galveston Saturday morning, okay?"

Paula was back in the foyer of her house, once more examining herself and liking what she saw as she downed the remainder of the vodka. She was thinking how generous she was because Amy was having such a difficult time raising her two children practically by herself; a weekend out of the city would be good for them. Paula was lonely. She had just realized that it was Friday night with nothing to do; she could not bear the thought of another Friday night in a Clear Lake bar under the pretense of waiting for a date. She had spent the last couple of weekends doing just that and was not happy with the results the next morning. As was typical for Paula, she saw no inconsistencies in the conversation she was having with her daughter.

"Mother?"

"Yes, Amy?"

"It must be my imagination; I could have sworn you just

invited the kids and me out for the weekend."

"Yes, honey, I did. What's wrong? Don't you want to come?"

Amy thought of the long, unbearably hot weekends of last summer and the many times she had called her mother asking if she could bring the kids out if only for a day to get away from the Houston heat. Not once had her mother agreed. It had simply not been a good time for company. She shook her head at the mass of contradiction and paradox that was her mother and replied, "Yes, Mom, we'd love to come. We'll see you about five or six this afternoon."

Paula's lightning-quick switches in mood and subject matter were legendary among her children and close friends, so Amy was accustomed to the sudden appearance of the "good mother" persona. She'd grown up being screamed at one minute, and then within another second her mother would convert to a caring and compassionate mother. This instability in their mother's personality and her drinking binges, which became more and more frequent as they grew older, were what had driven her younger sister and brother out of the house as soon as they had finished high school. Amy knew that her younger siblings thought her too weak to leave their mother, but Amy believed she understood Paula better than most. She knew Paula was drinking; these days she was almost always drunk but usually didn't show it until late into the night. She knew, too, that there may be some unpleasantness if Paula got really drunk because she could be dreadfully cruel when smashed.

Relieved that she would have company this weekend, Paula moved quickly through the large, silent living room and out to the garage where her Lexus was parked. She had decided against another vodka before she left, more because she had just brushed her teeth than because she was concerned about her driving skills. Paula had been drinking more or less on a daily basis since she was thirteen years old. Forty years later, her tolerance for alcohol was so high that she had to work very hard to get so drunk that she couldn't drive a car. Backing the Lexus out of the garage, Paula looked at the grass in the front yard; she really needed to water that lawn, she thought as she drove by the large once velvety, green lawn, now brown and patchy.

Paula glanced at her watch to see that she had over three hours before Amy and her children arrived, so she decided to take the long way to the store, along the street where she had first gone to school when they moved to Clear Lake from Washington. Slowing down as she passed by the elementary school, Paula pulled over to the curb where she stopped the car and could watch the mothers picking up their children.

She could almost see her ten-year-old self walking down the well-worn path from the school, swinging her book bag and hopping into the car where her mother was waiting. She had been so happy in those first few years here—maybe happier than she had ever been in her life before or since. Clear Lake was a wealthy city overall, but the city council had resisted the national obsession of throwing more and more money at the educational infrastructure in hopes that the quality of education would improve. The Clear Lake elementary, junior, and senior high schools in the new millennium were the same buildings where Paula and Lindsey had attended classes in the sixties and seventies and still maintained their ranking in the top twenty schools in the country.

Paula stepped out of her car, locked it, and began to walk around the large campus surrounding the large, red brick buildings. She was awash in memories as she strolled by the high school, listening to the sounds of the high school boys at football practice and the girls at cheerleading practice. Smiling at her memories, Paula did not see the four young teens racing toward her and collided with one of them, hard. The girl was tall, at least four or five inches taller than Paula and was staring down at Paula with a concerned and contrite expression on her lovely young face.

"Ma'am, I'm *so very* sorry! I didn't even see you. Are you okay?" If the girl had not been holding Paula's arms so tightly, Paula would have been flat on the ground, and she was still wobbly, so she was grateful for the strength she felt from the hold.

"I'm fine, honey, no need to worry at all," she lied as she tried to step back from the young woman and swayed, thinking as she did so that she had only had four vodkas so far that day and wondered why she was so unsteady on her feet. The girl quickly grabbed both Paula's arms once again to steady her.

"Ma'am, do you need our school nurse to see you?" Smiling, she added, "Mrs. Wallace is real nice. I'm sure she would be willing to take a look at you."

Paula smiled back and said, "Thanks, honey, I'm feeling much better now; you girls go on to your cheerleading practice and don't worry about me."

Frowning down at Paula, the girl asked skeptically, "Are you sure?"

Paula stepped back. This time her balance was back to normal, and the dizziness had gone, so she replied as she took four more steps now with confidence, "See? I'm just fine, thanks for your help. Now go to your practice; you don't want to be later than you are!"

The three friends who had been waiting started to bolt, but when they saw that their friend was not coming, one called out, "Caitlin, come on, she's warned us about being late!"

Paula nodded encouragingly to Caitlin, and the girl took off with her friends. The four girls raced along the walk like colts, their long legs flashing in the sunlight and their long, thick manes of hair streaming behind them. Paula stood watching until they were completely out of sight, remembering when she had worn that very same uniform. She couldn't believe it, but after all these years, the cheerleaders still wore the maroon, short pleated skirts with the long-sleeved, maroon turtleneck shirts and gold silk vest.

Walking slowly along the walkway that surrounded the football field, Paula thought about her high school years and the joy she had felt when she had made the squad. Her interests had been typically teenaged girl: making the cheerleading squad and dating one of the jocks on the football team. By the time she was thirteen and a freshman in high school, Paula had made the backup squad for the cheerleaders and was dating the quarterback of the football team who was a senior at the high school. Within six months, Paula had proved herself good enough to qualify for the team; she had worked really hard to get that honor, had taught herself basic gymnastics, and had practiced the routines endlessly at home. Looking back on what was happening at home, Paula was amazed that she'd been able to pull that off during her very first year of high school.

Life had changed radically for ten-year-old Paula when her baby sister, Lindsey, was born. At thirty-nine, Ann McCall was an "older mother" and had a lot less energy than she'd had a decade earlier with Paula. Although Paula was only ten, Ann relied on her help with the infant, possibly more than was warranted, claiming fatigue when her husband commented on the responsibilities that ten-year-old Paula was required to shoulder. Although Tom tried to persuade his wife to hire help, she would not hear of it, preferring to take care of her two girls and her large home by herself so that she would know that the tasks of the household such as cooking and cleaning were done the way Ann wanted them done. By then, Tom McCall was well on the way to achieving his status as the primary test pilot for NASA, so his hours were long, and his workweeks were frequently seven days long. Of course, young Paula did not understand the reason for her father's long absences, and she began to blame them on her new sister. Had Ann been more willing to ask for help or had she or Tom been more observant of the changes occurring in their older daughter, Paula's life and that of so many others may have turned out very differently.

Although Paula helped her mother out a great deal during those first few years of Lindsey's life, she began to become quite adept at fabricating after-school work: tryouts and studying for exams at the homes of friends. So lying became a way of life for Paula. She felt no shame at the deception; to Paula, the lies were the sole means of assuring that she had a life outside of being helpmate to her mother.

Paula had dated the quarterback and high school senior Ryan throughout her freshman year and throughout the summer before Ryan had left for College Station and A&M University. She wondered if the pictures were still at the house; Ann McCall had taken scores of photos of the young couple. Ryan was over six feet tall, and Paula was barely five feet. Ryan had been very blonde, and Paula, very dark; she had referred to herself and Ryan as Mutt and Jeff, but she was well aware of the engaging picture they made together. Paula slowed down and thought of Ryan; she had not thought of him in years. He had wanted to go steady with her, but she had been way too interested in all the other cute boys who were in the upper classes in her high school.

Because she had been dating Ryan as a freshman and because she was also a cheerleader, Paula was extremely popular and could have her pick of the boys at Clear Lake

High School in all the grades; not surprisingly, all the attention went to her head, and she decided to experiment. She remembered a party during the beginning of her sophomore year. Ryan had been home from A&M for the weekend, and he'd called Paula to ask if she'd wanted to go to the party with him. By then, Paula had become bored with Ryan; he liked her too much, she thought, and he was also too straight: Ryan would not drink and drive and hated it when Paula got drunk.

Thinking back on her teenaged self, Paula reflected that she had honestly never liked the taste of alcohol. What she had liked most was the notion of being *bad*—just a little wild and of persuading her friends to be the same. It became a kind of game to Paula; feeding the deception of being a good girl, helping her mother with her young sister, working hard to keep up her grades, while being fiercely devoted to cheerleading practice six days per week.

To Paula, the game became more and more enticing simply because she had so much power over Ryan; when she drank too much, Ryan would become very protective of her and stayed by her side most of the evening, afraid that one of the drunk testosterone-soaked other guys there would take advantage of her.

By nine the night of the party, Paula was already turned off by Ryan's overprotection and his concern about her drinking. That was the night she had met Tony. For Paula, Tony was perfect, the antithesis of Ryan—dark and brooding good looks with the same fascination with alcohol that she had; best of all, Tony looked like trouble in a James Dean or Brando kind of way. When she left the party that night with Tony, Paula knew that she would never hear from Ryan again, and she hadn't. A couple of times, out of curiosity, she had googled him and was not surprised to see that he had graduated from A&M cum laude and had gone on to Wharton for his MBA.

Glancing at her watch, Paula was stunned to see that two hours had gone by while she had been daydreaming. Turning abruptly to hurry back to the car, she stumbled again and grimaced as she felt the dizziness. Paula tried and failed to persuade herself that she simply needed more vodka, but unfortunately she was not drunk enough to extinguish what she knew to be true: decades of drinking the amounts of alcohol that she ingested daily had lethal effects on the body. She was surprised that she hadn't developed cirrhosis, but that was one of the reasons she inspected herself so carefully; she was looking for the first signs. Paula was all too familiar with the way an alcoholic dies; she had witnessed too many in her years as an ICU nurse, and she had a foolproof plan. *But surely not yet,* she thought, panicking momentarily. *Not at only forty-seven?* Stumbling again, Paula stopped, forced herself to take three deep breaths in a row, and was able to calm down enough to persuade herself that she had tripped on a rise in the smooth asphalt of the newly paved walkway.

Just ninety minutes later, Paula was back home, having torn through the grocery store in record time, and having bought everything in sight. The refrigerator was loaded with food that she hoped Amy and her kids would eat; there were steaks, hot dogs, hamburgers, and all kinds of fresh vegetables and fruits. She had also bought a chocolate cake for Amy's birthday even though she was a week late. Paula knew that Amy loved chocolate cake and figured that Amy would get a kick out of blowing out thirty-one candles.

Proud of herself for waiting this long for a drink, Paula grabbed a glass and filled it with ice chips from the refrigerator and filled the glass with Gray Goose vodka. She had bought three half-gallons of the vodka while getting groceries, and had been surprised when she put them away; she remembered that there had been two half-gallons there, but when she opened the door of the cabinet, there had been none. She had stood there staring at the empty section of the liquor cabinet where she kept her vodka and began to think out loud.

"I know I didn't drink one gallon of vodka in the last two weeks, that's not possible. I was in Randall's a little less than two weeks before and had bought two half-gallons then." She was sure of the date because she had bought a birthday card for Amy one week early; she'd just forgotten to mail it to her. Suddenly, Paula was furious at her housekeeper for stealing the liquor, for that was the only explanation; there was no way that she was now drinking a gallon of vodka a week, no way. But Paula stood rooted to the spot as she considered whether Maria would begin to steal booze after working for her and her family for over twenty years. Shrugging the dilemma off, Paula took a sip of her drink and decided to go look for those high school photos that she was sure were still around the house somewhere.

There were six bedrooms in the McCall-now-Livingston home, and Paula could think of only three places where the pictures could be. Lindsey's bedroom had been on the first floor, but her mother had permitted Paula to convert Lindsey's room to a hospital room when her heart failure began to worsen. By then, Lindsey's visits home were so sporadic that Ann McCall knew that her younger daughter would never sleep there again.

Paula walked down the corridor and turned into the wide doorway to look into the room. She had not been in this room since her mother had died. Dry-eyed, Paula surveyed the impeccably furnished bedroom with the adjoining bath.

The architect did an amazing job, she mused as she glanced at the handrails strategically placed through out the three-room suite. The room had been large to begin with, as were all the rooms in the large house; therefore, the contractors had needed to tear down only one wall to extend the southwest side of the room about thirty feet so that Ann could have a sunroom with three floor-to-ceiling glass walls extending to the borders of Ann's rose garden. The sun was just starting to set and cast long shadows on the cheery yellow and mint green paisley wicker chairs and couches. This had been Ann's favorite room in the house; she had spent hours in here reading and dozing in the sunlight. And on those days when she had the energy, Ann had walked the flagstone path down to the huge koi pond.

Paula was startled by the memory of the fish; she'd not thought of them for months. She wondered if they were dead because Ann had fed them almost every morning, and Paula had completely forgotten the things. Opening the door and stepping outside, Paula turned to look at Ann's rose garden, stunned to see the condition of the dying bushes.

"Oh my God, Mom, I am so sorry."

For the first time in many months, Paula stood still, remembering the three promises she had made to her mother as she lay dying in the hospital. Paula could visualize her mother as clearly as if she were standing there at this moment rather than nine months ago.

Despite Ann's request to the contrary, Paula had slept in her mother's room on a cot that the nurses had set up for her. Most of the time, Ann had slept, her body too depleted by the ferocious battle of maintaining her vital organ systems to permit wakefulness, but two nights before Ann had died, at precisely three thirty in the morning, Paula had awakened.

"Paula, Paula, are you awake? Please wake up, Dear; I need to talk to you."

Although the voice was barely a whisper, Paula had awakened from an exhausted sleep and had flown over to her mother's bedside. Taking the cold, skeletal hand, Paula could see the emaciated face of her mother in the hallway light outside the glass-enclosed cubicle of the ICU at Houston Medical. The once-beautiful face of Ann McCall was ravaged by illness and cachexia; her cheekbones, always prominent, now jutted out almost at right angles to her face, and her intensely green eyes were fierce and hot.

"Paula, I am dying."

"Mom, no, we've got another new drug to—"

"Paula, please, no more lies, please." Her voice had been barely audible, and Paula had to bend her head close to her mother's feverish face to hear her. "Promise me, Paula, no more lies." The effort was exhausting her, the time between words becoming longer and longer, and there was a cyanotic cast to her lips and nail beds that had not been there before.

"Mom, please stop trying to talk; you're exhausting yourself."

In a voice Paula had not heard in decades, she heard, "Paula McCall, you listen to me *now*." Ann had hissed the last word and had dumbfounded her daughter. Her voice had been clear and strong, like her mother of thirty years ago.

"Okay, Mom. Okay, right."

The sweat had been standing on Ann McCall's forehead; she was working harder than a marathon runner to have this last conversation with her older daughter. Paula had tried to extract her hand so that she could go to the sink and get a damp cloth cool forehead to cool her mother's feverish face, but those long, bony fingers had held on to Paula's hands with a tenacity that she would have thought impossible.

"Look at me, Paula." Paula had been looking around the room, hoping that she could grab some ice water or, better yet, some Vaseline for those dry, chapped lips. "Stop fidgeting and listen to me, Paula."

Paula had stared in astonishment at the dying woman

who now held her immobile. Ann's incredibly green eyes were clear and full of light; her voice, although low, had a strength that defied her condition.

"Your father and I made many, many mistakes with you and your sister."

Paula had started to interrupt, but Ann McCall tightened her grip even more and shook her head.

"But *you* are the one we destroyed, Paula."

Her mother had been looking up and over Paula's right shoulder as she spoke, and she was talking as if there were someone else there. Paula used heroic restraint to keep from looking at the place behind her that was so enthralling to her mother, but she did not want to upset her anymore than she was already, and so she kept her gaze focused on her mother. As she stood and waited for her mother to continue speaking, the force of her mother's words exploded in her mind: *destroyed* me?

Paula had thought this very thing for most of her life and had been supported in that view, at least tacitly, by the majority of the ten or more psychiatrists and psychologists whom she had started seeing when she was twenty-five. By the time she was in her thirties, she had switched to psychiatrists because they could prescribe drugs, and they did so, liberally.

But hearing her mother say this in the silence of a hospital room during a conversation that may well be her last had been more than Paula had bargained for; she had imagined hearing these words from her father and had pictured her response when he realized that he had ruined her life. But hearing them from her mother brought none of the feelings of jubilation and validation she had expected to feel; rather, Paula felt fearful and frightened.

"You are an alcoholic, Paula; you have been for most of your life." Ann McCall had paused, closed her eyes, but reopened them as she whispered almost inaudibly, "There, I've said it *finally*." There had been tears standing in her eyes then. "I never had the strength to face you and your disease honestly." Ann saw Paula about to deny her drinking and cut her off. "You just promised me, Paula, no more lying, *please*." Her mother's voice shook and broke with her last word. Paula had shut her mouth and swallowed the denial and the explanations and the justifications that were there at the ready, just as they had been so many years ago. The cyanosis around Ann's mouth had deepened; Paula could see her mother's lips turning bluer as she lay there.

Ann had seen the effort her daughter was making to keep silent and smiled a grim smile. "There's more, Paula, much more, and you are not going to like any of it, but you must hear this." Ann McCall paused for breath and drew in several shallow breaths. "We should never have paid for those psychiatrists, Paula, none of them. Your father was right; they didn't help you. They just helped you get addicted to drugs in addition to the alcohol." Ann had closed her eyes and sighed several times. Paula looked up at the monitor and confirmed her suspicion.

"Mother, your oxygen saturation has dropped to eighty-nine; in a minute the nurse will be in here to make you stop talking, so *please* let me put the oxygen mask on your face for just a few minutes, and then you can continue telling what you need to say."

The once-lustrous head of blond hair had nodded weakly. Paula watched her mother's face as her lips began to pink up with the oxygen and her heart rate started to drop back down. No longer could Paula see the intercostal muscles caving in between the ribs of Ann's painfully thin chest as she worked to breathe in the oxygen-rich air; a sign that she was no longer so air hungry, Paula knew. Looking up at the monitor, Paula could see the percentage of oxygen in her blood slowly begin to creep past 90 percent and she had permitted herself a small sigh of relief.

The sound of a car door slamming startled Paula out of her reverie; she stood quickly then swayed again. She tightened her lips and squeezed her small hands into fists until the dizziness passed, and she could walk through the garden around the side of the house to see if Amy and her kids were here. But the driveway was empty. Paula glanced at her watch and calculated that Amy and the kids should arrive within the next half hour or so.

Taking another generous swallow of iced vodka, Paula sat back down on the bench in her mother's former rose garden, closed her eyes, and let her mind return to that last conversation with Ann McCall.

Why aren't I furious at her for talking to me like this? Paula remembered asking herself as she had stood quietly by her mother's bed and watched her breathing ease and her face relax; Paula had thought—maybe hoped—that Ann had fallen back to sleep when she saw the hand that had been holding her own slowly move up and start to fumble with the oxygen mask.

"You want it off now, Mother?"

Paula had known the answer but waited for the slow nod before she removed the mask from her mother's face. Before her mother could say no, Paula had placed a straw in her mother's mouth and waited while she took several sips of the cool water. Oxygen was extremely drying to the mucosa, Paula knew; she also had opened the tube of lip balm the nurses had placed there and smoothed a generous amount of the balm on her mother's chapped and cracked lips. Ann McCall had opened her eyes, smiled at her daughter, and asked, "Did I ever tell you what a great nurse you are, Paula?"

She had, on many occasions, but Paula still loved to hear it.

"Good enough that you'll listen to your excellent nurse and decide to let yourself sleep and stop exhausting yourself?" Paula had been smiling at her mother, but she was hoping this conversation would end. She honestly had not been surprised at her mother's choice of topic if this were indeed their last conversation. After all, Paula had been expecting a talk like this since she had started secretly drinking at fourteen. When her parents had never addressed her drinking, not once, Paula had believed that there were only two reasons they had never said anything: they didn't know, or they knew but didn't care enough to confront her. She had always figured it was the latter. Paula had wondered just what was happening in her gentle mother's soul to make her engage in such an awkward conversation; Ann McCall had always been the peacemaker in the McCall family, never the agitator. Paula also had wondered what her mother had been staring at so intently in the dark corner of the hospital room; her attention had been so total on that spot as if she had seen someone there.

"No, Paula, this conversation is about thirty-five years overdue." That had answered one question for Paula; her mother thought her drinking had started when she had met Tony—not two years earlier.

Ann McCall's voice had been surprisingly robust, and her gaze was directed like a green laser on Paula's face. Very gently, Ann had reached up and traced her hand along the midline of Paula's forehead, nose, and lips. "I do love you, Paula. I hope you know that … but I was weak. Your father and I had so many arguments about you; he was convinced that we needed to do something drastic to put a stop to your crazy behavior, but I kept making excuses for you." Ann shook her head slowly back and forth. "Such a stupid, silly woman." She had looked at the horrified expression on her daughter's face. "Paula, I'm talking about me, not you."

Taking a surprisingly deep breath, Ann had pushed herself forward and up in the bed so that she could look more directly at Paula, accepting her daughter's support and additional pillows to prop her up.

Paula had pulled a chair over to the side of the bed and sat down, leaned forward, and said "Okay, Mom, whatever it is, just say it."

Ann had nodded. "When you started dating Tony, your father wanted to send you away to Thornton Hall in Connecticut; I refused and told your father that if he brought it up again, I would leave him. That was why your dad began taking all those risky assignments at NASA and began to stay in the pilot quarters rather than come home at night. He was furious at me for being so blind to what was happening to you." Ignoring the tears rolling down her cheeks, Ann had taken several quick shallow breaths and smiled as Paula wiped away the tears and then calmly accepted the oxygen mask that Paula placed on her face. When she had nodded at Paula that she could remove the mask again, Paula did so without argument. "Thornton Hall is a high school for kids like you were, Paula, one of the ten in the country where 'troubled teens' are immersed in an alcohol- and drug-free environment of discipline, academic, and athletic achievement. Had you gone there, everything would have changed for you, everything." Ann had been staring at her daughter's face as if seeing an echo of the person Paula could have been.

There had been no sound in the room aside from the muted electronics at the nurses' station continuously monitoring Ann's heart rate, breathing rate, and oxygen saturation. Paula was spellbound, for she had never guessed that her parents had considered sending her away to a private school.

She had returned her mother's gaze as she considered the implications of what she was hearing; Paula had never heard of Thornton Hall and could not imagine what leaving Texas and going to Connecticut would have been like at the age of sixteen. For once in her life, Paula Livingston had been speechless; this information about her parents' arguments about her, that she was the reason for her father's virtual disappearance from their lives, was a shock. Carefully keeping her expression composed to be one which would befit the concerned compassionate daughter, Paula's mind raced with the knowledge that she had been denied yet again by her selfish parents. What a difference this could have made in her life; grimly, she had thought of her famous younger sister who turned everything she did into gold. "Had I had the chances Lindsey had—"

Paula's resentful ruminations had been interrupted by Ann. "Your sister did the right thing, you know."

Paula's head had snapped back to look at her mother.

"I know, you both thought I was asleep, but I heard you begging Lindsey to write you another prescription and heard her tell you to go see that friend of hers who works with addicts. I heard every word. Lindsey was telling you the *truth*, Paula."

Paula had no longer been able to look at her mother, nor was she listening to Ann any longer; her mind had completely filled with images of her sister. She thought back to the early years when the four of them had been together as an almost-normal family.

Paula had been attracted to the riskier types of behaviors like drinking, like dating the wrong kind of guy, more because of the need to provoke a reaction in others like her dad than because it was something she enjoyed doing. Intellectually, of course, Paula had known that competing with a seven-year-old sister was patently absurd. Yet the bond between her kid sister and their father had gnawed at Paula. She missed nothing that went on between Tom McCall and Lindsey: the smiles, the looks, the mostly unspoken *connection* that the two had between them that excluded her and her mother. When Tom McCall and Lindsey *did* talk, their discussions were never about topics that either Paula or her mother had any interest in discussing. Initially, Lindsey and her father had talked endlessly about her career as a cardiologist, which both Paula and her mother thought was simply the palaver of a little girl and were each annoyed by the seriousness with which Tom McCall treated the ambition of his little girl. Later, their discussions had been about Tom's test flights; Lindsey had an extremely scientific mind and almost intuited the physics and theory behind flight and speed. Paula had no interest in such things; in fact, when McCall did attempt to explain to his wife and family the reason behind his long days at NASA and the challenges behind the designs of the planes, only Lindsey had listened, asked questions, and learned.

Most of us commonly refer to *envy* and *jealousy* more or less synonymously. But there are subtle differences between the two that negate the assumption that the two emotions are two sides of the same coin. While Ann McCall was jealous—saddened by the attention that her husband showered on his younger daughter rather than on Paula and on herself during the rare free time Tom McCall had at home; Paula's response was far more vicious. Ann's jealousy didn't originate from a wish that Lindsey be denied what she and her father had; Ann was only sad that their relationship was an exclusive one.

Paula's response had been purely destructive. Although Paula had no interest in the ideas that fascinated her father and younger sister, she determined to do everything she could do to destroy their closeness because she hated the fact that Lindsey had something she did not; and this was envy.

Such distorted thinking caused dreadful consequences in Paula's life. Initially, Paula's drinking had been a lark, a way to prove to her teen friends how bold and fearless she was and to prove to herself that she didn't care about her father; her dating Tony in secret while assuring her father that she broken up with the man was a way of asserting her power over her father, of showing him that he could not control her or tell her what to do. Paula's whole character became consumed by paradox as she made decisions intended to provoke a reaction or distress in another. Over time, she lost contact with her real self and her own desires, so driven was she by the need to influence the opinions, actions, and behaviors of those closest to her.

"I was jealous of her, too, Paula."

The statement had jerked Paula back to the conversation, wondering, not for the first time, if her mother were psychic. The green eyes regarding her then had been soft and filled with sadness and sympathy. "Of course, I know you're thinking of her; how could you not be?" The frail hand had reached out to touch Paula, and she took the cold fingers in her warm hand, rubbing them as she tried to warm her mother's hand. Ann had smiled. "That feels good, Paula, thank you."

Paula had looked at the exhaustion written on her mother's face. "Mom, why don't you see if you can get some sleep now? We can finish this discussion later, can't we?"

"I'm afraid, Paula, that we've wasted all the 'laters' we've been given, you and I."

Maybe it was the chilled, bloodless sensation of the hand that she was holding, but Paula had suddenly shivered, feeling cold, freezing. She tried to joke, "Mother, I think I should start quoting Edgar Allen Poe's *The Raven* right now; you're getting truly morbid." Expecting to see a smile when she looked at her mother, Paula had been dismayed to see Ann shaking her head. "Soon, Paula, I'll be asleep for a long, long time; I know what you want to do. I saw Dr. Stewart write the prescription when she came by this evening."

Dr. Stewart, chief of medicine at Houston Medical, had been in to check Mrs. McCall and had asked Paula if she could speak with her for a minute. Paula had stepped outside the cubicle and had leaned against the glass for a moment before standing straight again.

"Paula, are you okay?" Dr. Christine Stewart's face had been concerned, brows drawn together and eyes sympathetic.

Paula had smiled at Christine in appreciation. "I'm fine, Christine, thanks for coming by to see us. I'm just tired, that's all."

At that, Stewart had taken out her prescription pad and scribbled out a prescription for Ativan, the drug that Paula used to help her get to sleep and to calm down when her nerves got the best of her. Smiling at Paula, Dr. Stewart handed her the prescription. "I hope this will help you get some sleep. You look as if you could use about twenty straight hours, Paula."

Paula had been so grateful for the prescription that all she could do was nod in appreciation. When she had gone back into her mother's room, Ann had looked as if she was asleep; clearly, she was not. Looking at her mother, Paula had sighed and braced herself for the lecture she assumed was coming. Instead, this night of surprises continued in theme.

Without a trace of judgment in her eyes or facial expression, Ann had regarded her daughter steadily, her gaze unwavering. "You have been jealous of Lindsey since she was born, Paula. I knew it and fueled your resentment of her by demanding that you help me take care of this baby I didn't expect to have. Your father was concerned that I was expecting too much of a ten-year-old, and he was right. I was."

For the second time that night, Paula had heard that her father had been concerned about her and momentarily allowed herself to question the truth of her long-held bitterness at her father for destroying her life—but only for a moment. Their relationship had been decided years ago when he chose Lindsey over her; nothing could change that.

Although the light in her room was dim, Ann could see the effects of her words on the face of her daughter. Almost as if Paula's face were a mirror, Ann had seen the momentary hope and the yearning to believe that her father had loved her followed by the all-too-familiar mask of imperturbability that Paula wore. Inaudibly, Ann sighed. She hadn't really expected that the conversation could change Paula; that after all these years, her daughter would decide to make a life for herself instead of living in the shadow of her brilliant sister, but for a moment there … it had seemed possible.

Paula had yawned, loudly.

Ann had wondered why she was doing this; she would have no impact on her daughter. She knew that and had begun to open her mouth to admit defeat when she heard herself saying instead, "Paula, I made so very many mistakes with you and with Lindsey; you have no idea of how much I regret so many of my decisions." The pace and cadence of her voice picking up, Ann declared emphatically, "But your father and I did not destroy you, Paula; you did that all by yourself."

Ann had seen the mask break open to reveal blazing, blue eyes. "Mother." The word had been emitted through tightly gritted teeth.

"*No*, Paula, you will listen to what I have to say tonight. I'm done with listening to you justify unconscionable behavior to me."

Startled, Paula had blinked and sat back, almost as if she'd been slapped. Her mother had never talked to her this way.

"I want you to make three promises to me, Paula, and I want you to keep them this time." Ann McCall had searched her daughter's face as if she were memorizing each feature. "I want you to promise me that you will pay some attention to Amy and your grandchildren." The claw-like, bony hand had grasped Paula's and squeezed. "I want you to fake that you love her and them; I know you don't. You never have, but I want you to use your superior acting skills and pretend that you do. *Promise* that you will do this."

Paula had been sitting at her mother's side for close to a week and had left only for a shower, change of clothes, and yes, to fill up her flask. Her last flask was empty now; she didn't think she knew where there were any package stores open at this time of night, so she replied wearily, "Yes, Mom, I'll be a good mommy and grandmommy." What harm could it do, she had thought, if she could agree with her mother and maybe she could still grab a few hours of sleep?

Ann had studied her daughter and decided to lie to her, playing on her vulnerabilities. "You know that I have left everything to you—the house, the stocks, bonds, and the IRAs. You know, too, that the total worth is over seven and a half million dollars; what you do not know is that our lawyer will handle the trust and the payments to you. He has instructions that if Amy and her children, along with Tim and Trisha, are not well cared for by you, he is to change the executor of the estate from you to Lindsey, which will mean that you will have to go to her to access the trust."

The part about the lawyer and Lindsey were not fictional. Ann had known better than to place control of the entire estate into the hands of Paula; what Paula couldn't know was that Lindsey had steadfastly refused to discuss any of this with her or the lawyer; therefore, Ann did not know if her threat held any teeth. But Paula had seemed suddenly very attentive;

her look of boredom was gone, and she was staring at her mother as if at a specter. Ann smiled.

"Okay, Mom, you're right, I will watch out for Amy, Bobby and Sarah. I haven't done that very well, have I? I'll even call Trisha and Tim in California. I haven't talked to them in a while."

Fully aware that her daughter was acting, Ann had nevertheless been satisfied and continued quickly, "There are two other promises, Paula. I want you to promise me that you will try to get on speaking terms with your sister." Seeing her daughter's nod, Ann had added, "And I want you to take care of the fish and my rose garden." Sighing with exhaustion, Ann McCall had fallen back against her pillow to fall asleep. By three the next afternoon, she was dead. Paula had never spoken with her mother again.

Paula stood looking at the devastated rose garden, then reached into the pocket of her pants suit, and flipped open her cell phone. There in the address book was the phone number and mailing address of the landscaping service her mother had hired when the care of the yard and gardens became too much for her.

"Lucas? It's Paula Livingston, Ann McCall's daughter." She listened as the owner of the local landscaping service expressed his sorrow at the death of Mrs. McCall.

"Yes, thank you, Lucas, I appreciate it. But I wonder if you have anyone who has time today or tomorrow to come back here and revive what I have neglected."

Paula listened as he leafed through pages and was pleasantly surprised when he said, "I've got a man just finishing up in your neighborhood. He can be there in about fifteen minutes." Paula and Lucas discussed details and pricing for another few minutes, and Paula thanked him and shut the phone, deciding to explore the pond to see the dead fish. She approached the pond slowly, dreading the numerous dead golden bodies she would see and gasped when she arrived at the pond to see the huge goldfish swimming languidly around the large pond and playing catch among the water lilies her mother had bought years ago.

Sitting down, Paula reached into the pond to extract some pine needles and walked over to the bench, lifted the lid, and grabbed some flakes to drop into the pond. She was still standing there when she heard Amy and the kids arrive. Whispering to herself, "Okay, Mom, two down, one to go," she smiled as she walked back down the flagstone path.

❧

Alice laughed. "There is no use trying," she said. "One can't believe impossible things."

"I daresay you haven't had much practice," said the Queen. "When I was your age, I always did it for half-an-hour a day. Why, sometimes I've believed as many as six impossible things before breakfast."

—LEWIS CARROLL, *ALICE IN WONDERLAND*

23

Once the laughter subsided, Todd glanced at Steve Cooper with one eyebrow raised as if silently asking a question. When Steve nodded in reply, Todd cleared his throat and looked over at Rich just as Jansen had taken a good-sized spoonful of chocolate mousse and had raised it to his mouth. The rest of the group seated in Eleanor's library followed Todd's lead and watched Jansen place the spoon in his mouth and begin to swallow.

The seven were gathered around the roaring fireplace in a quasi-circle, where Cooper sat at one end of a brown leather couch with Kate beside him; each of the Philbin sisters was seated on a muted brocade wing chair on either side of the leather couch. Julie Grayson and *Houston Tribune* editor Jeff Simmons sat together on a floral upholstered love seat, and Jansen was sitting on a chocolate leather chair with its back to the fire. There was a large coffee table in the middle of the group where coffee cups and desserts now sat. Eleanor quietly interrupted the group's scrutiny of the unsuspecting Jansen as he enjoyed his dessert.

"Todd, excuse me but would you mind waiting until I finish my dessert, please?"

Eleanor had taken her customary three bites of the rich bread pudding that she favored about five minutes before, but she now had picked it up again and was taking small, dainty bites from her dessert plate. Immediately, all followed suit, and Rich was able to enjoy his chocolate mousse in peace.

Sitting back in the chair, Jansen grinned at Eleanor and Marguerite. "My compliments to Sophia and Samuel; two extraordinary cooks, because this meal was perfection." Laughing as he noted the mock shocked expression on Todd Kensington's face, Rich preempted the crack that he was certain would shortly emanate from his friend. "Todd is not accustomed to hearing me compliment chefs; he thinks I'm overly discriminating—"

Interrupting Jansen with a burst of laughter, Todd looked around the room very dramatically as only a trial lawyer can do and intoned, "Overly discriminating doesn't quite cut it, folks. I have known Rich Jansen for over twenty years and have never heard the man compliment any food but his own." The polite laughter following Todd's remark was a not-too-subtle signal to get on to the business of the evening; he took the hint.

"Rich, I did take the liberty of promising Dr. Cooper here that you would be happy to provide Kate with an explosive but off-the-record story about Lindsey. Would you be so kind as to enlighten all of us about your first two weeks as chief warden at the Huntsville Prisons?"

Jansen nodded slowly and leaned forward to take another sip of coffee. "Sure, I would be happy to do that." For some reason, Jansen's glance rested on Julie Grayson, who was sitting motionless next to Simmons; both of them seemed quite content to play a passive role in this unfolding drama.

Rich surveyed the group of people seated around him and then turned toward Todd to comment, "You're right, Todd, I started this job just two weeks ago, but I have to tell y'all, it feels more like two years." His slight Texas accent thickening from fatigue, Rich shook his head back and forth as he reflected on the sheer volume of information he had assimilated in the past fourteen days.

Watching him quietly, Kate Townsend knew exactly what he was experiencing; she could see the exhaustion in the shadows under his eyes and in the lines around his mouth as he spoke. Yet she understood the awe he was feeling as well, the sense that this thing was simply too big for any one person to shoulder. She doubted that Jansen had ever encountered anything he'd felt that way about.

"The off-the-record 'scoop' that Todd is referring to *really is* off the record." Jansen scanned the room, his expression grave. "One of the primary reasons that Greg Bell created a new position of chief warden at the Huntsville Prisons involves Lindsey and the former medical director of the Huntsville Prisons. The director filed a lawsuit against Greg Bell, his entire administration, as well as all wardens, and guards in all Texas prisons for permitting Dr. Lindsey McCall to practice medicine without a license at Huntsville Prison." Jansen's voice was subdued, his tone hushed. He stopped speaking to allow the import of his statement sink in. All eyes were riveted on him, and everyone looked stunned except Julie Grayson and Dr. Steve Cooper. Julie knew because Jansen had told her, but Rich wondered momentarily if Lindsey might still be communicating with her former colleague. But Cooper offered nothing except a very slow shake of his head, a pained expression carved on his face; Rich decided that Cooper was simply intuiting a rough idea of what had taken place, knowing Lindsey as he did.

Kate Townsend broke the silence in the room, regarding Jansen very solemnly. "Rich, I've no problem with off the record, none at all." She paused for a minute then added what everyone there was undoubtedly thinking, "But what is it with the saga of Lindsey McCall? Just when I think that her story can't possibly get more—" she paused, struggling to find the right word "—bizarre, it does!"

Jansen said nothing nor did anyone else, and he let a few more seconds go by to let the group mull over what they had just heard. Then Jansen began to explain, "The suit has been dropped, and the medical director has quietly resigned; thankfully, we've been able to keep this out of the media and plan to continue to do so. I'm sure there is no need to explain why the governor and I wish to keep this matter private." Once again, Jansen scanned the group assembled in the Philbins' living room and noted the somber nods; each of them was now remembering the media firestorm that hit Texas when control of the entire Texas prison system had been wrested from the state and placed under federal jurisdiction based on a successful class action suit won by inmates of the Walls at Huntsville. The blight on Texas had been dark and damaging; no one wanted to relive that nightmarish national scrutiny.

Nodding his satisfaction that his listeners appreciated the gravity of the information he was disclosing, Jansen said, "I met with Dr. McCall the morning of my first day on the job. Although there was extensive documentation about the incidents that had provoked the suit, there were gaps and inconsistencies in the previous warden's records and personal files.

"I audiotaped my conversation with Dr. McCall out of habit from my days as a homicide detective, but found the practice to be most useful because I later listened to that two-hour tape three times, or was it four?" Jansen directed his gaze to Julie Grayson; her almond-shaped, deep-brown eyes were fixed on his, but she revealed nothing. Without looking away from Julie, Jansen said, "I have interviewed hundreds of suspects in my years with the Harris County Sherriff's Department, but I have never encountered one like Lindsey McCall."

Now Jansen looked around the room. "Of course, I expected her to be different." Eying Kensington, Rich quipped, "You'd think that my good friend Todd Kensington would have prepared me somewhat even by just mentioning her looks?" At this, there were smiles among the people there who knew Lindsey: Julie, the Philbin sisters, and Steve Cooper. Jansen again noticed how carefully Cooper was listening to him. He wondered as he regarded the lanky, good-looking cardiologist just how close their friendship had been and then caught himself as he realized that he was alarmingly close to feeling jealous. Shaking off his unwarranted suspicions about Cooper, Jansen said, "She never claimed that she had not killed her mother. Not once.

"That just does not happen, ever. Every prisoner I have ever met cannot wait to tell you how innocent he or she is—not Lindsey McCall." Jansen shook his head as he thought back to his initial response to the beautiful physician. "If anything, she gave me all kinds of incriminating evidence against herself and what she called her dislike of caring for sick people, specifically her mother."

Rich knew the pace of his speech was picking up as was the emotion he felt while recounting the conversation with Lindsey. Of all those listening to his description about that initial interview, Steve Cooper seemed to be tracking better than anyone else present. Jansen's phrase about the dislike of "sick people" seemed to resonate with Cooper, almost causing him to wince. Then his gaze drifted across the leather couch to Kate Townsend, who sat vigorously nodding her head. Jansen lifted an eyebrow at the reporter, inviting her to comment, but she demurred.

Still looking at Kate Townsend, Rich continued, "Never once did she say anything critical of her sister, Paula."

Jansen was surprised when Kate remained silent, but Todd exclaimed, "That was the way she was during the trial—would not utter a word against Paula, even after the testimony that got Lindsey convicted." Kensington looked around the room at the sympathetic expressions. "Sorry, that was a tough loss." He paused for a minute and then looked over at Eleanor Philbin. "I don't think I've ever apologized, Eleanor, for—"

Eleanor looked sharply at Todd, her blue eyes blazing, and then cut him off, "We'll not have any of that here this evening, Todd. You have nothing to apologize for, nothing at all!"

Todd sat back, startled, and nodded like a schoolboy who had received a rap on his knuckles from the teacher.

Taking Eleanor's rebuke as a signal to move on, Jansen did so. "Lindsey explained that she had applied for work in the prison infirmary when she arrived at Huntsville. Naturally they accepted her, and she began to work as an aide." Jansen tried to ignore the pained expression on Steve Cooper's face at the idea of his brilliant friend and colleague working as an infirmary aide.

"Apparently the nurses and other workers in the infirmary took to Lindsey right away because she was willing to help with the dirty work." At this comment, Cooper grinned, immediately understanding the significance of the comment in the rigid medical hierarchy, which encompassed aides, nurses, doctors, and administrators. "But the prison medical director was insanely jealous of McCall."

Jansen paused and surveyed the group. "Ludicrous, when you think about it, isn't it? Here's a credentialed physician with a responsible position who is jealous of an inmate. Lindsey was probably very familiar with irrational jealousy." Jansen had been staring at the remains of his chocolate mousse as he paused, again immersed in the multiple injustices that seemed to plague Lindsey McCall. When he looked up, Julie Grayson was staring at him, the sheen of tears evident in her eyes.

"There were two incredible episodes between McCall and the medical director involving inmates with life-threatening emergencies. The first was over an inmate who died of cardiac problems that McCall believed to have been easily treatable. The prisoner died with McCall watching behind the doors of a treatment room while the intoxicated medical director did nothing but scream at McCall, seemingly enjoying her impotence." The only sound in the room when Rich stopped speaking momentarily to sip his coffee was the hiss of the fire and an occasional intake of breath at the mind-boggling story they were hearing. Steve Cooper sat motionless, his head downcast, and eyes closed.

"By the second event, Lindsey had decided that she no longer cared what would happen to her when she intervened. She knew this doctor was damaged and incompetent, and also dangerous to her because, of course, she was a felon, and felons can no longer practice medicine. A young boy was knifed during a fight." Jansen caught the looks among the group and explained the ready availability of instruments that could be altered and made into lethal weapons. Rich looked over at Cooper. "Lindsey explained that the knife had entered the lining around the boy's heart but not the heart."

Cooper nodded and explained. "Right, pericardial tamponade; you have time—not a lot, but some."

"Right, only Lindsey and the nurse were working that night—or so they thought. When the boy was brought into the infirmary, Lindsey and the nurse started to work on him when suddenly the medical director appeared; somehow the medical director tripped and hit his head against the door of the infirmary, leaving McCall to save the boy's life, which she did." Jansen was amazed that he had managed to say this last bit with a straight face; there were a few knowing smiles, but no one said anything.

Jansen paused to take a sip of his fresh cup of coffee, thanks to a recent Sophia flyby and began to wrap up his contribution to the purpose for this evening's gathering. "The medical director has withdrawn the suit and has resigned his position at the prison system. With the help of Lindsey's coworkers at the infirmary, the good doctor was easily persuaded of the benefits to him and to his career if he only went away quietly. We have been very fortunate to have dodged that bullet, so far anyway." Rich had no interest in naming any names or in emphasizing his role in this matter; the group seemed content to leave the story where he had left it, but he really didn't want questions either, and so he segued into the reasons he was sitting here.

Glancing at Kate, Rich declared, "With the exception of Kate and me, each of you has had a long history with Dr. McCall, and therefore a clear reason to take an active role in securing her release from prison. More than one of you has asked me either tangentially or openly why I am risking my job, bar license, and ethical obligations to my profession as a lawyer and my job at Huntsville."

Suddenly the air in the library was charged; the group seemed to be on the alert although no one had moved a muscle. "The answer is really quite simple; I do not believe that Lindsey is guilty. I don't believe that she administered her investigational drug to her mother. But I feel compelled to add my fervent belief that even if she had, no one in their right mind would have considered the act to be murder."

Jansen looked over at his friend Todd. "You have spent months vilifying yourself for thinking this case would be a slam dunk, that no grand jury would indict her, and then when they did, that no Houston jury would find her guilty. I think that almost any lawyer in the country would have responded the way you did, Todd. Had we still been partners in criminal defense, I'd have thought exactly the way you did. I still find it extraordinary that she was convicted." Todd smiled gratefully at Rich and was heartened by the warm smile and squeeze of his hand that he felt from Eleanor Philbin.

"And although I have an idea of how dangerous Paula Livingston is, I am certain that she knows what happened, that it wasn't her sister who gave Ann McCall the drug that allegedly killed her." Without diverting his gaze from Kate, Jansen added, "I appreciate very deeply the concern that has been shown to me by people I hardly know." Without thinking about it, Jansen turned to Julie Grayson, who had not uttered a word since saying hello to him and to the other members of the group assembled here this evening. "But I think I've no choice but to interview Paula Livingston on Monday; I've thought a great deal about how I'll explain to Paula my decision to intervene in this case." Jansen smiled slightly. "And I have decided that the only way to explain myself to Paula is to tell her the truth; it's easier to remember that way."

Julie's expression was grave, but she remained motionless and silent; she did not return Jansen's smile.

Jansen scanned the group, shrugged his wide shoulders, and suggested, "I'm done, folks, these were the cliff notes of my first two weeks at Huntsville. I'd very much like to hear a voice other than my own." Rich turned to Kate. "You had all the ingredients of a sensational murder story that would have sold a lot of copies of the *Houston Trib*. But the reason your series was so compelling—to me at least—was that you took a bizarre murder conviction of a world-famous TMC cardiologist and turned the whole case into a provocative social commentary affecting all of us. But I'll wager that you're eager to write the final story when we figure out what actually happened in that hospital room." Staring down at her lap, Kate was too preoccupied to notice that Jansen had asked her a question until Steve lightly touched her knee and nodded over to Jansen.

"I'm sorry, Rich, what were you saying?" Kate had been trying to work out just why she was so worried about his impending visit to see Paula Livingston; when speaking to Jansen, she had surprised herself when she had used the word *dangerous*. She was pondering why that adjective had come out of her mouth; Kate finally decided that it was because Paula was so *rehearsed*. Kate had always had the sense that she was speaking to a character—in a drama Paula was acting in. Of the numerous times Kate had met with Paula, there was only one occasion that she felt she'd penetrated through the facade to the real person, and that person had been deeply disturbing to her—the Paula who had briefly emerged had seemed *feral*.

Jansen grinned at her, "Your turn to talk."

Startled, Kate blinked and looked around the room. "I've not been following you; I've been sitting here trying to determine just what it is that bothers me so much about Paula Livingston."

"There's no Paula there anymore." Julie's soft brown eyes were dark and unreadable in the firelight.

"What do you mean?" There had been a chorus of voices asking the question; as if choreographed, Todd, Steve, Kate, and Eleanor were unanimous in their query.

Julie's posture changed very subtly. Jansen doubted that the others noticed, but after spending most of an evening and the following day with her, he could see a slight stiffening of her spine and forward tilt to her jaw—signals that she was girding herself to talk about subjects that were private, painful, and intrusive: her daughter and her alcoholism.

"I mean that there is no person called Paula there any longer; there are only the addictions and the alcoholism. That is what you sensed, Kate, and it disturbed you deeply. Paula's personality is gone, leaving only her craving and need." The clarity of her response and the straightforwardness with which she made the statement silenced the room.

Julie let it sit for a beat or two then suggested, "Let me give y'all some background on me to help you see why I say what I do."

Although there was an audible quiver in her voice, Julie was in complete command of herself as she addressed the group, most of whom she had never seen before. Their entire group was riveted by this slight math teacher as she addressed them. Because Rich was sitting in the firelight, he could see the sheen of tears standing in Kate's eyes, in Steve's, and in Todd's. He had no need to look into his own; he felt the sting. Watching Julie Grayson, Rich could feel only awe at the tremendous love and steadfastness this woman emitted as she shared the history she had experienced with the entire McCall family, but especially with her best friend, Lindsey.

Once more Julie smiled and offered, "Lindsey and I have been friends since we met in the first grade at Clear Lake elementary school. I spent more time at the McCall's house than I did at my own. We were roommates in undergraduate school at Rice University, and Lindsey was my maid of honor when I married my husband. Preempting the question that had to be forming in the minds of most, Julie looked over at Todd, "I wanted to testify at Julie's trial to mitigate the damage done by Paula's testimony, but Lindsey would not permit Todd to call me as a witness for her defense." Ignoring the two huge tears that slowly coursed down her face, Julie said, "Lindsey knew that I could discredit Paula—maybe sufficiently to alter the verdict of the jury, but we'll never know that now." Glancing quickly at Jansen, she said, "Lindsey never criticized Paula, *never.*

"Todd and I spent a lot of time talking about the way Lindsey affects most people, especially women; most of them dislike her without knowing anything about her." Julie frowned. "Lindsey is the smartest person I've ever known, and I've been around intelligent people for most of my adult life. But she is also spectacularly beautiful: One or the other is hard to take, but a genius who happens to be gorgeous?" She shook her head sadly. "So most people see in Lindsey what they expect to see: arrogance, condescension, egotism. But she is none of those things. She is simply one of those rare people who has never doubted her ability to do anything—anything at all." Then quietly, she added, "Like eradicate the systemic toxic effects of digitalis." She paused for a few beats. "You can imagine how crazy that makes most people, can't you?

"See, I knew that if I could testify at the trial, then I could humanize Lindsey for the jury and expose Paula's game for what it is."

Todd's head was bent down as if the weight of the trial were bearing him down once again. Steve Cooper looked at Kate and nodded his head; he totally understood what Julie was saying about Lindsey. He had seen it over and over again.

Suddenly, Julie's gaze met Jansen's. And she began to explain, "After you left the house today, Rich, I could not stop thinking about our conversation and the growing sense I had—and have," Julie paused and looked slowly at each of the faces regarding her, "that there is a confluence of events happening here and that it is providential, that none of us is here by accident." Noticing Eleanor and Marguerite's subtle nods of agreement and understanding, Julie's smile returned and widened. As if energized, she took a deep breath, looked at Kate, and said, "I said what I did about Paula because Paula's alcoholism and addiction to drugs was evident when Lindsey and I were still kids." Julie paused and stared into the fire; the silence in the library was absolute, as if even the roaring fire were holding its breath. "And God help me, that is what I would have said on the stand had I gotten the chance." Now smiling grimly, she continued, "And I could have provided a great long list of detailed examples; but about a month after Lindsey was convicted, I learned that my oldest daughter is an alcoholic; she started drinking when she was about twelve. My husband and I had no idea—we found out by accident." Whispering, Julie said, "Mark Twain once described forgiveness as the fragrance shed by a violet on the heel that has crushed it."

Jansen wished he were sitting closer to Julie; he could not imagine what these disclosures were costing her. Out of the corner of his eyes, he noticed that Simmons, Kate's lanky and taciturn editor, had moved slightly closer to Julie so that the distance between them on the love seat had narrowed enough for him to casually reach over to touch her forearm. Julie looked quickly over at him and half-smiled in appreciation. Todd Kensington sat with his eyes so lowered that he almost looked as if he were praying. Kate's mind was in turmoil, totally overwhelmed with the relentlessly lugubrious nature of this story and all who were involved in it. Cooper sat beside her, motionless.

Again, Julie glanced at Kate, a rueful smile on her lips. "When my husband, Ted, and I learned that our daughter had a serious problem, I began to educate myself about alcoholism. And after reading fifteen maybe twenty books on addiction and alcoholism, I started to realize that there is no consensus about treatment—nor is there a cure. I learned, too, that the theories about the reason for alcoholism varied with the background of the author. And what struck me was the certainty with which each author advanced his theory as *fact*. A priest friend of mine suggested a couple of books written by recovered alcoholics and their experiences with AA. For the first time, I understood that there is no single reason for any of this; but if the only tool that you possess is a hammer and it took a lot of money and countless years in school to find the hammer, then everything looks like a nail.

"Ted and I began to take our daughter to AA meetings and have learned what we know now is the truth about drug addiction and alcoholism. We heard over and over from those who *know* that when dealing with severe addiction and alcoholism the usual rules of human interaction do not apply; they *cannot* because that person—in this case, Paula—is no longer present. She has become *possessed* by the addiction." Julie paused to sip her coffee and stare at the fire. Everyone there had to lean forward to hear Julie's last comment. "My husband I were *determined* that our daughter Lindsey would not be lost to the syndrome of therapy and drugs."

"Let's let Julie take a break for a moment or two, shall we?" Looking over at Julie, Marguerite Philbin said with grave consideration in her eyes, "Dear, please let me ask Sophia for some fresh coffee for us all. Would that be all right with you?" Magically Sophia appeared within the next minute or two, and all cups were refilled as were the crystal creamers and sugar bowls.

Julie smiled gratefully at Marguerite as she sipped the now-steaming beverage.

Looking intently at Kate, Julie said, "One of the many reasons that I liked your series so very much, Kate, is what it points out about *us*." Pausing, she collected her thoughts. "About the American culture." Smiling, she confessed, "I have read Grimes' book cover to cover because he explains so clearly how we got here—this total abdication for our own physical and mental well-being to the professionals, for our loss of what we used to call common sense."

Appreciating Julie's interest, Kate suggested, "There is another author you would enjoy, Julie. Hank Reardon introduced me to Lewis Thomas and his writings back in the seventies and eighties. Hank was very fond of one particular observation of Thomas that is particularly evocative of what you are just saying. 'As a people, we have become obsessed with Health. There is something fundamentally, radically unhealthy about all this. We do not seem to be seeking more exuberance in living as much as staving off failure, ousting off dying. We have lost all confidence in the human body ... without the professional attention of a health care system, we would fall in our tracks ... the trouble is, we are being taken in by the propaganda, and it is bad not only for the spirit of society; it will make any health care system, no matter how large and efficient, unworkable.'

"Imagine, he wrote that in the early eighties!"

Julie had grabbed her purse and had written Thomas's name in a small notebook she carried; she smiled at Kate. "Perfect. And yes, I'll definitely read some of his books."

Looking up, she caught Jansen as he unsuccessfully tried to cover a yawn and glanced at her watch. It was approaching midnight.

"I hope you don't think me presumptuous folks, but my teacher training has kicked in to diagnose that we are all on information overload." Grinning, Julie looked around and was gratified to be met with smiles and nods.

Her smile fading, she looked across the table at Rich. "I don't know who else has asked that you forego your Monday meeting with Paula, but I am asking that you not see her until

I do. Paula's oldest daughter and I have maintained a friendship over the years, and Amy texted me on the way here. She was excited because Paula had invited Amy and her two children to spend the weekend with Paula in the family house in Clear Lake. Amy said she'd give me a call on Sunday after she and the kids got back home. I have a lot of admiration for Amy, as you might imagine; she's had a real challenge in her decision to keep a relationship with her mom."

❧

There is no blame in God.
—JULIAN OF NORWICH

24

It was one of those rare Sundays at the Grayson household where all six members of the family were home. Ted was traveling two weeks out of four, and Lindsey and the younger girls were all in soccer, which meant lengthy practices most nights of the week. Julie and Ted had capitalized on the occasion and had put together one of the family's favorite meals: Ted's grilled New York sirloin steaks, baked potatoes, and Julie's corn soufflé and broccoli with garlic cream sauce. Julie and Ted had opened a bottle of Stags Leap to breathe and had collected the four kids to sit for dinner just when the phone rang. Lindsey jumped to race into the hall, but Julie and Ted each rose from their seats at the ends of the long table to simultaneously exclaim, "Oh no, you don't, Linds, by golly the Grayson family will enjoy their Sunday dinner together today!" Realizing their identical crouched positions and words, Julie and Ted began to laugh; all three of the younger kids joined in, and finally Lindsey, too, had joined in the hilarity. By then the phone had stopped ringing but began ringing again immediately.

Julie, seated the closest to the kitchen, rose and waved at Ted and the family to signal that they should start. She heard the halting words of her son saying grace as she picked up the phone.

"Hey, Amy, what's up?" Julie listened for a few seconds and then interrupted to ask, "Look, Amy, are you at home?

We're just sitting down to Sunday dinner, and I'll call you back in about an hour or so, okay?" She listened for another minute or so then replied, "Sure, I'll check on her as soon as we finish cleaning up the kitchen." She looked at her watch to note the time and said, "I can get over there by five or five thirty, no problem."

Ted had heard her part of the conversation and was looking at her quizzically, but she gave him the look that translated to "I'll explain later; don't ask me now." All the kids except Charley knew what the look meant, but they all knew better than to ask their mother what was going on. Following the sumptuous dinner, Lindsey had surprised Julie with her offer to lead the cleanup of the kitchen if she could get some help. Amid a good deal of groaning, the tasks were assigned and the kitchen was on the way to being restored to its regularly clean and orderly condition.

Walking his wife out to the car, Ted had asked Julie if she wanted him to go with her; she did because Amy had sounded pretty worried, but neither parent thought it a good idea to leave Lindsey alone with the younger kids. Not yet anyway. She was doing well, unbelievably well, but they didn't want to move too quickly. She quickly kissed her husband and promised to call them after she had spoken with Paula.

Driving on I-45 from Friendswood to Clear Lake, Julie was happy she was heading south rather than north; the northbound lane was practically at a standstill with the volume of returning Houstonians from a weekend in Galveston. She hoped that most of the traffic would be cleared by the time she returned home, figuring that to be in about two hours. Julie reflected on what Amy had said about her weekend with Paula. She was worried because her mother had seemed resolved. When Julie asked what Amy meant by the word, she couldn't really explain other than to say that Paula had seemed almost serene and had been nicer to the kids than Amy could ever remember her being.

Although Julie did not see Amy a whole lot, she had invited her and her family over for dinner several times over the years, and Amy had reciprocated. Amy's husband was a Houston homicide detective and worked long, sometimes grueling, hours when he was on a case. Ted and Amy liked him a lot; he had stood by Amy for almost fifteen years and had withstood treatment from his mother-in-law that should have made him detest Paula, but he seemed to roll with most of her drama and became upset only when his wife was hurt by her mother. Apparently, Joe was out of town at a police training course in Dallas; Amy didn't expect him back until Wednesday.

When Julie had called Amy from her car phone after she had gotten on the road, she had asked Amy for details about her impressions of her mother and was somewhat disappointed when Amy was able only to repeat the same things she had said when she had first called. Julie had pushed Amy, asking, "Can you give me some examples of why you think she has reached some kind of resolution?" And Amy had answered that she really couldn't, that Paula was quieter than usual and repeated her earlier comments about Paula's atypical patience and kindness with the kids. Near the end of the fairly unproductive conversation, at least in Julie's mind, she had been about to hang up the phone when Amy suddenly said that she recalled something else.

"Mom hired Grandmama's landscaper back to take care of the rose garden and mow the lawn. You'll be pleased to see it, Julie; already the yard is looking happier." Amy was trying to sound happy about this surprise decision on Paula's part because Amy and Julie had discussed the sorry state of Ann McCall's prized landscaping on several occasions. Then Julie understood Amy's concern; this was unusual behavior on

Paula's part, and she agreed with Amy. This was significant.

Julie had not had a chance to talk with Ted about her Friday evening dinner involving Lindsey nor her part in the plan to uncover the truth behind the use of the then-investigational drug.

Julie had drunk only one glass of wine at dinner with Ted because she knew she'd be driving to Clear Lake. Now she wished she'd had at least one more. *Face it,* she mused to herself as she drove, *you're nervous.* The hands that gripped the steering wheel of the car were slick with sweat though the temperature inside of the car was almost cold; so she did what she always did when she felt like this: she prayed, hard.

As Julie pulled up to the huge white and still palatial house that she had practically grown up in, she felt the peace she could rely on when she remembered to pray. Her hands were dry, her heart rate was back down to almost normal, and she thought to herself, *We can handle this, can't we?* Secure in her belief that she was not alone, Julie got out of the car to enter a house she'd not been in for close to twenty years.

Walking up to the door, Julie knocked and waited. Nothing. Then she rang the bell, still nothing. The house was quiet, too quiet. She tried the front door, but it was locked.

Stepping back, she looked to see if she could see any lights in the house; it was dusk, and she knew Paula disliked the dark and would have all the lights on as soon as twilight approached. Julie said another quick prayer and walked around the back of the house toward the fish pond, Ann's rose garden, and the sun room that Ann McCall had spent so much time in. Julie took her time walking by the rose garden, feeling sad to see the shape of some of Ann's prized rose bushes and vainly trying to suppress the increasing sense of doom she felt the closer she got to this house.

Julie was unsurprised that the door to the sunroom was

unlocked; she could remember Tom McCall's admonitions to his wife and daughters to remember to lock that sunroom door. She could almost hear him in the stillness of the house, and she smiled at the memory.

Walking into Lindsey's old room that had become Mrs. McCall's when she became too ill to negotiate the stairs, Julie called out, "Paula, it's Julie Grayson. Amy called and wanted me to check on you; she was concerned when she left and—" Julie was yelling as loudly as she could as she walked into the hallway and on into the huge living room and saw what she expected to see. Paula was lying motionless on the seven-foot, white leather couch; Julie was sure that she was dead. But she walked over to the prone body and held the cold hand to see if there was a pulse. There wasn't.

Julie stood there dry-eyed. "Oh, Paula." It was a whisper that was uttered before she consciously thought the words. She struggled to stay upright under the torrent of sorrow and compassion that she suddenly felt for this woman and her regret for the many years of judgment she had imposed on Paula. Paula was lying on a couple of pillows and was dressed in a violet cashmere sweater and white, light wool slacks; her feet were bare and her toes freshly manicured. She looked as if she were asleep; the expression on her face was indeed peaceful.

Murmuring prayers, Julie took a deep breath and looked around the room but did not touch anything; this would be the medical examiner's case, of course; it was maybe homicide, but she felt that Paula had died as a result of her mixing her pills along with the vast quantity of alcohol she consumed daily. But then Julie saw what looked like a note fluttering in the breeze made by the air conditioner, along with the huge ceiling fan rotating lazily on the cathedral ceiling of the enormous living room. The piece of paper was balanced precariously between Paula's left thumb and forefinger and the large contemporary coffee table, which ran the length of the white leather sectional.

Wondering how she had missed it, Julie pulled her cell out of the phone and called Ted.

As soon as she heard her husband's voice, Julie said, "She's dead." Then she waited a beat to ask, "Ted, can you look up Rich Jansen's number for me, please? It should be in the address book I keep by the phone." Waiting for Ted to come back with the number, Julie wondered if she should call him before calling Amy or wait until she called Amy.

Taking down Jansen's home and cell numbers, she explained what she was thinking, "There's a note in her hand. I'm afraid she may have killed herself. Joe's in Dallas, so it will take him a few hours to get home, plus this is Clear Lake, and I'm thinking Rich's experience with Harris County homicide may help Amy in dealing with the police."

"You don't think they'll suspect Amy, do you?" Ted's tone was horrified, and as always when he witnessed the way his wife functioned in situations, which could paralyze most people, he was a bit in awe of Julie's coldly analytic abilities.

"Not at all but she *was* the last person to see her mother alive." She paused for a beat. "And, Ted, there is a very great deal of money involved here; Paula would have inherited everything I would assume because Lindsey was in jail when Ann died. And now that means Amy." She sighed and closed her eyes. "As always, nothing can be uncomplicated when any of the McCalls is involved."

She waited while her husband pondered what she had just said. Ted was a theoretical physicist; he was employed by a private research company in northern California just south of San Francisco but worked only two weeks out of every month in the corporate lab. The remainder of the time, he worked out of his lab at Rice University with two other physicists. Julie had met him while she was finishing her masters in theology at Rice, having completed her graduate degree in math the year before. They were instantly drawn to each other because of their dual interests in math and science and theology. While Julie was equally bright, her mind tended to be extremely practical and her outlook on life and people realistic, while Ted was an idealist and tender-hearted. The Grayson kids much preferred their father's discipline to their mother's.

Speaking into his silence, Julie asked, "Do you think I should get Amy's okay before I get Rich Jansen involved?"

She was grinning at her husband's instant reply. "Of course, you wouldn't do that without asking Amy first, Julie, would you? Tell me you won't just take over here, please!"

Deciding the best reply was a small lie, Julie answered, "Of course not, I was just making sure you agreed."

They quickly made their somber goodbyes before Julie dialed Amy s number. "Amy, it's Julie. I'm here at Paula's house."

Julie could hear Amy's boisterous eight- and ten-year-olds yelling about something. "Julie, wait a sec, can you please?" Then Julie heard, "Hey, you two, take it downstairs to the game room or outside, please."

Then Amy asked, "She's dead, isn't she?" Amy's voice was flat and weary.

"Yes, she is."

Julie held the phone, wishing there was one thing that could be said to comfort the oldest child of Paula Livingston. She closed her eyes, and as she prayed, memories of Amy as a baby flooded her mind. She had been a beautiful baby, but Paula could not stand the sight of her, blaming the child for her unhappy marriage to Tony and her enforced role as wife to a man she detested. Lindsey and Paula had been just eleven when Amy was born, so they spent their time playing and teaching the child while Paula worked. Later when Ann McCall became ill with the cardiomyopathy, Paula would bring Amy over to the house, along with her second child, a little boy, Tim.

"Does it look like she did it deliberately, Julie?" Amy was tearless. She'd shed too many tears while her mother had been alive; there were none left to shed.

"She has a note in her hand, Amy. Of course I've not touched it; we need to get the police over here. I'm sure they will want to check the house out and ask you and me questions." Julie waited about ten seconds to see if Amy would say anything else. When she didn't, Julie suggested, "Look, why don't you call Joe now and ask him to come home as soon as he can. Meanwhile, I'm going to call Rich Jansen; he's that fellow I told you about who is trying to help your Aunt Lindsey." Julie had told Amy only the bare outline of her visit with Jansen. Amy had asked Julie multiple times to explain how Lindsey had ended up in jail, but Julie simply couldn't tell her what she suspected, so she generally deflected the younger woman's questions as best she could. But Amy was smart, really smart, and Julie guessed that Amy suspected that her mother was somehow involved.

"Okay, yes, Julie, I'll call Joe now." She sounded grateful that Julie was making the decisions right now.

Quickly, Julie added, "Be sure and give Joe my cell number in case he wants to give me a call; I can tell him what I know about Rich Jansen. My guess is that they worked together at one point or another when Rich was at the sheriff's office."

Rich answered on the first ring. Julie could hear Mozart's "Requiem" blasting. "Hello." She could barely hear his voice, but when he had turned the volume way down, he asked again, "Hello?"

Dryly, Julie said, "You could not have selected a more appropriate opera, Rich."

"Julie?" His voice puzzled.

"Yes, and I apologize for interrupting your Sunday afternoon, Rich, but I am over here at Paula's house. She is dead. Her daughter Amy called this afternoon and was worried about her; she had spent the weekend with Paula and said that Paula had seemed different somehow—'resolved,' Amy said. And I see a note in her hand. Amy is calling her husband, Joe; he's with the Houston Police Homicide Department and is in Dallas at a training meeting. Maybe you two know each other." The words were tumbling out in her haste to get them said and in her relief that there was someone who could take this out of her hands.

Jansen had not said a word until he heard the pause signaling that she was done. "Stay there, Julie, give me the address, and I'll GPS it, should be there in an hour and a half give or take. I doubt that I need to tell you this but don't touch anything. I'm going to call Lew Armstrong, a good guy; he's a Clear Lake detective and will get there before I do, so let him in, okay?" She heard him whistle for Max and the door close, then he said, "What's that address?" After she gave it to him, he said, "Julie, leave your cell on, and if you can, stay off the line. I may need to call for directions; sometimes the satellite directions can get you pretty messed up." There was a click, and he was gone.

Breathing a deep sigh of relief that help was on the way, she jumped when her cell rang. It was Joe, Amy's husband who was leaving Dallas and racing back to Houston. "Hey, Julie." Joe was from New Orleans and had not lost that combination of East Coast and pronounced Southern-accented speech that was uniquely New Orleans. Joe was a typical Southerner, easy to underestimate for the uninitiated. "Thanks for going over there for Amy … thanks for saving her from being the one to see Paula this way."

Joe had grown up in the streets of New Orleans gangs and had every reason in the world to detest his mother-in-law. But he didn't; he never had. Amy's husband never complained about the demands Paula imposed on his wife, nor did he seem to resent Paula's imperious attitude when she was around Joe. And Julie loved him for it. "Amy said you were calling Rich Jansen." It was said as a statement not a question. "I'll sure enjoy seeing Jansen again … standing this time." The statement was made in Joe's typical laconic drawl, but she could guess at the emotion behind it; he must have been one of the policemen involved in that Houston shoot-out that nearly killed Rich.

Thinking of Rich's request that she stay off her cell in case he needed directions, Julie said, "He's on his way, Joe, said he should be here in about an hour. He also said he was calling a friend in the Clear Lake police, a guy named Lew Armstrong. Do you know him?"

"No, but if Jansen says he's good, he is. Am on I-45 now, Julie. I'll go home and will call you when I get there. I hope I get there before the police get to Amy, but that's unlikely since Jansen has called Armstrong, but thanks for getting Jansen down there; everyone knows Rich and admires him, seems like I'm saying thanks a lot. How about when all this is behind us you guys come over for some Cajun cooking?"

Smiling widely, Julie said, "We'd love that, Joe. Drive safely please." But he had already hung up.

Julie stared at the phone, preferring to look there than at the couch. Curious about the note and trying unsuccessfully to suppress her hope that Paula might have been compelled to tell the truth, finally, Julie could no longer stay in the cold, sad living room, so she walked back down the hall. She decided to wait outside for the Clear Lake detective to arrive.

Julie avoided Lindsey's old bedroom, going out of the house through a rear door that had been the back door of the house before the sunroom had been added. Walking around to the back of the house, she continued down the flagstone path to the koi pond, wondering if there were any still alive in there. When she reached the pond, Julie was delighted to see the bright orange flash of the fish as they languidly swam through the water lilies. There had to be at least seven or eight fish there, she guessed, and they were big.

Hearing the sound of a car door slam, Julie walked around to the front of the house and surprised a huge, black man slowly approaching the porch. "Are you Lew Armstrong?" The man had to be close to seven feet tall; as she got closer to the man, she realized she'd overestimated. He was probably about six foot six maybe seven. At five ten, Julie was not accustomed to craning her head back to look into the face of most men, but this guy was big, immense.

"Yes, I'm Armstrong; you must be Mrs. Grayson." There was no smile on his face; he had not reached out to take the hand she had extended, so she let it drop awkwardly. Then she saw a second man coming up behind the big, unfriendly guy. The second man had noticed Julie's attempt at a hello and reached out. "Hi, Mrs. Grayson, I'm Lew's partner, Kirk Mahoney."

"You'll need to come around the back, the front door is locked. This is how I had to get in when Amy called me to ask that I come over to check her mother for her."

The two men followed Julie back behind the house but not before she saw a look exchanged between the two. *Good Lord*, she thought, *I'm nervous, and all I did is discover Paula. How on earth is Amy going to feel when they start to question her about when and what time she had last seen Paula?*

They were all in the living room. Julie stood there while both men pulled out rubber gloves and began to look around. Armstrong approached Paula and surprisingly, gently for such a huge man, began to explore Paula for any sign of life or visible injuries. Finding none, he turned to Julie. "Is this how you found her?"

"Yes."

"Did you touch anything?"

"I picked up her wrist to see if I could feel her pulse—the hand without that note."

The opaque black eyes revealed a shiver of surprise before they became unreadable again. The huge, gloved hand reached down to pluck the note from Paula's hand. Reaching into his khaki sport coat pocket, Armstrong dropped the folded note paper into a plastic baggie. But Julie could see Paula's monogram on the paper, clearly identifying her custom-made note cards. Suddenly, Julie realized that she was going to cry, not just cry but sob, right in front of this huge, unfriendly cop. Then the doorbell rang, and there was Jansen, covering the foyer in long rapid strides, continuing into the living room. Max padded right over to her, sat down, and threw that ridiculously huge paw at her. Julie knelt down, trying with everything she had not to cry, but then threw her arms around the dog and sobbed.

She felt Jansen's arms draw her up so that she could stand with him and soak his white turtleneck with tears and mascara.

"Max hates to hear women cry." His voice was gentle with just a hint of humor. Looking over at the two Clear Lake detectives who were busying themselves with the details of their investigation, Rich asked, "Do you guys have any problem with my taking this lady home to her husband and kids?"

Armstrong started to say something then caught a look from Jansen and said, "Sure, go ahead. We'll need to question her further along with the daughter, but that can wait until tonight or tomorrow. This looks pretty clear-cut." Armstrong reached into his pocket to pull out and show Rich the folded note, and Mahoney showed Rich four empty gallon bottles of Gray Goose vodka he had found in the cabinet along with empty bottles of Zoloft and Ativan.

Julie had collected herself and had stood back just as Mahoney was showing Rich the empty vodka bottles and prescription drug bottles. She turned to Rich, her voice raspy but steady. "Have you read the note?"

He shook his head and raised an eyebrow at Armstrong who said, "We'll just need to dust it for prints, have the ME check her out, and then the family can have the note and the body; should take a day or two." Again, there was that unspoken exchange between Jansen and Armstrong, and the big man said, "Yeah, I guess early tomorrow morning, we can get everything done by then." He nodded to Rich and then grinned at him. Julie watched as Armstrong walked over to Rich and grabbed him in an awkward hug. "*Man,* it's good to see you." Armstrong kept the smile and turned to Julie. "Sorry about your loss, ma'am. We've already talked with her son-in-law—" nodding over at Paula's body "—we'll wait to question his wife until Joe makes it home from Dallas."

I use hate as a weapon to defend myself; had I been strong, I would never have needed that kind of weapon.
—KAHLIL GIBRAN

25

Okay, Mom, I'm late but late is better than not at all, right? I know you thought that I was lying when I told you that I would keep all of the promises I made to you, and you know what? At the time, I think I *was*; but then this past Friday afternoon, I walked out to your rose garden and looked at what had happened to all those bushes over this endless summer. And I felt sorry, Mom, really sorry, so Lucas is back and will have everything up to speed in no time. You always said that he could make anything grow.

Okay, you've noticed, I'm sure that I've started backward and have done the easier ones first. Now to Amy; I've changed my will—again—ha-ha! And have left the house—your house—to her and Joe. They will be happy here, and the kids will take great care of your goldfish; they are still alive by the way, Mom, through no fault of mine, they are there. Amy is also the executor of the will, and I did call Trisha and Tim this weekend, by the way, but didn't reach either one of them; at least they have a message on voice mail from Mommy dearest.

Lindsey? Well, that's the toughest one of all, so … I've got to stop for a minute here.

Okay, I'm back. I needed a whole lot of fortification for this next part, believe me. I can't tell you that I'm sorry about what's happened to Lindsey because I'm not. Actually, I'm pretty happy about it—it's been kind of neat seeing the great Dr. Lindsey McCall knocked off her high horse, but I did promise you that I would work on a relationship with her. This is all I can do, Mom.

I've asked your—now mine, now hers—lawyer to pay off Lindsey's house in West U because Lindsey will be out of jail as soon as they read this. I started giving you her new drug; she would not do it unless the ethics committee approved it for compassionate use. They never did make that ruling because I told Lindsey that I would take the stupid form over there. I never did, never intended to; if and when anyone goes through my stuff, they will find the undelivered form signed by Lindsey. But, Mom, at least you had that three weeks of feeling great, so it did help you for a little while.

Nothing else in your will about how you and Dad had divided up your estate has been changed. She gets half, and my half will be divided between Amy, Tim, and Trisha. I am told by the lawyer that your estate is worth over eight million dollars, so if the good Dr. McCall is sick of practicing medicine, she'll not need to work for the rest of her life.

That's all three promises, Mom, done. And I know you wanted to ask for a fourth—that I would stop drinking. But I think you knew that it was too late for me. I've just taken a handful of Ativan; I haven't been able to sleep for weeks and hope this will put me out. And of course, my friend Grey Goose, I'm out of vodka completely. I am so tired, Mom.

Good, I'm getting sleepy—hope I sleep for a good long time. And if I don't wake up, well, that's okay.

Paula

Once Rich had privately explained the importance of Paula's note to Armstrong, he had retrieved the note card and together they read the note. Now that the Clear Lake detective understood that this had been the sister of the TMC doctor who had been indicted for murder, Armstrong told Rich that he'd get a tech on the fingerprint match between Paula and the note that afternoon if Jansen could wait about an hour or so. Since the conversation with Armstrong had taken only a couple of minutes, Rich had asked Julie to wait in her car while he spoke with the detective.

It was almost dark as Jansen walked back down the walkway of the big house. He could barely see Julie's profile as she sat behind the wheel of her car. Opening the passenger door of her car, Rich sat and turned so that he could face her. Her eyes were red, and there were mascara smudges under her eyes; otherwise, Julie looked as if she had mostly collected herself. But the brown eyes that regarded him were filled with sadness.

Rich said, "She admitted she did it."

Julie let out a huge exhalation as if she had been holding her breath for the last ten minutes. Jansen could barely hear the whispered, "Thank you, God." But the sadness in her eyes seemed to deepen, and she closed her eyes for a moment, as if in prayer.

"Armstrong will release the note to me after he gets his tech to affirm the fingerprint match between Paula and the note; he'd also like some examples of Paula's handwriting so that the handwriting can be verified as hers, but he's pretty convinced that this is what it looks like. He's asking me to wait an hour or so for that to be done. I've already called Todd to start the paperwork for a no bill judgment on the *State of Texas vs. McCall* murder charge from the DA's office. Todd was confident there would be no argument from Masters. Given that we can get to a judge tomorrow, Lindsey should be out of jail by Tuesday, Wednesday at the latest." Rich was saying all this flatly, mechanically; he felt the way he imagined that Julie did: in shock, the way he used to feel back when he was in the Marines when he and his squadron were psyched up to head out on a mission, but the CO decided to delay at the last minute—all that adrenaline saturating the body now weighing him down.

"What do you want to do? Wait here with me? Go home?" Julie nodded to Rich without answering, picked up her cell, and called Ted. Rich started to get out of the car so that she could have some privacy, but she shook her head and signaled that he wait. He listened while she explained to her husband what had happened, clicked off, and said, "I'll head on home in a bit but a few questions first, please." Waiting for his nod, she asked, "What about Amy? Will they still need to interview her? I promised I would call her as soon as I knew anything." As Julie finished her question, her cell rang.

"It's Joe, Amy's husband; he's that Houston homicide detective that I told you about." As Julie flipped open her cell to speak, Rich wondered, *Joe? Is she talking about Joe Spencer?*

"Hi, Joe, yes, Rich is sitting right here." *There was no interest in the usual civility among them,* Julie thought as she handed Jansen the phone. *We're all too strung out to attend to courtesy.*

When Jansen took the cell to say hello, Julie could hear

the explosion as clearly as if the phone were still at her ear, "Jansen! How the blazes are you? Man, it's good to hear your voice!"

For the first time that evening, both Julie and Rich smiled.

"I'm doing fine, Joe, just fine." As Julie had suspected, Spencer and Jansen had worked together on multiple cases, and Spencer had been well aware of Jansen's close brush with death. She listened as Rich answered Joe's list of rapid-fire questions with one- or two-word replies. It sounded as if the Clear Lake cops would need to interview Amy, but their questions would be more or less perfunctory. He clicked off and handed Julie's phone back to her and waited for her questions.

Armstrong and Rich had discussed Paula's comments about the estate in her note and had agreed that finding the original will should be the responsibility of Amy and her husband as the direct next of kin. Although Armstrong had raised an eyebrow at Paula's description of the size of the McCall-now-Livingston estate, he did not see the inheritance as a factor that could incriminate Amy in any way, especially when the ME estimated Paula's time of death as somewhere close to three in the afternoon, about two hours before Julie had arrived. Amy had left Clear Lake early Sunday morning to teach her Sunday school class back in Bellaire, a fact that could be readily verified. Rich explained all this to Julie, who nodded in reply and was quiet for a beat or two.

Staring out the windshield of her car into the dark, the night illuminated only by a streetlight about fifty yards down the street, Julie asked Rich quietly, "How do you plan to tell her?"

The car was too dark for Jansen to see Julie's eyes, but she had turned toward him and sat quietly as he thought about her question. He had not given her question any thought, with all that had been happening and the accelerated pace they had reached in the progress of this thing. Jansen thought about Lindsey McCall, tried to imagine her response to the news that Paula was dead and that prior to her death she had written a note that would free Lindsey, and shook his head slowly.

"I haven't a clue, Julie; do you want to come out to Huntsville to talk with Lindsey with me tomorrow?" He doubted that she could get away from school for another day, but he wanted to give her the option if her schedule would permit the time from her classes.

"There is nothing I would like better, Rich. I have been sitting here trying to persuade myself that I would be the best person to tell her that she's free, that Paula had finally admitted what she had done." Julie paused and Jansen could hear the edge in her voice. "But Lindsey is not ready to see me, not yet. My sudden appearance in her life will call up more than she can handle right now." She reached over to switch on the map light in her car so that she could see Jansen. "I think you and Lindsey are connected in some way, Rich." Noting his uneasiness at her comment, Julie added, smiling slightly, "Yes, there's that, but more important than that, I think that you're an instrument." Pausing again, Julie was feeling her way through this conversation; she seemed to be realizing what she should say only moments before the words were said. Rich watched her face because the focus and attention of her eyes and facial structure were subtly different from what they had been moments ago. She seemed to almost crackle with the intensity of what she was saying as if she were some kind of human transformer. Although she was staring directly at him, Jansen was sure that she didn't see him.

"Yes, an instrument." Her words were stated emphatically, like a declaration; the alterations in her face and attitude dissipated, and Julie's brown eyes regarded him gravely. He wondered if he had imagined the earlier transformation. Julie extended her hand so that she was touching the lapel of his jacket. "Rich, she is going to be sure that she caused Paula's death; that belief, on top of her mother's death, may break her apart. You need to be prepared for the crushing guilt she will feel, and you will need to help her."

Jansen's head was reeling, and he could feel his head start to pound. He'd had almost nothing to eat since the dinner at the Philbin mansion the night before; he was suddenly light-headed. They both sat staring at nothing—Jansen wondering why he wasn't beside himself with joy, why Julie, who had every reason to be elated that her friend would finally collect the justice she deserved and would be freed from prison, was not relieved that she would no longer need to confront Paula Livingston.

"Do you know a priest that Lindsey could relate to, Rich?" When he looked at her in surprise, Julie declared, "Well, you *are* Catholic, aren't you?"

Jansen chuckled; she'd had no need to ask. "Yeah, I am." This whole episode was beginning to feel orchestrated in a way he could not understand but could sense. He thought back to that almost-mystical statement Lindsey had made within the first few minutes of meeting him—that there was a *reason* for her being there. Then when she had realized how crazy the statement sounded, she'd tried to take it back. Jansen had listened to that part of her conversation over and over again because it didn't sound crazy, not the way she had said it. Then when he and Julie had listened to the tapes of his interview with McCall, Julie had stared hard at him when she heard Lindsey make that statement; she'd known what McCall was talking about—so had he, and he'd thought a lot about Father John.

"Yes, I know a priest she could talk to."

26

Heading home on I-45 after following Julie to her Friendswood exit, Jansen picked up his cell to dial Father John. Although it was after nine on a Sunday night, the priest had made it quite clear that he wanted Rich to call him at any time that he needed to talk. He found the number of the rectory, hit the speed dial on his cell, and smiled when he heard the deep voice of the priest answer on the second ring. "Are you up for a couple of visitors, Father? One who needs a beer and a sandwich and another who'll he happy with a bone?" Poor Max had been waiting around patiently in the Mercedes while he and Julie had talked, and although the big dog loved coming with him, there wasn't a whole lot of room in the small sports car for an eighty plus-pound Doberman to stretch out; as a result, he'd been sitting upright in the passenger seat for a couple of hours now.

"Rich! How are you and Max? Sure, come on by, knock on the back door, and I'll make up some sandwiches. I was just hoping for someone to share a beer with. How far out are you?"

The state of Texas encompasses a vast geographical area that varies from densely populated cities like Houston and Dallas to areas so remote that four-legged and six-legged creatures were the main citizens; therefore, most Texans quickly learn to speak of travel time in minutes or hours rather than miles.

"I should be in downtown Houston in another thirty minutes, Father."

Rich slowed the car down to a crawl as he passed the cathedral. The searchlights illuminated the majestic bell tower, but high up and beyond the bell tower soared what Jansen considered the crowning achievement of the Co-Cathedral of the Sacred Heart. Gazing up at the over fifty-foot, illuminated stained glass window of the resurrected Christ, as always, he was awed by the magnificence of the artist's depiction. Rather than the weakened and pitiful representation of the Savior favored by artists of the last several hundred years, the Italian who had created this Christ had designed a warrior, whose humanity was perfected by a massive and muscular torso with a spectacular blood-red sacred heart flooding power and grace over the city of Houston. There had been a good deal of controversy when the window had appeared during the construction of the Co-Cathedral; traditionalists from all walks of Christianity had complained about the unorthodox nature of this Jesus. Rich loved it—had loved it from the first few shots he had seen on television, and he had taken to driving downtown at night so that he could see the brilliant colors illuminated by the bright lights within the church and reflecting through that crimson and sacred heart; each time Jansen viewed this Lord, he thought of the old Christian hymn "Onward Christian Soldiers." This was a general he could follow into hell.

Jansen drove around the block-long perimeter of the huge cathedral and came to a stop in front of the rectory; he parked the car right in front, whistled for Max, and within seconds, the Doberman was bounding up the steps. Before Rich got to the third step, the door opened wide, and there stood Father John with a raw bone for Max in one hand and a Grolsch for Rich in the other.

"Come in, boys, come on in!"

Max needed no persuasion; he had probably smelled the bone before the priest opened and was through the door. He sat in the foyer, his eyes riveted on the bone in Father John's hand.

The priest looked at Rich. "Can he have it?"

Rich nodded, and Max padded over to Father John to extend his paw. The priest crouched down to take the paw. "Hello to you, too, big boy, here you go." Max took the bone in his powerful jaws and stood with an expectant look in his eyes.

"Take it to Father John's kitchen boy, go ahead."

Max galloped down the hall and around the corner to the huge kitchen shared by four priests, an archbishop, and the cardinal. Jansen and Father John ambled slowly down to the kitchen where there were large and small tables, couches, and a formally outfitted dining table and chairs. Rich and Father John always ended up at one of the small tables with the most comfortable upholstered chairs that lined the walls of the generous space. Looking over to the table sitting in the corner by a window facing out on Jefferson Street, Jansen saw two thick ham and cheese sandwiches with a side of macaroni salad and chips sitting there; his stomach began to rumble loudly at the sight.

Rich took a seat and a sip of his beer and waited for John to say the blessing. He did so, and soon only sounds of contented chewing could be heard in the spacious room. At nine thirty at night, the residents of the rectory were either in bed or at one of the many social functions, which were occasionally command performances for the cathedral clergy.

Half of his sandwich devoured, Rich leaned back, pulled on the bottle of Grolsch, and said, "You are a lifesaver; that was the best sandwich I've ever had."

"Happy to be of service, any time. It is a good sandwich, isn't it?" The priest took another huge bite of his, then put it down, and patted his nonexistent paunch. "But not a good idea to make it a habit to eat this late—can turn to fat." Father John smiled down at Max, who was still happily chewing on his bone, then picked up his beer and eyed Rich over the rim. "How are you doing? Looking at the bags under your eyes, I'd guess that the new job has you hopping?" The priest fixed his keen gray eyes on Rich and waited.

Jansen had picked up the remaining half of his sandwich and had taken a decent-sized bite, which he was enjoying just as Father John asked his question; Rich nodded at him to signal that he had heard him and continued to chew as he regarded the man sitting across the table from him. Father John was an ascetic, Rich had guessed awhile back. The cleric's collar and black pants were a loose fit, and the planes of his long, angular face were very prominent, almost gaunt; the arms and hands, which loosely held his beer bottle, were thin but wiry. With his close-cropped gray hair, he could have been a military man, Rich mused as he regarded the priest, who sat calmly and keenly gazing back at him.

"I'm not sure where to start, Father."

"At the beginning might be nice," he observed dryly.

"It's a long and complicated story."

"Of course, it is."

Jansen chuckled at the man's acerbic style; there were no affectations with John, nothing superfluous in his body or in his speech. With a Ph.D. in clinical psychology from University of Michigan and a Ph.D. in philosophy from Rice University here in Houston, the priest had been a successful psychotherapist in Southern California with a thriving practice until he could no longer say no the "hound of heaven," a reference to a little-known poem by that name, a favorite of John's. He had been brought up as a Catholic but had stopped attending church in his undergraduate years while at Berkeley and had not entered the seminary until he was thirty-five. His age was one of the first methods that the Lord had introduced to teach him humility, John had observed wryly when he described a few very humorous classroom experiences in the seminary. He, a thirty-five-year-old, the forty-three other seminarians twenty-four or younger.

Rich sat across his kitchen table trying to collect his thoughts sufficiently to coherently explain enough of Lindsey McCall's story for the priest to get a sense of how she could be helped. Although John had shared only the sketchiest details about his life, Rich could see that the journey from Berkeley undergraduate student to his current post as rector at the Co-Cathedral had been anything but pain-free. Father John could get as close to understanding Lindsey's state of mind as anyone, Rich speculated.

❧

It was midnight by the time Rich and Max pulled into their New Waverly cabin in the Piney Woods, and both man and dog were sound asleep within seconds after hitting their respective beds. Rich's last conscious thought before exhaustion took over was a prayer of gratitude for all that transpired so far and for direction when he spoke with Lindsey once the judge had signed the DA's no bill judgment—an action which would expunge the initial indictment and conviction from Lindsey's record.

The stack of messages on Jansen's desk was an inch thick

when he got to his office at six thirty Monday morning. Ignoring them, he picked up his phone and dialed Todd's office. Todd answered himself as none of the receptionists made it into work at the hour most of the law partners did. Todd sounded as if he had been in the office for a couple of hours already, and he had wasted no time in creating the necessary documents. Peterson had faxed the entire record of the findings surrounding Paula's death. Once the fingerprint match had been ascertained by the Clear Lake crime tech, photos of the empty vodka bottles and empty prescription medication bottles along with the medical examiner's preliminary diagnosis of a respiratory arrest caused by alcohol and drug poisoning as the cause of death, there was sufficient evidence to rule Paula's death as suicide.

"Any guess as to what time the DA will sign off?"

"I brought over the whole file to Danny Simmons about ten minutes ago; Danny said he'd make sure Masters had it in front of his nose at his Monday morning briefing. Once Masters signs it, Danny promised he would personally get the document in front of Judge Weston before she hears her first case. We should have the green light by eight thirty."

"Thanks, Todd. I'll call Governor Bell to let him know."

"And I'll tell Eleanor and Marguerite; why don't you call Townsend?"

"I will, once we have the judge's signature."

Todd chuckled, "Good point. Listen, Rich, I'm due in court at ten for voir dire on a new case. I'll call you as soon as I hear back from Simmons."

He was gone. Jansen slowly hung up the phone while he stared at the beautiful sunset at Honfleur, grateful that he was no longer a trial lawyer. He felt a paw land hard on his foot, pushed his chair back, and grinned at his dog, whose long legs seemed to stretch the entire length of his enormous desk.

"Hey, big guy, looks like we've won one today. How about that for first thing on a Monday morning?" Then Rich got to work on the phone calls he needed to make beginning with Bell.

❧

"Good morning, gentlemen. Rich, Todd Kensington is on line two for you." Wanda stood smiling in his doorway with a small tray that held two steaming cups of coffee, a toasted bagel with cream cheese, and a bone for Max. Wanda brought the tray over to Rich's small table where he generally met with her to review the upcoming week, then sat down on one of the upholstered chairs arranged around the table, and called Max. Max had been sitting up since Wanda's arrival; he had learned to expect a treat when she came into the office. The Doberman looked over to Rich to get the okay to go get the bone, which Rich gave to him while picking up the phone.

"Is it done?" Rich sat drumming his fingers on his desk while he sat and listened to Todd wind up another call he had taken while waiting for Rich to pick up. The wait felt like five minutes or more, but Jansen knew it was really only ten seconds or so; his heart rate was up, and he was breathing hard.

"It's done; I'm faxing the declaration over to you now. I've also contacted the Texas Medical Association; she'll have her medical license restored by the end of the day. Eleanor Philbin has already spoken with Christine Stewart. Lindsey has her position at the medical center back, and the chancellor is calling a special meeting of the entire health science center at three this afternoon. He has agreed to have Kate Townsend as the sole member of the press at the meeting. I'm preparing a synopsis of what has taken place over the last three weeks, and either I will present it or he'll do it. Your name will not be mentioned."

Rich could say nothing. He sat at his desk with his head bowed, overwhelmed with emotion.

With some kind of intuitive sense, Kensington cleared his throat and said, "Look, Rich, you're going to have your hands full with Lindsey. Why don't you let me call Kate now?"

"Yeah, sounds good, I'll talk to you later."

There were two pairs of eyes staring at him when Rich hung up his phone and looked over at the table where his secretary and dog patiently waited. Both pairs of eyes were filled with concern.

Jansen smiled at them, placed his index fingers at each temple and rubbed for a moment, and then walked over to the table, took a seat across from Wanda, and quietly said, "Dr. McCall is free."

Wanda's hands flew to each side of her face as she exclaimed, "You did it, praise God. You did it!" Then the sturdy woman rose and walked over to Jansen where she leaned down to hug him, hard. Laughing and crying, Wanda returned to her seat and nodded to Rich, like a proud mother would. "Shall I ask Luke to go and get her … or do you want to sit by yourself for a spell and figure out how you'll tell the poor girl?"

Thinking that this woman was worth her weight in gold, Jansen nodded and said, "Yes, thanks, I would appreciate about thirty minutes; no interruptions." Glancing at his watch, he said, "So, Wanda, please ask Luke to bring her over at nine."

Smiling for all she was worth, Wanda took her coffee and walked to the door of his office. When she opened the door to leave, she turned around to ask very gently, "You are all right?"

Rich was sitting motionless, staring at the cup of coffee and the bagel. At the sound of Wanda's question, he looked over to her. "Yes, Wanda, I don't think I've ever been better." He blinked. "Thanks for the bagel."

Just as she started to open the door, Wanda turned back. "Rich? She'll need some clothes. How about I make a call to a friend who owns a boutique in Huntsville? She has some nice outfits and would make us a good deal on a few outfits for Dr. McCall."

"Great idea, Wanda," Rich exclaimed as he rose. He walked over to her, and gave her his credit card. "Thanks for thinking of that little detail."

When Wanda's knock sounded on his door, thirty minutes later, Rich was prepared; Father John's advice the night before had been very useful. He had suggested that Lindsey may well have suffered from some degree of post-traumatic stress (PTSD) during most of her life, explaining that the disorder was characterized by a flat affect or suppressed emotion and a tendency to intellectualize crisis points in life, such as her father's sudden death. The priest had listened attentively to the relationship between Lindsey and Paula, asking questions and adding inferences as Rich described what he had learned about the intricate dynamics among the four members of the McCall family. Echoing Julie's words, Father John had explained the phenomenon known as survivor guilt among sufferers of PTSD—that if he was correct in his diagnosis of Lindsey McCall, Rich could expect extreme sadness and probably guilt when she was told of Paula's confession and suicide. Jansen was well aware of PTSD and had seen its debilitating expression in the lives of Marines who had spent their lives post-combat in futile attempts to extinguish the ghosts of friends and colleagues who had been killed under fire. Jansen had watched these men try—and fail—to shoulder the burden of living when they felt they should have died along with their friends.

John clarified that survivor guilt is also seen in families, specifically between siblings with diverse skills and intellects.

In the priest's opinion, Lindsey had all the requisite ingredients for a double dose of survivor guilt: not only was she able to create the drug that could ameliorate her mother's failing heart but decades too late to help her mother, she also spent her life as witness to her ten-years-older sister systematically destroying her life and any possibility of happiness.

Hearing it stated in that way helped Rich connect the dots of Julie's comments about Paula, Lindsey, and Julie's prediction of Lindsey's response to the news that her life had been restored and that her sister had killed herself. But Father John had gone further than that—just as Julie, Todd, and Rich himself had done. John had inferred that Jansen's feelings about Lindsey were more than platonic. Very gently, the priest spoke of Laura, of the years that Rich had known her and of the love he had felt for her. Then he had fixed his gray, penetrating gaze on Rich and declared, "Laura would not want you to live your life alone, Rich; she would like nothing better than to see you with a woman again who you can love." Jansen felt the sting of tears again as he thought about the priest and the truth behind his words.

Now standing in the open door of his office, Rich looked right at Luke Preston, who stood grinning at him, and to Lindsey, who stood to Preston's left. When his gaze met McCall's, he felt that jolt, as if he had wet his hand and stuck it into a plug in the wall. She looked thin and solemn as she stared back at him.

"Luke, can you give Dr. McCall and me about fifteen minutes alone, please?"

Jansen stepped back and to his left to allow Lindsey entrance; following the direction of his extended arm and hand, the doctor took the chair that Wanda had recently vacated. She sat in the posture she had adopted four weeks before, her back erect, not quite touching the back of the chair, and her arms and hands resting loosely on the table; those extraordinarily green eyes were trained on him. She said nothing.

Heart hammering in chest, Jansen sat across from her and decided to go for it; he cleared his throat nervously and pointed to the papers that lay on the table in front of her. "Dr. McCall, Lindsey, the case against you has been overturned. You are free to go." Waiting a few seconds to see if there would be any response to his words, he paused. She was motionless but suddenly looked tense. "Your sister, Paula, has confessed that she injected your drug into your mother." Lindsey had been pale when she had sat down, now he saw her face just drain of color, she closed her eyes, those long eyelashes dark on the now almost porcelain cheeks. His voice now very gentle, Rich added, "Paula is dead; her confession was found in a note she had written before she lost consciousness."

At that, Lindsey's eyes flew open, again staring widely at him. "Suicide." She whispered the word but sat, waiting for his confirmation. When she saw his nod, two huge tears ran down her face, and her lips twisted into a grimace.

Jansen said nothing more; he felt strangely as if he had been torturing this woman: that each utterance he had made afflicted more pain on her already bruised and battered psyche. He sat back until the shocks she was receiving abated enough for her to react. She was staring over his head at the watercolors of Honfleur and, without shifting her gaze, nervously licked her lips. "I have no idea of what I am supposed to do now." Her face was devoid of any expression, and her eyes were huge and distant.

Thankful to Julie Grayson and to Father John for preparing him for this reaction, hardly a reaction at all to the news that she was no longer a prisoner and that she was once again free, Rich said dryly, "I'd suggest that we get you some clothes and get you some breakfast. You look like you could use a decent meal, Dr. McCall, and I'm buying."

With the faintest hint of a smile, Lindsey stared back at him and nodded.

❧

There is a really deep well inside me. And in it dwells God. Sometimes I am there too. But more often stones and grit block the well, and God is buried beneath. Then He must be dug out again.
—The Letters and Diaries of Etty Hillesum

27

While Lindsey returned to her cell to collect her few belongings and to discard her prison garb, Wanda placed the most important documents that required his signature in front of Rich and assembled the remaining papers in a manageable stack. "I think Warden Cleary can take care of the rest of these personnel forms and correspondence, Rich, if that's okay with you?"

Jansen smiled at Wanda, as the portly woman stood waiting at the door to his office. "Yes, he sure can, Wanda. Is Bob in yet? Do you know?"

"He's down the hall meeting with one of the guards; he should be finished in a few minutes. Do you want to see him before you and Dr. McCall leave?"

Rich had resumed scanning and then signing the pile of documents she had given him to approve, but at her last question, he frowned and looked sharply up at her, wondering if he had somehow telegraphed his thoughts or if his every move was completely transparent to her.

Wanda shifted from one foot to the other under his scrutiny. "Look, Rich, I simply took for granted that you would take care of her, at least for a while; someone needs to help that poor girl deal with what has happened to her over the last year of her life. But if you've assigned someone else to do that and are planning to stay for the day, then I can call some folks who have been wanting to see you. I've put off a lot of folks who are inventing reasons to come in because they're curious. You just let me know what you want me to do."

Once more Jansen thought about how much he liked this woman; there was no pretense, no hint of self-importance with her, and her method of communication with him was direct. Nothing was ever veiled or hinted at. He sighed deeply and decided to talk with her like the friend she had become.

"Wanda, let's talk for a few minutes." Rich was gesturing to his small conference table.

Nodding, she walked back across the office and took a seat, and when he took the chair across from her, she regarded him calmly, patiently.

"I'm not sure what I'm doing here. I'm sort of out of my element. Not here in this office, this job, but with *her* ...." Wanda regarded him kindly, while he stammered and rambled, ill at ease in his awkward attempt to explain something that he wasn't sure he understood. She made no attempt to help him express himself, to put words in his mouth; she merely listened.

"I have ... *feelings* for this woman." He'd blurted out the words, and he was horrified as he watched them shimmering on the smooth surface of the antique coffee table. With alarm, he looked at his secretary.

Wanda reached over to touch his hand and very tenderly said, "Rich, Lindsey McCall and you have been through a great deal of suffering in your lives." She patted his hand in an affectionate, almost maternal way. "You are a very handsome man, still young, and she is a beautiful young woman—and you are both available. Of *course,* you two would be attracted to each other—of course, you would." The Texas twang was thicker because of the compassion this kind woman was feeling in every pore of her body.

She held his gaze for another few seconds, smiling tenderly, and then the practical Wanda took control back and commanded, "Now why don't you get those forms signed. I'll ask Bob to come in to meet with you so that he and you can plan the week; Bob can handle the day-to-day stuff here just fine until you can come back." With that, she patted his hand one more time, then rose, and left his office.

Jansen stared at the closed door, shook his head, and smiled. Thirty minutes later, the stack of documents had been approved, and Bob Cleary was knocking on the door.

"Come on in, Bob."

Cleary walked in with a legal pad and pencil. He stood in front of Rich's desk as if he were still in the Marine Corps and reporting to his CO, body rigid and eyes directed somewhere over Jansen's head. Rich smiled at the younger man and rose to shake his hand. The two men sat at Jansen's conference table, and Jansen nodded at the legal pad that looked full of talking points that Cleary wanted to cover with Jansen.

Nodding to the pad, Jansen pointed toward the first bullet point and said, "Shoot."

Cleary coughed into his hand and then cleared his throat, "Excuse me, Sir, may—"

"Rich, please Bob. I'm not your CO, and this is not the Marines. And if you've got a question, just ask it." When he saw the dark flush appear on Cleary's neck and rise slowly up his face, Rich knew that he'd been too abrupt with him, but he was mildly annoyed at the kid's inability to shake off the indoctrination he'd received from the corps.

"Right, sorry … Rich."

While he waited for Cleary to ask the question that was evidently the most important as it wasn't written down, Jansen watched him recover his self-possession. Cleary had been a lance corporal in the Marines and had seen a good deal of action first in Iraq and then later in Afghanistan. Tall and well built, he looked like a model for the corps; the fact that he was also black was an extra attribute in Jansen's eyes. Over 40 percent of the prison guards were black; therefore, it was high time that Huntsville Prison promote an African American to the position of warden.

The flush still darkened his skin, but Cleary was back in control of himself. "The word out among the guards is that Dr. McCall is leaving—her conviction overturned." In this regard, the military and prison rumor mills were just alike and the accuracy of the intel just as accurate.

"They are right; her sister confessed in her suicide note to giving the mother the drug."

Cleary's eyes were so dark brown that they looked black, but they darkened even more as the man frowned in dismay. "Man, that lady just can't catch a break, can she?" He stared at Jansen for a moment and then turned to his list. Most of the items on it were routine and could be taken care of with ease. But the last one was dicey: "Galveston called this morning; they are releasing Devon Preston back to us. They want to get him back here this week." Cleary was talking about the young inmate who had been near-fatally stabbed but whose life had been saved by Lindsey McCall. Jansen had never talked about the boy with Cleary and wondered what his thoughts were on the kid and on his older brother, Luke; Cleary had, after all, worked at the Walls as a guard for a couple of years before being promoted to warden two weeks ago by Jansen.

Rich regarded him steadily. "What do *you* think about his coming back here, Bob?" Jansen kept his expression neutral.

Cleary responded instantly, "The kid would be dead within two hours of getting back here." Rich waited another few seconds to see if Cleary would take another risk, like offering his opinion about the attempted murder, the probable perpetrators, and maybe some thoughts on Devon Preston landing in Huntsville in the first place. After a few seconds, he did.

"La Emi failed in their attempt to murder this kid; now it's become a matter of a gang-wide mandate to restore their reputation. They won't fail a second time."

Jansen decided to push a little. "Bob, do you know Devon Preston?"

Cleary nodded and offered, "I do and I know his brother, Luke, very well; I believe what Luke claims about La Emi. I think the kid refused to join the gang, so they set him up for the robbery."

Jansen nodded in agreement. "Okay, so how do we protect Devon when he comes back here?"

Cleary looked at Jansen incredulously. "We can't protect him here; Devon was lucky. He had enough time to signal Luke that he was in trouble; this next time, there won't be any time to save him."

"So *Warden* Cleary, what are you going to do about this?"

Cleary smiled somewhat sheepishly now that he understood what his boss was expecting of him. "I'll call the warden over at Galveston, explain the situation, and tell him that we're going to work on an expedited review of Preston's case."

Jansen understood the man's reluctance to offer his opinion: Advancement in military rank and promotions in state and federal bureaucracies were frequently based on currying favor with the boss rather than making decisions and taking risks. Risk-takers were considered dangerous by those more interested in protecting their jobs than in developing future leaders. Cleary had just proven to Rich that he could think and would take the risk of expressing his thoughts; they could work together.

Rich smiled at his protégé. "Think you can hold down the

fort for me while I take a few days off?"

This time, Cleary's answering grin was genuine. "Absolutely, boss—no problem at all."

The two men rose and Rich opened the door to his office. Standing in the hall speaking quietly to Luke and Wanda was Lindsey, dressed in an olive-green cashmere sweater, light camel wool slacks, and a huge smile; she looked stunning. Those green eyes bore into his as she asked wryly, "Can you give me a lift? I seem to have misplaced my car."

She looked dazed as they walked down the corridors and waited while the massive sets of iron doors opened to permit their exit. Jansen gave her a good deal of space and let her set the pace as they left the Walls. Wanda and her friend had good taste. The new clothes fit loosely on her body; she looked as if in the few weeks that he had known her she'd dropped about five or ten pounds of weight that she didn't need to lose.

They stood in the bright sun outside the prison, and Lindsey stopped, turned around, and gazed back at one of the most notorious prisons in the country. Jansen waited while she stood there looking at the dreary buildings, formidable razor wire rounding the perimeter of the block-long prison, and the bleak, seven-foot, dark-red brick walls that enclosed the place.

Then turning to face him, she shielded her eyes against the sun and asked, "Where are we going?"

"To get you some sunglasses."

Lindsey started to follow him but stopped suddenly. "Where's Max?"

Jansen grinned. "We can't all fit in my Mercedes unless Max gets in the backseat; he doesn't like to do that, so Cleary is going to take Max home for me. Bob will meet us at the house in about an hour and a half. I figured we could get you some sunglasses and one of the Texan's great grilled chicken sandwiches and fries." Glancing at his watch, he added, "It's almost noon. Think you could eat something?"

Lindsey squinted at him, again shielding her eyes against the bright October sun. "Why are you doing this?"

"How about we save that until we get you some food?"

We must forgive all our enemies or be damned. To be a Christian means to forgive the inexcusable, because God has forgiven the inexcusable in you. To refuse it is to refuse God's mercy for ourselves.

—C. S. Lewis

28

Jansen and Lindsey sat in the back room at one of the fifties-style tables at the restaurant and waited for their orders. They had found a pair of retro sunglasses for Lindsey, which would work until they had a chance to get to some stores and shop for a more fashionable pair.

Lindsey sat across the table from him and was looking around the restaurant in fascination, as if the place were filled with priceless antiquities. Watching her drink in her ordinary surroundings, he could surmise what was going through her mind and senses: complete and total overload; she had not been outside Huntsville for over seven months, and she had to be struggling to absorb and adjust to the massive changes in her life and circumstances. Incredibly stressful, Jansen knew: a good stress—eustress, Father John had called what she was experiencing—but an enormous shock to her body and her psyche. For the hundredth time since he had left the priest's office Sunday evening, Jansen said a quick prayer of gratitude for the wisdom and counsel of Father John Tobin.

She'd not said a word since the purchase of the glasses and had apparently forgotten the question she had asked when they left the prison—a good thing because he hadn't a clue about how he would answer her.

The heavy-set redhead returned just then with two trays

of sandwiches and fries. Setting the plates before Lindsey and Jansen, she smiled at them both and in a deep East Texas twang asked, "Will Y'all be needing anything else right now?"

"Not for me, thanks." Jansen raised an eyebrow at Lindsey.

"I wonder if you have any malt vinegar for the fries?"

Surprised—and more than pleased—at her sudden interest in food, Jansen inquired, "Malt vinegar?"

Lindsey removed her sunglasses and directed those incredible eyes at him and smiled, a genuine smile revealing teeth that were perfectly white and even. "You haven't lived until you've had malt vinegar on your fries." She took the ketchup bottle from his hand disdainfully. "Sugar and food coloring, yuck. Try the vinegar first." Jansen's stomach had flipped over from the accidental touch of her long, slender fingers on his hand when she had grabbed the ketchup and with the realization that she was flirting with him.

Be careful here, my man, Jansen thought to himself as he worked to control the intense physical reaction that was threatening to overwhelm him. Father John had warned him about the likelihood of intense sexual attraction between them. The priest also took great care in explaining to Rich why consummating his desires would be a very bad idea right now if he hoped to have a long-term relationship with this woman. Jansen smiled as he thought about that conversation and how surprised he'd been that the priest had mentioned nothing about sin—about the Catholic prohibition of sex outside marriage.

Looking over at Lindsey, he saw her regarding him curiously.

"Is something funny?" she asked?

He was still smiling, but now at her fries. "I'm wondering where you got the idea for malt vinegar on French fries." It wasn't quite a lie, as he *was* curious, but then he remembered his honeymoon with Laura in northern France.

Simultaneously, they chorused, "Frites." And they laughed.

❧

Cleary was standing outside Rich's house when they pulled up next to his truck. Bob opened the passenger side door of his cab, and Max scrambled down the stairs of his Ford, racing over to find Jansen. Then he stood in front of Rich, wagging his stub of a tail and grinning. Cleary reached into the back of his truck and came out with a small suitcase. Bob carried the overnight bag over to Lindsey and handed it to her as he explained, "This is from Wanda, Dr. McCall; there are enough clothes to last you for a few days, including some for exercise—oh, and wait a sec." Cleary turned back to the Ford, reached in, and extracted three pairs of slacks, an assortment of sweaters, and tops and a bag filled with shoes. He smiled and handed the clothes to Jansen.

Accepting the suitcase with her left hand and fingering her new clothes with her right, McCall smiled at Cleary and Jansen. "Thank you, gentlemen. I trust you'll let me know whom I need to reimburse for my wardrobe?" She looked from Cleary to Jansen.

"We can talk about it later, Lindsey," Jansen replied as he draped the clothes over his arm.

Cleary looked rooted to his spot next to Lindsey and looked ill at ease, working up the nerve to say something. Jansen noted that Lindsey waited patiently while the man decided what to say.

"Dr. McCall—" Cleary began but Lindsey interrupted him first by placing her hand on his arm.

"Please call me Lindsey, Bob."

Jansen saw the tell-tale flush appear on the dark man's

skin, but he nodded, swallowed, then said, "I have never known a person who has been unjustly indicted and convicted of anything, Lindsey, never mind murder. I'd simply like to apologize to you on behalf of all of us in the Texas judicial system; I am deeply sorry for what you have had to endure during the last year." His voice was cracking with the emotion he was feeling.

Jansen was stunned and apparently so was Lindsey because no one said anything for a few seconds; then Lindsey impulsively threw her arms around Cleary, saying, "You have nothing to be sorry for, Bob, nothing at all, but thank you for saying that." Then she drew back suddenly as if shocked at what she had just done.

To lighten the moment, Jansen said, "Bob, take time for a beer with us, and Lindsey, do you like merlot?"

Those green eyes shining, she replied, "Yes, I do like merlot, I like it a lot."

Cleary begged off, asking if he could take a rain check, and soon, Jansen and Lindsey stood alone in front of the house. Max was prancing around Rich and staring at him with the intensity that only a Doberman can.

Watching the dog, Lindsey asked, "What does he want, Rich?"

"A run." He looked at Max. "We didn't get our run in today, did we, boy? Hey, you're a runner. If we hurry, we can get six or seven miles in before it gets dark. You game?" Before waiting for Lindsey's reply, Rich had unlocked the door, and he and Max were bounding up the stairs.

Jansen yelled over his shoulder loudly enough so that Lindsey could hear him, "Your room is on the left side across from my office. I'll grab new towels for your bathroom once we get back from our run."

Within five minutes flat, they were out the door and

heading through the dense Piney Woods forest, which surrounded the beautiful country home in New Waverly where Jansen currently resided. Lindsey could tell that Jansen was letting her set the pace; she had been running while in prison but on an inside track and only when Luke Preston could take the time to escort her out to the track. She could not remember the last time she had run in a forest; it had to be years ago. For the first mile or so, Lindsey slowed her pace every few seconds to look at one of the enormous pine trees, to smell its scent, to let this air, sunshine, and woods wash over her and to penetrate her very being—feeling something very close to happiness.

Lindsey knew that Jansen was adjusting his pace for her but he signaled several times that he didn't mind, that they had plenty of time. Even Max seemed willing to let her determine their speed; the Doberman would race off after a squirrel or rabbit and return within a minute or two, sides heaving, panting, and grinning to verify that all was well with his people. But within a mile, the endorphins began to kick in, and Lindsey began to increase her pace; incrementally at first, and then, unable to resist, she was running at her pre-prison time of a seven-minute mile. Rich kept up with her for about five but began to feel the muscles in his surgically repaired thorax and abdomen start to complain so slowed down. When Lindsey noted that he and Max were no longer at her heels on the narrow forest path, she stopped and turned around just in time to see Jansen pulling up his running shirt to mop up the perspiration pouring off his head and face and in the process reveal the extensive scarring from the surgical repair of his bullet wounds. She stopped and turned back around, concern written all over her face.

She was breathing heavily, the sheen of perspiration evident over her face, neck, and shoulders, but the color in her face heightened her beauty. "What happened to you?"

At first Rich had no idea of what she was talking about; his mind had thankfully turned off completely. He had been wholly immersed in the almost-unconscious movement of his body and the simple but exquisite joy of being one with all of creation. Returning to himself, he realized that she had seen the scars; so he explained the robbery, the multiple bullet wounds, his forced retirement from the sheriff's department, and six months of intensive physical therapy. Followed by Greg Bell's offer of the chief warden position at Huntsville, which included his country cabin in New Waverly.

While Jansen spoke to Lindsey, they had wordlessly agreed to turn back and walk along the path they had initially taken. By the time he had covered the whole story and answered her questions, they were back to the house.

Surprised that he had been talking for the entire hour that it had taken them to walk the five-mile return, Rich quipped, "Well, you asked." Generally, Jansen had developed the skill of deflecting personal questions rather than revealing too much about himself to employees, colleagues, and even friends. He had found that most people were more interested in talking about themselves and so never noticed. Lindsey was different. Pondering that difference as they walked up the path to the house, Jansen thought, *She listens exactly like Laura did.* Then he put the brakes on that line of thought with an effort.

"How about a shower, change of clothes, and a good bottle of merlot—sound good?"

Suddenly eager to get the conversation off himself, Rich went into the kitchen and called back to Lindsey, "I'll decant a bottle of merlot now, so it will be ready to drink in thirty minutes or so."

He heard Lindsey heading up the stairs with Max galloping behind her and followed her slowly up the stairs, exceedingly aware of how good it felt to have this beautiful woman in his house.

Hearing the water for her shower start, Jansen realized that he'd never checked her bathroom to make sure that fresh towels were out. He did not want to risk walking into her bathroom while she was in the shower, so he walked into his room to get clean towels and looked around because something looked different in there. After a couple of minutes, he noticed that the sheets on his bed had been changed and that the towels in his bathroom were a different color from when he had last showered here. He stood there puzzling about that and then remembered that Wanda had told him about a friend of hers who needed work and asked if it would be okay if she cleaned his house while he was at Julie Grayson's. Wanda assured him that she would show the woman around and would let her in and out of the house. Wanda had told him the price her friend charged, but now he couldn't remember. She had done an excellent job—the bathroom sparkled. Humming "Ode to Joy," Jansen stepped into his shower and turned it on full blast.

"This is a spectacular house, Rich" Lindsey exclaimed as she gazed around the great room, taking in the forest-filtered sun pouring through the floor to ceiling windows. "You said that the house belongs to the governor?" She sat with her legs curled up underneath her on the chocolate brown leather couch. Dressed in a light wool striped café au lait and choco-late-brown turtleneck sweater and dark brown leggings, Lindsey had pulled her wet hair back into a ponytail and looked more like a medical student than a thirty-something-year-old cardiologist. She was sipping her wine as she looked around the room.

The cool fall weather was holding, and the twilight promised a chilly night, providing an opportunity for Rich to try out the immense fireplace. He'd had to work at it for a few minutes, but the wood piled in the metal log holder was dry and was soon blazing. Max was splayed out on the thick sheepskin rug, which lay in front of the fireplace, dozing contentedly.

Jansen had finished showering before Lindsey and had prepared a quick pesto with sun-dried tomatoes and toasted bread for appetizers; the tray sat on the large coffee table, which was in reach of Lindsey. He stretched back in the coffee-colored leather recliner and smiled at Lindsey. "Greg called this his cabin." Chuckling, Rich explained, "He offered us—" pointing at Max "—a choice between the previous warden's house in Huntsville or this cabin." He took a swallow of the cabernet and let the full-bodied wine caress his palate for a moment before swallowing. "Max and I decided there wasn't much of a choice." And he smiled at Lindsey. The soft-filtered rays of the sun seemed to dance over the wisps of blond hair that had escaped the clasp she had used to fasten her ponytail; she seemed to be unconscious of her beauty. Watching her now, Jansen wondered at her personality. Being with Lindsey McCall felt like being with a guy; she was direct in her speech and was so far devoid of the confusing mind games that women often played. There was no artifice with her, and she had no need to talk incessantly. Right now, Lindsey was staring at the fire blazing in front of her; her face looked untroubled for the first time.

Feeling his gaze, Lindsey turned to look at him and raised an eyebrow and he knew what she was going to ask.

"Well?" The atmosphere in the room was suddenly charged; aware of it, Max lifted his head and looked around to make sure that all was well, then went back to sleep.

Jansen was surprised that Lindsey had let his explanation of the reason he had opened up his life—and his heart—to a complete stranger remain unsaid until now. Adding another to her growing list of attributes—patience—he kicked the recliner so that he was once again sitting upright and replied, "Do you want the abridged or complete version?"

Her gaze had not left his; her eyes were unreadable as she answered, "Complete … please." The last was added almost as an afterthought. Rich noticed that she was trying out aspects of what had to have been her former personality: commanding, forceful; he was happy to see that so soon.

"I didn't know it at the time, Lindsey, but at least 70—maybe 80—percent of the reason Bell created this new position of chief warden at the Huntsville Prisons was you." He waited a beat to give her time to react, but when she remained silent, her expression impassive, he continued speaking, "The suit that Pettigrew filed against you could have buried Bell's entire administration and brought the federal government back into control of the entire Texas prison system."

Her face betrayed no emotion, but her green eyes were now a deep shade of green and hardened; she asked, "How did you get him to drop it?"

"Surprisingly easily, actually; if you'll remember, I taped all of our conversations that first day: yours and mine, Monica's and Luke's. Just as Monica had predicted, Pettigrew had lied about the cause of death on many medical records, not only that of the inmate who died from the heat attack. There were also at least ten others he had been too incapacitated to care for and had falsified the reason for their deaths. Monica knew the names and the dates, so the records were easy to retrieve, and she was, of course, willing to testify to the truth of what had happened to the men."

"So Pettigrew dropped the case and handed you his resignation?" At the mention of Monica and Luke, Lindsey's face had softened, and she smiled wistfully.

Rich nodded. "Yes, and was happy to do it." He waited for a few seconds and then mused aloud, "Harvard Med, Mass General residency, then Duke University for three years, then nothing for four years; and then he shows up at Huntsville Prisons as medical director: something had to happen to get him started on his addictions." Jansen was watching Lindsey out of the corner of his eyes as he waited for her to express the rancor and bitterness she had to feel against the man who had contributed to such personal anguish. But there was none.

"I'd like to apply for his position." There was no trace of anger on her face or in her eyes; although the room had darkened, Jansen could see the excited glitter in her green eyes as she trained them on him. He stared at Lindsey openmouthed.

"What did you say?"

Somewhat defiantly, she replied, "The Texas Board of Medical Examiners has reinstated me; I have a letter that accompanies my license with quite a litany of congratulatory language. Would you like to read it?" Then suddenly, her face fell. "Surely you've not filled his position so quickly, have you?"

About all that Jansen could croak out in his suddenly raspy voice was, "No, Lindsey, the position has not been filled."

His heart lurched in his chest as he looked at this brilliant, dazzling woman who looked as excited as a three-year-old seeing Santa for the first time. "Good, I want that job, Rich." The words belied her childlike demeanor. Father John Tobin had predicted that Lindsey could have severe mood swings and may disclose surprising information to Rich as she began to deal with the reality of her new life, but nothing had prepared Rich for this one. He decided that the best course of action was the one he had practiced with this woman many times during their first encounter: silence.

Lindsey was looking at him now with an expectant look; deliberately misreading it, he asked, "Oh, sorry, would you like some dinner? We can have—"

She was shaking her head impatiently. "Will you at least consider me for that position, Rich?" Now satisfied at his answering nod, McCall asked, "Surely that's not the complete version of your story, Rich?"

Jansen shook his head, still amazed at the question she had just asked. "No, Lindsey, it's not." Suddenly feeling the need to fortify himself with another swallow of wine, he did so, took a deep breath, cleared his throat, and dove in. "From the instant I set eyes on you, Dr. Lindsey McCall, I was attracted to you, and once I heard your story that first day, I felt a compulsion to help you."

Rich paused to reflect on what he had just said and realized that yes, it was the truth; he had felt *compelled*. Jansen regarded her carefully to get a feel for how she was responding to what he had just blurted out. She sat on the couch looking *happy*, her eyes were very soft, she had a very slight smile on her face, and she was blushing.

"I listened to those tapes of our conversations three or maybe four times. I needed to understand more about how and why you had been indicted in the first place. So many details about your case didn't fit together." He stared hard at her. "And I *knew* you were no murderer; no one would have risked what you did when you saved Devon Preston's life—if she were a murderer." He chuckled. "The first day of my new job had not ended before I was considering putting my job on the line and maybe my law license by getting personally involved in your case. Then I called Todd Kensington." He waited for her to realize whom he was talking about, but she looked puzzled. "Your lawyer, Lindsey, he defended you at the trial?"

"Oh, I'm sorry, of course, I'm afraid I blanked out during most of those days." She looked embarrassed.

Jansen understood that now; withdrawal would have been her only defense. She certainly couldn't bury herself in work. He nodded and explained, "Todd and I went to law school together, and we practiced criminal defense law together before I decided to quit and become a cop."

Green eyes widened. "You're a lawyer, *too*?"

Chuckling at her emphasis, he nodded. "But I haven't tried a case in ten years, maybe more." Jansen glanced over at Lindsey, wondering just how much to tell her and then realized that he really had no choice; this was her *life* after all. "Todd is an excellent defense lawyer, one of the best in the state; I think I can count on my hands the number of cases he has lost, Lindsey. And your case seemed weird from the get-go; I couldn't imagine how it had even made it past the grand jury."

"When we talked on the telephone, Todd seemed fairly distressed when I started to ask him about you and your trial. He asked me to come to Houston later that week to meet him for dinner; that was cool because we'd not seen each other much during the last year; I'd not seen anyone …." His voice trailing off, Jansen felt acutely awkward as he thought about his own descent into hell.

Rich recalled Wanda's comments earlier in the day and realized for the first time that there were some similarities between himself and this beautiful creature sitting in his living room. Of course, Father John had instantly known it after hearing Jansen's description of Lindsey. After all, it was John whom Jansen had turned to in desperation when the long-suppressed grief from the sudden death of Laura five years before had become unendurable. John had carefully explained that the enforced inactivity following his injuries galvanized those agonizing bouts of grief; for those sorrows too profound to bear, many of us bury ourselves in our work—until something happens to make that impossible.

Interesting, Jansen thought wryly, *how easily we can recognize the defense mechanisms in others but totally miss their presence in ourselves.*

Rich had been staring at the flames while his mind had veered off his story and into introspection. Suddenly aware of the silence in the room, he glanced sharply at Lindsey. She was watching him intently, her eyes unreadable. Staring at her another minute, he realized that he *wanted* her to know him—what had happened to him. And he began to explain. "Five years ago, my wife, Laura, was killed in a head-on collision with a drunk driver on I-45; she died instantly. I buried her, and I went back to work the next day and never stopped until the day I got shot." Rich paused, eyes still on Lindsey; her eyes had closed momentarily but were now open. She sat motionless and said none of the usual things people said when something like that was revealed; she remained silent.

"The best antidote of all, work—until something happens and you can't."

Lindsey was nodding slowly, understanding written in her eyes and in her expression. She asked no questions, seemingly content to hear what he had to say in the order in which he decided to say it.

"I had literally just gotten back on my feet, physically and—" he hesitated "—psychologically when Bell offered me the job." Jansen smiled at Lindsey. "And it felt good, really good, to be functioning again, productive, and quite frankly, Lindsey, to be able to immerse myself in something, someone, other than me.

"Todd was jubilant that I wanted to get involved in your case because he was still punishing himself for your conviction." He stared at Lindsey; her expression was neutral—

interested, but passively so. Lindsey was acting as if he were talking about someone she barely knew; he had a sense of how Todd must have felt and began to feel annoyed at her passivity. But knowing that his next comments would evoke some kind of reaction, Rich stood up and adjusted a couple of logs in the fire, walked into the kitchen to retrieve the bottle of cabernet, and divided the second half of the bottle between them.

Rich sat back down but on the edge of his chair. Sensing the change in his demeanor, Lindsey uncurled her legs and pulled her knees up to her chin as if she knew she needed to adopt a defensive posture.

"The key to the state's case against you, Lindsey, was your sister." He waited a bit. "Her testimony was so powerful, so compelling, and so manipulative that the jury had no choice but to believe Paula to be the loving, self-sacrificing daughter and you to be the ruthless, callous daughter who had no capacity for loving anything but herself and her research." Jansen deliberately did not look at her; he couldn't imagine what pain his words could be inflicting on her, but he had to get this said. It was the truth, and she needed to hear it. "And then, you refused to let Todd do anything to negate that damage; Todd, who knew that Masters had won his case with Paula's testimony. And you wouldn't let Julie Grayson testify! You completely tied his hands." Jansen's voice had unintentionally risen as he spoke; maybe because of his sympathy for Todd, or exhaustion, or the unbidden sexual tension he was feeling, Jansen knew he sounded angry because he suddenly realized that he *was* enraged at her and at this entire pathetic mess.

"Julie Grayson knew your sister was an alcoholic and addicted to all kinds of drugs, had been for years, and you wouldn't let her testify?" Suddenly Jansen was standing rigidly, staring down at Lindsey; Max was now up and stood in front of him, amber eyes fixed on Rich while Lindsey McCall held her arms around her knees and sobbed as if her heart had broken. He stared down at her and added wearily, "You knew Paula had given the drug to your mother, didn't you? All this time, you've known it was Paula, just like Julie said."

Suddenly disgusted with himself, Rich walked out of the house and onto the porch, with Max padding softly behind him, his eyes anxious in the moonlight. "It's okay, boy, I've just been a total ass; Father John predicts it will take her days, maybe weeks, to feel anything, and in less than eight hours, I have the woman crying so hard that she'll probably never stop. Nice work, Jansen—*way to go.*"

Rich was pacing up and down on the porch, trying to talk himself into going back into the house, but he couldn't face her; he had no idea what he would say. He could feel the anger melting away, leaving profound weariness and sorrow.

But suddenly she was there, standing beside him, tears still rolling down her cheeks; but the shuddering, uncontrollable sobs had completely stopped. "Who is Father John?" Her eyes were enormous and still wet, but she'd regained enough control of herself to speak.

Jansen stared at her, dumbfounded, yet again.

"You were saying that Father John said that I wouldn't feel anything for days or weeks, but you'd managed to beat his prediction. Who is he?"

Rich shook his head, incredulity written in his widened eyes, astonished expression, and posture. Instead of defending herself and returning Jansen's accusations with verbal gauntlets of her own, Lindsey had accepted his outburst as justifiable and weathered the consequences; as impossible as it seemed to Jansen, she seemed ready to move on past all this drama. She was *curious.*

They gazed at each other; Jansen was first to chuckle, shaking his head in astonishment. Lindsey, watching him, also began to laugh until they were each gripped in hilarity. Satisfied that the human crisis had passed, Max sauntered down the stairs, found a bush to suit his needs, and trotted back up the stairs to find a more comfortable place to lie down on than the wooden porch. The Doberman stood in front of the door and waited for Rich to let him back in.

As he walked to the door to do so, Rich stopped, turned to her, heaved a huge sigh, and asked, "Can we leave Father John until tomorrow? You asked to hear the complete story, Lindsey, and that's it. Obviously I spent a good deal of time with Julie Grayson, learning about you, your sister, and your parents." He looked at her, intoxicated by the closeness of her, the scent of her hair, and suddenly realized that he had to get some distance between them. Rich stepped back and turned to open the door for Max at the exact time that Lindsey stepped forward, ending up between the open door and his arms.

They stood paralyzed staring at each other. Lindsey was motionless as she gaped at this handsome man who had completely transformed her life—literally had handed her life back to her and who seemed to understand her better than she understood herself. All these thoughts raced through her mind as she scrutinized the hard, angular contours of his face: the straight nose, the dark eyes, and the full, sensual mouth of the man standing before her. Without thinking, she reached up her hand to trace the slight cleft in his chin, when suddenly Rich roughly pulled her into an embrace. The front door slammed shut as he crushed her against his hard chest and body. Lindsey was suddenly overpowered by a desire she had never felt in her life. As the heat coursed through her entire body, everything felt as if it were on fire—every cell, every fiber, and she could not catch her breath. For the moment she clung to him, certain that if he let her go, she'd fall flat on her face.

With a groan, almost a growl, Jansen pulled away from her but held both of her arms tightly; his eyes were black with want and his lips swollen with the passion he was feeling. Breathing fast and hard, his voice raw and course with fierce longing, he said, "You *have* to help me here, Lindsey. It's way too soon,"

At that moment, Lindsey McCall fell in love; she lifted up her face and touched his lips to hers, welcoming the surrender, the power of a surging tide that enveloped and overwhelmed her, the *need*. "Why?" She breathed against his lips. "Why is it too soon?" She was pressing herself into him, wanting to become one with him in every way possible.

"I don't know," Jansen groaned in answer. Then with a supreme force of will, he gripped her arms even more tightly and pushed her away again, roughly panting. "Are you sure?"

"Yes yes yes, please, yes."

Two hours later, Lindsey and Rich lay in the tangled sheets of the master bedroom, drowsily murmuring, limbs entangling, and softly caressing each other. Jansen sat up, threw his legs over the side of the bed, and wondered at her splendid, perfectly formed body. "Dr. McCall," he whispered, "you are one spectacular-looking female specimen."

Grinning, her green eyes shining with life and with love, she rolled over, caressed his wide shoulders, taut and muscular chest, and belly, and replied in a guttural sing-song voice, "And you are Tarzan, me Jane." Her fingers found the scarring, and she sat up to look closer. "That was one hell of a surgical repair." Her long, slender fingers began to probe and explore.

Rich grabbed her hands. "You keep doing this and we'll never get out of bed!"

Laughing delightedly, Lindsey lay back against the pillows

and asked innocently, "Is that such a bad idea?" Then she squealed when she got a pillow in the face. "So we're getting up and going somewhere?"

"Nope, you stay right here. I'm going down to get another bottle of wine and some food; I'll be right back." Rich was back in minutes with the wine, his uneaten pesto with fresh bread, and some chunks of cheese. During the few minutes it took to prepare their light supper, he mused about the ramifications of what he and Lindsey had just done. When Father John had explained that sexual intimacy may not be compatible with a long-term relationship with Lindsey, Jansen had agreed; the wisdom of maintaining their boundaries at least until Lindsey had healed had been self-evident. And he'd had every intention of keeping their relationship platonic; he chuckled to himself while he waited for the bread to heat up, but he hadn't considered her in that equation. He'd not thought about what he would do if Lindsey changed his mind. He had never encountered a person so completely without guile. Lindsey McCall, for all her brilliance and staggering accomplishments, seemed strangely innocent, almost pure, and in great need of protection. More and more, he could see the Lindsey that Julie had described.

He thought about a long-ago conversation with Father John; Rich had been talking about his Beirut years as a Marine. Rich had confessed the almost ecstatic bliss he had felt when he'd killed the sniper who had ambushed his squadron and killed two seventeen-year-old kids from Arkansas. Jansen had never told anyone about the incident, pretending that he had successfully buried the memory; but it had crawled out in his nightmares during those six months of hell following his injury. Only this time, he saw the intense pleasure on his own face as he pumped the sniper's body full of bullets; the palpable evil on his own face awakened him night after night after night, his body drenched in sweat. John had listened to Jansen's recitation of the event, asked several questions, and placed his hand on Rich's bowed head, who was shamed by his own sobbing. The priest had said, "Perfection is not for the pure of soul; there may be virtue in sin."

Rich had raised his head and stared into the wise and loving eyes of the priest, stunned at the paradoxical statement and the non-Catholic doctrine that the statement implied. John had smiled and said, "Kahlil Gibran was a prophet; like many prophets, he suffered and was persecuted. He was excommunicated by the church because of writings like this one." Placing his hand on his chin, he mused, "But by the time of his death, I think he was brought back into the fold." He fixed his gray and intense gaze on Rich. "Fear, Rich: it's what killed Christ." The priest had said nothing more and had simply given Jansen the traditional Catholic absolution for his confessed sins. He wondered why he was thinking about that meeting now; maybe he was trying to rationalize what he had done just now?

The bread was hot, and he found a tray in Bell's well-stocked kitchen; he was able to carry everything in one trip, eager to be back with her. When he returned to the bedroom, Lindsey was sitting cross-legged in bed with his shirt on. Handing her a glass of wine, Rich propped up a pile of the decorative pillows from the bed and settled in beside her, setting down his wine on the nightstand at the side of the bed and handing a glass to her. He turned to look at her and reveled in the ferocious wave of desire that flowed through him; with difficulty Jansen restrained himself from grabbing her again. Her position and her decision to cover herself implied conversation; Rich expected Lindsey to ask questions about his analysis of the trial, Paula, or the content of his time with Julie, and so he waited.

"So who is Father John?" Her tone was inquisitive, the expression on her face and eyes bright.

Rich was more than happy to stay away from the emotionally loaded conversation of two hours before and smiled a slow smile. "I guess he's my spiritual director." She was surprised at the realization that a priest whom one saw frequently to discuss matters related to faith and to see for confession was indeed called a spiritual director. Now he gazed across the bed at Lindsey thoughtfully, his earlier passion gone. "My wife, Laura, had seen him for spiritual direction, and he had presided at her funeral mass. After she was in the ground, John had told me to call him when I needed to talk." His expression turned to one of chagrin. "He probably didn't think it would take me five years to come and see him." Jansen reached for his wineglass and lifted it as if to toast. Lindsey understood and picked up her glass; the two wine glasses clinked. "Here's to those of us who become expert at completely suppressing our emotions." They sipped their wine simultaneously and, as if on cue, put their glasses back on the nightstands beside them, and fell into each other's arms.

They spent the next two days sleeping, making love, running in the woods, switching off taking kitchen duty, and enjoying the contents of Bell's extensive fiction collection. Claiming that she'd not read a novel since graduation from medical school, Lindsey devoured three novels—a Lee Child, James Rollins, and Dean Koontz—while swinging in the hammock. The phone had rung repeatedly for Rich, and several times, Rich had been in his office for extensive periods of time. By unspoken agreement, they had not discussed anything regarding Paula, the case, or the future; they had taken pleasure in each other and the simple joys of exploring each other's body and heart.

On Thursday morning, Rich and Lindsey sat on the porch

drinking coffee after their ten-mile run in the woods. They could hear Max noisily drinking water in the kitchen as Rich confessed, "That's the first ten-mile run since I was shot." Leering at her, Rich said, "You're really good for my health, Dr. McCall."

"And you're not bad for mine either, Mr. Rich Jansen."

They sat quietly, enjoying the comfortable silence between them. They both looked ten years younger; sleep, good food, and the three days of peace had done them each a world of good. Lindsey had not had her recurring nightmare since she had left the prison, and Rich had enjoyed three nights of eight-plus hours of sleep for the first time in years.

Jansen eyed Lindsey, deciding it was time. "There are some folks who would like to see you, Linds." Without thinking, Jansen had adopted Julie Grayson's nickname for Lindsey. The first time he had called her that, she had startled, and he thought she was going to say something, but she hadn't; she had just smiled.

He had her attention; she didn't ask but waited for him to explain further.

Deciding to ease into it, he said, "Eleanor Philbin has called several times asking how you are, and so has Steve."

Green eyes widening, Lindsey echoed, "Steve?"

He waited until she figured it out.

And then in a breathy exclamation, she said, "Steve? Steve Cooper? Where is Steve? Is he still in Houston? Is he still working at Houston Medical Center?"

"Yes, yes, San Francisco, no, and no."

Lindsey was now laughing, so he decided to tell her about Eleanor Philbin's invitation. "Eleanor had invited us to dinner at her home in South Hampton tonight." He paused to see her reaction and was pleased to see Lindsey slowly nodding her head in tepid agreement.

"I don't think Wanda's daughter included clothes for dinner at Eleanor Philbin's home, Rich." *I don't have the right dress.*

Amused to hear the first typically female response from Lindsey, Rich chuckled, "Got that covered; we can stop at your house in West U on the way to Eleanor's early enough for you to change clothes and pack to come back out here."

"It's all still there: the house, clothes, my jeep—everything? How is that possible, Rich? Who paid the mortgage bill, the light bills?"

Jansen stared back at her and waited for it to hit. Lindsey's face showed complete confusion, then disbelief, and then complete and total anguish as she lost all control and began to sob just as she was able to whimper a soft, "Paula, oh my God, Paula had to have done that." There were more words, but Rich could understand none of them. Lindsey McCall sat on the porch and sobbed. Fifteen minutes later, she was still crying hard, but had recovered enough for her to try—and fail—to regain control of herself. Father John Tobin had told Rich to expect this and had prepared him for her loss of control to be total and for the weeping to sound as if her heart were breaking into smithereens, which was exactly what it was doing *again*. The priest had explained there would be many such bouts of grief; that Lindsey would be weeping for many long-buried losses, but that it was an essential step in the healing of her deeply wounded heart and psyche. The priest had said that it could take days or months, but that it had to happen.

After another ten minutes or so, very gently, Rich asked, "Do you want to know why you're crying like this, Linds?"

She could only nod.

"For years you've not stopped long enough to know how you feel about anything—anything at all." And then Jansen took her into his arms until the torrent of tears subsided.

29

On Monday morning, Eleanor Philbin had called Kate to give her the news about the discovery of Paula's written confession and Lindsey's subsequent release from jail. Eleanor had also shared with Kate her idea of having a very private gathering for Lindsey at her home near the end of the week. Did Kate think she could attend if all the parties were able to attend? Kate had suppressed her urge to bellow back that *nothing* could keep her from finally meeting Lindsey McCall. When Kate had driven Steve to the airport late Saturday night to catch the red-eye to San Francisco, Steve had mumbled something about coming back to Houston for the weekend; Kate suspected that this miraculous news and the chance to see Lindsey would make his decision quite simple.

Kate saw Cooper standing with his overnight bag as she waited in the long line of cars seeking friends and family members at William P. Hobby Airport. She tapped her horn a few times and rolled down the window so that she could wave madly, getting more than a few annoyed glances from more patient drivers. Finally, he saw her and jogged over to the car. Her breath caught as he arrived at her open window and gave

447

her a quick kiss; he had complied with Eleanor's request and wore a tuxedo. Kate thought he looked more like a young Harrison Ford than the Steve Cooper she had been hanging out with.

Cooper darted around the rear of Kate's Honda, opened the passenger door, flung his overnight bag into the backseat, and looked her over carefully. She was wearing the same dress she had worn the night of the Pulitzer Prize award dinner at the River Oaks Country Club. Steve's eyes traveled from the plunging neckline down her thorax and the mid-thigh split in the white ankle-length dress and then pursed his lips for a long and slow whistle of appreciation. Kate could feel her face heating up under the pressure of those sexy, brown eyes of his.

Shifting restlessly under his gaze, Kate teased, "Remember, Dr. Cooper, we're just good buds here, so stop with the heavy-duty, sultry looks, please. This girl is only human, after all!"

Cooper leaned over, tipped her face to kiss her, and murmured, "You're right, Kate, but you look beautiful in that dress, good enough to—"

Kate pulled herself away, glanced quickly at the time, and said, "Steve, we need to move. Eleanor wants all there before Lindsey and Rich arrive."

"Lindsey and Rich." Cooper's eyes had cleared, his mind now on the evening ahead. "Lindsey and Rich," he repeated thoughtfully. "Does that mean those two are an item ... already?"

Kate was pulling out into the traffic at the airport and was focused on the crazy drivers trying to cut her off to get into or out of the line she was in. Shaking her head at the insanity of the other drivers, she shrugged. "This is all I know." And she told him the sketchy details of Julie Grayson's discovery of Paula's body early Sunday evening. Cooper peppered her with questions, most of which she answered that she did not know because Eleanor had told her only the barest of details, but she did know that Lindsey was staying with Rich at his house in New Waverly. Eleanor had also given Kate the number of Rich's cell phone if she wanted to call him to ask him for more information. Kate had thought about calling and then decided that she would leave them alone; these two deserved some peace and quiet, and if there was something happening between the two of them, then even better. Kate had attended the briefing at Houston Medical that past Monday and had been jubilant as she's written the front piece proclaiming McCall's freedom for the Tuesday edition of the *Trib*.

Deciding to let Kate give her full attention to driving, Steve closed his eyes for a catnap, wondering about Lindsey and Rich Jansen hooking up; the more he thought about it, the better it sounded to him. Jansen had impressed him last Saturday night.

Earlier that same day, about sixty miles north of Hobby Airport, it had been a couple hours before Lindsey could give Jansen a watery smile, indicating that the worst of the torrent was over. She gazed at him, the love in those deep emerald eyes so evident that it stunned him for a moment. But then she said very softly, "You're right, Rich." Then she reached her left hand over and touched his cheek so tenderly that it took his breath away. "Bet I look pretty awful, right now."

"Even with mascara running down your cheeks and your eyes kind of red, Lindsey McCall, you are the most beautiful woman on earth."

Shaking her head and chuckling dismissively at Jansen's compliment, she asked, "So who else will be there at Eleanor's tonight?" The speed with which she had pulled herself together was remarkable.

Deciding to ease into it, he replied, "Hank Reardon." Lindsey raised an eyebrow at that but said nothing. "Christine Stewart." Jansen saw a slight smile but again, no comment, "Kate Townsend." He was expecting the frown and lack of recognition. "She's the reporter who wrote that series on you for the *Houston Tribune*."

"Why on earth is she going to be there? I don't know her."

Her voice had risen a notch. *A little distrustful*, Rich thought. "I think you would enjoy reading the series of articles she wrote; a month ago the woman was awarded the Pulitzer Prize in journalism. I have all four in my office; why don't you read them this afternoon?" He smiled and lightly touched her arm. "I assure you that after you read them, you'll be as eager to meet her as she is to meet you."

Hesitantly, a little dubiously, Lindsey compressed her mouth together and lifted her eyebrows. "Okay, if you think I should read the articles, I will."

Jansen chuckled, "You have the expression I'll bet you had in college when they told you that you couldn't take all sciences, that you were required to take liberal arts, too."

The accuracy of the remark hit home, and she laughed, relaxing. "Who else?"

"I'm not sure if Boyd Masters will be there or not." The Houston district attorney was embroiled in a vicious campaign for the office of mayor of Houston. Boyd had written Lindsey a long apology along with the affidavit that confirmed her release. Rich didn't think she had read his note; the last time he had seen those papers, the note still remained in a sealed envelope. Rich had not seen it, but Todd Kensington had had given him an idea of its contents.

"And of course, Steve Cooper, Todd Kensington; Jeff and

Ellen Simmons, the editor of the *Tribune* and his wife; and Julie and Ted Grayson. That's it—eleven of us plus Eleanor and Marguerite." Rich was intentionally talking through her widened eyes at the mention of Julie but stopped talking now to gauge her reaction; he had not informed her that Father John Tobin would be there also because he could not figure out how to explain his presence to Lindsey.

Lindsey sat with her hands over her eyes, tears again streaming down her face. "Rich, I cannot see Julie and Ted. I simply can't do it." Jansen waited for a few minutes while she calmed down and looked at him.

"What?"

Jansen sat and looked at Lindsey with all the love, pride, and admiration he felt for her as a woman and as a person; he could feel the energy moving out of him and could see her respond in the softening of her mouth and eyes. "You can do this, Lindsey, my love," he said gently.

Eleanor had explained that she had asked the others to be there by seven and had asked Rich if he and Lindsey could be at her home by seven thirty on Thursday evening. When he made the commitment yesterday, Rich had thought a seven thirty arrival in downtown Houston would be simple, but he had overlooked the fact that Lindsey would need a dress, which meant going to the house she had not seen for almost a year. Following their earlier conversation, Lindsey had been upstairs reading in her room for a couple hours; she had agreed to see Julie but was obviously dreading the encounter and had accepted his recommendation to get some rest before they left for Houston. Rich figured they would need to leave New Waverly by four to have enough time for Lindsey to get to her house, get dressed, grab some clothes to bring back to Rich's place, and make their seven thirty arrival time at Eleanor's home.

He waited until almost three and knocked on her door to see if she was awake; hearing nothing, he knocked again and heard a muffled response. Fearing that she was crying again, he opened the door to find her lying sleepily on top of the bed, clearly just waking up. Lindsey stretched, smiled, and patted the bed beside her. "Come lie down with me for a minute."

Rich was tempted; she looked like a child, hair tousled and sleep written all over her, but he smiled and said truthfully, "You have no idea how much I would like that, but I'm afraid we can't; we should leave shortly."

Thirty minutes later, Rich and Lindsey were headed to Houston. Fortunately, there was little traffic, and they were exiting the 610 loop onto Bellaire Boulevard by a quarter to five. Lindsey's directions were excellent, and within twenty minutes, Jansen pulled into the driveway of a chocolate brown wood shingle house on the corner of Edloe and Bissonnet. Lindsey turned to Rich and chuckled, "I'll bet you were worried about a resurgence of the waterworks, but there's no sentiment for me with this house—I slept here, that was it."

Julie had told Rich that she'd talked with the lawyer responsible for the McCall estate to request that someone clean the house, tidy up the scant landscaping, and leave the key in the trellis around the side of the house. Rich got out of the house, found the key, and opened the door to the garage.

Lindsey walked through the door that Rich held open for her and said, "See what I mean?" The furniture was sparse and utilitarian, and the carpeting was an outdated, dark brown shag.

"Yes, I see," Rich said as he took in the colorless, unimaginative, and rather dreary living room. "I wouldn't want to spend much time here, either." Jansen followed her into a bedroom through a hallway at the southern end of the house.

Light was streaming into a fairly large bedroom window through white, transparent drapes with open white blinds. The bed was queen-sized and sat on a simple Adirondack frame and headboard; it looked comfortable. To the right of the bed was a closed door of a small closet. There was a light pine antique dresser and a nice-looking large matching antique armoire, which was used as a second closet. On either side of the bed were two unpainted Adirondack nightstands with small lamps on them. The walls were painted white and were unadorned. Lindsey watched while he scanned the room.

"I like it; simple and comfortable ... needs some art, though."

She smiled and opened the door to the closet and studied the contents while Jansen enjoyed watching her move. She wore tight jeans and a sweater and had spent some time on her hair. It fell loosely to her shoulders in natural-looking waves and looked like spun gold in the sunlight streaming through the large window. Apparently finding what she had been searching for and turning around holding a glittery gold evening gown, she asked him, "Think this will do the trick?"

Lindsey brought out a suitcase and began opening drawers to retrieve underwear, jeans, shirts, and sweaters. Jansen took the piles from her arms, opened the bag on her bed, and suggested. "Let me pack those for you, Linds. Why don't you go get dressed?" Jansen spied a couple of pair of casual shoes and running shoes in her closet and packed those as well. Ten minutes later, he heard, "Okay, what do you think?"

The dress fit her like a glove, emphasizing all the right curves contrasted with her lean, athletic torso, and ended two inches above her knees, showing perfectly toned thighs. She had added a few badly needed pounds in the last few days and looked more beautiful than any movie star he had ever seen.

Jansen gasped and then gulped, "Dr. McCall, I believe your

public is waiting your arrival."

Lindsey grinned, spun around on her sandaled heels, and said, "Okay, let's roll, Mr. Rich Jansen."

As they headed down Bellaire Boulevard toward the medical center, Lindsey suddenly said, "Rich, can you stop here for a few minutes, please? We don't have to be at the Philbins' until seven thirty, right?"

The sun was setting right in Jansen's eyes, and so he could not see where she had been pointing until he had made the right hand turn and then the second right hand turn into St. Vincent de Paul Catholic Church. Lindsey said nothing but opened the door as soon as he had turned the ignition off. Jansen stepped out, locked the car, and slowly followed her into the front of the church. He watched her from the foyer of the spacious contemporary church as she walked down the aisle, her head up and fixed upward and straight ahead, finally choosing one of the front pews and kneeling there, head bent.

What was she looking at? He wondered and realized that she had been staring at the enormous crucifix. Rich genuflected and sat in one of the last rows of the church, pulled out the kneeler, and prayed as hard as he ever had in his life—mostly in gratitude for the miracles that were happening in his life.

It was seven thirty on the nose when Rich and Lindsey drove through the black metal gates and pulled to a stop in front of the mansion. This time Samuel was waiting, and smiled at them. "Welcome, Mr. Jansen and Dr. McCall."

When they walked into the drawing room, once more it was Eleanor who spied them first. "Lindsey, my dear, dear girl, welcome." She smiled at Rich warmly. "Thank you for bringing her here, Rich, thank you." Her warm blue gaze was thanking him for much more than the transportation.

Rich scanned the room quickly and saw that everyone had made it except for Masters; he was guessing that the slight blonde older man standing next to Kate was Hank Reardon; he could feel the man's energy from way across the room. Eleanor and Marguerite had thought of everything; in the corner of the great room was a baroque trio: a harpist, cellist, and violinist playing Mozart or Bach softly. Everyone was in evening clothes, and there were flowers everywhere. A young woman approached Lindsey and Rich to ask if they would like a glass of champagne. Rich started to reach for glasses for them but stopped when he realized that Lindsey had not moved. Her eyes were riveted on Julie Grayson.

Nodding to the young woman, Rich said, "Later, thank you." Rich put his arm about Lindsey's waist just as she started to cry and then sink to the floor, murmuring something that sounded like, "Julie, I am so sorry. How can you ever forgive me?"

In an instant, Julie was there helping Lindsey up and leading her through the door that she and Rich had just entered. Eleanor signaled to the trio, and the music was instantly a good deal louder, and soon the guests were mingling and carrying on with their conversations. It had all happened so quickly that Rich didn't think many people noticed, but at least one had caught it. Rich watched the slight, energetic man disengage himself from Christine Stewart and Marguerite Philbin. Jansen accepted a glass of champagne from the young woman who was circulating the room with a tray filled with glasses of champagne and sipped it as he smiled at the approaching man.

"Hello, Rich Jansen, I'm Hank Reardon, and I wanted to introduce myself to you." The magnetism of this man was almost tangible; Rich could feel himself being drawn in by the smile and the sense of genuine warmth. Rich took Reardon's extended hand and returned a firm handshake.

Without any preamble, Reardon's startling blue eyes

looked directly at Rich and said, "Eleanor has suggested that you and Lindsey may be developing a deep friendship, and I wanted to take the few minutes we have to tell you what a wealthy woman she has become." Reardon spent the next few minutes reviewing the first two quarters of profits for the sale of Digipro and the percentage of the profits that were Lindsey's by contractual agreement between Andrews, Sacks, and Levine, the pharmaceutical company for which Reardon was CEO. The numbers were staggering; Lindsey was a multimillionaire, and Reardon predicted that the sales would increase exponentially for the foreseeable future.

Reardon had guided him gently to a side of the room where no one could overhear their conversation. "Look, I can only imagine what you and Lindsey are dealing with right now; I wanted you to know the scope of her earnings and that I have taken the liberty to open up an account for her at my bank in Lausanne. Perhaps you and Lindsey would accept an invitation to my home once your lives are more settled, and we can talk more then. Until then, Rich, here is my card with my personal numbers on it." Reardon leaned forward slightly closer, and his whole face lit up with the smile that he beamed at Jansen. "Lindsey is one of the most remarkable women I have ever met; you have my most fervent wishes for hers and your own happiness." With that, Reardon strode back across the room.

Rich sipped some more champagne and was looking around for Father John when he saw Julie and Lindsey standing in the doorway, both women looking radiant. If Lindsey had been crying, there was no sign of that now. Her makeup was flawless and fresh, and she had an arm around Julie, whispering into her ear something that must have been hilarious because both women were dissolving into giggles. Julie was dressed in a simple and stunning long, black dress with a single strand of pearls at her throat and two teardrop pearls in her ears. Her dark hair was swept up and away from her heart-shaped face, and she looked lovely. Jansen stood smiling at the contrast between the two.

Lindsey spotted him, said something quickly to Julie, and walked over to Jansen. She leaned close and began to say something when the music was suddenly toned down, and Eleanor Philbin picked up as if nothing had ever happened. Eleanor's face was wreathed in smiles as she crossed the enormous room to take Lindsey's hand and Rich's hand. She commanded, "Now come, you two."

Apparently this had been orchestrated because Reardon, Marguerite, a woman he did not recognize, Kate Townsend, and Steve Cooper had formed a line; and the rest of the gathering fell in behind them. Jansen realized they had formed a receiving line of sorts and that each person intended to speak to Lindsey, to offer her their congratulations or their sympathies—whatever was proper in this most bizarre of situations. Rich managed to suppress the smile he felt threatening to erupt and managed to look appropriately genteel. But then he caught Kensington's eyes and almost lost it again.

"Lindsey, dear, we all thank you for joining us here this evening." The warmth, love, wisdom, and sincerity flowing from this woman erased all the cynical thoughts he had been having about this evening, and her next words expunged the awkwardness and discomfort that he expected everyone in the room was feeling. Eleanor stepped to the side so that she was directly in front of Lindsey and placed both hands on her arms as she leaned forward to say, "There is no way that anyone can wipe out the last year of injustice, humiliation, and suffering that you have endured. But we hoped that this evening would be a way for each of us here to express our sorrow for the past and our joy for the future."

Tears were standing in Eleanor's eyes and in Lindsey's.

Eleanor dropped her hands and stepped to her right so that her sister, Marguerite, could approach Lindsey. Marguerite just gazed up at Lindsey from her diminutive height of four-feet-something and smiled. "You are a remarkable creature, my dear: beautiful and brilliant; all of this has only made you stronger." And then she reached up a tiny hand to caress Lindsey's cheek.

Hank Reardon was next, he grinned, and echoed Marguerite with a wicked grin: "beautiful, brilliant, and rich, Dr. McCall." Then the smile faded, and his expression became grave. "Just like everyone here, Lindsey, my heart aches for all that you have had to endure to get you to this place, but we don't seem to be able to make it through this life without suffering. Somehow we make it through to the other side." And then, Reardon turned to Marguerite. "Finding that indeed we are stronger." Turning back to Lindsey, he said, "I just wish that Simon could have been here to see that you did it; you created a drug that has already revolutionized the treatment of acute heart failure."

Kate Townsend was watching Reardon as he spoke to Lindsey; there were dark shadows under his eyes, tangible shadows of grief for the recent loss of his beloved wife, Peg. Hank Reardon was no stranger to deep suffering.

She smiled to herself as she thought of the spontaneous call to Hank that she had made Monday morning; Reardon had answered the phone himself and had bellowed out a cheer when Kate told him that Lindsey was free. When Kate told Hank about the private gathering at the Philbin mansion planned for the next Thursday evening, Reardon had answered that he'd not miss this for the world and had thanked Kate profusely for keeping him in the loop. Kate stood quietly scanning the room, and she thought of that evening at the River

Oaks Country Club. Although it had been scarcely three weeks ago, it felt more like three years. Except Paula, they were all here; all those people who had been so involved in the creation of her series, the steps leading up to the Pulitzer awards. Kate recalled those moments at the table when she had been overcome with anguish about Lindsey McCall, still in jail while Kate had profited by her story in a manner far beyond her wildest dreams. Just then, Kate and Eleanor met each other's gaze. Kate smiled in wonder at the prescience of the woman— her certainty that they would help Lindsey. And here she was, Lindsey McCall, free. Miraculous, Kate thought, downright miraculous.

When Dr. Christine Stewart stepped in front of Lindsey, Jansen could feel the chill emanating from the woman as she smiled a smile that never quite reached her eyes. She did not touch Lindsey but stated coolly and professionally, "Lindsey, as Chief of Medicine at the Houston Medical School, it is my distinct pleasure to welcome you back as a tenured full professor with a 20 percent raise in salary." Stewart turned to smile at Reardon. "And to let you know that Hank Reardon has fully endowed the first Dr. Lindsey McCall Chair of Cardiology and Cardiovascular Research with you, of course, as the first chair."

Dr. Stewart took a deep breath, hazel eyes glittering, enthralled with her last and best offer when Lindsey raised her right hand as if to ward Stewart off. Then Lindsey stepped forward to touch Christine's hand and began to shake her head, all the while looking at Stewart kindly, almost sympathetically.

"Christine, thank you for your generous offer … offers; but I cannot accept them, not any of them."

The silence in the room was profound.

Jansen stole a glance at Steve Cooper, who caught his gaze

and nodded very slightly to Rich.

Lindsey turned to Rich and astonished him by declaring, "I have asked Rich to accept me as medical director for the Huntsville Prisons, if he will have me; I know now where I belong … finally."

Lindsey had extracted a promise from Rich the night they drove back to New Waverly from the Philbins' celebratory gala: One week without the outside world—seven days with no talk of anything but food, good wines, Max, and one another. On the Sunday afternoon prior to their re-entry into their newly shared world, Lindsey, Rich, and Max sat in the great room reading and listening to Sibelius.

Jansen looked up from the paperwork that he had postponed all week to glance over at the woman who had taken residence in his heart. Lindsey seemed to be managing the radical changes in her life with hardly a misstep, but Jansen was worried that decisions and commitments just two weeks after she had been released from prison and learned that her sister had killed herself could be cause for regret later on. It was strange, he mused, because he felt as if he had known this woman from the instant he had met her, yet he didn't really *know* Lindsey; he didn't know if she normally made decisions quickly or what movies she liked or books she liked to read. He thought about the certainty with which she turned down Christine Stewart last week: that she had walked away from the life she had prepared for since she was seven years old still felt rash, almost reckless to him.

"I know you think we need more time to process everything that is happening to us, Rich, and I know you are worried about me and whether I need time to *recover* from almost a year in prison." In the fading afternoon light, she looked calm, almost serene. "What I don't think you understand is that the time in prison served as time to recover from my *life*.

"See, I thought that working sixteen out of every twenty-four hours was normal—no, that's not right. I didn't consider it normal ... *normal* held no interest for me. I knew medicine would be all-consuming, so I decided to believe that nothing else was interesting, nothing but medicine and research. And it worked, just fine. Until that day that I knew I had the right modification to the molecule, I never expected to feel the letdown, the despair that I felt when I knew I'd done it. All those years of work and I didn't care about any of it. It was simply another milestone which had been reached." Her voice was low, reflective. "You see, Rich, I didn't have clinical practice to go back to. I was too afraid to touch a patient again."

Lindsey told him of the patient she had lost during a cardiac catheterization and of her inability to force herself to do another cath. The man had been young, fifty-two years old; she had found no disease but inexplicably he developed a fatal dysrhythmia and died. She had tried to go back to the cath lab, but she could not do it. So the research had been her solace and the former chair of medicine, Simon Bayer, had supported and believed in her and had introduced her to Hank Reardon.

The indictment was a relief, Lindsey told Rich; once Digipro had been formulated, she no longer had the excuse she'd always had to keep her away from her mother and her sister. Lindsey had known that Paula had given her mother the premarket formulation of the drug; she had suspected, too, that Paula never took the necessary forms over to the committee who could have approved the use of her drug on her mother.

"But it couldn't have saved Mother's life; it was too late for that, way too late."

She thought back to her emotional outburst upon seeing Julie Grayson when they first arrived at the Philbin party, took a deep breath and declared, "I have a daughter Rich, you met her when you were at Julie's but I have not seen her since she was born."

Eleanor's housekeeper had directed her and Julie to a lovely set of rooms worthy of the name restroom at the request of Eleanor. Adjacent to a lavatory was a dressing room with one mirrored floor-to-ceiling wall, brightly lit with halogen ceiling lights and an assortment of chairs and small couches where a few chairs were placed in front of the mirror for cosmetic brush up while the remainder were placed in shadowed corners of the large, spacious room and were grouped around tiny decorative tables, inducing whispered conversations.

Lindsey had been oblivious to their surroundings while the torrent of tears, regret, and recriminations gushed out and finally slowed to a trickle. During the tumult, Julie had just sat next to her while she held the hand of her best friend. Only when Lindsey's shaky, shuddering breaths signaled that the worst was over did she speak.

"I think I have a couple of bottles of Kendall-Jackson in the car; shall I go out and get them?" Her almond eyes danced, and a quirky smile played on her lips.

Lindsey had replied with her best try at a giggle, but it sounded more like a sob.

Still holding Lindsey's hand tightly, Julie declared, "She's beautiful, Lindsey, truly beautiful."

Her loving, brown-eyed gaze held Lindsey while she described their daughter. In answer to the unspoken questions she saw reflected in the watery green gaze directed at her, Julie replied, "She looks nothing like you, Linds; it's amazing really—except her eyes. She has your eyes—same shape, same color."

Julie Grayson paused as she pondered the best way to describe the child Lindsey McCall had delivered a little more than sixteen years before.

Slowly and gently, Julie described her daughter Lindsey and waited for Lindsey to interpret the description.

"She looks exactly like Paula." The whispered response was closer to a breath, full of wonder.

The next several minutes were filled with the simple details of the Grayson household, of their three younger children and their busy lives. Julie had decided that she'd reveal only what Lindsey was asking to hear, no more, not now.

"Does she know?"

"She knows that we adopted her, Linds; we told her several years ago. We have not told her that you are her mother."

Lindsey had sat quietly next to her friend while she tried—and failed—to cope with the waves of conflicting feelings: a confusing mixture of joys, sorrows, and gratitude, along with memories threatening to engulf her.

She had looked over at her best friend. "I really don't know what to do with all this, Julie. Do I meet her and explain why I couldn't raise her myself? Is that the right thing to do?"

Julie regarded Lindsey intently as she answered as truthfully as she could, "No, Linds, not now, not yet anyway." That green gaze felt like twin lasers to Julie as Lindsey listened to her. "Maybe one day, but not now." Her friend had stood and then pulled Lindsey to her feet while she led her over to one of the chairs sitting in front of the mirrored wall.

"Now, let's repair that beautiful face of yours, Dr. Lindsey McCall. Your public is waiting."

Rich waited until he knew Lindsey had no more to say then walked over to where she sat, feet curled underneath her. Gently, he pulled her to her feet to hold her tightly against him, whispering into her hair, "You could not have selected a better mom for her, Linds."

Waiting a beat, he stood back to look at her and then broke the somber mood. "Time for some culinary action, Doctor. Kate and Steve will be here in a couple hours; we have work to be done."

END

AFTERWORD

Why a second edition?

The Fragrance Shed by a Violet is a work of fiction. The characters and institutions are works of my imagination. However, the theories and data described in Kate Townsend's first article of her investigative series, in Julie Grayson's experience with alcoholic treatment, and Lindsey McCall's skepticism of psychiatry are based on fact.

While doing talks with a variety of groups last year, there were a surprising number of questions about the material grounding Kate's initial article for her Murder in the Texas Medical Center series. There were numerous questions as well about the big business of medicine and research. Therefore, Kate's article has been lengthened in this edition to include more detail about the history of medicine and the possible reasons for a criminal conviction of a doctor engaged in the practice of medicine. To that interest, I have included a list of references for those who may be interested in learning more about these complicated subjects.

I was also asked about Kate's award of three Pulitzer Prizes. Included in this new edition is information about how three Pulizers could be awarded to a single journalist along with some fun purely Texas comments from the chair of the committee.

The many typos and a few editing errors in the first edition were obstacles in the flow of the story. They have been resolved.

For those interested in reading more about the growth of medicine as big business, clinical research, what Kate calls the extended alliance between the law and medicine and sources for the data quoted in her article, I recommend these books:

John Abramson. *Overdosed America: The Broken Promise of American Medicine.* New York: Harper Perennial, 2004. Abramson writes powerfully about the inferior medical care of Americans by virtue of its commercialization.

Marcia Angell. *The Truth About the Drug Companies: How They Deceive Us and What to Do About It.* New York: Random House, 2004. The former editor of The New England Journal of Medicine reveals extensive examples of collusion between medicine and pharmaceutical companies.

Peter Breggin. *Medication Madness: The Role of Psychiatric Drugs in Cases of Violence, Suicide, and Crime.* New York: St. Martin's Press, 2008.

Guy Clifton. *Flatlined: Resuscitating American Medicine.* New York: Rutgers University Press, 2008. A former chief of neurosurgery, Clifton writes candidly and disturbingly of the current state of American medicine.

James Le Fanu. *The Rise and Fall of Modern Medicine.* New York: Carroll & Graf Publishers, 1999. British physician and columnist Fanu explores the explosive growth of medicine and offers intriguing reasons for the rapid decline of research seen in the latter two decades.

Eliot Freidson. *Professional Dominance. The Social Structure of Medical Care.* New York: Atherton Press, 1970. Eliot Freidson revealed the fallacies inherent in Talcott Parson's idealized professional view of the physician through elegant studies which showed physicians to be no different from any other population.

Eliot Freidson. *Professional Powers: A Study of the Institutionalization of Formal Knowledge.* University of Chicago Press, 1986. A fascinating follow up to Freidson's earlier work; using the alliance with the courts to demonstrate the growth of power within medicine.

Victor Fuchs. *Paying the Piper, Calling the Tune: Implications of Changes in Reimbursement.* Frontiers of Health Services Management, 1986. Fuchs created the model demonstrating that at a certain point, added medical treatments no longer improve care but accelerate the decline.

Jay Katz. *The Silent World of Doctor and Patient.* New York: The Free Press, 1982. An intriguing and readable account of the alliance between the law and medicine in creating the autonomy of physicians.

Talcott Parsons. *The Social System.* New York: The Free Press, 1961. It was Parsons who popularized the concept of the professional in using the physician as a model. In doing so, he elucidated the attributes mentioned in Kate's article.

Professional Judgement: A Reader in Clinical Decision Making. Eds. Jack Dowie and Arthur Elstein. Cambridge University Press, 1988. An extensive analysis of uncertainty, variation and error in medical decision making.

Donald Schon. *The Reflective Practitioner.* New York: Basic Books, 1982. A brilliant and insightful examination of medical decision making.

Paul Starr. *The Social Transformation of American Medicine.* Basic Books, 1982. Starr did write this Nobel Prize winning book while on the faculty at Harvard and he was denied tenure by the university. Dr. Starr has been at Princeton for the last several decades.

∾

Just as Julie Grayson did, I read more than fifteen books in my attempts to understand drug and alcohol addiction. The two most helpful to me were "The Big Book": what Alcoholics Anonymous calls their bible. And a book that Jeff Speirs sent to me: *Drinking: A Love Story*, by Caroline Knapp, 1996. These were the two sources which finally helped me visualize Kate's sister and to walk a few miles in her shoes.

The list of those who were instrumental in helping me write this story is very long, too long to list here. But there are a few people without whom I could not have done it:

John Wilder, Margaret Caddy, Susan Toscani, Eleanor and Marguerite Philbin for giving me the permission to use your names, Jeff Speirs, Warren Diepramm, Assistant District Attorney Montgomery County Texas, former ADA Houston, Dr. Marie Francoise Doursout, Assistant Director Research University of Texas Medical School at Houston, Nancy Cleary, Karen Kibler, and Father Paul McCollum.